Marty Whimpel

and the Curse of the Acne Pimple

Book 1

Written & Illustrated
by

Jim Tatton

ISBN: 1453795758
EAN-13: 9781453795750
Electronic copy ASIN: B003VD1EP8
LCCN: 2010914457

For updates and information about upcoming books visit my blog at **http://martywhimpel.blogspot.com**

Cover design by Jim Tatton

Acknowledgements

I'd like to dedicate this book to my loving and patient wife, who, without her constant encouragement this project would have died in the hand-written form, also to my grandmother Pearl who instilled in me a love of reading and the magic that can come from escaping into the World of Books. My son also played an intricate part in getting my book this far, I wanted to prove that if you set your mind to it, you can accomplish anything, it's the best example I can set for him I hope he learns something from it. I would also like to thank those who have given feedback and help with editing, because without your keen eyes this book would make no sense. Finally I'd like to thank you, the reader, without you I am just writing a journal really, and I already know what happens in this story. If *you* are touched by Marty's story, I'd love to hear about it, I'm anxious to continue the series and I'd love it if you would share it with your friends and family members. Email me at **martywhimpel@yahoo.com** or check out our blog at **martywhimpel.blogspot.com**

TABLE OF CONTENTS

PROLOGUE

To Whom This Letter May Reach,

You have already showed potential by recovering this note.

I hope this reaches you in time. The government has taken control of everything. There are mandates against free-thinking. The Tribunal of Progress doesn't want you to think on your own, they want you to become mindless drones with only one desire, making more money and getting further ahead in the business world. They are trying to crush creativity and free-thinking, don't let them win!

This is not the way it has always been, don't believe their lies. There was a time, not long ago, that we were able to read books, hold knowledge in our own hands and exercise our creative ideas.

The only thing that has meaning is learning. Don't let them tell you anything different. You've got to take the future into your own hands. The schools have been taken over by androids. They have been programmed to not allow questions. Your parents have chosen the life that you now live.

It has not taken much time for this change to take place, everyone in town wanted the same thing, more prestige, more power, more money, and less "wasted" time spent reading or interacting with their peers. They also have closed off the old town and are finishing work on this wall that will separate the past from the future. Whatever warning they are going to put here…don't pay it any heed. You MUST learn from the past so that you don't repeat the same mistakes that we made.

We were so excited that we had graduated to the computer age, none of us could have imagined that the next generation would take it this far. I hope that I'm still alive when you find this note. I promised that I wouldn't die before I passed on my legacy, but it is increasingly depressing to see the greed that has taken over Scat-town. I have almost given up hope for the future, whoever you are, you are my last chance.

There have been walls built blocking out the view of the old town, but it is still there, with trees, grass, and homes that have been abandoned in the pursuit of "happiness" that never paid off. Planes that fly overhead have been tampered with by the government making it impossible to see anything that they don't want you to see.

As the glass skyrises and metal roads take the place of the familiar landscape I realize I am a stranger here. If you, like me, feel that there is more to life than what you have been told you are correct! The monstrosity that you know of as home is proof that humans really can cage themselves like animals.

If you haven't decided to take the challenge yet, let me tell you this, you would be saving not just one world, but two. Time, an unheard of asset that no one can buy, and very few people keep track of, is of the essence to another world, one with which you will soon become very closely acquainted. To find out more, come visit me, beyond this wall across the old town you will see a hill in the distance. On that hill is my home. I pray that I'm still there when you come to find me.

Nicholas Chrismon

Chapter 1
There must be a beginning...

Upon the lonely hill behind the cracked shutters and peeling paint of a rundown cottage is concealed one of the world's greatest wonders. Unlike the other seven, now in museums, this alone is left of a time that is not-that-far-distant but completely forgotten. The time I speak of is the "Age of Books." An ancient figure behind the faded blue and white gingham curtains slowly shook his head as he gazed out on the "modern madness." The steel barrier could easily be seen over from his vantage point because the holographic force fields were only designed to block the view out, however he could see the glass and metal high rises that now scarred the once beautiful landscape and wished for just a moment that the view were blocked for him as well.

He slowly shuffled to his well-known recliner and gingerly sat down. On a nearby table lay the beloved tale of Rapunzel, that flaxen haired beauty, which, just moments before, he completed for the umpteenth time. Gazing at the faded cover he smiled. It was just yesterday, maybe the day before that, he first read this now forgotten story, wasn't it?

"Oh, how time has flown, Marty! I wish you were still here, and then we might be successful in reviving the books. I don't think I can do it on my own."

"Nick, don't ever forget the power of one voice, you doubted before, now *you've* got to believe."

It came so suddenly and seemed so real Nick turned and looked from whence the voice had come, then, slowly, dejectedly, he sank back into his once comfortably stuffed "story chair." His chair, just like he, had seen better days. The cover was threadbare and so worn you could barely make out the floral pattern that had once been so cheery and bright. Laying his head back on the sagging cushion he sighed, the sound quite raspy and thick.

A slow trickle of hot tears again burned the back of Nick's eyelids. He wiped at them ashamed, not because he had anyone to impress, but because he wished he had the determination and strength that Marty once had.

"I will try, dear friend, you know I will." As the words were still on his lips Nick's head began to droop, and ninety-six year old Nicholas Chrismon slipped into a quiet slumber filled with memories of better days.

A constant knocking slowly roused Nick who, even though he was ninety-six, still had very good hearing. He looked around confusedly wondering what it was that had awakened him. Then, somewhere from the back of his mind, the recognition crept forward, "The door," he said aloud. "Someone is at the door."

No one had visited him in over twenty years, so he almost didn't recognize the sound of the knock. He stood, cursed his slowness, and prayed his visitor would have patience. As he came around the corner of the library he was in direct line with the front door. Through the partially sheer curtains he caught a glimpse of a group of some kind, all different sizes and shapes. "Children," he gasped, "Marty, it's the children!"

He shuffled faster pausing only slightly in front of the mirror in the hallway the ancient reflection startled him, "Who *is* that?" he thought. Reaching up to straighten his hair, the reflection smoothed its silver hair with a gnarled and wrinkly hand he sighed and mumbled, "It's me, but I just don't feel *that* old." Again, focusing on the front door, he turned covering the last few remaining feet in a moment then reaching forward he slowly opened the door.

The movement of the door made the entire group on the porch freeze, eyes wide with shock, as someone, older than death by the look of him, came into view. Their fear quickly fled when they saw him smile nervously. His hands shook as he tried to open the door further to welcome them in.

When he spoke, it came from a far away make-believe time and place, but his voice was welcoming, gentle, and kind. "I've waited so long to meet you, come in, please come in."

The ice of apprehension melted off of all of the visitors except the tallest, most dashing youth, Billy who stuck out almost a head taller than his peers. None of them had any idea what they just stumbled on or how many laws they had broken, but the group stepped forward as one. When he spoke again each youth stopped to catch every word, "I'm forgetting my manners," he softly chided himself, "My name is Nicholas Chrismon, but you may call me Nick."

"My name is Chante Lation it's nice to meet you Nick. This is my cat, Crispy," The girl with the bright red hair startled Nick into extending his hand; she shook it and continued into the house. He noticed she had stopped just inside, "Yes, dear?"

"We found your letter."

Nodding with understanding Nick smiled and his face folded like a rumpled bed sheet, there was no real pattern to it, but it seemed to know which wrinkle went where. Instantly at ease, Chante smiled back at him then stepped past him venturing into the unknown before her peers. She waited just inside as they watched her open-mouthed for the next volunteer.

Following closely behind Chante was the pixie-like girl who looked like she held enough energy to run a small country. "Hi, Kimber Nayshon, I've wondered for the longest time if anyone lived beyond the wall, it's nice to finally find out." She too shook his gnarled hand with her tiny doll-like one.

"Billy Cripton here, nice place." The gruff exterior hid a very young, but very nice looking boy. He was definitely one of the leaders of this group and by the look of him; he probably played most sports as well.

Nick's blues eyes found a friend in each of the children and they were quickly put at ease. Even though this was their first meeting it's as if they were coming home.

Before long Nisha Richards, Wendy Orway, Saul Leeder, Weston Mils, Josh Callins, and Alden Blaines had come in to gather again along the inner hall waiting to see what Nick would do next.

One lone girl was left standing on the porch. She looked around her and realizing she is the very last, stepped forward. Her head was bowed, "I'm Menalee Bosun, it's nice to meet you sir."

It came out in little more than a whisper. Nick leaned forward then with his hand gently brought up her face to meet his gaze. The soft intake of breath was unheard but the aged figure had frozen in place, the look on his face was that of sheer wonder. Finally after an uncomfortably long pause, he spoke, "I think we've met before...but you were a few years older."

Nicholas Chrismon

This comment made everyone including Menalee wonder if this old man had gone completely crazy. The young people jostled each other as they tried to figure out exactly what he meant.

After what seemed like a year, Nick snapped out of his trance and dropped his hand to his side, "Uh, sorry. You just look very much like a dear friend of mine from the past. Did I hear you correctly that your name is Menalee?"

"Yes sir, that is right."

"Remarkable, even your names are the same," he shook his head in disbelief and moved to the side to let her rejoin her friends.

He stepped past the line and continued down the hall, when he turned around he realized the line of children was still where he left them. The soft murmur of curiosity floated to his ears, "What a strange place."

"I like it."

"He's a little loo-loo."

"Yeah, but he's nice."

"What are these things all over? There are piles and piles of them."

This last comment came from Nisha, a thin, pale and rather out-spoken brunette, who, by the look of it, had just captured everyone else's attention. The chuckle that came from Nick caused all the young people to turn back to the elderly man.

Nisha, feeling like she was being mocked, became defensive and piped up, "What's so funny? I just wondered what all this stuff is."

"I'm sorry, Nisha," Nick became instantly contrite; "I just forgot you had never seen books before."

"Books?" Billy interjected. "What are *books*?"

Again, by the sheer quietness of it, Menalee's voice was heard, "I thought that books were just a myth. I didn't think books ever really existed."

"Oh, Menalee my dear, not only did books exist, but books are the reason I exist." Again Nick had hushed the crowd of children.

"Here, let me hand you each a book, then we can talk in the library."

Nick moved to a nearby crate that was stacked on top of others. He reached inside and began searching among the titles, "Chante, you first, this is a book of poetry, sonnets actually on happiness."

Chante grasped the book, still holding Crispy, when Nick spoke to her, "You can let your cat down, I think he is as curious about my house as you are."

As she let Crispy down he gingerly made his way to a stack of books, sniffed at them, and arched his back in a mighty stretch, then letting out a satisfied purr, curled up on the rug, and dozed off.

Nick's voice continued calling out, "Wendy, here is the story of *Cinderella*. Kimber, *The Tale of Tom Thumb*. *Beauty and the Beast* for you, Menalee." Nisha was growing impatient but Nick proceeding quickly made it so she couldn't voice her opinion. "Alden, *Grimm's Fairy Tales*, Josh, *Sherlock Holmes*, *King Arthur* seems right for Weston, Saul, the story of *George Washington*..."

Here he paused, moving to the shelves on the opposite wall, pulled out two more volumes and, "Billy, *The Emperor's New Clothes*, for you, and last but not least, *Aesop's Fables* for Nisha." Now he turned on his heel and called over his shoulder, "Come this way, follow me."

As the visit grew longer it was as if Nick were being recharged, he lead his parade down the rest of the hall and turned into the library. Making his way to his "Secret Stash," he pulled out a book with a red cover and sat down in his 'story chair.' He motioned at the floor around him, "Take a seat."

As the children all seated themselves in a semicircle around Nick's chair, he noticed that they were all clinging to the books as if they had become a part of them.

Nick, seeing this, smiled and thought, "Marty, it's working..."

A hush settled over the group as Nick opened the front cover and turned the first few pages, then something small, round, and copper slipped out of the book and fell onto the carpet. Chante leaned forward and picked it up.

"What is this? It looks quite old."

"Oh, it's a penny," Nick said without interest, but the soft murmurs again caught his attention.

"A penny, is that what he said?'

"Don't know, but it sure looks neat."

Nick chuckled again, realizing that he had created quite a stir, "It's a coin we used to use to buy simple candy or drop into wishing wells, or fountains."

"Oh, it's magic!" explodes Kimber.

"No, it's not magic we used to call it 'change.' It was something we would use to purchase things... it was...

money," Nick attempted, running out of words.

"*Money*? You didn't have riles and pinnets and trecles? How weird!" Billy challenged.

"No, Billy we had pennies, nickels, dimes, quarters, and sometimes fifty-cent pieces."

"I think I get it, but can you tell us how much it is?" ventured Menalee.

"Well Menalee I don't know what you use for money now, I have not been in town for almost fifty years. I only ventured close enough to leave my note on the edge of town just before the wall sealed me off completely twenty years ago."

"Wow! How do you live here without going into Scat-town?"

"I'll explain that later, did you kids want to hear a story?'

"If that is what is in the *book*," Billy had a hard time with the word "book", "I think that would be tercellent!"

"Is that *good*?" Nick wondered aloud.

"Yeah it is," reassured Saul.

"Great, then let's begin," Nick cleared his throat and began:

"Come on in," the old man said.
His face was like a book I'd read.
Filled with lines and surprises
Lots of spies and disguises.
He smiled, reading my blank look
He said, "You've come to find a book."
"Yes, that's right," tentative came.
He smiled and handed me the same.
My hand grasped the old cracked cover
Eyes turned down to look it over.
The title on it nowhere found
The old man gave not a sound.
My excitement rose, I caught my breath
But the man was still as death.
I glanced back up and caught his eye
A faint smile was his reply.
I opened it, the book, you know

The pages turned, out came a glow.
The wind picked up and blew my hair
And when I looked no one was there.
I looked back down into its pages
Witnessed the dawning of many ages.
I glanced around when I was done
And found myself, again, alone.
Time has passed and so have books
Packed in boxes, shelves, and nooks.
I've collected, read and treasured
What I've seen cannot be measured.
All I have to leave behind
I have tucked into my mind.
So listen close, I'll bend your ear
Yes, that's right now gather near…
This story begins ages ago now
Listen close, don't question how.
The boy, once upon a time,
Was a dear friend of mine.
He was cursed with the "acne pimple"
His name, you see, was Marty Whimpel.
He was amazing, such a guy.
I still sometimes question why,
He chose me to tell his tale,
Since he did I've shared it well.
I see you still have questions many,
Well, gather here and see this "penny."
"A penny? What on earth is that?"
Said a girl holding her cat.
"You must listen, please, don't talk
Now let us begin to walk
Through the ages, back in time
So you can meet this friend of mine…

Nick glanced around at the rapt faces gazing up at him, and realized they were all leaning forward in anticipation.

"Do you like it so far?" He asked.

The only answer was nods of affirmation.

"Well, do you find anything odd?" Again he queried.

"Wait," Chante snapped, "it sounds like us, and you even talked about my cat!"

"Yes, now you see why I was so surprised to finally meet you all today. You see, our story has been written for so many years, I have just been waiting for us to live it," again Nick cleared his throat, "Okay, let's go back so you can meet my friend Marty."

Chapter 2
Introducing Marty Whimpel

Thursday, May 18, 1990   **Groomsberg, Wisconsin**

In a darkened bedroom in a small house on Oak Grove Road a young boy sits crouched under his covers. The faint light glowing through the lump of sheets is the only sign of life. Under this mountain of blankets is Marty Whimpel; he's hunched over an open book with a flashlight in his hand. He is reading aloud, but quietly, "the...ca...car...carpet...sw...sw er..swerved...and..A...Ala...Aladdin...al...almost...fell...off." Here, Marty paused, the yelling from outside his covered fortress sounded only slightly muffled.

"Don't tell me your lies anymore!" the shrillness of his mom's voice meant she was close to crying.

"Oh, don't you worry, I won't be 'lying' to you any...more." His dad grunted, he sounded like he was carrying something heavy; as he walked past Marty's room he stopped, and called back toward the bedroom, "Don't expect me to come back, you have two weeks, then this place is sold."

"Fine, just leave," the tears choked Charlotte Whimpel's voice, "We'll be gone by then," she finished as the front door opened. There was no response before the door slammed shut.

Marty threw back his covers, swung his feet to the floor and padded to the window that glowed faintly from the streetlamp outside. He pulled the curtain back enough to see into the driveway where Samuel Whimpel's Chevy Corsica stood, doors ajar and trunk open. His dad threw one suitcase into the trunk and slammed it shut. Then he turned and looked at the house, directly at Marty's window, and shook his head in disgust. He turned back to the remaining garment and carry-on bags, chucked them in the back seat, shut the door and jumped into the driver's seat.

The angry roar of the engine, as he started the car, cut

through the night. The Corsica, backed out of the driveway, disappeared into the inky blackness; its taillights looking like an angry animal retreating into its cave.

"He's never coming back."

Marty's voice startled himself in the silence. Only then did he hear his mother's muffled crying from down the hall. He turned away from the window and debated whether he should go to her. His concern for his mother won out over the anger at his parents so he opened his bedroom door, turned right, passed the bathroom and stopped in the doorway to his parent's room.

At eleven-and-a-half Marty was quite thin, awkward, and very self-conscious, his hands never knew what to do so they commenced to twist his pajama top as he leaned against the doorframe.

"He's gone."

It wasn't a question.

Charlotte looked at Marty and repeated again, "He's gone."

"Okay," Marty didn't know what else to say.

The next thing caught Marty like a punch in the gut, "We're getting a divorce."

Divorce! Marty wanted to shout, but he caught himself and asked, "When?"

"Whenever he gets the papers, I guess."

Charlotte Whimpel was a beautiful woman, but right now her shoulder length chestnut brown hair was rumpled, her blue eyes were puffy and red, her dainty nose was running and she looked almost younger than her son.

"I'm sorry Marty, I don't know what else to say," she seemed utterly defeated as she sank back against her pillows.

"Mom," Marty stepped further into the room, "We'll do okay, I'll...we'll be fine." His anger gave way to the fright of a child, and then that gave way to the pain he saw his mother going through. *His* fears would have to wait; right now his mom needed him.

"How are we going to live?" She asked the ceiling.

"Have you called Grandma Pen?" Marty's attempt at a solution only brought a new rush of tears.

"No, how can I tell her Samuel's gone?" Charlotte sobbed and turned her face into her pillow, muffling any further sobs. Marty climbed onto the bed and sidled alongside his mother's huddled frame. He reached out and began smoothing down her hair. Just that simple act caused his mom to visibly relax, her sobs subsided and, after a few minutes, broken only by a slight shudder occasionally, she slipped off to sleep.

He took the quilt that was folded at the foot of the bed, spread it over her sleeping figure, tucked it around her, and shut off her bedroom light. Then, tiptoeing back to his room, he left the front room light on, just because. He went into his room, closed the door quietly, climbed into bed, wrapped himself into a cocoon of blankets and began humming softly to himself, then his own tears came. Hot, salty, and bitter he let them pour down his cheeks unchecked. Finally they subsided and he stretched out onto his bed staring at the slightly glowing window barely blinking.

Friday, May 19, 1990

He must have dosed off because his room was now filled with early morning light. The faint sounds from the kitchen floated to him, it had all just been a nightmare. He stretched, pushed back his covers and got out of bed. His eyes burned a little, then he remembered crying. Was that real? He opened the door and made his way down the hall to the kitchen. Turning left into the sheer whiteness of the kitchen was almost blinding this morning. He stopped in his tracks.

His mother looked like one of those cheesy robots on T.V. She was moving around doing things, staring unseeingly ahead. Her makeup was undone, her hair was uncombed and she was still in her wrinkled silky pajamas. Finally she realized he was standing there and flashed an unfelt grin, "Morning sweetie, breakfast will be ready in a minute."

He wanted to just hug her, but instead he said, "Okay," and moved toward the dining room avoiding a glance toward his dad's chair. He sat, trying to soak everything in, but couldn't shake the feeling of emptiness the house now had.

After a few minutes Charlotte entered the room carrying two plates of eggs and ham, she placed them on the table and slid into her seat. Taking his hand, she gave it a squeeze and asked, "Whose turn is it for the blessing?"

Dad's, it was left unspoken, then, swallowing over the lump in his throat he said instead, "Mine." They bowed their heads and blessed the food avoiding anything about the new void in their lives and pretending everything was the same, "Amen."

"Amen." Hers came much more quiet than usual, then, "thank you."

"No problem, mom, let's eat," this forced cheerfulness was wearing him out! He just wanted to scream and hit someone, mainly his dad, and tell him how unfair this was, but then he smiled and added, "Don't want the chicken to get mad at us for wasting all her hard work."

This brought a soft chuckle and an appreciative glance that again said 'Thank You' without words. They ate; he picked up his plate, took it to the kitchen and placed it in the sink. Suddenly Marty realized he was not going to stay in this house anymore. The thought hit him quite hard. After all, he grew up here and he had many fond memories either here or at the school library with Mrs. Rousekewitz.

"Mrs. Rousekewitz! I have to tell her!" This thought tore at Marty's insides. "Rousy" as he affectionately caller her was like an adopted grandmother to Marty. She had never had children of her own so the students at Mt. Bloom

Elementary were her kids while they were there and many came back to visit often. That's what Marty had planned to do, too, but if he were going to move, would he still be able to see Rousy? He almost asked his mom, but decided against it. She was in enough pain right now.

Marty rinsed off his dish and left it to soak in the sink. He showered quickly and dressed for school. He dressed extra nice today, there were only three days left of school after the weekend. He wanted to leave a good last impression on his teacher, but mostly on Rousy.

He looked in the mirror on the back of his door and checked himself over. His dust brown hair was staying down for once without extra coaxing. He was wearing a jungle green shirt, which made his eyes look green, even though his eyes were usually blue, they were chameleon, and they changed with what he wore. His eyes were his very favorite feature. In his mind it was the only exciting thing he owned. The nose betrayed his relation to his father, but his mouth was his mother's. Overall he wasn't too fond of his appearance, but he was proud that he resembled his mother more than his father at this moment.

He breathed a silent prayer to have strength at school and not break down, reached out, opened the door and stepped out into the hallway, "Mom, I'm ready!" he cried.

"Okay, one sec, I'm putting my face on."

Marty loved that expression, when he was younger he actually thought that his mom had her face in a jar and she was putting it back on for the day. Now he knew it was just her make-up, but still, he liked the saying.

Charlotte came out of the bathroom fluffing her hair, she stopped, smiled at Marty and twirled so her skirt flared out, "How do I look?"

"Uh, great Mom, really smashing!" Marty was caught off guard; his mom looked much younger than her forty-eight years.

She giggled, came forward, hugged Marty, then taking him alongside headed toward the front room. "Do you really think so?"

"Yeah Mom, where did you get that outfit, it's beautiful!" Marty was genuinely impressed.

"This old thing?" She dropped into an exaggerated southern drawl, "Why suh, I do buleeve yo' fluhtin with little ol' me!"

"Oh Mom, I love you!"

"I love you too, Marty. Let's get going so we don't ruin your perfect record."

Marty really didn't care if he ruined his attendance record; he only had it because his mom was always so punctual. He just went along for the ride.

"Mom, what are you going to do today?" he asked it as carefree as he could, but secretly he wanted to know if he should call home to check on her later.

"Oh," her brow furrowed, "Well, I think I'm going to call Grandma Pen and then go from there."

Grandma Pen or Pearl Pentel, Charlotte's mother lived in a small town in Utah. She had been living there forever as far as Marty knew, he had never heard of her living anywhere else. He thought for a minute, what was the name of that town where she lived? Scant? No, Scamp? Oh yeah, Scat-town, that's it. Marty had only met Grandma Pen one time, that had been two years ago when he traveled with his mom to his Grandpa Rufus' funeral. That had been the first time Marty had been on a plane. That had been a lot of firsts in his life. First plane ride, first meetings, first funeral, first time out of Groomsberg. Well now he was the first person he knew whose parents were going to get divorced. He hated firsts!

Sure, sometimes they were great, but usually they were reeking masses of garbage.

"I agree!" Alden interjected.

Nick stopped reading and lowered the book to look at

the somber face of the young boy. It was rounded with youth, but it also carried a look of worldly wisdom and sadness that shouldn't be part of any child's countenance.

"My parents got divorced too," Alden continued, "I can completely understand what Marty is going through."

Nick nodded sympathetically and asked, "Would you like some time before we continue?"

"No, I'd like to hear how Marty deals with it, maybe it will help me."

"Alright then, we'll continue," Nick looked down again at the book and quickly found his place.

"Where are you?" Marty's mom queried.

This snapped him out of his thoughts, "Oh, I was just thinking about Rousy," he lied, "I think she would have been a great mom, it's too bad she never had kids."

Charlotte smiled, "You're really going to miss her aren't you?"

"Well, I can still go visit her, its not like Central Junior High is *that* far away." Maybe this test would get him the answers he wanted.

"Maybe," Charlotte sidestepped the situation by changing the subject, "You sure look nice today."

"Oh, thanks," Marty knew this was going to be bad if his mom wouldn't even comment on whether or not he could visit Rousy. Well, he had better plan for the worst and be pleasantly surprised with anything better.

The Toyota Tercel pulled parallel to the curb in front of Mt. Bloom Elementary, Marty opened the door and hopped out.

"Aren't you forgetting something?" His mom had leaned over with her cheek turned toward him.

"Oh, yeah, sorry," he leaned back in, pecked her on the cheek, "Love ya, mom, have a good day." He turned and ran off in the direction of the trailers behind the school where the library was located.

"Rousy! How are you?" Marty called as he stepped

through the door into the library.

"Shhh, Marty, you know this is a library," Sheryl Rousekewitz chided, she tried to look stern without much success. "Oh come here and give old Rousy a hug!"

Marty dropped his book bag on one of the plastic chairs by the computers and hugged Rousy.

"My goodness, did you grow more?" he was almost past her height, but she didn't mind at all.

"Oh Rousy, you always ask that, I was just here yesterday!" Marty said in mock exasperation.

"Has it been that long?" Rousy played along.

"Sorry I didn't write, I know how you worry." Marty loved playing these games with her.

Marty looked at this silver haired lady, her generous bun bound at the nape of her neck. She had some flyaway hairs that made it look like she had just woken up. Marty loved this woman almost as much as his own mother. All of a sudden the tears broke through and started racing down his cheeks, "Oh, Rousy," He grabbed her around the neck.

She was completely caught off guard, "Honey, what's wrong?" She patted him on the back, trying to comfort him even without knowing the problem. After a full minute Marty finally pulled away, his face flushed, tears wetting his cheeks. He gasped for air, "My...parents...Oh Rousy!" He shook his head and put his face in his hands.

"What's wrong with your parents, Marty? Did something happen?"

He nodded his head, his face still in his hands.

"What is it? What happened?"

"They're...getting...divorced!" it was muffled because he spoke into his hands.

"Oh, honey, I'm so sorry, is there anything I can do?" Rousy's motherly instincts were working overtime.

He shook his head, "There's nothing anyone can do. Dad hates me!"

This caught Rousy by surprise, and she leaned forward taking Marty's shoulder, "What? Your father doesn't hate you!"

"Oh yes he does, it's because I can't do anything right! I'm so clumsy and stupid; He's embarrassed to be my dad."

Rousy waited until Marty had stopped his personal belittling and then said, "I don't think your parents are getting divorced because of you. Usually people get divorced because they just don't see things the same anymore or they just fall out of love with each other..." This insight caught Marty off guard, before he came back in with more of his weaknesses, he looked at Rousy. She was sitting down now, looking at the hands folded in her lap.

"Rousy, how do you know about divorce?" She looked up sadly, the answer written clearly in her eyes.

"You...you're divorced?" This blew Marty away. Rousy nodder her head slowly the overhead lights catching her half-moon spectacles as she did so.

She spoke quietly, it came from far inside her, "Lewis was my one true love. I thought we would be together forever..."

Marty sat down beside her, still watching this new side of Rousy.

"Then he started working late, going on business trips..." she laughed softly, "How blind could I be?"

Marty shrugged, not knowing what else to do.

"Finally he came home from one of his 'conferences' and told me he no longer loved me." Her head bent down toward her lap. Then Marty saw something that twisted his heart, she was crying!

"Rousy, I..."

Rousy looked up and shook her head, "No, Marty, you need to know it's not your fault, just like it was not my fault. It's been almost forty years since Lewis left me, for most of those years I blamed myself. I don't want you to go through that. Lewis made a choice. Unfortunately that choice affected me. It changed my life. If he hadn't left me, I never would have gone back to school, graduated in Library Science, and taken this job as a Librarian."

Mrs. Rousekewitz "Rousy"

This made Marty stop, "You mean you would not have been here if you were still married?"

Rousy shook her head, "Nope, I'd have stayed home and raised a family, but now I have thousands of children. I enjoy watching you all grow up and then come back to visit me." Her head came up, her shoulders pulled back and she looked past Marty, into her past or off into the future, Marty wasn't sure, but she looked triumphant.

"Lewis may have left me, but he didn't break me, he lost me. I have gone on to live, that's what you need to do Marty, live, be the best *you*, you can be."

"But how, Rousy? I'm not good at anything. I look funny, I stink at sports, I can't draw, I can barely read, the only accomplishment I have is a perfect attendance record, I could be a potato and get that!" Marty now looked at Rousy and she looked deep into his eyes.

"What do you *want* to be Marty?"

"What?" Marty wasn't expecting to be quizzed right now.

"What do you want to be? Think about it. That is what you need to find out, as soon as you know that, nothing can stop you!"

"You really think so?" Marty asked doubtfully. He turned away.

"I know so," the conviction in Rousy's voice made Marty look back at her.

"What do *you* think I could be?" he hoped she would help him.

"Anything, and I mean *anything*!"

That was it? That was all the advice he was going to get?

"Okay," he knew it came out a little sarcastic but he couldn't help it.

"Marty, just think about it over the weekend, and on Monday come with a list of things you want to be. Can you do that for me?"

"Yeah, I'll try. Thanks, Rousy, I better get to class." He hugged her again, grabbed his bag and headed out of the library as the first bell rang.

The remainder of school passed without consequence and the final bell signaled the end of the day. Marty made his way toward the front of the school to wait for his mom. As he waited, Rousy's challenge ate at him, "What do you *want* to be?" Again he shook his head, "I don't know Rousy, I just don't know."

The Tercel honked and pulled alongside the curb. Marty waved, and climbed in, "Hi Mom, did you have a good day?"

She smiled, but he could tell her heart wasn't in it. She looked as if she'd been crying again but he didn't press the matter.

"How 'bout we go out tonight?" She forced cheerfulness.

"Sounds like fun, Mom, where are we going?" he played along trying to stay cheerful himself.

"Let's go to PJ's, we haven't had pizza for a while."

"Sounds good. I talked to Rousy today."

"Oh, how is she doing?"

Marty wanted to tell her about Rousy's divorce, but decided against it. "She's fine, she just told me I should think about what I want to be, why would she want me to do that?"

"She cares about you and can tell you're having a hard time growing up," Charlotte wiped at her eyes and turned to Marty, "So, have you thought about it?"

"A little, but I haven't come up with anything yet." This was sort of true, he had actually thought of hundreds of fantastic things but had shot them down one at time for various reasons: Too skinny, too stupid, too young, why try?

"You know you can be anything you want. You have so many opportunities that I never had," Charlotte's eyes twinkled as she looked at her son.

Her encouragement sounded very similar to Rousy's, but a little different, "What do you mean, mom?"

"If you decide now, you will have six more years to prepare while you are in school, that's almost eight years before I decided."

"Really? Was that when you met dad?" Marty was

intrigued. This was more than he knew about his mom.

"Yes, that was the year that Samuel Alden Whimpel walked across campus and into my heart," her voice had become dreamy like a schoolgirl.

"Alden? I didn't know that was dad's middle name."

"Marty's dad had *my* name?" Alden's voice was filled with wonder and a touch of disgust. "I don't know if I want to be named after a guy who walked out on his family."

"But Alden, weren't you named after your grandfather?" Nick questioned from behind the ancient cracked red binding.

Alden was a little surprised that Nick knew about his family, but being reminded about his grandfather helped him to feel better about his name. He loved his grandfather; he was the only person who ever acted like they cared about him.

"Can we get back to the story?" Billy was becoming impatient with all of the interruptions.

Nick looked over at the dashing youth, "Yes, Billy, we can resume with the story, *if* Alden agrees."

"Well, Al, what do you say, can we get on with the story?" Billy requested.

Alden nodded to Nick, who cleared his crackly throat and read:

Charlotte explained, "I know, he hated it so he was always 'Sam' to his friends. He was tall and broad shouldered. I loved his wavy brown hair and the way he smiled made my heart melt."

"How old were you?" Marty felt safe to ask questions that were along the line of the conversation, then he wouldn't have to talk about what he wanted to be.

"I was twenty, he was twenty-four," she sighed, "It seems like yesterday, it's been twenty-eight years! I can't believe it."

Marty looked at her, she was wiping at her tears quietly. He reached down, fetched the box of tissues from under his seat and handed her one.

"Thanks," she dabbed at her eyes and turned to Marty, "We'll be all right, Marty, really we will." Her reassurance was more for her than for Marty, but he didn't let on that he knew as much.

"I know mom, we have each other, we'll be fine." Marty watched his mother out of the corner of his eye; she seemed to be doing better. Good, he thought to himself, I've got to stay strong, for both of us.

A few hours later Charlotte and Marty were seated at PJ's waiting for their supreme pizza, heavy on the olives.

"So," Charlotte began trying to make this a natural transition into a conversation, "I called Grandma Pen today."

"Oh, how is she doing?" Marty could sense his mother's tension gauge raise about 50 notches so he tried to keep his expression as calm as possible.

"Well, she's sure lonesome since Grandpa Rufus passed away. I said we may come to visit her, what do you think?" She held her breath and Marty could tell she was really hoping for his approval.

"Sounds like fun, mom," his mother heaved a sigh of relief before he continued. "Is this 'visit' for an extended period of time?"

Charlotte's look would have been almost humorous if Marty didn't know the serious nature of the conversation, "Where did you get all these big words all of a sudden?"

"I've been working out what to say all day," Marty was proud of himself for taking such a big part in their decision making.

"Oh? So, were you expecting us to go to Grandma Pen's?" Openly curious now, his mother leaned forward.

"Yeah, I was pretty sure we would leave, and I don't know anywhere farther than Utah to go to."

This time his mom's chuckle was sincere, "You got that right. I guess we could have gone to the black hole of Calcutta," she paused to watch Marty's reaction, "but I don't have any relations there."

Marty laughed, he loved his mom's sense of humor, "Is there really even a black hole of Calcutta?"

"I'm not sure, but I would have done some research before we moved there."

"Mom, wherever we go, I don't mind," he sighed. "I just wish I could take Rousy too."

Charlotte was touched by the deep affection that Marty had for his librarian, "You're going to miss her, aren't you?"

"Something awful, especially..." his voice died off.

"Especially, what?"

"Well, today when I went to talk to Rousy about the divorce, she told me she's been divorced too."

Charlotte was not expecting this, "She told you that?"

"Yeah, she was married and then her husband Lewis fell out of love with her, at least that's what she said." He thought deeply for a minute, "Is *that* what happened to you and dad?"

Charlotte nodded, shook her head, and then spoke, "Well, sort of, your dad fell out of love; I'm still stuck in it."

"Love sounds a lot like glue," Marty observed.

This brought his mom's eyes up to meet his, "It is, sort of, so you have to be extra careful where you put it, because it's super strong and you might get stuck to something that doesn't want you there." She sighed, "That's what happened to me anyway."

"Well, Mom, I still love you and I don't think I put my 'glue' in the wrong place," he smiled and grabbed her hand.

"Oh, sweetheart, you always know just what to say." The pizza arrived and they enjoyed eating in silence. Then Charlotte looked at Marty and asked, "So, have you thought about what Rousy asked you to do?"

Marty nodded.

"Are you going to share with me?"

"I'm not sure yet, so I can't share with you," he thought

briefly, then finished, "but when I figure it out, I'll let you know."

Charlotte Pentel Whimpel

She smiled, "Okay, I guess I can wait."

That night Marty sat in his room at his desk well after his mom went to bed. In front of him were a blank piece of paper and three new pens (just in case one ran out). He stared at the page until the lines became blurry and he leaned forward onto his folded arms as he fell asleep.

Chapter 3
Somewhere

The trail was worn and rocky; Marty stumbled, but caught himself before he fell. He looked over his shoulder, unable to see what was chasing him, but sure it was still there. He turned back to the trail and plodded on. He came to a fork in the trail. One path went down, and the other continued up. He chose the left side, the one that headed up. He couldn't go down, he knew that wouldn't help. How he knew he wasn't sure, he just knew it.

While picking his way along the constantly rising trail it suddenly became covered in a tangle of branches. He fought against them, getting scratched but not caring, he had to get through. Suddenly the branches were gone and the trail was clear again. He pushed on, his goal was at the top, he knew that much, but what was on the top?

The shrill screech made him cover his ears, it came from overhead. He looked up, but the sun blinded his vision, what is it? Marty stopped, looking for cover, then seeing none, he turned back toward the trail. He was sweating now and reached up to wipe his forehead, the saltiness becoming sticky. He pulled his hand away and looked at it, it was covered in blood!

"Why is Marty bleeding? Is this a dream or something?" Nisha asked, stopping Nick in mid sentence.

Nick smiled at the vocal brunette and then looked at the rest of the group. Their faces showed signs of concern, anxiety, and curiosity. "It will all make sense in a moment. Just wait Nisha, you will soon find out."

Nick found it endearing that the children were getting so involved with the tale he had to tell about his friend. Finding his place in the aged volume, Nick started reading again.

Marty knew he was going to be sick, he started getting dizzy, and then he was falling unable to catch himself.

Saturday, May 20, 1990

Marty sat up. He looked wildly around, but he was seated at his desk again. "What happened?" he asked aloud. That had been too real to be a dream, but now that he found himself in his room in his house in Groomsberg Wisconsin, he knew that is exactly what it had been.

He looked at his desk and found the pile of papers scattered, only a few were left in place and those were damp with sweat. That was when Marty realized *he* was damp with sweat too. *The dream had been so real, what was it about? Where was I trying to go? What was that thing following me? Why was I bleeding?* This was just the start of his questions.

Only after all these questions rushed forward in his mind did he realize that the sun was up and shining in his window. What time was it? He glanced around and saw his clock radio was blinking. The power must have gone out sometime during the night. The overhead light that Marty had left on when he fell asleep wasn't on, "The power surge must have popped the bulb," he thought. Rising from his bed, he flipped off the switch, grabbed the chair, and climbed up to retrieve the dead light bulb. He reached around the light shade and...nothing was there.

Marty quickly unscrewed the little fastener that held the glass shade in place, holding the shade with both hands he brought it off of the fixture. He almost dropped the glass cover, there was nothing there. Empty sockets where two light bulbs had previously been!

"Is he still dreaming?" Nisha interrupted Nick, her forehead wrinkled with concern.

Nick's loving smile again met Nisha's questioning gaze, "Patience, Nisha, patience."

Once more Nick found his place and began.

"Marty stepped off the chair and placed the glass cover

on his bed and sat down. Suddenly his knees felt very weak, what had happened after he fell asleep? His mom would not try a prank like this just to freak him out, but who did? Marty's mind was trying to figure out how to ask his mom without raising a lot of questions.

The thought struck him so quickly he almost shouted with joy, *I'll just check around the house quietly to see if the power went out and then ask mom about it, yeah, that's it.*

He made his way to his door and quietly opened it, slid into the hallway and down to the living room. He looked at the clock, nope still the right time. Wait! This clock was battery operated, he chuckled at his forgetfulness. He turned and walked back down the hallway past his room, then past the bathroom and turned into the kitchen. He glanced at the microwave it too read 8:12 a.m. No, it wasn't a power outage. Prickles on the back of his neck stood up. A hand slowly settled on his shoulder, and he swung around ready to Karate chop his opponent!

His mom laughed, "My goodness Marty, you sure are jumpy this morning!"

"Sorry, Mom, you just startled me," he tried to cover up his over-excited behavior.

"Want some breakfast?"

"Yeah, sure, need any help?"

"No, it will just be a few minutes. You can go lay back down."

"No!" Marty snapped so fiercely his mom looked at him concerned.

"Are you all right sweetheart? Did something frighten you?"

This is where he could spill all, about his flashing clock, his missing light bulbs, and his bizarre dream, but Marty shook his head, "No, Mom, sorry I snapped, I just didn't sleep very well, I was thinking about what I wanted to be."

Even to him this excuse sounded lame, but his mother

nodded, "Okay, well just watch some cartoons or something."

"Yeah, I think I will," he turned and made his way back toward the living room, avoiding a sideways glance into his bedroom. He flopped down on the couch and flipped on the TV. Soon he was laughing over the antics of *Slap Happy Pappy and the Mushy Muskrats*. His mom's call to breakfast caught his attention. He clicked off the TV and headed into the dining room. He avoided looking at his father's chair and took his seat next to his mom.

"My turn for prayer," she piped up.

"Yeah, that's right," he smiled at her, they held hands, bowed their heads and she began praying.

Silently Marty searched his brain, *What kind of hallucinations am I having?* He thought deeply about this until his mother squeezed his hand.

"Are you asleep?"

"No," he hesitated.

"Did you hear the prayer?"

"Yeah, sorry, I was thinking," Marty's brain raced for an excuse "I need some new light bulbs, mine burned out."

"Already? I just put some new ones in," then stopping, she thought, "Well, maybe it has been a while. I'll get you some after breakfast."

Whew! That was close, Marty thought, *that covered the problem and changed the subject!*

Breakfast finished, they put their dishes in the sink. "Do you want to help me clean?" Charlotte was fishing to see what Marty had been doing.

"Sure Mom," he really didn't want to clean, but it would keep his mind off of his room.

"I thought we could start to pack things we don't want so we can give them to charity."

"Okay," he said, not really registering, then, "What? Oh, you mean we are going to "pack light" for our visit to Grandma Pen's?"

Delight at Marty's willingness to play along during this horrible crisis touched Charlotte, and she began to cry.

"Mom, what's wrong?" Instantly Marty was to her, the concern written plainly on his face.

"Nothing, I...this is all so much to make you go through..." her voice trailed off.

"Mom, it's not your fault, dad made a choice," Rousy's words fit here very well, "don't let that choice break you. He's the one that's losing."

Charlotte turned to Marty, "You're not quite twelve and here you are giving your mother advice on coping strategies."

"Sorry," he shrank back a bit.

"No, it's okay, that's really excellent advice, thank you Marty."

Bouncing instantly back he hugged her, "You're welcome, any time, and I won't even charge you for it!"

This brought laughs from both of them. "Well, on to our cleaning spree!" She smiled and he followed her into the hall. "You tackle your room and I'll get mine." While this sounded fair to her it struck fear into his heart.

"Uh, okay, sounds good," this was the only thing he could say that wouldn't worry his mother.

They parted, his mother going down the hall into her room, and Marty made his way into his where he froze in the doorway. The clock was no longer flashing it was showing the correct time. Even more, the light cover was back in place and the light was on.

He turned around and rubbed his eyes and turned again facing his room. Yep, the clock was fixed and his light was on. Had he been imagining things before? Maybe, but he doubted it. He flipped the switch and the light turned off. The light coming in from outside was bright enough; he didn't need his overhead light now anyway.

He walked into his room, shut the door, and sat on his

bed, still running through his actions of the morning. He slid along his bed until he was stretched out with his head resting on his pillow. Rolling onto his side, he felt something poke him in the back. He sat up and turned around. There, right where he had left it two days before, was his book of stories. He reached out, picked it up and realized that it was oddly warm to the touch. Prickles rose up the back of his neck again, this was way too strange.

He flipped open the book to where he had been reading, *Aladdin and His Magic Lamp*. He had been reading this when he heard his dad leave, he hadn't picked it up since. As he flipped through the book to see the illustrations, he came to two pages that were stuck together, "I don't remember that," he muttered to himself as he laid the book on his desk to try and pry them apart. As he pried, he felt the heat again. This time it was centered on the stuck-together pages.

He continued prying until finally, as if by magic, they gave way. He gasped at what he saw. There, inside the book, was a place, it would have been an illustration, but it was moving just like a miniature television screen. He watched intently to see what he could find out about the place in the picture. There was a bridge over a small river, the river rippled as the wind rustled the leaves on the trees and also bent the long grass. The river gurgled along, but this couldn't be, it was inside a book! He kept trying to rationalize this but, at the same time, he couldn't pull his eyes off this unknown land.

Suddenly, a small face appeared, as if in close up on TV, it screamed, "Help me!" and then it turned and the creature flew over the bridge and disappeared.

"This is insane!" Marty still tried to explain this away, but he couldn't. As he considered what to do, he heard the shrill shriek from his dream coming from the book. He froze, cold sweat breaking out on his forehead. That poor creature, whatever it was, was being hunted as he had been in his dream. He had to help it, but how?

Chapter 4
When a Doorway Opens

Marty's gaze fell upon the writing on the page opposite the moving landscape, it read:

> The fairy-like trillos, Scrimt and Sayvd,
> For their master, worked and slaved.
> Sweat and toil were their lot,
> Gold paid for freedom goes for naught.
> They were cursed to lives like this,
> Only freed by love's first kiss.
> Their master is the witch Bismorda,
> You'd be blind to kiss, well, sorta.
> Only if you keep in mind,
> This one act so true and kind,
> Would bind the trillos to you forever,
> And they would not forsake you, ever.

So he had to help these "trillos" okay, but how did he get in the book? In answer to this question he looked down at the page and noticed a small picture of a door at the very bottom. In microscopic print it said,

> "Open door, take key,
> any door will portal be."

Intrigued, he touched the door and felt the wood of it under his index finger. It was so small how would he get it open, and when he did, how would he get the key?

He quickly looked around and found...nothing. What was he looking for?

Something small enough to open a miniature door...tweezers!

He had a pair in his drawer; he retrieved them and was all ready, when he heard his mom approaching.

He shut the book and slipped the tweezers into his pocket. "Look natural," he told himself, then remembered he was supposed to be going through stuff for packing.

He raced to his closet and grabbed armloads of clothes, took them from the closet, turned and dropped them on the floor. He had just got his third load dropped when the doorknob turned and his mom entered.

"Wow, you're really cleaning out your clothes, that's a good place to start. The ones that don't fit anymore can go in one pile, then take out the stuff you never wear, that should leave you with a manageable amount." Then, to herself, she muttered, "I wish I didn't have so many clothes. It's going to take me so much longer than you." She smiled and stepped back into the hallway, "Well, I'll let you get back to work, see ya in a while." With that she pulled the door shut and retreated back down the hall.

When he heard her go into her room he jumped over the pile of clothes and again opened the book. The stuck together pages were easier to pry open the second time and he found himself again looking at the same scene of the bridge and river.

He turned his attention to the small door and extracted the tweezers from his pocket. Using them he carefully tried to pull on the door, but it wouldn't budge. He had to turn the knob, but how? What would make the tweezers grab the handle? Something sticky…gum! He would use just a dab of gum in the tweezers to make them sticky. Again he went to his desk, rummaged through two drawers before he found a stick of *Chewy Bubbles,* his favorite gum. He popped it into his mouth and furiously chewed trying to get it soft and sticky. After he had worked it into a normal gum consistency he bit off a miniscule piece and placed it in the tweezers. He pushed the tips together and…Voila!

He had a sticky "hand" to use on the doorknob. He again worked at the door and it came open.

There, inside the shallow opening, lay a key. He cleaned off the tweezers and picked up the key with them. He let it fall onto his extended forefinger; it was so small he could barely see it! How was this supposed to change a door into a portal?

Even as he thought this, the key began to buzz quietly, become warm, and enlarge until it was the size of a normal house key. It may have been a normal sized key, but it was nowhere near normal!

It had a weird creature wrapped around the handle part, but it was all metal. He looked closer and it looked like....well nothing he'd ever seen before, but that was the same case with the trillos up until twenty minutes ago.

With the key in his hand he realized that he was now risking the wrath of Bismorda, whom he had never seen, for Scrimt or Sayvd, whichever one he had seen. This was truly crazy! Again he looked closely at the key and was amazed at the detail.

It looked like a dragon, well kind of. It had wings and a long neck, then it had the body of a snake, it was all wound up on the key. The key part was like one he had seen in an antique book once. It had just a single tooth and then a rounded protrusion on the end.

How was this supposed to work on my door?

He took a glance at his bedroom doorknob, his heart sank, there wasn't even a keyhole in it!

Before he gave up he decided he would look closer, after all, he had missed the door in the book at first glance too.

He stood up and made his way to his door, he gripped the key tightly in his fist, as he got closer a strange glow surrounded the doorknob, and he bent to examine it.

There, right in the center, a keyhole had appeared!

He put the key in place and turned it, it clicked, and then stopped. Marty, for some reason, thought that something more would happen. After all, what was so magical about a simple "clicking" sound? He withdrew the key from the knob, and the glow dimmed. Placing the key in his pocket, he reached out, and turned the knob. It turned easily in his sweaty hand and he opened the door.

The first thing he heard was the sound of running water. He glanced around the door and was greeted by a world dimmed somehow by a shadow. The river flowed not two feet in front of his own two feet and there was a brick wall opposite him. It took a moment to realize where he was, then it hit.

I'm under the bridge!

Stepping out the door and onto the grassy bank, he pulled the door closed behind himself. The bank was very narrow; he made his way to the mouth of the bridge and looked out. The colors that hit him were so vivid he squinted. He had never seen such green! Walking out into the sunlight he continued along the banks for a few feet then he remembered why he was here, the trillos!

Looking at the bridge behind him he was surprised to see the illustration from the book in real life! He walked back to the bridge and crossed it slowly trying to think what to do next. The trillo had flown over the bridge in this direction, where was he going?

Then Marty saw it.

About a mile away there was a building, at least it looked like one, tucked into some softly rolling hills. That must be were the trillos were being held prisoner!

Determined now, he set out to free Scrimt and Sayvd. His walk was an easy one. The path was smooth and tamped down.

Smiling, Marty began picturing himself as he laid out his plans, this was going to be easy.

First, he would walk in, demand the trillos be set free, then, if necessary, throw water on the witch and watch her melt. That was how you took care of witches, wasn't it? The path he was on led him lazily through the countryside. He enjoyed the walk; it was nice and cool with a light breeze blowing.

The sun overhead was warm on his back.

Then the sun dimmed, "Must be a cloud," Marty thought aloud.

He continued walking and, sure enough, the sun came back out.

Then for some reason, prickles raised on his neck, and he felt that something was behind him. He stopped, listening intently, but no sound followed. He started walking again, but the sound of his feet hitting the path was gone, there was no sound!

Now he was really starting to get frightened, how could he hear someone following him if he couldn't hear his own footsteps? He glanced quickly behind him, but wasn't surprised to find just an empty path. Cold sweat beaded up on his forehead.

It was beginning to be like his dream!

He started walking faster on the path, trying to think, his heart racing. The trail was getting a little steeper now and the trees more dense, he broke into a run. No sound anywhere, it was suffocating him, there was no way all sound could be blocked! Whirling, Marty lost his balance and almost fell on the path, but caught himself just in time. He looked around himself, shielding his head with one arm raised, the other coming out to stop any blows aimed at his chest.

Qualf

Nothing attacked.

Nothing moved.

Nothing came close.

And whatever it was, NOTHING began to close in.

There was nothing behind him but, even as he thought that, he knew he was wrong. This "nothing" was still following him, he could feel it. The feeling was growing stronger with every second. He turned and ran with added strength up the ever-steeper trail. He came to the fork in the path one going down and the other going up just like his dream. Flashes of his nightmare filled his mind.

Next the screech would be coming; he knew it, then the blood. He had to change the dream, but how? Stopping; he looked around, there was nothing sharp anywhere on the path to defend himself with.

All he saw were rocks jutting out of the hard ground. Falling to his knees, Marty tried to scratch at the ground around one of the rocks.

Wait, the key!

He remembered he still had it in his pocket. Pulling it out he looked at it. The creature wrapped around the key looked different, it had moved! It was now coiled down around where the key should go into the lock. Staring at it for a second in disbelief not comprehending how a key could change he thought something that made his heart stop, *I can't get back to my room without this key!* Then the next thought hit him, *Maybe whatever is following me wants this key too...I'll bury it!*

That sounded good. Marty stepped off the path into the shaded dirt under the trees. He fell to his knees and dug easily into the loosely packed dirt then he saw leaves flutter down slowly around him. Looking up, he could see that something had just landed in the trees above him because the branches were dangerously bowed under the weight of something enormous. Squinting to look closer he couldn't see anything except the branches hanging down under a great weight.

"It's invisible!" he whispered, but no sound came out.

Apparently, whatever it was wasn't going to harm him or he would have been eaten by now so he turned his focus back to the key. He shoved it into the shallow hole and covered it quickly. Standing, he turned back toward the trail.

No, he needed some way to mark the spot so he could find it again. Searching his pockets he found a penny.

It would work.

After placing it on the small mound he turned again to leave, glancing back just once at the area he then stepped back onto the path. About ten steps later he realized that he could hear his footfall on the path and the rustling of the leaves, even the sound of a distant bird, the sounds were back, all of them!

"Was the creature gone?" Menalee's timid voice halted Nick in his reading.

Looking over the binding at her large hazel eyes, "Yes, it was Menalee," Nick looked around at the large upturned eyes of the group and asked, "Were you frightened?"

The answers were varied, but most of the boys acted brave and the girls acted relieved that the creature was gone.

"Let me tell you all a secret," Nick's voice took on a conspiratorial tone and they all leaned in to hear, "Marty was never so scared as when he retold this story, every time I heard it, I was scared too."

Then, clearing his throat, Nick refocused on the small print of the page of the aged book in his lap.

For some reason Marty felt safer without the key in his possession. Could it have led the creature to him? How? He pondered on this as he continued up the hill. The trillo's cry ringing in his memory made him speed up his pace; he had to help them *if* he could. In a short time the path came out of the woods and stopped right in front of the building he had seen from a distance. "Building" was the best word that described it. He stopped to see if he could find a way in.

As he circled the structure he studied it. The front or what should have been the front was a type of castle-looking thing. It had the big turrets of a castle but no front entrance. The top of the wall was notched at intervals, also like a castle, but there were no sentries posted to stand guard on it. As he went around the side he came upon what looked like a giant aquarium instead of another wall, everything was under water behind glass. There were some very strange things moving around inside that Marty had never seen before. After looking for another moment he found there was no hint of a door on this side either so he pushed on to try and find a solution to this current dilemma. He continued to what should have been the back and found something that looked like a shed off in the woods.

Taking note of it, he turned back to study the third wall of the "building," this side was like the inside of an oyster, but Marty had never seen a wall made of it before.

It was breathtaking.

The iridescence glimmered in the semi-shade changing from white to pink, to purple, and then to blue as he walked along the length of it. Again, there was no door or entrance of any kind.

"Well, there's only one wall left," Marty said, to no one at all as he turned one more time to view the last length of the structure. If the iridescent wall was stunning and strange to Marty, this final one was mind boggling. It was filled with tiny prisms, or something that looked like prisms, running the entire length of the wall. Overall it looked similar to a kaleidoscope, but on a much larger scale. This final wall did not have an entrance of any kind either. Marty actually realized he had not expected one, and that was strange.

Retracing his steps along the prism wall, he remembered that odd little shed behind the building; he figured he would see if there was anything in there. He made his way toward the rundown shed. As he approached it he could see the weeds that were grown up around it and almost decided against it.

"Oh, it can't hurt, I'll give it a try."

He was at the door to the small wooden hut that was probably the gardeners' by the looks of it. He pulled on the handle and was surprised to find the door opened easily.

Inside wasn't a dirty old shed, instead he found a set of granite stairs that lead down to an ornate entryway. This was impossible; this entry couldn't fit in a tiny shed! Then he realized all of the unbelievable things he had seen recently and decided to give it a try. Marty stepped through the door and onto the stairs, making his way down the giant staircase into the mammoth entryway.

Entryway to Castle

What caught his attention was a large carpet running the length of the floor and up the stairs stopping right at his feet; it was so ornate that it could only belong to a very wealthy person. Before realizing what he was doing he was descending into the gilt and glamour of the elaborate entry hall. He glanced back at the door he had just come through but now it was a large oak door carved beautifully in very intricate patterns of fairies and forests. Turning back to face the entryway he heard the faint sound of wings approaching.

Looking around he was able to just make out that there was movement then he saw two small hovering objects. Just as he spied them they started getting closer, but not much bigger. There were definitely two of them and they moved quickly. Suddenly they were in his face. One of them was the creature he had seen earlier in the book, it looked like a boy and he was accompanied by what looked like a girl.

Their wings hummed quickly as they scanned Marty up and down. He too was scanning them, taking it all in.

The relative silence was broken as the male trillo spoke in a high-pitched barely audible voice, "It's you! The one with the book! You've come to save us!"

This brought a large smile from both of the creatures. Marty was bursting with questions: *Why me? Where is Bismorda? Where am I?* But instead he could only nod and say weakly, "Yes, that's me."

"I am Scrimt and this is my wife Sayvd, we are slaves to the witch Bismorda," squeaked the male trillo.

"Yes, I read that in the book."

Then recovering as quickly as he could he lamely tried to sound like a hero, "So, where is Bismorda?"

This stopped both of the trillos. They looked at each other, "You mean you didn't meet her? But how did you know how to get in?"

"I searched until I found the small shed in the back, that's all."

"Oh, he must be a wizard!" Sayvd spoke for the first time her voice even higher than Scrimt's if that was possible.

She tried to straighten her minute dress and she fidgeted with mini scissors that were in her skirt pocket.

"No, I'm not a wizard!" Marty was shocked by the idea, "Wizards don't even exist, I'm just a kid!" then he demanded again, "Where *is* Bismorda?"

Shocked in their own right the trillos reiterated, "Wizards *do* exist and so do witches, Bismorda is a witch and you're here to save us from her, she left some time ago with no explanation."

Scrimt had now become nervous as well and was pulling at his long shirt-like outfit. He began muttering something that Marty only caught snippets of, "...light...invisible...the key...kid"

Marty was getting frustrated with Scrimt very quickly, "Can you at least tell me what Bismorda looks like?"

"She was once beautiful with long flowing purple hair, flower-like grace and her nose nicely pointed," replied Sayvd in a dreamy voice as she touched her own miniscule nose, remembering better days.

"Then, those wicked sisters came from Zanth, and they put a curse on her because they were jealous," Scrimt continued.

Zanth?" the name caught Marty by surprise. "Where is *that*?"

"Oh, it is far away, but they heard of Bismorda's beauty and hunted her down," almost in tears Sayvd's tiny bottom lip quivered, "the curse made her a horrible monster that terrorized this land. She took us prisoner."

Scrimt nodded sadly at the memory, "We were the only ones left above water and not transformed."

Things were suddenly becoming clear to Marty, "You mean this building," he made a sweep with his arm at the surrounding structure, "is the whole kingdom?"

"As far as the eye could see," Scrimt and Sayvd said in unison.

"You still haven't answered my question," Marty tried again, "What does Bismorda look like?"

Finally Scrimt and Sayvd looked at each other, evidently something passed between them because when Scrimt spoke, it was with conviction, "She is invisible."

"Then how do you know when she is here or not?"

Again the trillos froze, except for their wings. "Sir,"

Sayvd began quaking midair as she spoke, "You can tell, believe us."

Sayvd & Scrimt

Marty realized he wasn't going to get much else out of the trillos about Bismorda. Then Marty had a thought, it crept out of the back of his mind and he said it before he had completely thought it, "Is she the creature that followed me, the shrieking, giant, something that landed in the trees and broke them? Does sound stop around her?"

It all came out so quickly that Marty, as well as the trillos, now froze. The questions hung in the air, unanswered vocally, but answered by the silence.

Bismorda *was* the creature!

Again Marty's thoughts spilled out before he could fully form them, "The poem said that you would be freed only by love's first kiss, how am I supposed to help?"

This question the trillos *could* answer, they gladly

began chattering, but at the same time, and it got so jumbled Marty had to hold up his hands to stop them. "Okay, one at a time, please."

"If you only knew Bismorda," Sayvd was rapturous, "I know you would love her."

"We have some old paintings of her that we had to hide so she wouldn't destroy them," Scrimt started to float deeper into the castle, followed by Sayvd, and Marty decided to fall in line.

As they led him through the entryway Marty glanced to his left and right. Huge cave-like recesses opened up on both sides. They were so deep Marty couldn't see the back walls of either one. One thing was sure this building was making Marty feel very small and insignificant. Suddenly Scrimt and Sayvd stopped in midair and Marty almost ran into them but stopped just in time. He looked at what they were staring at but saw nothing.

Then he heard it too, nothing, just like in the forest.

No humming wings on the trillos, no chatter, no footsteps echoing hollowly into the blackness of the side rooms, nothing. That's when he knew that Bismorda was back.

He looked for somewhere to hide but suddenly knew it was useless. The shriek inside the hall was so overpowering that Marty fell on the ground and curled into a ball while covering his ears. His world swirled and engulfed him.

Chapter 5
A Calling Awaits

The whirring in Marty's ear brought him back to consciousness. He didn't open his eyes; he was frightened what he might find. Instead he tried to use all his other senses to analyze his surroundings without moving. Something fluffy under his head set it on an incline, his hands were resting on either side of him they lay on something soft and silky. A tightness across his chest suggested something restrictive as it continued down the length of his body it felt like he was in a sleeping bag or something like that. He was startled suddenly by voices that spoke within inches of his left ear.

"Oh, I hope she didn't frighten him to death, she meant well, she just can't speak," the voice continued, Marty's mind raced, he had heard that voice before, but where? "He's our our only chance. Oh, Scrimt, I hope he's not dead!"

That's it! Marty remembered the trillos, Scrimt and Sayvd, the reason he had come here, wherever *here* was. He ventured to open his right eye just a crack and tried to surmise where he was in the building. The light was dim and coming from somewhere to his left, it could have been a window or a door he wasn't sure. Since he couldn't make out much through only the slit in his eye, he thought he might try whispering to Scrimt and Sayvd.

"Psst, Scrimt, Sayvd, is it safe?"

The chatter in his left ear stopped abruptly.

Then there was a muffled squeak followed by an almost unheard, "Yes."

Marty's eyes opened and he turned his head. The trillos were near the tip of his nose so he had to cross his eyes to try and focus on them. They saw his difficulty and backed up a bit.

"Oh sir, we're so sorry she scared you like that," Sayvd was twisting the hem of her dress, revealing her miniature bloomers, looking more distraught than ever.

It was Scrimt who spoke, "Will you ever forgive us for lying to you?"

Whatever Marty had expected to hear, this was not it, "What?" he began to sit up, but he got a head rush and had to sit back on the pillow "What do you mean, 'lying to me?'"

Marty barely took notice of the enormous bed in which he found himself. The surrounding bedroom was also lost on Marty.

"Scrimt, tell me what you're talking about!" Marty had lost interest in whispering.

"Uh, the whole reason you are here..." Scrimt searched for the right words, "Bismorda wanted you, she saw you through the book, and she has been watching you for ages. When you appeared she knew you were *the* one."

"*The* one?" Marty calmed down, now interested in this new twist in the story.

"The one that could break the spell," Sayvd broke in, "So she had us come to you in your dreams, make you want to know about us."

Scrimt again took over, "We took the light devices and hid them."

"I changed your time keeping box," Sayvd admitted painfully.

"Then, when you left we fixed things to make you wonder," Scrimt hung his head.

"Well it worked!" Marty was a little curt with the trillos even though he felt relieved that he hadn't been going crazy.

"We have never had anyone find the book to Qualf with your gift," Scrimt came back a little defensive, "Believe me we *have* looked."

"My *gift*?" Marty was now extremely curious. As far as he knew all he could do was be punctual.

"A Yulesaychaater," the trillos said together.

"A what?" Marty was confused.

"A key gatherer!" Scrimt exclaimed.

"Say it again please?" Marty was impressed with the name.

"A Yule-say-chaater," Scrimt slowly repeated.

"A yool-say-chaw-ter?" Marty tried.

"Yes." Scrimt and Sayvd smiled at each other, the tension easing.

"So what exactly is a key gatherer?" Now genuinely interested Marty leaned forward.

"Someone who has the ability to enter the world of books," Scrimt explained slowly, letting this sink in.

"Someone who has the power to help if needed. That is why we had to get you here."

"I see," Marty was easing into his newfound place of power, "So, if Bismorda wants me here, why was she trying to kill me?"

"She wasn't, she just wanted to make sure you got here without the sisters of Zanth finding you."

"Oh, well that makes me feel a *little* better," then, he remembered the incident in the entry, "If that is true, then what just happened in the hall?"

"That, well, that's the way she talks," Sayvd explained.

"You mean she can't say words?" Marty was perplexed by this new development, "Why can I hear her but nothing else?"

"She controls what you hear when she is around." Scrimt replied, sadly shaking his head.

"Can I see the painting you were taking me to?"

Marty decided he would see what he could do, since he was already here.

Also, if he considered what he had just been told as the truth, he may be the only one who *could* help.

Scrimt and Sayvd looked at each other, a spark passing between them, then they both smiled.

"Right this way," Scrimt rose in the air, followed

closely by Sayvd, and bringing up the rear was Marty as he climbed out of the plush bed.

That's when it hit him, "Wait, who put me in this bed?"

Both Scrimt and Sayvd twirled in midair, "Oh, that was Bismorda," as if that were the end of the conversation. The questions multiplied in Marty's brain until he couldn't keep track of all the side questions and decided he would just accept that it was so. He followed behind the trillos, they left the bedroom and emerged in an endless hallway lined with hundreds of rooms on the left side and long windows on the right. The sun was still high in the sky.

"What time *is* it?"

"Time?" Scrimt and Sayvd asked together.

"Yes, is it time for a meal? Or bed time? Or what?" Marty couldn't believe he had to explain everything, *were these trillos really that slow to catch on?*

"Oh, that," Scrimt finally understood, "Where the sun is you mean?"

"Yes!" He was finally getting through to the simple trillos.

"Once we break the spell," Scrimt explained, "the sun can go down again."

"You mean it has been day time since the spell was cast?"

Both trillos nodded sadly.

"But when do you sleep?"

"We don't," it was said by both, "We haven't for ages."

"So, time is frozen?" Marty began to understand.

"Yes."

Marty now had a new resolve to solve this problem as soon as he could, "So, where is that painting?"

Scrimt moved to the next room and tapped on the door lightly, it swung open slowly and Marty rushed forward. Inside there were piles of tapestries and tables of intricate workmanship.

Everywhere he turned was more stuff. "So where are they? Or it, however many you have."

"Right here," Sayvd was hovering near the wall where large frames were leaning against it.

There were three of them. Marty slowly dragged the first to where there was an open square of carpet and turned it toward the light. His eyes met the face of someone not much older than himself, she had shoulder length lavender hair, elf-like pointed ears, a long thin nose and a pointed chin. Her eyes, like his, were his favorite feature. They resembled those of a cat, greenish yellow with a long black pupil in the center. She was wearing some kind of Greek-style robe that pinned at the shoulder with an ornate gold brooch shaped like the serpent on the key.

She was truly breathtaking!

"That was when Bismorda was just a witchling," Sayvd dabbed her eyes and continued.

"It was just before the War of 320 wasn't it, Scrimt?"

"320?" Marty was caught off guard. "As in 320 *A.D.*?"

"Well, when else, silly?" Sayvd floated over and hovered near Marty's right shoulder, "Wasn't she lovely?"

"Yes, she was," Marty didn't know what else to say.

He'd never seen a human-like person with cat eyes, but they were intriguing. He almost commented about his own eyes, but then thought better of it, why would the trillos care if his eyes changed color with what he wore?

"So what does, I mean, *did* she look like before the curse?" Marty continued, wanting to get on with this.

"Well, that would be the third painting then," Scrimt said knowingly.

"Okay, let's see that one," Marty returned to the frames and picked up the one closest to the wall and slid it out.

Again making his way to the open square of carpet he looked at this painting, he was surprised to see that the picture was the same except for a few alterations. She was now wearing a dress that looked like something from a Shakespeare play from his Mom's yearbook. Her hair was also much longer it dropped down her back, how far Marty wasn't sure. But the one thing he found most interesting, she hadn't aged at all.

"That was in 1624," Sayvd's voice was choked and she buried her face in her hands.

"The paint wasn't even dry before the Sisters from Zanth dropped in unannounced to pay Bismorda a 'visit,'" Scrimt's shoulders were hunched forward and he looked defeated.

"That was over 300 years ago!" Marty was shocked.

"Our kingdom has been searching ever since."

"So, how do I kiss Bismorda if I can't even see her?" Marty was not going to be scared away. Being their last hope, he couldn't turn his back on them.

"You mean you'll help us?" Scrimt did a flip in the air and rushed toward Marty stopping inches from his nose, a smile spreading across his face.

"Thank you, sir. Oh, thank you!"

"You can call me Marty, instead of 'sir' if you want."

"Oh, what a noble name!" Sayvd sighed.

"Really? I always thought it was kind of stupid myself," Marty admitted.

"Oh, no, Marty is a dashing name," Scrimt agreed, "Named after Mars the God of War."

"Wow, really? I didn't know that. So, how do I save the kingdom from this war?"

"Oh, it's easy; all you have to do is kiss Bismorda."

"I know that, but how do I do it if she is invisible?"

"Well if you stand in front of a mirror, you can see her reflection, but you can't turn away or she will eat you." Marty gasped but Scrimt pushed on, "that's part of the curse, if you break eye contact she has to eat you, even if she does not want to."

Marty gulped, steeling himself, "Okay, I'll do it." Marty headed for the door.

"Wait, the kiss, we haven't told you about the kiss."

"I know what a kiss is," Marty was still trying to remain patient as he grabbed the doorknob.

"In your world, yes, but not in ours," Scrimt explained.

"How is your world different?" *aside from all the strange creatures, magic, curses, portals, and never aging* Marty added silently, *oh yeah and witches.*

"A kiss is," Scrimt was searching his brain, "I think it is a pat or a pet in your world. Does that sound right Sayvd?"

"Yes, I think that's right," Sayvd nodded.

"Oh, okay, so I have to keep eye contact with her reflection, then pat Bismorda and the spell will be broken?"

"Yes, that is correct," Scrimt agreed.

"Okay, I think I'm ready," Marty straightened to his full height, "take me to a mirror."

Sayvd stopped Marty with, "But do you know *where* to pat Bismorda?"

Marty stood still; he had just about made the biggest mistake of his life, "Uh, no I don't, where *am* I supposed to pat Bismorda?"

"But, Marty, you know where to pat her, think," Scrimt urged.

"Think?" Confused, Marty began babbling, "I'm here in the kingdom of Bismorda about to pat an invisible creature when I see her in a reflection, but I can't break eye contact or she will eat me and I'm supposed to think?!"

As he breathed heavily from this release, again from the back of his mind a thought came.

"I must touch her heart," he spoke aloud, "but, how do I touch her heart?" His right hand stole to his chest as he asked this question.

He could feel his own pounding heart, it calmed him, and he knew.

Again he turned to Scrimt and Sayvd and they were both nodding, "Okay, *now* I'm ready, let's find that mirror!"

Scrimt and Sayvd flew ahead of Marty as they made their way back to the entranceway. The whole time Marty didn't let his hand leave his heart, he looked like a patriot in a parade marching behind the flag, and that's what he was, someone fighting for freedom! Marty took little notice of his surroundings as they passed the rest of the tall doors and windows of the hallway, and then turned into the entranceway, it looked different, over one of the side caves, the one off to the left, actually, there was a monstrous mirror. From this angle it reflected the opposite cave perfectly except for a slight glint from the overhead chandelier. It gave it the look of a small lake frozen over and turned on its side, then Marty gasped.

Scrimt and Sayvd spun around, "What is it? Did you change your mind?" the concern was evident in their voices.

"No, it's just, that," Marty pointed at the mirror, then his hand dropped to his side, "it is so *magnificable!*"

What Marty meant to say was 'magnificent' but as usual, when Marty used large words it got all jumbled. Scrimt and Sayvd didn't disagree, "Yes, it is," they nodded as they continued into the entranceway.

As they pulled up in front of the mirror, Marty took his place, right in the center, Scrimt floated on his left and Sayvd on his right.

Finally they both spoke at once, "Good luck," and they were gone.

Marty did not know what to do to pass the time, nor did he know how long he would have to wait, so he began to whistle.

It wasn't any specific tune it was just being made up as he went along.

Then the sound was gone, he looked at his reflection, his lips were still puckered as if he were whistling, but there was nothing coming out; Bismorda was close!

Marty froze.

He wanted to look to the side so badly his neck started to hurt from holding his head still. Then his right hand made its way back to his chest to find a wildly racing heart. He tried to calm it as something appeared at the edge of the mirror. Marty bit his tongue so he didn't scream out, it wouldn't have made a sound anyway, and he stood his ground waiting for the inevitable.

It was a snout and it was huge! The teeth that protruded from the mouth were sharp and menacing, curling down toward the chin, full of poison no doubt. Saliva moistened the rough scales of the jaw as the tongue flicked in and out. Next came the eyes, cold, hard, black, and deadly, he locked onto them with his own. Here was the head of something very large; something that looked like a dinosaur then it hit Marty that this was a dragon! The neck slithered into view it was at least ten feet long and deep oily green, then there were wings deep purple with highlights of lavender, folded along the massive body, twitching to unfurl and flick him like an annoying bug.

It kept coming, the creature was endless!

There were no claws or feet like the dragons he had seen in fairytale books, it was more like a snake. Marty had seen this creature before, of course! It was the same one as on the key! Marty's heart was starting to settle as the tail finally came into view. This was no stranger, he knew it, it was the creature on the key! Its head came to rest on the marble floor parallel with Marty so they were side by side staring into the mirror. Massive and intimidating, the coal-like eyes stared back at Marty as if he were wrapped in bacon and lathered in barbeque sauce.

It reared up, exposing the smooth underbelly. The abrupt movement startled Marty causing him to sidestep, but he was careful not to break eye contact.

Building up his courage, he moved sideways again until he was within arm's length of the massive body. Reaching out with his left hand he ran it along the cool, smooth skin until he felt it, the first throb of a heart. He ran his hand higher along the monster's belly until he had it, a strong heartbeat under his hand. He looked deeply in the eyes of the creature as he matched his heartbeat to that of the pitifully cursed Bismorda.

As their heartbeats synchronized the black eyes softened and started to lighten to a green and the pupils formed into the cat-like ones in the painting. Along the skull lavender tufts of hair began to appear and that's when Marty felt something that made his blood freeze.

He had to sneeze.

Bismorda as Dragon

The itch at the back of his nose made his eyes begin to water. If he sneezed, the spell would not only stop working he would be eaten! Swallowing, biting his tongue, and focusing on the beat of their hearts, he made the tickle disappear and only then did the beast's head begin to shrink, the snout turned pointed, the chin lengthened, arms began to extend as well as legs from the sides of the massive body. The tail retracted and everything began to shrink.

Within ten minutes the only things left of the creature were the olive green color of Bismorda's gown and the purple of the wings that had transformed into the luxuriant lavender tresses flowing down her back. Marty let his hands fall from their chests in unison, he was completely worn out. Visibly he sagged, as did Bismorda.

She looked much worn but she was anxious to thank her hero. "Oh, Yulesaychaater, thank you, I could never repay the kindness you have just paid me."

There was a foreign accent that Marty couldn't place that tinged her speech. Rushing forward she surprised Marty by taking him in a huge hug, he quickly blushed.

It was when Bismorda finally broke their embrace that Marty really got a good look at her. She was wearing a floor length gown of deep olive green velvet, with a latticework front covering an ivory under dress.

She had not aged one day!

The green catlike eyes were amazing to behold, the skin of her face was a pale ivory, as though she hadn't seen the sun in ages, her cheeks were full, but not plump, and her chin was slightly pointed. Protruding from the sides of her head, through her shining unbelievably purple hair, were the pointed tips of her ears. Her lilac hair fell well below her waist, long and straight, glowing in the light from a nearby window. She stood almost the same height as himself and he thought that they could actually pass for the same age. That was when Marty looked around at their surroundings again and realized that the entrance hall had changed drastically too.

The gray granite had been replaced by white marble and there were many windows high on the walls, letting in the light of the outside. Tapestries hung from the walls and the floors were covered with ornate carpets. Crystal vases overflowing with exotic blossoms glistened from antique tabletops as they caught the bright sunlight. The sight was truly breathtaking and it was not lost on Marty's searching eyes. Suddenly Scrimt and Sayvd were both there hovering between Marty and Bismorda.

"Oh, it's you, you're back! Congratulations! Great work Yulesaychaater Sir! Thank you for saving us," they went on, but Bismorda raised her hands to quiet them.

"I can never repay this debt Yulesaychaater, but if you ever need help in your world I will try to come to your aid," Bismorda smiled, it was a flash of bright white that left Marty with butterflies in his stomach.

"Well, thank you Bismorda for trusting me enough with your entire kingdom, even your life," *Did that just come from me? It was so refined!* Marty did not speak like that usually, but he impressed himself anyway. He bowed to Bismorda, Scrimt, and Sayvd, turned and started up the grand staircase. His job was done; he didn't look back as he pushed open the oak doorway leading back into the shed. However it was not into the shed that Marty emerged, but out onto a grand set of white marble stairs, similar to the ones inside.

The sun hit the stairs and made them glow. Marty squinted as he walked down to the ground. Only then did he turn back and look at the astounding sight that was Bismorda's castle. The high pointed towers, graceful walls, large entryway, servants lined along the walls, and the beautifully colored flags snapping in the soft breeze.

Then he realized the sun was further down in the sky than when he had come. Time had returned to normal in Bismorda's land once more.

Marty again turned away from the castle and started down the now much wider path that led up to the front of the castle. Many creatures and people greeted him as he walked down the hill, and it surprised Marty that they all bowed reverently to him. As he came to the place he had buried the key he was met by a grand sight indeed. Just off the path was a large marble statue of him perched on a large concrete stand with a small plaque set into the base. He could not help himself he had to see what it said. Approaching tentatively he looked around him and, with the statue watching over him, read the delicate inscription:

Bismorda

From this day may this statue stand
To our hero "Marty the Grand."
He came to Qualf of his own choice
And saved us all, let us rejoice!

Marty was touched, then he looked up at the statue and his eyes caught something glinting in the sun, right above the level of his head. Reaching up he ran his hand along the small ledge till he was holding two small items in his hand. One was his penny; the other was the key, with the snake-like dragon form of Bismorda back in place curled around the head of the key. He dropped them both into his pocket and turned back to the road. Going down the much wider and more level road was easy and he made good time.

As he descended from the top of the hill he realized the countryside was quite covered in small houses, huts, fields, and other forms of life.

Bismorda truly had a beautiful kingdom! He was surrounded by the call of unusual birds and bugs as he exited the forest. In a short time Marty was back at the bridge, he again crossed it and made his way beneath it. The door to his room was right where he had left it; opening the door he entered and closed the door behind him. He leaned against the door, with his back to it and he found himself smiling. His eye fell on his clock and was surprised to find that only an hour had passed. He still needed to transform his room back to his world before his mom came to check on him.

Turning, he hesitantly pulled the key out of his pocket. Again the doorknob glowed red-hot from within as the key drew closer, the keyhole opened and he inserted the key into its place. The simple click sounded; he pulled the key out and the knob returned to its normal brassy color. Quietly turning the handle he peered out, it was his hallway again!

He was home.

Moving to the pile of clothes he attacked this simple chore with added zeal; after all he was now the Yulesaychaater!

Chapter 6
Big Boys DO Cry

That night, after only breaks for a late lunch and dinner the house had been divided into two sections, what to keep and what to not. Items from the keeper piles of clothes, simple furniture and other odds and ends were, for the most part packed into boxes and labeled. All the rest had been boxed, bagged, hauled, and stacked in the garage. The only things left out were essentials for the next four days. Thursday morning they would gather these few things, lock the front door and head to Utah. Probably never to return.

Marty lay in his bed, staring at the ceiling and listening to the house settle around him. Like a pro he knew every sound this house made, where the floor creaked, and the way to get to the fridge without waking his parents, he was going to miss it. His eyes started itching with the inevitable tears that were going to surface. He let them come. Laying there, alone, in the dark the tears streamed down his face and suddenly Marty smiled.

Why was he sad? This could be an awesome adventure! There would be a new school *that* he wasn't really looking forward to, but he was sure there could be many more adventures like he had today. Scrimt, Sayvd, Bismorda, and the other creatures now had a place inside of Marty. He slipped his hand under his pillow and found the key. It was cold, but he didn't care, he held it and remembered his great adventure. He slipped off to sleep with a smile on his face, still clutching his *first* key. Qualf.

Sunday, May 21, 1990

Marty woke at first light, jumped out of bed, and sat at his mostly empty desk. He had stacked the paper and pens again before he went to bed and today he was going to do his assignment from Rousy. Starting his list with adventurer, hero and next he wanted to write Yulesaychaater, but he didn't know how to spell it. Then he realized his list would look very strange, since he was the only one who knew of his gift. He'd never heard of it before and doubted if anyone else had either.

This stopped his hand in its tracks and made him think, *What did Rousy say exactly?*

Searching his brain he finally remembered, "Oh, yeah, it needs to be things I *want* to be." He went back to his list, keeping the first two items, but decided against writing down Yulesaychaater, because this was a gift, not something he had particularly wanted to be. He bit on the end of his pen and thought of some more things that he wanted to be. Suddenly, as if struck by a bolt of lightning he sat up, "She never said this had to be what I wanted to be when I grow up, or what I wanted to do for a job, but just what I wanted to be!" This opened the floodgates of Marty's brain, there were thousands of things he wanted to be! He wanted to be good at sports, a good student, a good reader, a good son, a good example, but most of all he wanted to be the best Marty Whimpel he could be! Continuing to list things until both sides of one page were filled, he then stopped, looked back over what he had written, and nodded his approval. Speaking quietly to himself, "Thanks Rousy, for helping me see what I really wanted, I'll never forget you."

The rest of Sunday was quite laid back. Marty and Charlotte watched a few movies together, ate their meals, and just enjoyed each other's company. Then, just before bed, Charlotte poked her head into Marty's room, "So, did you think about what you promised Rousy?"

Marty nodded, "Yep, I wrote it all down this morning before you woke up."

Surprised, Charlotte asked, "Oh? Want to share with me?"

Marty thought first, then shook his head. The look of disappointment on his mom's face spurned his next comment,

"At least not yet, okay mom?"

She smiled weakly and started to retreat when Marty arose from his bed and approached her, "Mom," it brought her head back in, "I love you, thanks for understanding." Leaning forward he kissed her on the cheek.

This time she smiled genuinely, "I guess I'll understand better someday maybe, but I'll be content to act like I understand now."

"Thanks again Mom, g'night."

"Good night sweetheart, "Charlotte turned and padded down the hall.

Marty turned back toward his bed, why couldn't he tell his mom? It wasn't that big of a secret. Why was he waiting to tell Rousy first? Marty shook his head, he didn't know, he just was that was all. With that, Marty crawled back under the covers, lay down, and was soon asleep.

Monday, May 22, 1990

Marty woke and prepared for his last few days of school. Somehow, now that he knew he was leaving, he wanted to make a good impression on everyone at the school. Taking extra care, he got ready. Choosing a blue shirt that would make his eyes stand out, he then selected a pair of clean khaki shorts and his white canvas shoes. Glancing in the mirror at the final effect, he smiled, he liked how he looked!

After breakfast his mom dropped him off at school. Making his way back to the library trailer, he entered it, and closed the door soundlessly. He found Rousy sorting through the final turn-ins of the year. Today would be her last day until next school year, the last two days the library would be closed. Looking up she stopped mid-sort. She smiled, "Morning Marty, you look like you have had a good weekend."

Marty couldn't trust himself to speak; all of a sudden

he was choked up and could only nod. Coming around the counter she pulled out two chairs. Motioning for Marty to sit in one she sat in the other. As he sat down, he stared at his hands, not daring to face Rousy. Their knees almost touched and he smiled, finally looking up. Then the tears started to slowly trickle down his cheeks, "Oh Rousy, we're moving! Mom and I are going to live in Utah with my Grandma Pen. I'm going to miss you so much!" He stopped and looked at Rousy.

Her eyes were glistening behind her half moon spectacles as she spoke softly, straightening her silver strands of flyaway hair absent-mindedly, "I thought you would be, that is what I have been preparing for this weekend, one last goodbye."

Two silent tears followed the well-worn tracks down Rousy's face until they dripped off her chin and fell into the folds of her skirt. Then she spoke again, "I figured the assignment might be the last impact I may have on your life," she paused, dropped her head, then in a whisper she asked, "Did you do it?"

Marty leaned over his bag, unzipped the main compartment and pulled out the piece of paper he had written on the day before. He handed it to Rousy. She wiped at her tears with the back of her age-spotted hand and tipped her head so she could use her spectacles to read his paper, "An adventurer, a hero." Here her voice broke, "I know you can be a hero, Marty, after all you have saved this old lady by being the grandson she never had."

Marty put his hand over her wrinkled one that was holding the paper; they sat in silence for a moment, not needing to say more. She handed him the list, not reading anymore, she shook her head. "You are quite a wonder Marty Whimpel! Heaven help the person who tries to stand in your way!" Their eyes locked for a minute, "Come give me a squeeze!" He fell into her arms as she was seated, they hugged and cried silently. The sound of the bell brought them back to reality. "You better run along now, I don't want to be the reason you don't get that perfect attendance plaque!"

Marty grabbed his bag and hurried to the door, he turned to look back at Rousy, "Bye, Rousy, I'll keep in touch!"

The door opened and shut and Sheryl Rousekewitz was left alone among her books to shed quiet tears over another one of her children gone off into the world, but not just any child, that was *her* Marty!

Thursday, May 25, 1990

The next two days were full of final things at school and at home to keep Marty busy. After collecting his unsigned yearbook, attendance plaque, and report card he was ready to leave for Utah, but he had to wait until today.

He and his mom were just finishing loading the Tercel with all that it could hold and more. They had both just carried out the cooler with their snacks for the first part of their trip and turned to look one last time at their house. Charlotte came over and stood by Marty, her arm resting on his shoulders, "Say good bye to our old life Marty, we're out to find a new one!"

Marty turned to look at his mom, how he admired her spunk! Here she was, not even a full week after the final fight, the tears were gone, at least for the moment, and she was ready to head back to her hometown with him in tow to start a whole new life. His arm came up, hugged at her waist and he nodded. They climbed into the Tercel, Charlotte revved the engine, they both waved as they pulled away from the curb, away from Oak Grove Road, away from Samuel Alden Whimpel, away from their old life, and started on the road toward their new one.

Chapter 7
A Whole New Life

Monday, May 29, 1990

After 4 days and close to 1500 miles Marty and Charlotte Whimpel in their Toyota Tercel pulled up alongside the curb in front of 5443 South Farnsworth Drive. There was a small sign over the mailbox, made of wood, claiming the name of Pentel. Marty and Charlotte looked at each other, smiled and got out of the car.

In the front window the curtains were pulled aside and there was Grandma Pen waiting with a big smile on her face. She met them at the door just moments later with arms wide open. The smells that greeted them were of fresh baked bread and Grandma Pen's special scent. Marty tried to place it. It was a mixture of flowers, soap, and baked goods. As he hugged her he breathed it in deeply.

Pearl Pentel was about to have her 81st Birthday and oh what a pearl she was! She measured all of 5 feet 2 inches tall and that was standing tall! Her silver white hair haloed her round shaped face. Anti-style she wore silver cat-rimmed glasses that framed her smiling eyes and matched her hair. Dressed in a simple housecoat she looked comfortable and loveable, it was a pale blue that almost matched the color of her house and her eyes.

Marty felt at home instantly, it was like the feeling he felt in Rousy's library, safe and warm and loved. Finally, Grandma Pentel spoke, her voice was like a song of laughter, "Well, the road warriors have triumphed! How would you both like some fresh hot bread and homemade jam?" Marty would soon find out that few things compared to Grandma Pen's homemade bread and jam.

Quickly they were herded into the kitchen, shown where to sit, given a plate and served steaming hot bread with a pat of butter on it, already melting as they watched. Then came the bowl of strawberry jam, with a delicate little spoon that reminded Marty of Grandma Pen, it was small, silver, and looked as though it were a million years old.

Doling out a liberal helping onto his bread, he spread it around, and took a bite. Up until that very moment, hour, and day, Marty had never tasted anything so good in all his life. It was like a hug on the inside. He felt warmed all the way through and couldn't help but smile. Grandma Pentel had watched this closely, she was finally going to be able to dote on her only grandchild, and she could hardly contain her joy!

They all finished their bread, washed it down with a glass of milk and decided to start emptying the car. Grandma Pentel was selected to hold open the front door, since she was advanced in age and couldn't lift much at all. Marty and Charlotte made trip after trip to bring their clothes and other few belongings into their new home and placed them in the already prepared guestrooms.

Marty's new room was downstairs, this was an adventure in and of itself, Marty's old house had only been a single story and now there was a ground level and a basement.

This would be a great source of excitement, having the basement all to himself! His imagination was already planning the first exploration.

His mother's room was upstairs right next to Grandma Pen's. This room was also of interest because it was like entering a time warp. It had many things from when Charlotte was still living here, from her childhood and teenage years. Posters of Elvis and other by-gone musicians plastered her walls. The carpet was a soft pink, like cottoncandy. The bedspread was frilly and girlish. Ragged stuffed animals lay in a small heap by the pillows near the head of the bed, there was even a record player in the corner with a stack of the large black plate-like objects waiting as if she had just left the room for school. Marty was a little bewildered as to why his mother's room would have stayed untouched, but then he remembered she had been the only child of Grandpa Rufus and Grandma Pearl.

Pearl Pentel

Marty reluctantly left the fascinating chamber to continue unloading the car. The final trip from the Tercel brought more than a little joy. Grandma Pen told Marty to rest for a while, the unpacking could wait. Then the peppering began, she showered them with questions about the trip: *Were there any problems? Had they seen anything exciting? Did the car run okay? Did they eat enough?* And so many more.

Pearl had never been one to allow even the smallest event to go undissected and this trip would not be the first one. Charlotte smiled wearily and answered each question posed while Marty curled up right where he was and fell fast asleep.

****

Off in the distance a shimmering light beckoned tantalizingly. It danced as if it were alive. Marty made his way toward it in the jostling waves. Looking around he saw that he was on a small boat surrounded by teeming waves.

Becoming frightened that his skiff would capsize he was startled when a soft sound came through the semi-darkness calling him, "Maartyy...come...Maartty." Again Marty looked to where the light was and he felt calm, it was getting closer. The waves were getting rougher and the voice louder as well, "Marty...come on...Marty!"

His body was shaking in the rowboat as it rose and fell on the waves.

Then he could feel a hand on his arm and he sat up, eyes wide looked around warily, realizing he was in his Grandma Pentel's front room. His mother, who had been shaking him still held his arm as she crouched near the sofa. She was looking at him with concern in her eyes.

The sun had advanced in the sky outside and Marty realized he had been asleep for quite some time. He again looked into his mother's face and smiled, trying to reassure her that he was fine. He said, "Sorry mom, I was just in the most interesting place."

"Good dream?" Grandma Pen leaned forward questions already bubbling to the surface.

Marty turned his attention to his grandmother, "Yes, I saw a light of some kind off in the distance, I was trying to get to it, but the tiny boat I was in was moving very slow on the water. I didn't even see what the light was; I was trying to find out."

"That sounds nice," Pearl sighed, "I like it when dreams are nice and peaceful. Sometimes I have some frightening ones, like this one I had about a killer potato..."

Marty wanted to laugh right out loud, but the sudden look of distress on his grandma's face caused him to choke it back. But in his mind he thought, *A killer Potato? Why, or rather, how could there be such a thing?*

He tuned back in to hear her say, "and it would keep rolling toward me, I was frozen and couldn't move," then she shuddered and hugged herself, rocking quietly.

Charlotte, who had remained quiet this whole time, then spoke, "Maybe I should be more concerned for you mom, Marty's dream doesn't sound nearly as terrible."

She turned and smiled at Marty, "I was just trying to wake you so you could climb in bed, but you sure were deep into that dream, it was like waking the dead."

"Sorry, I guess I'm a little worn out," Marty smiled weakly, again feeling the desire to close his eyes in sleep.

"Well, you can go to bed, just brush your teeth quick and move the stuff that's on your bed, onto the floor. We can worry about unpacking for the rest of the summer."

Marty nodded, grateful to be excused and made his way to the stairs. He flipped on the switch and descended to "his" basement. Making his way past shelves of bottles filled with fruits and sauces, all homemade, in the back of Marty's mind he couldn't help having the feeling that it was like a mad-scientist's laboratory with strange things in bottles lining the walls. Then he passed a literal wall of toilet paper, he had taken little notice of it before, but found it interesting now, he would have to ask Grandma Pentel why she had so much. Turning to the right he entered his new room. He flipped on the switch and sent light into every corner of the room.

It was strange how much Marty was now watching each light he was seeing, then he realized what he was doing. He was trying to figure out what kind of light he had seen in his dream. It still wasn't clear what the light had been. Maybe he would dream about it again when he fell back to sleep.

Shifting half a dozen boxes to the floor, he pulled back the covers and almost fell right into bed, but he remembered his mom's final words, "just brush your teeth quick…" With a little effort he found his book bag, which had been his carry on luggage for the car, unzipped it, and pulled out his toothbrush and toothpaste. Leaving the bag open, he walked into the small bathroom off of his bedroom, and flipped on the switch. This was the first time Marty had seen "his" bathroom. Stopping just inside he marveled at how grown up it made him feel; this was going to be so cool to have his own bathroom!

It was decorated in shades of pale yellow and white, from the door the toilet was directly on the left, the shower kiddy-corner and the sink was straight ahead. There was a small mirror over the sink that hid a small medicine cabinet. Stepping to his sink he looked at himself in his mirror. He brushed his teeth, watching himself. This was all new to him, he had never watched himself in his own bathroom before, he was thoroughly pleased.

Even with this new novelty, sleep was still pulling at Marty and he quickly finished, placed his toothbrush and toothpaste in the shallow cabinet, closed the mirror and left the bathroom, turning off the light. He didn't even bother changing his clothes; he did kick off his shoes, slipped out of his pants, and climbed in between the sheets.

In no time he was back on the small boat, moving toward the distant light.

He never did make it to the light, but he didn't mind for some reason, he just enjoyed the constant rocking of the boat and slept peacefully through the night.

Chapter 8
In Dreams It Came

For two weeks Marty continued to have this same dream, never getting any closer to the light, but then one night as he was once again in the skiff something started floating toward him on the waves.

As the object drew near he squinted, for some reason he knew this had come from the light, whatever it was he would accept it gladly. Finally it was within reach, he leaned over and plucked it from the waves. It was a book!

Turning it over in his hands, he examined it, there was a lock holding it shut. The corner was engraved with some ancient writing that Marty could not make out, strange symbols that someone from a time long ago had known. To Marty's surprise he reached in his pocket and pulled out a key, this in turn fit the lock, and opened the odd book. As Marty opened the front cover, he woke up.

Looking around in the darkness he realized he was sitting up in his bed. His hand was out in front of him and he was holding something. There was no need to turn on the light, he knew what it was, it was the book! Pushing his way out of bed he fumbled for the light switch not letting go of this unseen wonder, afraid he might lose it in the light.

Flipping on the switch, the glow of the electric light again flooded the room. Looking down he found clutched in his right hand the book from his dream. The cover was worn and Marty could tell it was very old. There were engravings on what should have been the back of the book and on the spine. A metal bar fastened over the edge of the book held it closed. The locking device had a hole that was X-shaped and Marty was curious what the key would look like that fit it.

He remembered in his dream how he had reached in his pocket and found the needed key. Shrugging, he decided to try it, why not? Walking to where his pants were on the floor; he searched the pockets, and found a little bit of pocket lint, but no key. Moving back to his bed with the book he sat down to study the cryptic writing. He wasn't that great of a reader, but this was definitely not English!

The Book from Marty's Dream

The markings were a combination of slashes moving in a diagonal pattern from the top left corner across to the bottom right, meeting the spine on the right side. Marty had never seen a backwards book before, and it was intriguing. Tracing the characters or symbols with his finger he tried imagining the person who could have made them but the image was blank, he couldn't picture them at all. Finally he decided he would just keep the book in a safe place and study it later. Lifting up the top mattress he laid it directly on the box spring, assuming that in his bed would be as safe as anywhere, and dropped the mattress back on top of it. It made a lump, so he mussed the sheets to hide the protruding portion, turned, and walked out of the room, flipping off the light as he passed.

He went past the wall of toilet paper again and made a decision to ask grandma today *why did she have so much of it?* After all it had been two weeks since they had arrived, and he hadn't asked her yet. So, for the moment the strange book slipped to the back of his mind.

He came out of the door at the top of the stairs and turned left into the kitchen. The smell of biscuits and gravy greeted his hungry nostrils. "Mmm, Grandma, it smells delicious!"

"Well, sit on down I've been waiting for you to get up," she swatted playfully as Marty pulled out a chair and sat down.

That's when he realized there was only one plate on the table, "Did you and mom already eat?" He twisted in his chair to see Grandma Pen's hunched back as she peeked into the oven at the biscuits.

Today she was in a soft pink housecoat the same color as his mom's carpet. He smiled, amazed at how many colors of housecoats she had. She turned, "Yes, we ate early; your mom had a job interview."

"Oh, that's right, I forgot," Charlotte was going to try to be hired as a secretary at a local office, just to provide for them. "Did you wish her luck for me?"

"Well, I wished her luck, and she's been gone for over and hour, so I think that's a good sign."

"Yeah, maybe it is," Marty agreed.

Marty was trying to think of a way to steer the conversation to the wall of toilet paper, but he couldn't think of how to do it. That's when he decided to find out more about Grandma Pentel in general, and it might work its way out. "So, what did *you* do as a job Grandma?"

"I was a teacher for thirty-five years."

"Really, what did you teach?"

"I was an English teacher," Pearl perked up she hadn't talked to anyone about her passion for years.

"Did you like it?" Marty was now a little hesitant, English was not one of his strengths.

"I loved it Marty, in fact, I wanted to keep teaching, but grandpa and I wanted to travel, so we retired the same year."

"What did he do?" Marty realized he knew so little about his grandparents; it was fascinating to get a chance to find out more.

"He taught too," Pearl said dreamily, "In fact I met him my first time at faculty meeting."

"You taught at the same school?" This could get good Marty thought.

A steaming plate of biscuits and gravy was placed in front of Marty as Grandma Pen sat down next to him at the table, ready to continue their discussion.

"I think I should begin when I was a young girl, then you'll understand the real Pearl Ingalls Pentel."

Marty dug into his biscuits and gravy, anxious to hear this story and grateful to have the chance.

"I was born on July 10, 1909 to Victor and Patricia Ingalls, the third child of 9."

"9?" Marty swallowed a mouthful of biscuits and gravy, then spoke again, "Wow, you must have never been lonely." He smiled as Grandma Pen shook her head and chuckled.

"No, not back then I wasn't," She continued, "My father wanted a boy, you see, I was the third girl in a row, so we all got to go fishing with him, we camped, and learned all about gardening. We were all 'Daddy's' girls. He wouldn't let us be girly, no frills for us, we all had overalls and large shirts to wear from our earliest years. Actually I have some pictures of us, when you're finished eating we can look at them."

Marty was nearly done he finished wiping up the last bit of gravy with the final chunk of biscuit, popped it into his mouth, chewed, and smiled, "That was great Grandma thanks!"

"Do you want some more?" She was ready to dish up a second helping.

"Oh no, I couldn't, five biscuits is plenty, thanks!"

"It's five biscuits '<u>were</u>' plenty since they are now on their way to your tummy," Pearl corrected lovingly.

Marty didn't really pay attention to the correction, "So, can we go see your pictures?"

Pearl laughed, "Yes, dear they're in the small room, I'll be right there."

Marty stood, pushed in his chair, and walked across the hall into what was called 'the small room,' Marty still didn't understand this title, it wasn't really that small, but, oh well.

He sat down on the olive green sofa and was momentarily reminded of Bismorda, not because the sofa was smooth or cold, but the color was almost identical. Smiling to himself over his recent adventure, he realized that Grandma Pentel's birthday would be coming up in just a few weeks. What could he get for her? That was still a mystery, so was this next adventure. He only had to wait a moment before Grandma Pentel appeared.

Opening the sliding closet door she exposed a shelf assembly filled with photo books and a coat bar filled with old winter coats and empty metal hangers. The smell that escaped was quite different from any Marty was accustomed to it was a mixture of leather and fur along with old paper and a strong odor Marty couldn't place. Pearl selected the oldest looking book and carefully extracted it from the shelf. Turning she sat down next to Marty. The cover of the book was some kind of leather, Marty guessed, at one time words had been embossed in gold but now all but the letters P O AL U were worn off.

Marty found this a funny title for a book, "PoAlu? What does *that* mean?"

"Well, Marty, it used to say Photo Album but like the

best of us, it's showing its age now too." Smiling fondly at the cover she continued, "I remember when I was in high school, I had just started my first job at Woolworth's and this was my first purchase."

"What year was that?" Marty asked eagerly.

"Let's see, I graduated in '27 so it was the summer of '25, just after my sixteenth birthday." Pearl went on, falling easily back the almost seventy years.

"Back then the '20s were called 'the Jazz Age' because of the popular jazz music and I knew I'd be able to get my picture taken at some of the jazz clubs and wanted a book to keep them in."

"I remember how busy the street was that day as I walked along 4th North and Main Street and the whole town, it seemed like, was driving around in their new Model-T Fords. The year before was when they became very popular. Can you believe it cost $300.00 in '24?"

"Wow, I bet mom would have loved to pay that for a car, I think she paid almost that much a month until she had the Tercel paid off."

Pearl chuckled, "You have to remember that back then we were lucky to make $2.00 a day, most people made $1.00 a day. So $300.00 was a whole lot of money! Well, here, let's look through these pictures."

Opening the ancient cover she revealed black pages with black and white square photos attached at the corners by small holders. That's when the unknown smell hit Marty, it was the pictures!

Marty leaned forward to look closer at the grainy images of a forgotten time. "Is that *you*?" he excitedly pointed at a young woman wearing a bell-like hat hugging her tight curls, dressed in a knee-length strapless gown with stockings up to her knees and black high-heel shoes strapped on her feet. As she smiled she was twirling a long string of beads.

"Yep, that's me. We were called 'flappers' back then,

can you guess why?"

"Cause of the beads? You're swinging them around, is that it?" Marty guessed.

"Not quite, when we danced we kicked our heels up and kind of flapped our arms, it was great fun. Some gals even had real pretty beaded dresses with lots of fringe that would swing as they danced. See Marty it was the age of women's liberation. We were no longer required to be restricted by men. In 1920 we even got the right to vote. It was a new age for us. World War I was over and we women were able to work outside of our homes. My mother stayed at home but Abby, Ruth, and I worked at different jobs."

"Where is this Grandma? You're in a funny dress thing, but it looks like a beach."

"That is at the beach by the Great Salt Lake and I'm wearing a swimming suit not a dress."

"Really? That sure is a lot to be wearing to swim!"

"Actually I think that now girls wear far too little to go swimming," Pearl replied frankly.

"Who is this?" Marty pointed to a picture of her and a young man.

"That was my beau Winston Clements," Pearl smiled at the picture and Marty could tell she was reliving the date, "He took me to the school dance, this was a picture my father took before we left. I was a senior that year. I remember just a few weeks after the dance in May of 1927 Charles Lindburgh flew alone across the Atlantic Ocean, that was some big news! That same year the 'talkies' came in."

"What are 'talkies?'" Marty puzzled.

"That's a movie with sound."

"What did you watch them *without* sound for?"

"They were exciting! The words were printed on the screen between scenes so you knew what was going on. Then a piano player played to add the effects. I still remember the hours we spent at the movies, by the radio, or playing games as a family."

"Didn't you have a T.V.?" Marty was fascinated, how could the world have been so different?

"No, dear, that didn't come along 'til your mother was young. As teenagers we listened to the news, concerts, opera, and one of my favorite shows *Amos 'n' Andy*. We would all sit around the radio as a family, all nine kids and mother and father. It was a great time for us. Ruth and I loved to play Mah-jongg while we listened."

"Ma-what?"

"Mah-jongg, it is a Chinese game that was a little like dominos and a game of matching mixed together then stacked up on top of each other."

"That sounds like fun," this was really enthralling, to be taken back to a different time.

"Oh, Marty, it was, I wonder if I still have my old Mah-jongg set."

"I'd love to learn how to play."

"We'll have to try and find my old set and then I can teach you, dear. Oh, and we listened to sports, too, 1927 was a record year for Babe Ruth, 60 home runs! Can you believe it?"

"Babe Ruth, isn't that a candy bar?"

"My goodness, Marty, this *is* quite a thrill to be talking to someone who is from such a different era. If someone had told me as a young girl that we would have movies in our homes or that people would walk on the moon, I would have said they were crazy!"

"Grandma Pen, you have seen so much, this is really neat! It makes me think more about what is around me."

"Good. You need to learn to be grateful for the many conveniences you have been blessed with. In October 1929, we all got a rude awakening and realized we had been taking much for granted when the Stock Market crashed in New York and started the Great Depression all over the country."

"What was that?" It sounded ominous to Marty.

"Well, it was when a lot of people lost all or a lot of their money. Do you remember the musical *Annie*?"

"Yeah, Mom loves that show!" Marty was excited that his grandmother had finally mentioned something he could relate to his own life, so that the story would seem even more real to him.

"Well that is a representation of what happened during the Depression, the rich, like Daddy Warbucks were *really* rich and the poor lost everything."

Marty shook his head, "That doesn't seem fair."

"It wasn't. It was during this time that *Little Orphan Annie* came out on the radio along with 'soap operas.'"

"But I thought those were the mushy love shows on T.V.," Marty protested.

"That's what they are today, but back then they were programs like *Dick Tracy*, *Superman*, and the *Lone Ranger*. They were called 'soap operas' because it was detergent companies that paid the money to put them on the air. In hopes that it might bring some sort of comfort or reassurance that we would all come out all right."

"Oh, that's interesting to know. So, did it make you feel better?"

"Yes and no. It was at this time frills were cut, our toilet paper was much the same as fine sand paper and was very uncomfortable to use. Actually when Grandpa Rufus and I got married, we promised each other we would never *not* have toilet paper again. So we saved up and would buy extra when we shopped. You've seen our supply downstairs I'm sure," She smiled, her eyes twinkling behind her glasses.

So that's why she had so much toilet paper, now it made sense. Marty just nodded, he didn't want to break Grandma Pearl's story line.

Just then Charlotte's head peeked around the doorframe, "Hi, I'm home!"

"Oh, Charlotte, you startled us, we didn't even hear

you come in." Pearl smiled over at Marty again, "Marty and I were just going through my memories. I hope it wasn't too boring."

"No way, it was really cool Grandma!" Marty's enthusiastic response pleased both Charlotte and Pearl.

He then turned to Charlotte, "Mom, did you know why Grandma has a wall of toilet paper down stairs?"

"The Great Depression," Charlotte giggled at Marty's surprise. "You forget Marty, Grandma Pen *is* my mom, so I've heard her stories, but I'm glad you two have had a chance to talk."

Pearl and Marty smiled at each other pleased that she approved. Then Pearl asked, "So, did your interview go well?"

"Yes, I'm surprised you didn't notice I was gone," Charlotte feigned hurt, "I've been working away and you two have been here chit-chatting."

"My goodness! You started today?"

"Yes, it's almost five, didn't you know?"

"Well, we talked right through lunch and totally forgot about the time!"

As if Marty's stomach heard her, it rumbled and they all laughed.

"How 'bout letting Marty and me help throw dinner together?"

"That would be lovely, dear."

Pearl closed the photo album and pushed off the couch to stand. "Goodness, I've shouldn't sit so long, my bones will never forgive me," she chuckled.

Marty jumped up to join her, "What's wrong with your bones Grandma?"

"Oh, just old age, it's slowing me down, sweetheart."

"Well you *have* been through a lot, I think you earned it," Marty smiled as he put his arm around his Grandma's waist, and they walked together into the kitchen behind his mother.

They threw together some salad and had dinner. After dinner Marty pushed his plate away and asked, "Grandma could we play Mah-jongg?"

Pearl chuckled, "Well, we can look for it, I think I remember where it is."

"How did you learn about Mah-jongg? And what *is* it?" Charlotte was now interested.

"I thought you had heard all of Grandma's stories," Marty joked. When his mother gave him her look, he continued, "Well, it's a Chinese game that's a mix between dominoes and a matching game. It came out in the '20s." Marty answered knowingly, pleased that he could inform his mother of something he had learned that day.

"Hey, I didn't tell you when it came out," Pearl was surprised.

"Well you told me how old you were, I just figured it out," Marty blushed at having gotten caught.

"So, do you still have it, Mom?" Charlotte asked, now intrigued.

"I know I do, I just need to remember where," Pearl paused, "it may be in the small room closet with the other games."

"What other games *do* you have, Grandma?"

"Oh tiddly-winks, marbles, and some other fun ones, I think my old Monopoly is even in there," Pearl was pleased that Marty was so interested in her life, she had thought there would be problems raising a pre-teen with her daughter, but now she felt much better about it.

Marty was up and headed out the door, "I'll look grandma, I should be able to see onto the shelf."

"Okay, honey we'll be right there," Charlotte smiled after her son then turned to her mother, "Thanks for entertaining him today, Mom."

"My pleasure, you have a fine young man there."

Charlotte's eye brimmed with tears and her voice caught as she looked after him, "I know..."

Pearl reached out and touched her daughter's arm, "We are going to be just fine, I'm so proud of you for not letting this get you down."

Wiping at her eyes Charlotte cleared her throat, "I'm really excited about this job, I actually can't believe he just hired me like he did."

"So what will you be doing?" Pearl pried gently.

"Well, I'm in charge of any correspondence, I'm also to keep the files organized and by the looks of his office he hasn't had anyone for a while," Charlotte smiled, "but that's job security."

"Grandma!" Marty called from across the hall, "I think I found it, but it's in between some other games, and I can't reach it."

"OKAY, dear," Pearl called back, then turning to Charlotte, "Can you take a chair for him to get it down?"

"Yeah mom, I can," she instantly understood what her mother was doing, building Marty's independence, and she was grateful for her wisdom.

Taking one of the kitchen chairs into the small room, Charlotte handed it to Marty and he climbed on it, easily reaching the desired height. Pulling out a prehistoric box that was barely holding together, Marty revealed it as a tar black color and it had a fitted lid. Stepping down off the chair the three of them sat side by side on the sofa. Marty slid off the lid and revealed a box full of pieces, the size and shape of dominoes but they were dark gray. There were markings on them, some were pictures, but there were others that looked similar to the writing on the book of his dream!

Marty gasped.

His grandmother leaned in, "I know, aren't they *neat*?"

All Marty could do was nod his head, he still couldn't believe that his book may have come from China! The etchings certainly looked similar he would have to compare them later. Right now he wanted to learn how to play. Taking the box with them they moved into the kitchen and sat down around the table.

"I remember just like it was yesterday that I purchased these with my pocket money for Ruth and me to play," Pearl reminisced as she arranged the Mah-jongg tiles into a pyramid-type building in the center of the table after mixing up the blocks.

Marty watched with fascination, "So is it always set up like that?"

"No, there are actually many ways to set it up, but this is one of the easiest," as she completed the structure she paused, then reaching forward selected two of them from the edges of the structure.

"So, I have now played first. It's your turn."

"OKAY," Marty stuck out his tongue from the corner of his mouth and screwed up his face in concentration.

Suddenly his eyebrows raised and he selected two more tiles that matched, "Your turn, Mom."

Charlotte leaned forward and played her turn. They continued and the tiles dwindled, then at Grandma Pen's turn, she sighed, "I guess that's the end of the game, I can't find any more matches!"

"But there's still more blocks left," Marty protested.

"Yes, but if you can't see the matches it means they are probably stacked on each other and now play has to stop," Pearl explained patiently.

"Oh, I see," Marty, conceded, "Can we play again tomorrow?"

Pearl giggled, "Of course we can."

They cleaned up the blocks and Marty slid the lid back into place. "Thanks, Grandma, that was fun. Can I take them down to my room? I'd like to study the engravings some more."

"Sure sweetheart, that's fine, enjoy yourself."

Marty tucked the box under his arm, leaned over, gave his grandma and mother a peck on the cheek, and headed downstairs. This time as he passed the wall of toilet paper he paused, trying to imagine not using this simple convenience, and uttered a silent prayer of gratitude for simple pleasures. Turning into his room he again illuminated it with the flip of a switch.

Removing the book from between his sheets he laid it out on his bed. Then plopping down beside it, he took the box of Mah-jongg tiles out from under his arm. Again removing the lid he smoothed out a place on his sheets and dumped out the tiles. He began finding those with the strange slash-like writing on them and putting them in one pile and replacing the others with simple pictures in the box. After he had all of the ones with the writing left he began comparing them to the cover of the book.

He found a few that could have been matches to the cover markings they looked like / and \ and –. *But what did they mean?* Instead of answering Marty's questions, it just created more. Marty puzzled over this for quite a while, and finally he could feel sleep creeping into his eyes and they started to droop. Changing his clothes, he put the book back between the mattresses and climbed into bed.

As he nodded off to sleep he puzzled over the strange slashes some more until he found himself back in the small skiff bobbing on the waves.

Chapter 9
Don't Pick the Red

There was something different this time. Marty looked around to discern what was different in the boat and realized someone else was there with him! It was another kid his same age. He had short blonde hair and slightly bucked teeth. His blue eyes were wide as he looked at the light in the distance, but he continued rowing.

Who was this? Why was Marty dreaming about a complete stranger? Was he seeing the future?

That's when Marty realized the reason he hadn't been moving in his other dreams, he hadn't had anyone rowing the boat! Having this other guy in the boat was helping him immensely; they were coming up on the light quite quickly. It stood far back from the shore somewhere above them as they ran aground on an empty beach. The light seemed to be floating in the clouds.

Marty and the other boy worked together as a team, pulling the boat up on the sand to secure it, and then congratulating each other for doing so well. This other youth was almost the same height as Marty and he guessed they were well acquainted; the only thing that bothered Marty was he didn't recognize him at all! Suddenly the other boy pointed toward the light and Marty turned to look, the clouds had cleared to reveal a huge candlestick with a large taper in the holder with the wick alight. For some reason Marty smiled and tugged at his companion's arm, urging him forward, closer to the warm glow encircling the comforting light.

As they drew up to the base of the candlestick he felt a comforting wave surround them. Marty stopped to marvel at the trees and shrubbery along the way, from each plant, books were hanging, as if they were fruit. There were some trees that still had blossoms made of pages, but others had fully ripe books hanging off the weighted boughs. They ranged in color to all the shades of the rainbow and were dazzling to behold.

The light from the candle cast a warm glow over this entire garden making it feel welcoming and peaceful. Marty and his friend looked up to admire the candlestick and could feel the love that it had for them. Marty's reasoning whispered in his ear, "How can a candle love?" Shaking off this reasoning he gazed admiringly at the flickering light.

Then a soft voice floated to Marty, "Go ahead, Marty, pick a book, any one you desire, but keep in mind, don't pick the red, pick the blue." The voice faded and Marty looked around again. His companion was doing the same; apparently he had heard the voice too. They split up and searched among the trees for the one they wanted the most.

There were exotic lime colored ones that drew Marty for a moment, he turned to see where his friend had gone, and found him poking around a low shrub covered in violent red books. He was about to warn him when the shrub took a bite at him! His friend stumbled back and fell on the ground. Marty rushed forward to help him. Reaching his side he reassured him that he was okay, but he was visibly shaken. As he comforted him the images around him started to fade and swirl.

Marty sat up, the room was dark, but it always was, being in the basement. He looked around to see what had made him wake up, but wasn't sure what he was looking for. Beginning to lie down again he had a creeping thought that made its way to the front of his brain, "What color was the strange book that he had found?" The warning being fresh in his mind he decided to check.

He slid from his bed and flipped on his light, squinting in the sudden brightness, he paused, waiting for his eyes to adjust. Then he stepped to his bed and pulled the book out. Disbelief filled him making his throat close he stared at it there in his hand. It was much worn, but he could tell it was a very dark red, almost a black. He looked at it not seeing anything but the color now, it was definitely red, and he was afraid of what he might find in this book. The excitement he had felt at finding what language it might be actually chilled him now, what if he had figured out how to open it?

What could have happened?

He remembered the boy in his dream that had almost been eaten by the bush of red books. Suddenly he felt prickles stand up on the back of his neck; someone had sent this book to him hoping he would open it. *Who had power over dreams?* He remembered the confession of Scrimt and Sayvd about how they had come in his dreams. It made him wonder who else had the power to alter his dreams.

Then it hit him, *Bismorda could help!*

She might know where the book had come from. Maybe she would even be able to read the writing. He would have to pay a visit to Qualf and talk with Bismorda. Soon.

After deciding this he checked his clock. 8:00 a.m. he better get upstairs if he wanted to see his mom off before she went to work. Changing quickly he ran upstairs, but only after making sure his secret was safe between the mattresses. The smell of bacon and eggs greeted him as he emerged in the kitchen. Pearl and Charlotte were seated at the table talking quietly when they heard him come upstairs.

He smiled, "Morning Mom, morning Grandma."

He bent and kissed them each on the cheek then took the remaining seat at the table. Pearl pushed the pan of eggs and bacon in Marty's direction sweeping off the lid as she did so. The steam cloud dispersed and Marty grabbed the spatula to serve up his portion.

He looked up at his Mom and Grandma, they were both eyeing him lovingly. Smiling he ducked his head as he filled his plate, now feeling self-conscious of how much he was taking.

Finally Grandma Pen's voice broke the silence, "Don't worry dear, eat up, we've already had our fill."

Marty looked at his grandmother and smiled appreciatively, she had read his thoughts. He could now eat and not feel guilty about his mammoth appetite. For some reason he couldn't eat enough, it was actually kind of a pain to be eating so much.

Now his mother spoke, "You must be hitting another growth spurt."

She smiled sadly, "Soon you'll be too big for me to keep in line."

"Don't worry mom, I'll kneel down if it will make you feel better," he smiled lovingly at her.

"You better not grow *that* much," then she paused, thinking, "Well you may do just that, Grandpa Rufus was quite tall and your dad is pretty tall.

"It won't be fair to have a son that is taller than me," she played.

"Promise mom, I won't let it go to my head!" He shoveled another scoop of eggs into his mouth.

"Goodness Marty, slow down," Pearl chided, "You may bite the bowl off the spoon if you're not careful."

Marty slowed just enough to not bring too much more attention to himself.

Before long, Charlotte pushed back from the table and rose, "Well, I better get to work, Marty you help Grandma today around the house." Marty nodded that he would do just that without breaking his eating stream. Charlotte turned in the door, waved briefly, then exited through the front room.

Pearl turned to Marty, "So, what *were* your plans for today before your mom volunteered you to help me?"

He swallowed and looked up, shocked at her willingness to hear his opinion, "Well, I was kind of wondering where the library is here."

Where did that come from? Marty asked himself. He had not planned to say it, but it sounded believable.

"Oh, it's just a couple blocks away. Would you like to go?"

"I don't want to drag you along, can you just explain how to get there?'

"Nonsense, I'd love to go for a walk. I haven't been to the library for years, it could be fun," Pearl said optimistically.

"You sure you're up to it?" Marty wondered aloud.

"Yeah, let's go out on the town!" It seemed that Pearl had dropped ten years at least.

Marty wondered what she would wear; he hadn't seen anything but her multiple colors of housecoats.

Pearl spoke again, "Give me a minute to get myself together."

"Are you gonna put your face on?" Marty wondered, using his mother's term.

Pearl laughed out loud, "Yes, that among other things. Will that be okay?"

"Sure Grandma this will be fun," Marty was surprised that he meant it.

He had grown to really enjoy the time he was spending with the peppy lady who was his grandmother. "Can I look at your other games while you get ready?"

"That's fine, just remember you'll probably need a chair to get them down," Pearl went back to her bedroom and Marty dragged a chair into the small room to use as a ladder.

Marty looked at Tiddly-Winks, a bunch of plastic disks that were all different sizes. He read the box and found that the game was quite easy to play. Then he realized something, he didn't have any problems reading the instructions. He didn't even stumble once. Surprised, he looked at the box again. Maybe it was because the instructions on the box were so easily written. Yes, that must be it, he convinced himself. His thoughts returned to the object of the game. You were supposed to hold one disk and use it to flip the other disks. It seemed quite easy; he'd have to ask Grandma Pen to play it sometime.

Marty turned back to the closet and his eye stopped on some large flat books that were under the stack of games. He worked the books out and replaced the box of Tiddly-Winks so he could hold them; there were six fairly large books. Stepping down off the chair he sat on the couch. The top one had a faded pink cover and a picture of a woman braiding her long hair. *Rapunzel* was written on the cover under the picture. These books looked really old Marty thought, not as old as his dream book, but they were old anyway. He placed *Rapunzel* on the sofa beside him. The next had a pale green cover and again an illustration placed to reveal what was inside, the title *The Emperor's New Clothes* Marty registered somewhat questioningly, but moved to the next four volumes *The Three Dogs, Aladdin and His Magic Lamp, The Three Brothers,* and *Puss in Boots.* Each had a picture, its own distinct color, and the title printed clearly on the cover.

Pearl's call brought him out of his thoughts as he was admiring the covers, "Okay, Marty, I'm ready." He looked up and was surprised to see Pearl dressed very elegantly. She had on a navy blue skirt with a smoky blue blouse tucked into it. It was buttoned up, leaving only the top button undone, and she wore simple pearl earrings. She had on nylons and black leather slip-ons. She looked ready to go out to dinner.

Marty jumped up. "Wow Grandma, you look beautiful! Should I go get dressed up? I feel a little too much like a kid."

Pearl Chuckled, "Well minus the fur and horns, you are still quite young."

Marty was thrown off guard, "Fur and horns, what do you mean?"

"A kid is a baby goat. Marty, I was making a joke." Pearl explained.

"Oh," Marty let that sink in, then smiled, "That was pretty good Grandma."

"Well, let's shove off, shall we?"

Some of the things Grandma Pentel said were so different they made Marty smile. She was such a fascinating woman. He was again grateful for his Grandmother. They walked the two blocks and turned into the parking lot of the local Scat-town library. Seeing them walk in the elderly librarian leaned forward, "Howdy Pearl, how are you these days? I haven't seen you since…well it was before Grace died, but after Mertyl, so it must have been, well…three months ago." Marty was fascinated by the way this woman kept time; he made a mental note to question Grandma about it later.

Pearl nodded, "Yes, Tessie it has been that long. I've been a little busy getting all my plants in, and then my daughter and grandson moved out here a few weeks ago." She paused in her explanation, gently pushing Marty toward the counter, "This is my grandson Marty, Marty this is Quintessa Winchester, Tessie for short, one of my best friends. We went to school together."

Marty couldn't help but stare, there were other people as old as Grandma Pen? This was almost too much to handle, but he nodded, "Nice to meet you ma'am." He took note of her posture, she was ram-rod straight and had bright red lipstick and her fingernail polish matched. *It doesn't really match her outfit*, Marty thought. She wore a teal ensemble similar to Grandma Pen's, but she had a gold chain necklace and gold bulb earrings. Her hair was steel gray and she wore it pulled back fiercely from her face and fastened in a braided bun at the base of her head. The glasses she wore were perched on her beak-like nose and she peered at him over them.

He didn't usually judge people, but she looked much more fierce than his grandma. She was currently analyzing him as well, lips puckered as if she had just bit into a lemon. Marty got the distinct feeling that she did not like children.

"Yes, *Marty*, was it? Do you have a library card?"

"Uh, no ma'am I just moved here from Wisconsin a few weeks ago, but I'd like to get one, if I could," he looked at Grandma Pentel to see if this would be okay.

She nodded and smiled sensing his uneasiness with Tessie.

"Yes, Tessie let's get Marty a card, I have a feeling he'll be using it a lot."

Tessie took this chance to cut Marty out of the conversation, "Okay, Pearl, he has to sign here on this contract, and if he misplaces his card," she looked sideways at Marty distastefully, then continued, "it will be a dollar replacement fee."

Both Marty and Pearl nodded, showing they understood. Marty signed twice and was given a Scat-town library card. He pocketed it, excused himself and went browsing.

Tessie's intense hiss sliced at him and he turned back toward the circulation desk, "Don't mis-shelve the books, if you look at something, place it on the red shelves that are clearly marked."

Marty turned again and made his way to the computer catalog. He typed in: Subject-plants. This in return brought up a large database of available plant books. He didn't know what he was looking for, but he thought he would look busy so Tessie wouldn't hiss at him again. His thoughts returned to the books he had found in the closet. Clearing the search he typed in: Fairy Tales. Many titles came up and Marty scanned them for any that caught his attention, then one leaped off the screen: *Asian Fairytales and Folklore.* He found the location, wrote it down and went on a search. Finding the area that had all the fairytales and folklore books he quickly located the book.

Picking up the book, he flipped the pages until he came across some illustrations, then he found one of the symbols from the book, he was sure of it. He snapped the book shut and made his way to the front desk. As he approached Tessie and Grandma Pen were talking in whispers across the desk. Tessie stopped abruptly and pasted on a smile, "Did you find what you were looking for?"

Man, she is like a robot.

"Yes, ma'am, I did," he handed the book and his card to Tessie.

Taking both, she scanned them, rubbed the spine on a metal square in the desk, then handed them back with a slip of paper.

"It is due back in two weeks."

"Okay, thank you ma'am." He turned to Grandma Pen expectantly.

"Let's go home Marty," then to Tessie, "it was good to catch up with you again. See you soon I hope."

"Probably sooner than you think, Helen Lantry isn't doing well," this sad news followed them out the door.

Marty turned to Grandma Pen, "She is your *friend*?" he stopped there not wanting to say something he would regret.

Pearl smiled back, "Well Marty, she is one of the only people around that I still know from the old Scat-town."

"Oh," Marty was glad that he had not said more.

Then Pearl cut into Marty's thoughts, "But I did give her a piece of my mind about the way she treated you," she chuckled, "didn't you see her smile when you came back?"

"Yeah, it was kind of scary," Marty admitted honestly.

"Don't let Tessie get to you, she just never married and never had children so she is a little apprehensive around them," Pearl explained.

"Is that why she looked at me like I was an insect?" Marty asked.

Again Pearl chuckled, "I *told* her that nothing gets past you."

"Well she did, it made me uncomfortable. I actually felt a little like I had turned into a worm or a fly by the look on her face."

"Oh, Marty you have such a way of describing things," Pearl looked adoringly at him.

"Oh, I was going to point out some of the sights on our way back. That building over there," She pointed at the

Laundromat, "used to be the old *Depot*, I used to take your mom there for candy and milkshakes. You should ask her if she remembers it sometime." They continued down the street and as they passed houses Pearl would say who used to live there.

When they finally got home, Marty excused himself, raced down the stairs under the guise that he was going to read, closed the door and quickly found the dragon key. He'd kept it stored in one of the drawers in his dresser. Gripping the fairy tale book and the key he went to his bed. He extracted the unknown book from between the mattresses and now with all three he had his hands full, thinking quickly he grabbed his book bag and tossed the books in and zipped it shut. Flinging the bag over his shoulder he approached the door. The knob glowed, the keyhole opened, and Marty's heart raced as he put the key in and turned it. When the simple click sounded, Marty removed the key, and exited his room closing the door behind him.

This time his trip to the castle wasn't frightening at all. Again he was greeted by people and creatures that bowed reverently as he passed quickly en route. He passed the statue that was a likeness of him without even a glance over his shoulder and before long he came to the opening on top of the hill with the breath-taking castle of Bismorda standing just where he had left it.

A trumpet sounded as he hurried up the steps and the doors opened, he was surprised to be greeted by Bismorda herself, how had she known he was coming? Then he remembered, oh yeah, she's a witch. She took him inside and they made their way to the sitting room, one of the large doors that had taken the place of the huge cave on the right side of the entry. It was lavishly furnished in deep shades of purple velvet and gold trim.

Marty dropped his bag and sat down where Bismorda pointed and she took the seat opposite. He paused to catch his breath, as he did, she spoke, "Marty it is so good of you to return, what a pleasant surprise."

She smiled and then continued, "I didn't really think you would return, after all you are a Yulesaychaater, and I am a mere witch."

It hit Marty that she was blushing, was she flirting with him? Marty did not have time to flirt, not now, he was on an important mission, besides he didn't know the first thing about girls, let alone ones that were 1600 years old. He leaned over to his bag, unzipped it and withdrew the two books. Dropping the bag back to the floor, he extended the ancient one toward Bismorda, "Have you any clue what this says?"

Bismorda's brow furrowed, "Well, it is a very ancient script, but it says *SPELLS*."

"Spells?" Marty was now interested, "Have you seen a lock like the one on this book?"

"Only once before, but that was many years ago, it was a very powerful lock and actually had no key hole, but was opened by magic."

Okay, thought Marty, two out of the three, now for the final one, "Do you know where this book comes from?"

"It's from a small country near Korea and China it is unknown to mortals, but well-known to me. It's actually close to Zanth, do you know where that is?"

Marty shook his head, Zanth...he had heard of it before, "Wait, isn't that where those witches are from that cursed you?"

Bismorda nodded, visibly disturbed, "The country is called Zilthowl. I thought that it had been destroyed though, so I don't know how you came to find this book."

"It floated to me in a dream," Marty explained.

"Really?" Bismorda was now curious, "How long ago?"

"A few days," Marty answered, "I woke up holding it."

"So, someone sent it to you in a dream?" Bismorda

voiced the same thought Marty had had that very morning.

"Who would do that?" Marty asked.

"There are many who have been looking for the Yulesaychaater, so it could have been anyone."

"I had a dream where I was told that red books are bad and the blue ones are good," Marty recalled, "does that make any sense to you?"

Bismorda thought deeply for a moment, as she did, Marty noticed her pointed ears twitched as she thought. Finally she said, "Tell me exactly what was said."

Marty thought she didn't hear him so he repeated, "I was told that red books are bad and blue ones are good."

"No, Marty, did the voice say, 'Don't pick the red, pick the blue?'" Bismorda attempted in an airy replica of the dream voice.

"Oh, yes that's what it said," Marty agreed as he brushed along his arms where goose bumps had appeared.

"Interesting…" Bismorda again thought, her ears twitching once more, "tell me more about your dream."

"Well, I was in a small boat on the ocean, the book floated to me and I picked it up. Then I woke up holding the book."

"When did you hear the voice?" Bismorda questioned, she was now leaning forward with interest.

"Oh, that was a different dream," Marty resumed, "the one where the voice spoke to me, I had it last night."

"Tell me about it."

"Well, I was back in the boat, but this time someone else was in it with me. He was rowing and we were going towards a light. We landed on a beach and found a garden of books with a huge candle in the center of it. That's when I heard the voice."

Bismorda looked a little dazed; Marty had to ask, "Are you alright?"

She nodded and when she spoke it was in a whisper,

"Do you mean you met a Checkpohmer?"

"I'm not sure what that is, but if it was the big candle then yes."

"Oh, Marty, I'm sorry I keep forgetting you know nothing about the language of the books, a Checkpohmer is a book watcher. It takes many forms, but usually it is a large source of light, guiding people to the center of where books are born. There are only a few of them left."

Marty must have looked puzzled for Bismorda continued, "Something, or someone has been trying to destroy the breeding grounds for books. The garden you visited in your dream sounds like one that I have heard of on the Island of Bicolotern. It's off the coast of Australia, again unknown by mortals, but vital to our existence."

"Oh, I see, but you still haven't answered the red and blue question," Marty tried to reroute Bismorda back to their original conversation.

"Oh, well that is usually true. Red books contain most spells or witch craft centered subjects, but sometimes there are many great truths put into red books, then locked against careless eyes."

"Is this a good book or a bad one?" Marty wondered.

"It contains spells, or says it does," Bismorda reasoned, "I wonder…"

"So, you're not sure?" Marty was a little disappointed.

"I'm not sure Marty, I'm sorry I couldn't be of more help."

"No, actually you've been a great help I know a lot more that I did before I came here," then he remembered the fairytale book, "Oh, I got this in the library today, I thought you might like to see it." He handed the book to Bismorda, her eyes were round with wonder.

She took it reverently, "I've never seen a book from your world, it *is* very different."

Flipping it open she scanned the pages, she ooed and

ahhed as if she were watching fireworks. Then she gasped and spoke in a whisper, "These are my old friends, they are all here, well there are quite a few of them missing, but I know all of these well."

Marty was pleased that he had made Bismorda happy.

She closed the book and returned it to him, just as reverently as she had taken it. "Marty, please promise me you will help guard the books."

A little confused by this comment he responded, "I will, Bismorda."

"There are evil forces brewing that want to erase the world of books, you must not let that happen," Bismorda's tone made Marty pay attention.

"I won't, Bismorda, I promise," he said now with conviction.

"Best of luck on your quest to find the key to the book of spells!"

Marty was startled by Bismorda's frankness, "But how did you...?"

"Remember, Marty, I *am* a witch!" She smiled, her brilliant white teeth shone.

Marty put the two books back in his bag and pulled it over his shoulder, "Well I need to get back, Grandma might wonder where I am."

"Yes, well, your welcome is never worn out here, Marty. Feel free to stop by anytime."

Bismorda led Marty to the front door and stood there until Marty had disappeared from view. Then she called Scrimt and Sayvd to her, they appeared quickly and listened as she instructed, "Marty has just informed me that he has been to the island of Bicolotern in a dream. A large candle was guarding the garden there."

At this both Scrimt and Sayvd gasped, "A Checkpohmer!"

"Yes and it sounds like quite a powerful one, I need

you to find out if it is on our side and what its human form is. If we can get Marty acquainted with it we may have a powerful bond, if it is not on our side we must keep Marty away from it at all costs. Now go, but return as quickly as you can." Scrimt and Sayvd nodded and flew off in the opposite direction to that which Marty had taken.

Bismorda stood looking off at the horizon and spoke softly "Oh please, let this Checkpohmer be on our side. If we could get a Checkpohmer and a Yulesaychaater, we may just survive!" With that she withdrew into the castle and closed the door.

****

Meanwhile, Marty was just arriving at the bridge where he re-entered his room and turned the key. He opened his door, dropped his bag on the floor and headed upstairs.

There he found Grandma Pearl in the small room looking through the faded orange book titled *The Three Brothers*, he knocked quietly at the open door. She looked up and smiled. "I used to read these stories to your mom when she was young, where did you find them?"

"They were under the games in the closet," Marty had forgotten that he had left them lying on the couch. "Sorry I didn't put them away."

"Oh, that's quite alright dear, I haven't seen them in years. It's funny I didn't even think about them, but seeing them again brings back so many memories," wistfully Pearl looked back at the book, hesitated, then asked, "Do you think it would be silly if I read you one, just for old times' sake?"

Marty shook his head, "No, Grandma I'd love to hear one." He sat down on the sofa next to Pearl. Clearing her throat, she flipped to the front page and in a clear distinct voice she started, "Once upon a time there were three brothers, they had names like anyone else but everyone had called them Tall, Fat, and Foolish for so long their real names had been forgotten." The story unfolded and the brothers each went on a personal search for fortune. They found it after encountering a little old man in a bright pink hat, but because of a stingy innkeeper the first two lost their treasures and only when the final brother, Foolish unknowingly outwitted the innkeeper did his brothers receive their treasures back.

After the story finished Pearl paused, looked at Marty, his eager face turned toward her, and smiled. "Wow, Grandma, that was great! I love the way you read stories!"

"Oh Marty, that was a lot of fun, I haven't done that in ages. I had forgotten how much I love to tell stories."

"You should do it more, you are really good."

Pearl colored, "Really? I only read to your mom, but I certainly enjoyed it. Oh, I read to my English classes too, does that count?"

"You read to your classes? I bet everyone loved it!" Marty said honestly, "I wish my teachers would read, they just tell us what to do then sit there and stare at us."

"Oh, Marty, I'm sure they don't!" Pearl said knowingly.

"But they *do* Grandma! They make us feel bad for them because they are teachers."

"I hope you're just exaggerating," Pearl's voice now filled with concern, "That would make school just awful."

"I don't think teachers like being teachers; at least that's how they act." Marty continued, "but it sounds like you loved to teach, and I bet your students loved your class."

"I hope so," Pearl did hope that she had never made any of her students pity her because she was a teacher.

She changed the subject, "You ready for lunch?"

"Yeah, want some help?"

"I would love some."

They walked together into the kitchen both lost in their thoughts. Pearl remembering her years of teaching, Marty now wondering if there was a fortune out there for him, like the brothers in the story. They ate lunch and then they cleaned, Marty helping like he promised. Charlotte came home, they ate dinner and when it came time, Marty went to bed.

****

Just as the sun was setting in Qualf, Scrimt and Sayvd flew to where Bismorda was waiting, in the sitting room. They hovered within inches of her in their excitement. Bismorda spoke first, "Well, if I'm reading your faces correctly, I'd say we are on our way to a mighty alliance of a Checkpohmer and a Yulesaychaater."

Scrimt and Sayvd nodded enthusiastically, Scrimt spoke, "You'll never guess what, or I mean where the Checkpohmer is."

"Tell me," Bismorda was like a youth, giddy and impatient.

"Well the Checkpohmer is employed at Rosewood Junior High School," Scrimt explained.

Sayvd couldn't let Scrimt have all the fun, "That's where Sir Marty will go to school!"

This news was received joyously and the three of them went to bed truly grateful for this good omen.

****

The months of summer break slipped by quickly, too quickly if you asked Marty, and soon it was time for school to start.

Chapter 10
When The Bell Tolls

Saturday, August 18, 1990

Marty received his schedule, looked it over and read aloud, "First period will be Physical Education with Mr. Hank Thickett. Second period is Pre-Algebra with Mrs. Mabel Faleswell. Third Spanish with Mr. George Wolden, fourth Science with Miss Violett Baumer, fifth Music with Mr. Delbert Bachenheim, sixth History with Miss Malvina Culbreth, and seventh English with Mrs. Samantha Penn." He breathed and looked over the folded paper at Charlotte and Pearl, smiled weakly, and said, "Sounds like a lot. I hope I remember where I am supposed to go, and when."

"Oh you'll do just fine, Rosewood is easy as cake to find your way around," Charlotte piped in, "Here, I bet they included a map with your registration. Let's see." She grabbed the envelope, extracted another folded page and smoothed it on the kitchen table where she and Pearl had been seated when Marty entered with the mail. Charlotte looked at the mass of lines and numbers that represented Rosewood Junior High School and nodded her head. Marty looked over her shoulder and gulped, *I'm supposed to find my way around that maze?*

Charlotte pulled out the chair, motioned for Marty to sit and said, "I'll get a bunch of highlighters and we'll map out your route at school, Okay?"

Marty nodded numbly as he continued to stare at the labyrinth that he was expected to conquer at the age of 12. He had recently celebrated his birthday. It wasn't a big affair, since he only knew Grandma Pen and Charlotte the three of them had just gone out to dinner. He had a new watch and some new clothes for school as evidence of his newly acquired age.

Other than that Marty still felt the same and now he

was being asked to accomplish the unthinkable task of remembering seven classes in order and in the right place in a complicated maze called Rosewood.

Marty shook his head as Charlotte entered and began color-coding Marty's attack strategy. When she was finished Marty looked at the result, well, this *might* help, now there were only a few lines amid the mass of squiggles on the map. He smiled gratefully at Charlotte, "Thanks, mom."

"Now, let's see which hall your locker is in." She looked up to find Marty studying the map intently. He hadn't heard her. Looking at the registration slip she found printed clearly in the top-right corner E-325. She tapped Marty's shoulder, then when he lowered the map she leaned forward, "Your locker is here." Pointing with her finger to a place midway down the line marked "E". He heard her this time, "My locker? What is that?"

"Where you put your books."

"You mean, I don't have a desk?" Marty was stunned.

"No, you move everything from one room to another or leave it in your locker."

"Can I just carry my books?" Marty tried.

"Well, you could but it would be pretty heavy!" Charlotte reasoned.

Marty was now desperate, "Can you go with me to school on the first day?"

"Oh Marty, you'll have plenty of time to learn what to do at orientation."

"Orientation?" Marty was confused, "What is that?" All these unknown words seemed to be piling up on him.

"That's where the school lets you explore an experimental day, going to your classes. You'll meet your teachers briefly and then move on to your next class."

"When is that?" Marty was amazed at his mom's wisdom.

"Well, it says here at the bottom of your schedule,

Monday, August 20th at 6:00 p.m. Parents welcome."

"So, will you go?" Marty requested expectantly.

"Of course, dear, I'd love to," Charlotte stood, "Okay we have two days until school kind of starts, do you want to celebrate? Let's go out to eat!"

Marty and Pearl were surprised, but pleased with the suggestion.

They went out to eat at *Posey's* a small restaurant downtown with delicious French-fries and milkshakes. When they returned home, it was late; Marty went down to bed and fell quickly to sleep.

The waves were back; it had been over two months since Marty had been in the skiff.

He immediately turned and saw the same boy rowing the boat, but could tell this dream was later than the original one, they both were confident and knew the way. They climbed out on the shore of the beach and were quickly again in the garden of books.

The voice again floated to Marty, "Bismorda said you would be coming soon, I'm so glad you are finally here. We must protect the books…" Marty turned to his unknown companion, he was looking through the books on the various shrubs, he hadn't heard the voice. Marty realized he was the only one who could hear it. It was meant for him.

Again the voice spoke the last three words, "Protect the books…"

Then Marty woke, the question he asked aloud, "How?" was left unanswered.

Marty puzzled over how he was to "protect the books" for the next day and a half, then a more immediate threat to his existence took over, orientation.

Monday evening found Marty and Charlotte in the crowded front office of Rosewood Junior High; they had been put in the blue group that would tour the school prior to the mock school day. They had one hour to complete the tour. Marty could already feel the walls closing in on him as he fell into line with a horde of parents and students being led by a teacher in a "blue leader" t-shirt. The pointing and instructions became way too much for Marty to handle and he started trying to orient himself, first finding landmarks, and then counting available hallways. He quit at 110 (the number seemed excessive but math had never been his strong suit).

For some reason it seemed like he was getting more and more lost, instead of being pointed in the right direction. Amidst this confusion he caught sight of something that made him stop dead in his tracks. The student behind him ran right into him, and they created quite a traffic jam. Marty was still craning to see what had made him stop and wasn't really aware of the disturbance he had created.

He had seen the boy from his *dreams*.

Charlotte finally pulled Marty out of the traffic of bodies, and they stood off to the side as the others passed. When they were alone for the most part, she asked him, "Are you okay? What just happened?"

"Uh, it's all so confusing, I started to get dizzy and I just stopped," Marty hoped this sounded believable because he knew the truth didn't.

He couldn't just say, *Oh I just saw a boy who was in my dreams, we discovered a giant candle and a garden of books.* No, he definitely couldn't tell her that.

She looked concerned, "Are you going to be okay?"

"Yeah, maybe we should just sit down for a few minutes until they go through our schedules."

"That sounds like a good idea, follow me sweetheart, I'll take you to the stage area where we're supposed to meet everyone else."

They began walking down the nearest hall; Charlotte said it would be a straight shot, so Marty agreed. Halfway down the hall Marty felt a warmth envelop him. He stopped, looked to his right and saw the library doors like a like a great big set of hands beckoning him to enter. Feeling sheepish he asked, "Could we check out the library?"

Charlotte beamed, "Sure, I wonder if Mr. Candletier is still here, he was such a wonderful librarian."

A face peeked around the corner about fifteen feet from the door and broke into a contagious smile, "Charlotte Pentel! My goodness, come in child!"

Marty watched as his mother seemingly dropped twenty years and hurried into the library. He followed close behind. As they arrived at the point where the face had first appeared, a tall, white-haired man rounded the counter and greeted Charlotte with a quick embrace. They separated and looked at each other, affection clearly written on their faces. Then Charlotte remembered Marty, "Oh, Mr. Candletier, this is my son, Marty."

"No! You're too young to have a grown child!" His genuine shock made Charlotte blush.

"Oh, Mr. Candletier, do you realize how old I am? It's been thirty-six years since I first came to Rosewood, I can't believe you haven't changed at all."

Marty watched this interchange in wonder. This elderly man had more energy than a freight engine, but he must be close to Grandma Pen's age. His white goatee curled at the end and bobbed as he talked. He had a full head of gleaming white hair. Marty was fascinated how it caught the light. It danced like fire.

When Mr. Candletier finally turned to Marty he extended a hand of long, spindly fingers that reminded Marty of a spider's long jointed legs, but it didn't frighten Marty at all. Instead he shook hands and was surprised at the warmth and strength in the older man's grip. Locking eyes with him he felt a jolt of electricity. His eyes were like liquid blue flame behind his glasses. He smiled and when he spoke Marty could feel the words in his veins.

"It is a pleasure to meet you, Marty. I hope we shall become good friends while you are here at Rosewood."

Marty could feel the power of his words and, oddly, he had felt that power before. He just couldn't place it. Then Marty responded after an uncomfortably long pause, "Oh, I'm sure I'll become one of your frequent visitors, I've always spent a lot of time in the library."

Charlotte smiled and put her arm around Marty, pulling him to her.

Then she spoke, "It is so good to see you again, Mr. Candletier, I still can't believe you're here."

"Oh, they're going to have to drag me out of here or blow up the school!" he chuckled.

"Well, I know Marty will be in good hands if you are here. Do you know if anyone else is still here from my time?"

Ignatius Candletier furrowed his brow for a moment, "Well, I don't know of anyone who is still here, but I know some who have come back." Here his mouth twitched not allowing the wanted smile to escape.

"*Oh*, who has come back? And what do you mean by *come back*?" Charlotte gave in to the bait.

"Well, a Mr. Reed Wright has been teaching here for a few years, he came to us after quite a stint in Salt Lake City." The mischievous grin now broke free.

Charlotte visibly blushed and Marty was now extremely curious. "Who is Mr. Wright?" He asked Charlotte.

"Oh someone I knew a long time ago." Charlotte mused.

"He'll be pleased to hear that he was so important to you," Mr. Candletier interjected sarcastically.

"Fine, if Mom won't tell me, will you Mr. Candletier?"

Ignatius looked over the tops of his glasses at Charlotte, until she finally nodded faintly. "Your mother and Mr. Wright used to be an item."

Charlotte blushed an even deeper shade of red.

"What does that mean?" Marty was now openly confused.

"Marty, it means Reed and I used to date, we were a couple," Charlotte explained.

Finally understanding Marty nodded his head, "Oh, I see."

He thought to himself *Now was it that difficult?* But kept silent.

"Charlotte, you might also be interested to know, he's still single, but you didn't hear it from me."

This little gossip session was clearly closed unless Charlotte persisted in knowing, she didn't, so Marty was left hanging.

Mr. Candletier went back behind his counter and leaned over to face Marty once more, "Make sure you come and see me now. I'll be looking forward to seeing you, Marty."

Again Marty had the distinct feeling he had heard that voice before, but couldn't place it.

Marty and Charlotte left the library, but now Charlotte seemed very preoccupied. Suddenly she said, "I need to use the restroom, Marty."

"Okay, you know where it is, I'll follow you."

They turned left at the library entrance and the restrooms were right there. Marty was surprised, he hadn't noticed them when they walked down here before. Now he made a mental note, from the library the restrooms are on the left. He waited outside as his mom went in. A few minutes later she emerged and Marty had to look twice, was this *his* mom?

She looked totally different. She had almost no makeup on, she had washed it off, then she had put on a little lipstick and simple eyeliner. Her shoulder-length hair had been brushed through, it had been up in a ponytail, and was now hanging with a light curl inward at the ends. He came forward his mouth opened, but no words came out.

"Marty, close your mouth, it's hanging open," Charlotte reached forward, placed her hand under his jaw, and slowly closed his mouth. Then she smiled, "What? You act like you've never seen your mom before."

Marty finally found words, "Mom, you're really pretty, why do you wear all that makeup?"

Charlotte shook her head and shrugged her shoulders when she spoke her eyes were glistening, "I tried to get your dad to notice me, he seemed to like younger women with lots of makeup, so I tried to be that kind of woman."

The sadness was evident in her voice.

"You shouldn't have to hide behind makeup, Mom. You look a lot younger without it." Marty confided.

"*Really?*" Charlotte didn't believe him.

"Yeah Mom, I didn't recognize you when you came out. You don't need a lot of makeup, I think you're beautiful!"

His honesty finally convinced Charlotte and they turned again heading toward the stage. They passed the library and kept going. Down the hall they passed a few classrooms, the doors were propped open and they were vacant. Marty had now established a way of orienting himself; the library was the new center point of his inner map. To the right were some classrooms, he would identify them later, but they were now on his inner map, too. The hallway intersected another hallway, but Marty was not going to get lost again. He had found his center. To the right was the office and to the left another hallway. He could see beyond the office to the front entrance. He had done it!

To the left was the stage and others were already gathered there. Marty and Charlotte turned and in seconds were seated on the stairs in front of the stage. In moments there were hundreds of people converging on the stage to start the mock day. Marty spied the blond boy again. He was with two tall and thin people, Marty decided they were his parents. There were definite similarities in their faces, but the unknown boy's parents both had dark brown hair, in contrast to his short, blond buzz cut.

Marty wanted to get the boy's attention but didn't know how to tactfully do so. Then he thought, *What would I tell him? Oh, I met you in my dreams, just thought I'd say Hi? No, that sounded really crazy and I don't want to freak him out.* He would have to act natural, but what *was* natural? Marty had never had a friend before, he had always felt too awkward and inadequate, so he didn't know how to 'naturally' acquire one. *Well, I'll just wait for an opportunity to meet him. Yeah, that should work.*

Beside Marty, Charlotte was scanning the crowd, too. Then she saw him. *I can't believe it, he looks almost exactly the same!* Her palms started sweating as she looked at his blonde head bobbing above the masses. *He always did stand out in a crowd, he was six feet six inches and slim. He's wearing his age well,* she thought. *I like him with glasses.* Charlotte found herself making mental notes of what he was wearing, *a white shirt and tie, he always did dress up. I never knew he went into teaching.* Her thoughts were interrupted by Marty poking her.

"Mom, they said we're supposed to start, let's go to first period."

She looked down at Marty, love filling her eyes. "Okay, what is it?"

He consulted his schedule, "Physical Education with Mr. Thickett."

"Okay, that's in the gym, let's go." They stood and joined the mass of others making their way back to the hall they had just recently come out of. Marty was surprised to find the boy and his parents just a few people in front of them.

He heard him say, "Dad, I have Physical Education with Mr. Thickett first."

The boy's father responded, "Okay, well, let's see if we can't find out where that is."

Marty turned to his mom, "Hey! They're looking for the gym too, should we show them where it is?"

Charlotte had not heard the boy or his father speak, but agreed with Marty that they could help. They walked up alongside them in the hall and Marty turned to them, "I heard you say you're looking for Mr. Thickett's class, that's where we are going, if you want to follow us, my mom knows the way."

Marty's confidence caught them all off guard. Charlotte looked at her son, surprised at how well he had done that, then nodded and pushed to the head of their small group, "Follow me!" They made their way past the library hall and continued until this hall again intersected a different hall. Where it made the T intersection Charlotte pointed, "There's the gym straight ahead."

They all went inside, sat on the bleachers close to the front, and waited to meet Mr. Thickett. A bell sounded and the crowd quieted. There was a movement off to the right as a heavy-set, middle-aged man made his way to the front. His voice boomed out, "Welcome students and parents! This is going to be a great year for Rosewood's football team! I hope you will all come out to support us!"

Charlotte looked at Marty, "It sounds like we have come to a pep rally instead of school."

Marty had no idea what a pep rally was, but he nodded anyway. He looked again at the man in front who was going to try and teach Marty how to be fit, when he, himself looked like a bad advertisement for fast food. Quietly Marty leaned over to the blonde boy and whispered, "What else do you have on your schedule?"

They compared and every one was the same! Marty looked at the top of the paper. The name printed clearly on the left corner was Chrismon, Nicholas. Another sidelong glance told Marty that Nicholas had seen Marty's name, too. They nodded to each other as a silent greeting, then turned back to the boisterous Mr. Thickett.

The rest of orientation went by smoothly, Marty and Nicholas moving with confidence by the end of the evening.

The thing that caught all of them by surprise was the fact that Marty and Nicholas had lockers next to each other. Marty knew it was fate, but everyone else thought it a neat coincidence. When orientation was over they finally got a chance to talk for a moment.

Charlotte held out her hand, "I'm Charlotte Whimpel, and this is my son, Marty."

Nicholas' mother took Charlotte's hand, "Janet Chrismon, this is my husband Tom, and our son, Nick. It's so nice to meet you. Thank you for helping us around tonight."

"No problem, my pleasure," Charlotte reassured them, "Are you new here?"

Janet continued, "Yes, we just moved in over the weekend, it's lucky we found out about this orientation, but we had written the school ahead of time and Nicky's schedule was waiting at the house."

"Where did you move in?" Charlotte was curious.

"Oh, we're on Maple, Tom, what's the number again?" Janet's brow furrowed.

"212," Thomas Chrismon was happy to let his wife talk while he stood back. He was not the social one and any chance he had of escaping direct conversation he gladly took.

Charlotte spoke, "Oh really? Maple is just around the corner from Farnsworth that's where we live. We just moved in, too. Well, actually I'm back after many years of being gone, but my son moved back with me."

Janet and Thomas nodded their heads.

Marty found it strange that divorce wasn't even mentioned, but he didn't care, it was better that way. He didn't want to seem abnormal after just meeting Nick. After all Nick still had his parents, *both* of them, and he'd probably think it weird if Marty didn't. Finally they said their good-byes.

Marty and Nick promised to find each other the next day at school, and they all went home.

Charlotte felt a little depressed that she hadn't run into Reed again, *but there are always parent teacher conferences!*

She smiled to herself as she prepared for bed. Her mind went back to before Samuel when Reed had been 'the one,' *what had gone wrong? Why did I lose my Mr. Wright? Well, maybe that doesn't matter now, maybe I've been given another chance to try.* With that she climbed into bed and fell asleep.

Meanwhile, Marty was downstairs in his room preparing for bed and puzzling over a few things that had bothered him. *First, Mr. Candletier, how could he look the same as when Mom knew him thirty-six years ago? Everyone changes and no one that is that old lives forever. How old was he? Next, why did what Mr. Candletier said sound familiar to me? I have never met him before.* With these questions still tumbling in his mind, Marty climbed in bed and drifted off to sleep.

The light ahead bobbed in the cloud cover as Marty and Nick got closer. The clouds parted and the candle came into view.

Marty sat up in his bed, wide-awake, *Mr. Candletier is the candle!* Laying back down he tried to reason with this realization but couldn't. *How could Mr. Candletier be a librarian at Rosewood and a giant candle, or Checkpohmer on the island of Bicolotern?*

With this question unanswered, Marty fell back to sleep.

Chapter 11
Divulging A Secret

Tuesday, August 21, 1990

The morning dawned and Marty knew it was going to be a great day, he knew that Mr. Candletier and the Checkpohmer were one and the same, he didn't know how, but he was determined to find out.

He got ready for school and went up to the kitchen. The smell of hash browns and eggs met him as he seated himself at the kitchen table. Both Charlotte and Pearl watched Marty anxiously, when they saw no apprehension they breathed easier. He must have calmed down after the orientation the previous night. They ate their breakfast together then Marty left for school.

He would be walking the three blocks to the school because they lived so close.

As he came to the corner of Farnsworth and Maple he met Nick and they greeted each other warmly. They had become fast friends without a lot of chatter. Arriving at school they suddenly realized there were older kids there too, why had that not occurred to them sooner?

Because it was a Junior High School there were 8th and 9th graders at Rosewood as well as the 7th graders who had attended orientation the night before. Nick and Marty made their way to their lockers without incident. Shortly after arriving Nick had his locker open and was depositing his book bag and lunch, but Marty was still trying to negotiate his locker combination.

He thought the numbers *25 right, 13 left, 19 right, open...not open.* He then would spin the dial and try again.

The fourth time in a row, still nothing, panic was starting to seize Marty.

Nick broke into Marty's thoughts, "Let me try."

Marty showed Nick the numbers written on a slip of

paper, now sweat soaked and crumpled in Marty's hand.

Nick opened it on the first try, turning with a smile, "I think they can smell fear," he whispered conspiratorially.

Marty had to laugh at his tone. He really liked Nick and was glad they were now friends. Marty put his bag in and shut the door.

Now it was his turn at light humor, "Okay, let's go get fit with fat Thickett."

They both laughed as they headed off to the gymnasium. The classes until lunch went well. They got to pick their desks in Pre-Algebra, so they sat together, in Spanish they also sat together, science class was set up in tables so they chose two seats out of four and they were joined by a boy named Toby Bond and a girl named Monica something. Marty couldn't pronounce her last name, therefore he couldn't remember it. Toby seemed pretty nice talking to Monica, but he threatened to punch Nick if Nick looked at him. So the first day of Science didn't leave any lasting friendships on their table except for Marty and Nick's.

At lunchtime Nick went to his locker to get his sack lunch as Marty got in line in the cafeteria. The plastic tray in front of Marty held some sort of mystery sauce they called gravy, but he couldn't figure out why they would put gravy on hotdogs. As he made his way to a table where Nick was already waiting he made a vow that he would never again eat school lunch!

Marty sat down and Nick looked at Marty's tray, his face wrinkled in disgust and Marty said, "My feelings exactly!"

Nick tore his peanut butter sandwich in half and offered it to Marty.

After hesitating he took it gratefully.

The only thing on the tray that was recognizable was the milk so Marty felt safe drinking that, grateful his lunch hadn't been a complete waste of his $1.25.

After lunch they made their way to music class. Mr. Bachenheim greeted them each by name at the door. This impressed both Nick and Marty as they passed on into the classroom. The seats were in a semi-circle around the piano and the rows were raised by a set of bleacher-like risers. On the board was written, in a quickly scrawled hand, a musical note and to the side it read, JUST A NOTE.

Marty looked at Nick who was also puzzled by this obvious statement. They sat down and waited for others to arrive. As a girl with two long braids entered she looked at the board and laughed. She laughed and laughed, the tears pouring down her cheeks.

Marty and Nick were totally bewildered by this and finally Nick leaned over and whispered, "Maybe it's a girl thing."

They agreed that this might be it, but were still dumbfounded as to the point of it.

Finally the room was filled and only two other people had found the message remotely funny. Marty and Nick were still at a loss when Mr. Bachenheim stepped in, his mass of brown hair sticking out in all different directions, his eyes magnified by his spectacles, his odd assortment of a button-up sweater and blue jeans with loafers showing his obvious lack of fashion sense.

He pointed threateningly at the board and shouted, "This is the only kind of note I want in my class!"

This took everyone by surprise and everyone was silent, they didn't even dare to breathe. Then, as if he had become a totally different person he sat calmly at the piano and spoke so quietly everyone leaned forward to hear him, "Now I want you to all make two lines around the room, shortest girl to tallest girl and shortest boy to tallest boy."

Everyone stood and did as they were told; amazingly there wasn't even a sound, no one wanted him to yell again.

Marty and Nick were right next to each other in line

because of their similar heights. They were also two of the tallest boys, since this was the seventh grade only class.

Mr. Bachenheim then hit a chord on the piano and everyone froze.

He again spoke quietly, "I want each of you to come forward and sing up and down the scales for me, please, starting with Amy."

The girl with the braids went forward and trilled out notes that Marty didn't think humans could hear.

As she finished Mr. Bachenheim only said two words, "Soprano, there," and he pointed to a section of the risers.

This was repeated for every student pausing only to tell each their part and pointing out their seat. It was a given that the shorter would be on the closest row and on up to the tallest in the back row. Marty and Nick both ended up as tenors and were placed right in the center of the back row.

The excitement in the room was now a silent frenzy; they were all in their parts and ready for the adventure of music, but the bell signaling the end of class cut their excitement short.

Before they left Mr. Bachenheim called, "Remember where you sit, so we will be ready to start singing tomorrow."

The murmurs as they exited were varied.

"He's a little weird."

"I think he's great."

"All the real musicians were crazy, he fits in."

"I think it will be fun."

Nick and Marty agreed that Mr. Bachenheim was different, but he would be interesting, which was much more important to them.

They arrived in Ms. Culbreth's history class and sat near the front.

Very shortly they would realize what a mistake that had been.

When they had come to orientation the night before,

the fact that parents were present may have tempered Ms. Culbreth, but now the parents were gone and her full wrath was unleashed. Sitting behind her desk, her black beady pupils in her severely pinched face glared at each pupil as they entered, daring them to ask a question. Black covered her from head to toe. She had a black blouse tied at the throat with a red bow, a black floor-length skirt, visible only under her desk, covered all but the tips of her pointed black shoes. It was as if a black-widow spider waited ready to pounce on any unsuspecting victim. Eyes unusually large behind her thick spectacles looked completely white except for the specks of black still glaring at each tasty morsel.

Her age was unknown and would remain that way.

No one dared speak.

The bell to start class broke the spell. The silky grace with which she rose caused the class to visibly cringe in their seats.

Her voice broke the stillness; it was unearthly, "Welcome to class. Those of you who came to orientation last evening, it was a pleasure to meet your parents."

She smiled; it looked painful, "This year we will be studying history."

Gliding across the front of the classroom like a specter, it looked like she was floating, well, you couldn't see her feet beneath the long skirt anyway.

Suddenly she leaped forward, supporting herself on her two stick-like arms, landing on Marty's desk and she spoke again. "My name is Ms. Culbreth, not Miss, not Mrs., but *Ms.* Culbreth!"

Her breath was putrid.

Marty almost gagged, but didn't dare move.

She continued, "In history we study the past and learn from it, so we don't repeat it. Therefore, plan on learning it, so you *don't* repeat my class!"

Raising herself to stand erect again, she spun in place

so that her back was now to Marty, and glided over to the chalkboard.

She picked up a piece of chalk and wrote swiftly in a swervy script on the board: *U.S. History, Any questions?*

She then glared over her shoulder daring anyone to follow the instructions.

When no question was asked, she smiled again, this time it slowly spread and looked like she had gas. She replaced the chalk and approached her lectern standing front and center for all to see. The droning then began and for the next 40 minutes history was again killed by *Ms.* Malvina Culbreth.

After the bell rang she gave the assignment of reading two chapters by the following day, no one complained, they wrote it down quickly and gratefully escaped into the hallway.

Nick and Marty made it all the way to their lockers before they spoke. Marty started, "Man, she's like death. That class is going to be awful."

"Yeah, Ms. *Killbreath* will definitely suck any fun out of history, that's for sure!" Nick agreed.

"What's next?" Marty almost didn't want to know.

"English with Mrs. Penn," Nick reminded him.

Marty giggled, "Oh, yeah."

He giggled because he could still see Mrs. Samantha Penn on the night of orientation.

She had been the only teacher that Marty had instantly liked.

Did she look comfortable? That's the best word Marty could find to describe her.

Her hair was set in a perm, but slightly disheveled, she had large glasses that had gone out of style years before, her outfit was all polyester, a flowered shirt and yellow bell-bottoms, her shoes were Velcro strapped, and, best of all, she was a little scatter-brained. Marty could tell immediately when she had all of the parents and kids come in and sit on the floor instead of at desks.

Yes, Marty was looking forward to Mrs. Penn's class. They got their notebooks and headed off toward English class, grateful they only had Ms. Culbreth once a day. When they got to Mrs. Penn's door, the lights were out, but a sign read, COME IN, MAKE YOURSELVES COMFORTABLE.

How fitting!

They went in and squinted in the dimness, trying to make out the classroom, they finally saw lumps in the shadows move and realized that they were other students. Some were sitting cross-legged on the floor; others lay down, sprawling every which way. Marty and Nick sat on the floor not sure where Mrs. Penn was, then they saw her.

She was sitting cross-legged on her desk.

A large string of beads down her front seemed to emit a faint glow and she had a headband on.

Her clothes consisted of a baggy shirt with fringe and tassels, her pants looked gray in the limited light, but they could have been white. With her eyes closed behind her glasses, hands resting, palms up on her knees, she looked like a yoga teacher. Then as quiet settled once more they could hear her humming. It was not a tune, but more of a buzz. Marty found it strangely soothing and began to nod off when the bell to start class sounded.

Mrs. Penn stayed where she was but spoke to the class in an intoned chant, *"Make yourselves comfortable. Today we will learn to* hear *feelings."*

Everyone looked at each other in the relative gloom wondering what was going to happen. Mrs. Penn finally unfolded her legs and slid off of her desk. She stood looking down at the class, out of her over-sized glasses, and spoke without chanting this time. "How does *pain* feel?"

Letting the question hang for only a few seconds she answered herself, "Everyone knows how pain feels, but what does it *sound* like?"

Marty looked around.

Some students had their faces scrunched up in concentration, others were looking around, only two sat defiantly not willing to even try. Finally Marty let his mind wander, what *did* pain sound like? Words started floating up in his brain like — slickery, crackilicious, and smotley, but he didn't dare say any of these because they sounded silly.

Then without warning Mrs. Penn took a plate off of her desk and dropped it heavily into the metal garbage can. The shattering sound rolled around in the semi-darkness, then she spoke.

"That is one sound of pain, can anyone describe it?"

At this a few hands went tentatively up daring to try.

Amazingly one of them was Marty's.

Mrs. Penn peered into the gloom and selected Marty, "Yes, Mr. Whimpel, what would *you* describe that as?"

Marty gulped, "Uh, sort of, smotley?"

There were some titters around the classroom but Mrs. Penn came forward, "Say that again," she was excited.

"Smotley," Marty said it a little louder.

"Yes! *Smotley!* Great! Anyone else?"

That was it? No question of what smotley was? No yelling because it wasn't even a word? She just accepted it.

Marty knew at that moment he was really going to like Mrs. Penn's class. After a few more feeble attempts by the other students Mrs. Penn turned on the lights and approached the board. She wrote out the word "Smotley" and asked, "Now what might that mean?"

Turning to Marty, her eyes twinkling, they told him without words she wanted the other students to try and explain it without Marty's help, at least for now. The room was quiet, not silent; the students were shifting under the pressure. Marty almost laughed out loud at some of their faces.

There were some with pained expressions, this was clearly the first time they had been asked to use their imagination, even though Mrs. Penn hadn't called it that. Finally Nick raised his hand. Mrs. Penn saw it and called on him immediately, "Yes, Mr. Chrismon?"

"Uh, scary?" Nick was really trying but was still unsure.

"Okay, scary, pain *is* scary, good, so smotley means *scary*, what else?"

She opened this up to the remaining students.

Nick sighed deeply that his answer had been accepted.

Suddenly one of the two defiant ones from earlier made a movement, it could have passed for raising a hand or scratching his head, Mrs. Penn saw it and responded quickly, "Yes, Mr. Wildern?"

"It's like Motley Crew."

This wasn't a question. It was also deeper than most seventh grader's voices.

Marty turned and looked at the one who spoke. In the light he could tell he was a 'tough guy,' he was built like a wall, large and flat. He almost looked two dimensional, but his head was thrust out making a contrast to his stiff body.

Dressed in blacks and dark grays, he was making a definite statement.

Like Ms. Culbreth Marty now feared 'Mr. Wildern' whatever his first name may be.

He refocused on Mrs. Penn as she wrote scary and Motley Crew on the board under the word smotley.

She was nodding, "Okay, painful, scary, Motley Crew, does anyone know what Motley means?"

At this no one moved and the lesson began.

She continued, "It means mixed or misfits, how is it painful to be a misfit?"

This question hung in the air, no one wanted to admit they were misfits, then she went on, "As a girl, my family didn't have much money, so I didn't get the most stylish clothes, I always had to buy second hand things, and I *hated* it! But as I grew up I found that there were many things more important than fitting in."

She let that sink into these fresh new seventh graders who were on the brink of self-discovery. After a moment of quiet, she explained, "I found out that people can be cruel, hateful, and mean. Oh, I was the brunt of many jokes. The popular kids thought it funny that I was always alone at lunch. They never once came over to eat with me, or say hi. So I want to ask you, was *that* pain?"

Here were Mrs. Penn's pains being bared to the whole class, and she wanted them to comment on them?

Again surprising himself Marty raised his hand, "Yes, Mr. Whimpel?"

Marty swallowed over the lump that had risen in his throat, "I have never been able to read very well, actually I never did *anything* well, and at my old school everyone made fun of me, too. So I know that being a misfit *is* pain and the sound is awful. It's like the sound of screeching brakes, the smell of burned toast, and the burning of tears all mixed together, and I hate it."

Marty had been so into letting his feelings flow, he had forgotten that he was surrounded by his peers. As he finished this realization flooded over him, but somehow he didn't care. He looked up at Mrs. Penn whose face was turned toward him, the look of love and thanks on her face were like an unseen hug to Marty's heart.

It was okay to be a misfit.

Suddenly Nick's hand rose. Mrs. Penn called on him and he started, "I've gone to five schools in six years because my dad is in the military. Every time I made a friend, I had to say goodbye, finally I just chose to not try, make it on my own, but it was lonely, and I didn't like it at all. Finally when my dad asked me what was wrong, I asked him to stop moving us around, and so we moved here a few days ago. Now I feel like a misfit again, a brand new school, house, and neighborhood, but yesterday I met Marty and now I'm *not* alone."

Marty could feel himself choke up.

He had helped Nick feel welcome without even realizing it would mean so much to him. Suddenly the room was filled with hands that were raised. In turn each pupil shared how he or she was a misfit. Finally *Mr. Wildern* shared his story and Marty instantly felt sorry for him.

He began softly, "My name is Ben; I'm new to this school, too. I was held back two times in sixth grade. The first time was because I missed a whole lot of school, the second was because I *skipped* a lot of school. You might think that's the same thing, but it's not. The first year we found out my mom had cancer, so I missed a lot of school to be with her. We would go on trips and do things she had always wanted to do. Then she got bad and couldn't travel, so I stayed with her while my dad worked. She died at the end of the school year. The school made me repeat sixth grade, I was angry at them, but I also had to skip school because my mom's death hit my dad hard, and he started to drink. He lost his job, so I had to go around and try to find ways to make money. I couldn't make enough, so we lost our house and moved into a shelter. The only clothes they had that were big enough were either gray or black so I had to wear them. Finally dad snapped out of it after he went to counseling at the shelter. He stopped drinking and got a job. We got an apartment and some stuff to put into it, but we still didn't have a lot of money, so we went to the Salvation Army store and the only stuff there that fit was black or gray, so here I am in black and gray."

He held out his shirt and looked at it, "A lot like Motley Crew."

He smiled, it was slow and faint, but it was a smile.

Mrs. Penn spoke reverently, "Thank you, thank you *all*

for trusting me enough to share your stories. I want this class to be a safe haven for you, so whatever has just been shared does not leave this room. We share our stories, writings, problems, and joys with each other. We are all like a group of friends. I hope that the feelings that you have heard today will help you out in the hallways here at Rosewood and out in the world for the rest of your life."

She paused, smiled warmly, and added, "Thank you again for sharing with us, and I trust that you will all respect each other from this day forward."

The class looked at each other and smiles were shared. The whole room was a large warm blanket, keeping each student safe. The bell rang and no one moved, quietly Mrs. Penn spoke, "I'd like you each to write out something about the sound of feelings. We'll share them tomorrow. You're now excused."

Almost in slow motion people got up off the floor and exited the room. The class proceeded quietly down the boisterous halls of Rosewood, still thinking of how they had changed in Mrs. Penn's class. Marty and Nick made their way to the library, Marty knew where they were going, Nick just followed. They walked into the welcoming atmosphere of the library. Mr. Candletier looked up as they entered, smiled, his eyes twinkling, leaned over the counter, and asked, "What took you so long, Marty?"

He was clearly joking so Marty played along, "Well, the car ran out of gas, and we had to walk the remaining hundred miles, but we made it."

Nick watched as this interchange took place, then suddenly he was staring into the flame blue eyes of Mr. Candletier and he froze in place. Ignatius extended his hand in greeting and Nick took it mechanically, not taking his eyes away from Mr. Candletier's. Just as suddenly Mr. Candletier smiled and began chuckling, "Hello there, my name is Mr. Candletier, what's yours?"

"Uh, N....Nick, ... Nicholas Chrismon, sir."

"Okay, Uh Nick Nicholas Chrismon, do you have a nickname that is a little shorter?" Mr. Candletier's eyes twinkled behind his spectacles.

Nick broke out of the trance finally, "Yes, Nick, that's what most people call me. It's nice to meet you, Mr. Candletier."

"Well, Nick and Marty, pick your poison."

This comment made Nick and Marty stop, look at each other in bewilderment, and back at Mr. Candletier.

"It means what do you want boys? Like, what kind of book are you looking for?"

Comprehension hitting them, Marty and Nick nodded. Marty spoke first, "Adventure." Nick thought for a moment, "Me too."

Ignatius explained how the library was set up, "I have a color code here, according to your grade level Red for 9th Grade, Yellow for 8th Grade, and Blue for 7th Grade. The only reason I have them split up like that is you will read certain books each year in your classes; I expanded it to similar subjects and reading levels. So now you know which books to choose from. Follow me and I'll take you to your next *adventure*."

With that, Mr. Candletier strode out from behind the counter his long legs covering distance quickly as Marty and Nick hurried along behind. Mr. Candletier turned abruptly into a row of books and stopped half way down the aisle. Marty and Nick stopped behind him and looked where he was pointing. There on the shelf, clearly marked by colored dots along their spines, were the 7th grade adventure books. As he was retreating Mr. Candletier looked over his shoulder and reminded, "Don't pick the red, pick the blue."

His eyes twinkled at Marty as he turned and went back to the front counter.

Marty was still looking where Mr. Candletier had been,

his thoughts racing.

He knew! Mr. Candletier knew who Marty was, he knew he was a Yulesaychaater, and he knew that Nick had accompanied him on the adventure to Bicolotern.

Finally a soft poke in the back reminded Marty that Nick was still there. Marty turned and Nick showed him a book about Robin Hood. He whispered, "I think I'm going to read this one, what about you?"

Marty grabbed the nearest book and held it out, "This one," he showed it to Nick before he looked at it himself.

Nick's face registered shock and he looked at Marty, who then looked at the book.

Marty's mouth dropped open too, the book was titled *The Adventures of Nick and Marty!*

They took their selections to the counter, still not believing the book in Marty's hand. As they laid them on the counter Mr. Candletier's eyes raised from the computer catalog, "Did you find what you were looking for?" his eyes crackled and sparked.

Marty found his voice, "Yeah and quite a lot more."

"Glad to know that the library still keeps up with the times," he wasn't going to say anything more about the book, Marty could tell, but he tried one last time.

"How long is the check out period?"

"Robin Hood is due back in two weeks," Ignatius was all business.

"What about the other book?" Nick wedged in.

"What other book?" Mr. Candletier was all innocence.

"This one," Nick pushed the book across the counter at him.

"That's not one of mine," he smiled slyly as he turned the spine toward them, "See, no sticker. It must be one of yours."

Marty stared at the place where the sticker should have been, but there was nothing.

Why hadn't he noticed that before?

As they continued to puzzle over this conundrum they started to leave, only to be stopped by Mr. Candletier, "You'll find that starting at the *beginning* will be the most helpful way to get to the end."

Ignatius smiled again, his eyes still dancing blue flames, as the boys left the library. Then he spoke softly to himself, *"Good luck Marty, I know you can do it."* Then he added, *"Nick, you're in for the adventure of your life."*

"Boy was he right," Nick chuckled as he closed the cracked cover and looked out at the faces filled with wonder that were looking back at him.

"What do you mean he was right?" Chante questioned, "What kind of adventure did you have?"

"Did you go to the Island of Bicolotern?" Menalee ventured.

"There, among others," Nick teased unwilling to give the adventure away too soon.

"Others?" their voices chimed. Only Billy remained quiet.

"Do you think that would have been a great adventure, Billy?" Nick was very perceptive of Billy's apprehension. "To go to other places?"

"Yeah, I guess," was his non-committal response and he began fidgeting with *The Emperor's New Clothes* in his lap.

"What about school?" Weston posed, "that sounds like quite an adventure to me. To have real *live* teachers that cared what you thought and felt."

"And they actually talked to you not *at* you," Wendy's nose wrinkled at the thought of her experiences at school of being talked at.

"I wish we had that," Nisha said longingly, "what would it be like to have a teacher who actually read our papers and gave us responses to our questions?"

Nick was surprised by these comments about school, "What kind of lessons *do* you have at your school?" he wondered aloud.

"Oh, most of them are just recordings of the text from

our computer screens placed in a vocalization unit programmed to present on a certain day," Saul explained unenthusiastically.

"Our teachers are droids, that don't think or feel," Alden continued, "they are forced to repeat whatever they are programmed to say, the school Aminzar makes sure that no feelings are expressed and no thought is given the chance to grow. It might be dangerous." Alden spoke from first hand experience, his mother had served under the Aminzar for seven years and as a result had completely forgotten Alden existed, he had been forced to live with his grandfather who was unable to care for him long before he fell ill and was taken away.

The aged and infirm were taken to 'the home' where no one ever saw them again.

Alden had tried to find his father, but because he couldn't locate him was forced to go back to his mother's house where he had to watch out for, cook, and clean for himself.

His mother was still under the influence of the Aminzar and since Alden could do nothing about it, he suffered in silence.

"That sounds awful," Nick empathized, "why do you keep going?"

"It's against the law not to go," Chante clarified, "if you're caught, you get taken to 'the home.'"

The group shivered collectively, they all knew someone or had heard of someone who had gone there and they didn't want to take the trip themselves.

"Can we go back to Marty's world?" Nisha begged, "I like it there."

"Yes, can we?" eight other voices agreed, only Billy sat silent.

"Certainly," Nick complied.

Picking up the red covered volume once more, he opened the yellowed pages, found his place and began reading again with a renewed amount of gratitude for the time period in which he had been born.

The trip to their lockers was done in a haze they were halfway home before either of them even spoke, "What do you think?"

They both asked at once, stopped, looked at each other, and began laughing.

"This is really weird, but so cool I can't believe it," Nick marveled.

"I can believe it, I just don't know how he *did* it," Marty wondered.

That caught Nick's attention, "You *can* believe it? Do things like this happen to you a lot?"

Marty stopped, looked at Nick, and leaned forward, "Can you keep a secret?"

Nick nodded, unable to speak, and leaned forward too.

"I am a *Yulesaychaater*," Marty whispered.

"A *what*?" Nick was at a loss, *I just met this kid yesterday and now he is speaking some weird language I can't understand. What have I gotten myself into?*

"A Yulesaychaater, or a key gatherer," Marty explained slowly, winning Nick's confidence quickly back.

"Okay, so what?" Nick did not comprehend Marty's words.

"A key gatherer can..." Marty searched, "well, he can gain access to books."

"I can do that at the library," Nick still didn't see the point, nor was he properly impressed.

"No, I mean I can go into books, wherever the book is talking about, fairy kingdoms, whatever."

Nick's face began to show the first inkling of understanding, but his eyes were still clouded, Marty waited for a moment, the clouds parted and Nick asked quietly, "You mean you can actually *travel* to wherever the book is taking place?"

Marty nodded and Nick shook his head in disbelief, "But that's impossible, what if it isn't even a real place?"

"Every place in any book is a real place…somewhere," Marty's words were as much for himself as they were for Nick.

They stood there for a minute longer and then Nick spoke, "How did Mr. Candletier get a book with our names on it?"

Now Marty would have to share even more strange knowledge, finally he decided this might take a while, "I'll explain everything, but let's go to my Grandma's house, so I can show you some stuff. It might help you understand."

Nick agreed then remembered, "Oh, I need to tell my mom where I'm going, let's just say we're studying, and we'll have a few hours."

They walked along Maple until they reached Nick's house and went in. Janet Chrismon was seated on the sofa in the front room she looked up, smiled at both Marty and Nick and stood up, "How are you Marty? How was the first day of school?"

She kissed Nick on the cheek and gave him a squeeze.

Nick promptly blushed and threw a look at Marty that said, *Please don't tell anyone.*

Marty nodded silently so Nick could see his secret was safe.

Nick pulled away from his mom slowly and asked, "Would it be okay if I go over to Marty's to study?"

"You have homework on the first day of school?" Janet looked a little doubtful.

"Yeah, two chapters for Ms. *Killbreath*," Nick didn't even realize he had used the nickname he had made up for their teacher and continued, "An assignment in Math, and a writing assignment for English."

Janet smiled at her son, "My goodness you've grown up quickly. I still can't believe you are in Junior High School."

She got a bit teary eyed and tried to cover it by wiping at her face with the back of her hand.

"It sure is dusty here in Scat-town, it makes my eyes water."

"Don't worry mom, I'm sure I'll be around for a few more years at least," Nick attempted to lighten the mood.

Mrs. Chrismon brightened, "Of course you will, that's fine if you go over to Marty's, just be home for dinner."

Here Marty spoke, "Do you want our phone number, just in case we're busy studying and forget the time?"

Impressed with how responsible Marty was Janet replied, "Sure, Marty that would be great, then I can call your mom and chat sometime too."

"It's 825-0000. Pretty easy to remember, I think Grandma Pen got the first number when the phone was invented!" Marty quipped.

"Oh you character! She's not *that* old! Your mom said that your grandmother is 81."

Janet was again impressed with her son's new friend's sense of humor with his next comment.

"You're right! I forgot they didn't even have electricity 'til she was a teenager!"

At this, Janet laughed, she couldn't help herself.

Marty confirmed, "We'll be sending Nick home for dinner, but if we don't finish, can he come back over later?"

Thinking briefly, Janet nodded, "I think that can be arranged. Oh, which house is yours? Just in case I want to drop by to talk with your Grandma sometime."

"5443 South Farnsworth, it's the blue house, with the white shutters. Anyone can tell you if you ask for the Pentel's house."

"Okay, well you two have fun, don't work too hard," She shooed them out the front door and watched as they walked away.

"Your mom is really nice, Nick," Marty complimented.

"She seems to like you too," Nick chided, then under his breath he added, "brown-noser." And they both chuckled.

"Oh, a brown-noser am I?" Marty feigned hurt, "I didn't hear you trying to stop me, you must have been too busy taking notes."

"Actually, I kind of was," Nick admitted sheepishly, "you really have a way with my mom."

They rounded the corner onto Farnsworth and arrived at Grandma Pentel's house, she was seated on the park bench on the front porch in her pale pink housecoat, checking her watch and then peering out at the street in the direction they were walking.

As she saw Marty and Nick approaching, she arose.

She spoke before they got to her, "What took you so long? I've been worried."

"Sorry grandma, we went to the school library and then over to Nick's house to get permission to study over here. Oh, this is Nick, Nick, this is Grandma Pen."

"Pleased to meet you ma'am," Nick stepped forward and extended his hand.

Grandma Pentel took it and they shook briefly.

"Nice to meet you too, Nick, come on in, you both must be starving!"

Nick looked over at Marty and grinned, he could get used to being spoiled by Grandma Pen. They all walked inside and the heavenly scent of fresh-baked cookies and bread wafted over them, hugging, and welcoming them home. Nick stopped and breathed deeply, enjoying this novelty. In the kitchen a few minutes later Marty and Nick had a large slice of fresh bread layered in butter and jam, along with two cookies apiece and a large glass of cold milk.

They ate in silence except for the satisfied grunts of the thoroughly pleased. When they had polished off all of their fresh made bounty they stood, took their dishes to the sink and deposited them there. Then Marty bent, gave Pearl a kiss on the cheek and a squeeze, and said, "That was just what I needed, thanks a lot Grandma!"

Nick nodded in the background but Grandma Pentel spoke up, "Come give Grandma Pen a squeeze!"

She held out her arms and Nick, though surprised, stepped into them and gave her a genuine hug.

Marty now explained, "We've got homework, so we'll be down in my room. We'll see you in a bit."

With that Marty grabbed his bag, motioned with his head to Nick, and headed for the stairs. When they had reached the basement Nick walked slowly along, eyes wide, as if he had just entered a treasure trove. Marty allowed him to gawk, remembering his own feelings when he first came downstairs. They proceeded all the way to the wall of toilet paper, when Nick's eyebrows went up. Marty only said, "The Depression, I'll explain later."

Entering Marty's room Nick whistled, "Man you have got the coolest house, this is like your own 'batcave!'"

Marty hadn't thought of it like that before, but it was true nonetheless.

He shut the door and turned conspiratorially to Nick, "Okay, you ready to hear the *whole* story?"

Nick dropped his bag and sat on the floor as Marty did the same, "Yeah, tell me the whole thing, and don't leave anything out."

Marty then related his adventure in Qualf and the changing of Bismorda back into a witch. He produced the key from his drawer as proof. Nick held the key and admired it. The story had just begun however and Nick settled in as Marty retold the dream of the boat, Nick, and the Garden of books. Then he came to Mr. Candletier.

"He is a Checkpohmer, a book watcher, he and I are supposed to protect the books."

"What books?" Nick was fascinated.

"All books, there is an evil power that is trying to destroy them, or take them over," as Marty explained he pulled out the book from between his mattresses.

Nick leaned close to inspect it, running a tentative finger along the lettering.

Suddenly Marty had a thought, "Would you like to meet Bismorda?"

"What do you mean? Travel with you to Qualf?" Nick could not have been more surprised, but even as he asked he was nodding his head.

Marty smiled, "Okay, let's go."

"You mean, right *now?* Don't we have to get stuff ready?"

Nick began travel planning in his mind.

"What stuff? We'll be there in about fifteen minutes," Marty tried to simplify this even further, "Just watch."

He picked up the key that was next to Nick on the floor, stood and went to the door. Nick rose to stand beside him, watching his every move. The key was near the doorknob, it glowed and the keyhole opened. Marty turned to Nick, "Let's take our adventure book to show Bismorda, it's in my bag."

Nick retrieved the book bag, handed it to Marty, and watched. Marty proceeded to empty the bag of all but the adventure book and slung it on his back. The turn of the key produced the same click and when the door opened the now familiar river flowed at their feet. Nick stared unbelieving until Marty turned, and beckoned him to follow. Exiting the room, Nick pulled the door shut, and joined Marty on the sun soaked banks of the river. Turning they crossed the bridge and started their brief hike to Bismorda's castle. Halfway up the trail Marty pointed out the statue of himself, Nick wanted to look closer so they detoured for a moment.

"You have a statue made of you, Marty. That is so cool, do you feel famous?" Nick was in awe.

"Not at all, you're the only other person I know who has seen it."

He smiled briefly at Nick, reassuring him he was not

stuck up in any way. The remainder of the trail was clear as usual and they came into the clearing that was the courtyard of the castle. A quick gasp behind him told that Nick was struck by the beauty as Marty himself had been. That's when Marty noticed something odd, the castle was still gleaming but no sound came from the grounds at all. No one was on the castle walls to alert the inner chambers that visitors were approaching. Cautiously Marty shushed Nick with his eyes. Mounting the stairs increased the sense of foreboding that was creeping over Marty. The front door was open, just a crack, and Marty's heart leaped in his chest. Nick was close behind him, proceeding with the utmost gravity as Marty reached the front door.

A dark burn around the metal of the handle was the only significant difference Marty noticed as he pushed the door open with his foot. Slowly it swung open revealing a dimmed interior, Marty looked up at the giant chandelier and saw that all of the lights were out. For the first time Marty realized they weren't electric lights, they were a type of candle or something similar to it, they had all burned out and the remnants were hanging, melted, coating the beautiful crystalline prisms. Fear crawled up Marty's back slowly, like a chilled hand, raising goose pimples on his arms and neck. Glancing around he could tell there had been a major struggle; chairs were overturned in the sitting room, dark patches here and there where the carpet had been scorched.

"There was a fight," the walls seemed to say sadly, "We could do nothing."

The flutter of a paper caught Marty's eye. He went to the desk-like side table, and retrieved the single sheet of parchment. On it in a rapid hand was scrawled the following message:

Marty Whimpel thinks he's grand
The Zanth witches need a hand
After a teeny-tiny struggle

All the kingdom we now juggle.
Bismorda seemed to think that you
Might be the one to help her through
If you are the one with gall to spare
Come and fight the Oh Rah's stare.
The only chance to be set free
For the kingdom, this will be.
Match wits with us, you may survive
But if not we still will thrive.
Dare to cross the threshold dear
The time may feel plum soaked with fear.
Turn around now go back home
You are weak and we are strong.
Our beauty freezes you like stone
We are two and you are one.
By chance that you still read on
You may truly be the one
The only Yulesaychaater left
You broke our curse and left us miffed.
If you will come again to fight
Upon your gift we'll shed a light.
We're sure that you still question why
Such a gift for you small-fry.
Take the offer free them all
Don't back up against the wall.
All we say will come true
Come on Marty, we wait for you.
Signed,
Grisele & Mopel

The paper shuddered slightly as Marty looked at Nick, who had read it all over his shoulder.

"What are you going to do, Marty?"

Soberly Marty looked back at Nick, "The only thing I *can*, I'm going to fight them and save the Kingdom of Qualf."

His determination was contagious, "I'm going too!"

Nick insisted.

Nodding, Marty retrieved the book from his bag and read the cover, "It says *The Adventures of Nick and Marty*, it's meant to be."

Marty tried to feel the confidence he should, but it was hard as the silence of the kingdom enveloped them.

Chapter 12
Discovery Of A New Ability

Slowly Marty and Nick became aware of their surroundings again. The reality of the huge empty castle began sinking in as they turned to leave Marty folded the witches' note and slid it into the front of the book. Only then did Marty fully understand that he was carrying a book all about Nick and himself, he stopped, looking again at the cover he thought, *I wonder what it says about us…*

He opened the cover fully and a slight cracking noise echoed all over the vacuous hall, Nick turned, realized Marty had stopped, and returned to his side. Together they read about their first meeting, first day of school, and first trip to Qualf. They finished with the end of the poem and their commitment to fight for Bismorda's kingdom. The book was writing down what they did, but more than that, the other pages had writing, but Marty couldn't understand them. They were in a foreign language of some kind, but as the story unfolded for Nick and Marty it was translated into English or the language Marty used in his world. Thoughts rolled around inside Marty's head so quickly he couldn't recognize most of them when one suddenly came out his mouth it caught them both by surprise, "This book was written in the language of books at the beginning of time and only now is it getting translated because we have answered the call."

Nick's face slowly, almost imperceptibly, registered the gravity of this statement. Someone, somewhere, ages ago saw them doing what they were doing right now. That was really hard to believe and Nick voiced his doubt, "But that can't be possible! No one can see into the future!"

Marty looked at Nick and spoke simply as if he were addressing a much younger child, "Explain the door then."

Sputtering Nick couldn't give voice to his feelings. Marty nodded his head, "See, you can't explain it in our language, *only* the language of the books can hold that truth."

Words spoken by Bismorda suddenly flowed back into Marty's brain, *"Sometimes there are many great truths put into red books, then locked against careless eyes."*

He fumbled around with Bismorda's words for a moment and spoke, "Nick, we need to find the key to the book of spells. That is the only way to get to Zanth that I know of. We have to do that before we can do anything else."

Nick could see the logic in this and nodded his agreement.

"There's nothing else we can do here right now, let's go back and do our homework, maybe that will help us to think some more."

Turning once again to leave, something on the floor caught the sun's rays and sent a small rainbow of light dancing onto their path. Bending down Marty retrieved the object which he turned over in his hand a few times and still had no idea what it was. It looked like a feather, except it was some kind of glass or crystal. But it couldn't be glass or crystal because it was soft and flexible. A sound flooded into Marty's head, this object was buzzing! Suddenly it floated out of Marty's hand until it was hovering at eye level. It began spinning and Bismorda's voice filled the chamber, "Marty, I hope that you will figure out how to use this trillo wing, it is my only chance. Grisele and Mopel Zanth are back! They are attacking the whole kingdom this time. Most have already been taken captive. I have but minutes and not much hope except in you. I hope that you have found the Eyahge'er, his name in your world is Nicholas Chrismon. You must come together, you are very powerful alone, but together you will be unstoppable."

Here the sound crackled and died, the wing came to rest on Marty's out-stretched palm again.

"Eyahge'er, what is that?" Nick was bursting with pride at being mentioned by this unknown voice.

I wonder which trillo sacrificed their wing Marty

wondered.

"I have no clue, and I don't think we'll find out until we free Bismorda."

"So where do we start?" Nick was sold on the idea now.

"Well, I'm sorry to say this, but I think it has to start back at my house with our homework."

"Why?" Nick's elation bubble had been burst.

Marty reasoned, "Because I have no idea where to find the key to the book of spells, and we can't just stay here in Qualf 'til the key drops in our laps."

Nick agreed reluctantly, "Okay, let's go."

Curiosity got the best of him as they started to leave and he burst out, "Can I hold the trillo wing?"

Marty almost laughed, but remembered this was Nick's very first adventure, however poor it was. He handed the wing to Nick who accepted it as if it had been an Olympic torch he held it above his head for all to see.

Unfortunately, no one was there to see.

Marty led Nick back through the deserted entrance hall and they were almost to the front door when a thought occurred to Marty, *Could Bismorda have a book that might help us?*

Marty realized he had never been anywhere in the castle but the entrance hall, sitting room, the large bedroom, and the storage place that had held the portraits of Bismorda. They should look around and see if anything here may be of use on their journey. After all Bismorda *was* a witch wasn't she? She must have some spell books of her own. The suggestion of a quick search was warmly accepted by Nick since this was his first time in a castle, not to mention a fairytale castle in a remote and unknown part of the world.

Turning back to face the large entrance hall they decided to explore the two rooms off to the left first. Even though they could cover more area if they split up they heeded Bismorda's advice and stayed together. The first room proved to be a kind of observatory, there were telescopes of all different sizes pointing at many unknown destinations. After peering into two of them Marty noticed that the room had no windows. So how could the telescopes see anywhere? He also noticed the light was a constant that radiated from the walls, no switch necessary. Nick was plastered to one of the larger scopes and was muttering various exclamations. Marty approached him and as he did the scope's side reflected the light in such a way that Marty saw a name flash on the side – *Xenoxia* was what is said.

Marty let Nick stay occupied with Xenoxia as he walked around the room and found the names on each one Thimmelwood, Aerif, Cotolspik, Ninsh, Faeson Wil Blanch, the names were extraordinary but Marty wasn't finding the one he really wanted.

He began to read the names aloud, "Mikelswain, Poisentre, Zanth, *Zanth*! Here it is!"

At Marty's excitement Nick forsook the thrills of Xenoxia and approached Marty's side as he put his eye up to the eyepiece. He had to squint because it was very dark inside the scope.

Then it hit him, it was night in Zanth!

After this was established he peered closely to try and see any signs of life. Lightening tore across the blackness as if Marty had been inside a big bag of cereal and a Giant had torn it open to reveal a blinding light. It made Marty jump. Immediately he was upset with himself for having let the small amount of light escape, he had to use it as a resource to see the land. Peering into the scope once more he waited, seconds later lightening again lit the landscape and suddenly the picture froze. Marty was surprised when he heard Nick beside him, "What did *that* do?"

"Huh? What did *what* do?" Marty pulled back from the scope and turned to Nick.

"I pushed the button on the side as I saw the reflection of lightening on your face. I was just curious what the button did to the picture."

"It froze," Marty pondered this for a moment, "like a camera."

Marty looked into the eyepiece again and the lightening was frozen in the sky, lighting up the black forest on the horizon. The sky was a deep smudgy purple filled with swirling tarry clouds. Marty saw waves crashing against a rocky shoreline, then out of the craggy shore rose up a large mound of something he couldn't distinguish. He'd have to try and catch another phase of this unusual landscape. He pushed the button and the view was again plunged into near-blackness. As the sky rumbled visibly, Marty prepared to push the button again. The next flash of lightening came and Marty caught the new view of the landscape. This new picture made Marty catch his breath. Nick's voice sounded close by, "What? What's wrong?"

Marty backed away and let Nick look. There, caught plainly in the lighted frame, was a huge skull. Its size was massive when compared to the trees alongside it. Nick's question voiced Marty's own feelings, "What is *that*? I mean I know it's a skull but it's *HUGE*!"

Trying to assemble his thoughts Marty ventured, "Maybe it's stone. Like it was carved into a mountain or something."

Even as he said it Marty drew up again to the scope. It certainly looked like a skull, then the broken, twisted rocks caught his attention, they weren't rocks they were bones! Some kind of gargantuan beast or the remains of it were piled here in the scope of Zanth, but why? Again Marty depressed the button landing the view in blackness, then he saw it, a faint glow coming from the sockets of the eyes. It looked like a flame was deep inside somewhere. Could it be possible that this skeletal skull *was* Zanth?

As weird as that sounded it made sense.

He finally spoke, "Nick, I think that this *is* Zanth. Look at the view in the dark, can you see anything unusual?"

Nick peered into the inky blackness and the faint glow in the sockets caught his attention too, "The eyes have a light coming out of them!"

"Exactly, like the skull has a fire deep inside it!" Marty exclaimed, "Now we know what the place looks like we can plan for our attack."

"Let's go!" Nick was fired up again.

Marty agreed but in a different way, "You're right, we need to get back before we're missed!"

Nick began to protest, but realized the wisdom in Marty's reasoning.

If he got in trouble he wouldn't be allowed over to Marty's and then he would miss out on their adventures.

"Okay, let's go attack our homework at least it's a start on the evil power against us!"

Marty laughed at Nick's corny joke, "Sounds like a plan."

Without searching further, they exited the castle and made their way back to the bridge. Upon entering Marty's room, they turned the key, and were back in Grandma Pen's basement.

They plopped down on the floor, Nick opened his hand, palm up, and revealed the trillo wing, "*Our* first adventure!"

Marty nodded as he reached out, grabbed his history book, picked it up, and said, "Our *second* adventure!"

Nick moaned and got his book too. They decided if they read out loud it might go faster, so they took turns, Marty started. As he started reading the words flowed easily and were said with feeling.

Nick interrupted, "Were you lying?"

This caught Marty off-guard, "What?"

"You said in Mrs. Penn's class you didn't read well, that's not true!"

Marty realized that Nick was right; he had no difficulty with reading at all.

When had *that* happened?

He had not even noticed a change, or had he? His mind flashed back to the beginning of the summer, *the Tiddily-Winks box, I noticed then. But when had it changed? I struggled with the poem of the trillos, before I met Bismorda, but that was the last time I remember having a problem with reading.*

He acknowledged Nick's question and statement, "It *was* true, but then I saved Bismorda…" he let his explanation trail off, the thoughts tumbling over each other.

Nick's eyes got big, "You mean she made it so you could read? Maybe that's how she repaid you!"

Of course!

Marty remembered the last time he saw Bismorda, she had blushed and acted shy, she thought he had come back to thank her for the gift, he even showed her a book he had checked out.

I thought she had a crush on me! Man did I screw up! I didn't even think to thank her. He only nodded to answer Nick's question. Then he set to reading again, the words flowing freely.

His thoughts floated out to Bismorda, *Thank you, my friend, for helping me. I will come rescue you; I just need to find out how. But I will. I will.*

Chapter 13
A Day In Two Worlds

After getting through their history and half of their math assignment there was a soft knock on the door. Both Marty and Nick looked up, Marty called, "Come in!"

Charlotte poked her head into the room and smiled, "Nick, your mom just called, dinner is ready. Our dinner is ready too, Marty. How 'bout taking a break?" Then, as an afterthought she added, "I guess your first day was okay, aside from all the homework, right?"

She laughed at Nick and Marty as they both pulled faces of anguish.

"Okay, sorry. Touchy subject. Anyway, take a break and come eat. Nick, you can leave your books here, your mom already said you could come back when you're done eating. In fact, she and your dad are going to come over and visit me and Grandma Pen when you come back."

Charlotte retreated and Nick turned to Marty, "I'll keep thinking what we can do to find the key or any other clues."

Then he fished in his shirt pocket, "Here, I don't want mom finding this if I forget to take it out."

He passed Marty the trillo wing ceremoniously. Taking the wing, Marty stood and deposited it in his dresser drawer beside the key to Qualf.

Nick turned and made an off-hand observation, "Time doesn't pass the same in Qualf as it does here, does it?"

Marty shook his head, "No, I'm still trying to figure it out too, it just doesn't make sense."

"I'll bring my wristwatch when I come back, then we will know the time while we are gone," Nick gave a hopeful look at Marty.

Marty thought, then spoke, "Okay, we need to return to Qualf and explore some more tonight anyway. With a watch we can be sure we're not gone too long."

They exited Marty's room and made their way upstairs. Nick left and Marty sat down at the table. He could tell he was going to be the center of attention at dinner and asked jokingly, "So, what did *you* guys do today?"

If he had had a camera the looks he got from Charlotte and Pearl would have been priceless.

"Oh no you don't mister, tell us how school was," Charlotte persisted.

"It was really interesting," pausing, he thought which one to start with, Killbreath or Penn?

He decided to wedge Killbreath between the two positive ones with a smattering of the morning classes.

As he told them of Bachenheim's class and how he was going to be a tenor, he caught Charlotte's attention and she mumbled something to herself. Marty stopped mid-sentence, "What was that mom?"

"Oh, Reed used to sing tenor, that's all."

Marty tried to place the name Reed, when it suddenly hit him, "*Mr. Wright?*"

Charlotte nodded, "That's just odd, sorry, your father never liked to sing so I never thought to see if you liked it. I just thought you signed up for music to try something new."

Marty was curious now, "Do *you* sing mom?"

Pearl responded, "Oh your mom has a beautiful voice, she used to be in all the shows in school. In fact, isn't that where you met Reed dear?"

She didn't add in her sudden questions of why Reed was now on Charlotte's mind, she didn't think it was her place so she kept silent. Re-routing the discussion Charlotte questioned Marty, "So you like Mr. Bachenheim then?"

"Yeah, seems a little crazy, but I think he will be good."

Here, Marty went on with Ms. Killbreath, Pearl stifled a chuckle, "You don't mean *Malvina* Culbreth do you?"

Marty was struck by the name, "Is that her first name?"

Pearl nodded, "I remember her in my classes, she was

always a very rigid stickler for rules."

This was too good, "*You* taught *her*?"

"Yes I did, she was never interested in extracurricular activities. I tried to get to know her, but she was one student I never did find out much about." Pearl shook her head, "I always wondered what happened to her."

Marty finished up with Mrs. Penn's class.

Charlotte commented, "She seemed delightful on the night of orientation. The way she had us all sit on the floor was charming. I'm so glad you enjoyed her class."

Dinner finished as they chatted and Marty had a thought, "Grandma, do you have any other fairytale books?"

This was a little off of the subject they had been on, but Pearl instantly switched to his wavelength, "You mean like the one I read to you?"

Marty nodded, "Yeah, like that."

Shaking her head Pearl answered, "I only kept those few books of fairytales, I have a lot of other books downstairs in the study, but Grandpa Rufus and I didn't hang on to many children's books."

"Oh, that's okay I was just curious. I just really liked those, that's all."

Charlotte spoke quietly, "Don't you still have *your* stories mom?"

"I don't think Marty would be interested in those dear."

"Why not? Those were *my* favorites growing up," Charlotte confided.

"Really? I didn't know that."

"Grandma, did *you* write some stories?"

"Oh, I never wrote them down, I just told them to your mom. I made some up, and some I was told by *my* mother."

"Mom, you really should write those down! They are treasures! I would love to have a copy."

"Me too. Grandma if it's anything like how you talk

about history, I would love them. I can tell."

Pearl blushed beneath her careworn wrinkles at having so much attention directed at her, but then straightened a little and said, "Maybe I'll do just that while you two are busy with work and school. It would give me something to do."

That said, the doorbell rang, Marty jumped up, "That's Nick!"

He raced to the door, opened it, and let Nick, his father Thomas, and his mother Janet Chrismon in. Entering from the kitchen Pearl and Charlotte greeted their guests and led them into the living room. Nick and Marty excused themselves and headed downstairs, the adults chatted amiably in their absence. Safe once again in the confines of Marty's room they quickly synchronized Nick's wristwatch to Marty's clock and were off to Qualf to see what they could find to rescue Bismorda and save her kingdom.

Dusk was nearing as they reached the castle, this would be the first time Marty had seen Qualf in anything other than full sunlight. Because of the dimness of outside, inside the castle was dark as pitch. Luckily the glow from the observatory cast light into the entrance hall. There was also a faint glow coming from under the second door, the room they had yet to explore.

"Was someone else there?" Nisha broke in with concern in her voice.

"I bet it was the Zanth sisters waiting for Marty and Nick," Wendy wagered.

Weston reasoned, "If they were there, Nick wouldn't be here," then he looked at Nick, "isn't that right?"

Nick's smile spread slowly across his face like ripples in a still pool, "My goodness, it seems as though you have all been transported to Qualf with me and Marty. Does it seem real to you?"

The nods of assent were proof that these children had indeed become wrapped up in Nick's tale of his friend Marty.

"Would you like to guess what happened?" Nick

offered.

"I want to know what *really* happened, so you'll have to keep reading," Menalee insisted. Then realizing the others were looking at her she added, "Please."

"Menalee, nothing would give me more pleasure," Nick assured her with a smile and a nod. "Is that what all of you want as well?"

Again nodding in the affirmative caused Nick to raise the book and find his place:

"Moving along the wall they reached the second room on the left and got the door open. The sight before them made them both gasp. This room had been, at one time, a rather organized laboratory by the looks of it, but there were books flung all over the place and the smell of spilled chemicals filled the air.

"They were looking for something...but *what?*" Marty wondered aloud.

"Come on, Nick, let's try to straighten this place up."

They gathered the books and began putting them back on the shelves as they did so a page from one book fluttered to the ground. Marty bent and snatched it up. Letting his eyes run down the page he called to Nick to get his attention, "Come and see this, it may help us."

The page, also known as a leaf, had come from some sort of book of maps or something like that. But this specific page was filled with information in a cryptic poem. It went like this:

Zombies still have skin
Aliens come from worlds within
No one lives to see their faces
Tombs are filled from far off places
How to conquer these bad witches

Why are they made up of stitches?
Inky blackness covers over

Leaves may shrivel from the clover
Love wax cold, fear will spread

Won't you join those of the dead?
If you don't like the mirror's view
Never let them look at you.

"It is very strange," Nick agreed not quite understanding how this could help.

"Check out the first letter of each line, it spells ZANTH WILL WIN. But if I am reading this right we cannot look the witches in the eye, we have to use a mirror."

Impressed, Nick commented, "How did you get that out of the poem?"

"Read it again and see if that fits," Marty challenged.

Nick did so and a look of understanding spread over his face, "It's like you seeing Bismorda! Only in the mirror is truth revealed."

This comment made Marty stop and think, "Wait, say that again."

"Only in the mirror is truth revealed," Nick repeated obediently.

"Follow me!" Marty dashed out the door holding the page in his hand.

The darkness of the entrance hall was oppressive after the lighted laboratory, they stumbled to the sitting room and Marty fumbled around in the dark until he announced, "I found it!"

Nick had been waiting at the door, not trusting himself in the darkness; he started to come forward as Marty met him, or rather bumped into him. They both staggered, caught themselves, and rushed back to the light of the lab. Moving into the light of the room Nick looked back and saw Marty was holding a hand mirror. It was ornate and obviously a woman's looking glass. Marty pressed the mirror into Nick's hands, "Hold this."

Taking two steps back, Marty held the page so he could view it in the mirror, the words transformed themselves as he watched. They now read:

Only light can break a spell
Hear our words and know full well.
Reach the land when sun is high
After dark you'll surely die.

Inside the skull of the chukaht
Silence reigns where sight is naught

Vision lost from youth these two
Avenge their wrongs on all they knew
If e'er you want to stop the fear
Nixing it will take a year

Pose a question they can answer
Rivalry will stop the cancer
Invite them to help your problems solve
Dark work may soon dissolve.
Even small things do the trick

Failure cut them to the quick
Always remember, though you're small
Love will conquer over all
Live the life you know you should
So the world has more good.

This poem was much more difficult to figure out. Marty and Nick traded places, Nick read through the new poem with brow furrowed, "Are we supposed to ask the witches for help?"

"That's what I got out of it too," Marty puzzled, "I thought they were bad."

This conflict of ideas was hard to understand. How

could they get near enough to the witches if their gaze froze people? The mirror would work in this case. Next to stop the witches reign of evil they were supposed to ask them for help? Help with what? How was asking them for help going to stop them from being bad? And what did the message mean, OHRA IS VAIN PRIDE FALLS? Instead of getting more answers the questions kept piling up.

Marty looked at Nick, "Let's go, what time is it?"

Checking his watch, Nick looked at Marty, "6:30."

Barely an hour had passed since they left, but they would have to hurry back to finish their homework. Marty grabbed the mirror and page, looked around the room and found a cloth bag. Grabbing it, Marty shoved the two items in and as an afterthought grabbed the whole book that had held the page, and shoved it in as well. Last item of business, what would they use for light on their way back to the bridge? Stabbing in the dark Marty's eyes swept the shelves, resting on a book with a sun engraved on the binding.

"Why not?" Marty grabbed it and peeked under the cover, a blinding light shot out, he smiled and looked at Nick, "I think I'm finally starting to understand this place."

"Good, cause I'm still completely lost," Nick admitted.

"Let's go," Marty called over his shoulder as he stepped into the entrance hall.

Cracking the cover while holding the book vertically in front of himself Marty created a very strong beam of light that shot out ahead of them, illuminating their path.

"This is the coolest place I've ever been to," admired Nick, "and if that poem is any sign, this is just the beginning."

Marty nodded and they left. A half moon cast eerie shadows on their return trip the only sound that echoed back to them, the sound of their footsteps. Luckily the light from the book assured them a stumble-free stroll down the mountain.

As the bridge came into view, "Amazing, they got

everything," Marty muttered.

"Huh?" Nick was now lost again.

"The Zanth sisters took every creature from Qualf, they are incredibly powerful."

Agreeing to what he didn't know, Nick nodded. Re-entering the room they returned to Grandma Pentel's basement with the turn of a key. Checking the clock they realized that a little less than an hour had elapsed during their absence.

With many ideas pouring through their heads, they completed the math assignment and were just finishing the English homework as Charlotte called from upstairs, "You guys done yet?"

Marty opened his door and called back, "Yeah, almost, mom, five more minutes!"

With the finishing touches in place they ascended the stairs and emerged in the kitchen.

"Well if you guys are going to have this much homework every night, we may just have to become good friends," Janet teased, looking sideways at Charlotte who was smiling too.

Pearl chimed in, "You're welcome to come over anytime. It's so good to have another nice family in the neighborhood."

Thomas Chrismon was totally taken off guard at the next comment, "Give Grandma Pen a squeeze!"

With this she wrapped her arm around his waist and brought him into a hug. At 6'7" Thomas literally towered over this petite woman and made her look even smaller than she really was. Having been in the military for twenty years he was used to standing at attention, and he wasn't used to getting hugs except from his wife and when his son had been small. This outward pouring of affection from a practical stranger rattled his gruff militaristic exterior. He bent down and patted her on the back looking thoroughly confused as

Charlotte and Janet exchanged amused looks.

"Don't worry dad, she does that to everyone!" Nick was helping to ease the situation as Pearl chuckled, "What? Everyone can do with a good squeeze can't they?"

On this note the Chrismon's headed home in the softening light of dusk. This second sunset for Marty was a little surreal, having already seen one in Qualf. Nevertheless he enjoyed the brief waves and then retreated back into the house.

"Honey, did you have any questions about your homework?"

"Nope, thanks though mom. I think I'm going to go down and read before bed. G'night."

Kissing both Grandma Pentel and Charlotte he was soon down in his room re-reading the poem both with and without the mirror. Storing all of his acquisitions in the bag and putting it under his bed he looked at the book of spells that still lay on the floor, it was when he saw the book that his breathing quickened and goose-bumps prickled over his arms, the witches had been looking for *this* book at Bismorda's!

Someone else had sent it to him, and all this time he had attributed it to the Zanth sisters. Now he wondered anew, who *had* sent this book to him? Piles of new questions still unanswered were un-stacked and stacked again in his brain as Marty nodded off to sleep.

Chapter 14
Once Upon A Dream

The path ahead was weaving in and out of the trees, a faint pink was bobbing in front of Marty's eyes but every time he tried to see what it was he couldn't lower his gaze. He followed this unknown source until he saw a cottage in the distance. The next thing Marty knew he was holding a key. It was shaped like some strange mask and the teeth of the key were oddly X shaped.

He felt that he had been to the cottage before and the key was somehow his present or treasure, trying to memorize the look of the key he woke up.

Wednesday, August 22, 1990

Staring around in the darkness of his room Marty realized he was searching for something. He felt around on his bed. Just a moment ago he had something, what was it? Realization dawning, he stopped groping around in his rumpled sheets. The key from his dream was *still* in his dream, he didn't receive the second dream object quite as easily as the book of spells. And yet, the dream still meant something, but what? Climbing out of bed Marty got ready for school.

Making sure everything was together for his assignments he threw the strap of his book-bag over his shoulder and raced upstairs. On his way to school Marty mulled over his dream. Nick's voice behind him brought Marty out of his thoughts, "Hey Marty! Wait up!"

Slowing to a stop Marty spoke before Nick was all the way caught up to him, "I had another dream Nick!"

Registering this with a little shock, Nick's eyebrows went up, "What was it this time?"

"I was walking along in the woods and I came to a cottage I've never seen before, then I was holding a key and the teeth were shaped in an X."

In awe, Nick spoke, "The *spell book* key!"

"That's what I thought too, but I woke up and didn't have it in my hand."

"Maybe it's another adventure!" Nick said hopefully.

Marty nodded distractedly and added, "I just don't understand the pink."

"The *pink*? What pink?" Nick was curious.

"Oh, in my dream something kept moving right in front of me. It was pink but I couldn't move my head to see what it was," still not fully comprehending it himself Marty tried to explain it to Nick, "It was leading me to the cottage."

"Hmmm, maybe it was a strange creature like the trillos," Nick ventured.

"I've thought of that, but I can't come up with anything."

By this time they had arrived at their lockers and were now prepared to go to P.E. class. As they sat on the sidelines of the gymnasium Mr. Thickett appeared looking thoroughly squeezed into the regulation black t-shirt and grey shorts. The discomfort was evident on his face as he began shouting for order. Quickly everyone became aware of the fact that since he was uncomfortable *they* were going to be uncomfortable. Today was the start of the fitness tests to see where they "measured up" physically. This battery of tests was comprised of running, push-ups, sit-ups, pull-ups, and rope climbing. The classes for the next two weeks, they were informed, would be like boot camp.

Great, Marty thought, *we're in the* Army *now!*

By the end of all of these instructions Mr. Thickett was panting from exertion.

"Why do we have to prove how fit *we* are to a man who definitely isn't?" Nick whispered.

Marty shrugged, his own thoughts were racing ahead wondering how he would survive the running test. The push-ups would kill him, he'd be embarrassed by the pull-ups. And the rope climb? He would rather be publicly flogged.

Moments later Thickett's orders ceased and his command to, "MOVE!!" brought the whole class to attention. The mass of students began moving in a herd around the perimeter of the gymnasium floor. Soon the crowd had thinned into a single file line more than half were panting and wheezing. Surprisingly Marty and Nick were doing quite well. They weren't winded nearly as bad as they thought they would be and soon the bell to go rang out clearly.

Trooping off the floor they looked at each other, Marty's look said, *How did we survive that?*

Nick's shrug readily answered, *I haven't a clue.*

On the way to second period they had a chance to talk about the apparent miracle of first hour, "Maybe it's because we hiked to Bismorda's castle twice yesterday," Nick finally wondered.

"You know, that's probably it!" Marty agreed.

These adventures were paying off in *their* world too! Entering Mrs. Faleswell's room they took their seats, got their homework out, and prepared for class. As they waited Mrs. Faleswell waddled into the room, she was a dumpy sort of woman in her mid-fifties, her hair was cropped closely to her round head and it almost looked painted on. It was graying and that fact plus her over-sized thick glasses gave her the look of an owl. Her fashion sense was clearly unconscious because it was far worse than Mr. Bachenheim's. She seated herself and revealed her knee high sock tops where they stopped just below the knees and her knee length skirt that didn't quite meet them. Pasty white knees that hadn't seen the sun in probably twenty years almost matched her blinding white Velcro strapped tennis shoes.

The saying on her t-shirt today was, *Don't you just love cats? They're Purrrfect!*

Placed below this was an almost frightening

caricature of a cat's head. Marty wondered where the rest of the cat was, but the bell to start class brought him back to reality. Clearing her throat Mrs. Faleswell flipped on the notorious over-head projector.

"Pass your papers class, we're going to correct yesterday's assignment," the nasally voice rolled around the silent class.

The students looked at one another in confusion they hadn't learned the lesson yet! Their assignment had been given with the instruction that today they would go over the principles, some examples and any questions from the assignment, then they would correct it. Now they were being told to pass their papers *before* they had been instructed! A hand went up slowly in front of Marty; it was a girl with short blond hair.

The movement caught Faleswell's eye, "Yes?"

"Um, Mrs. Faleswell, I thought we were going to go over how to do the assignment, *then* correct it."

A collective sigh issued from all the students, the oversight had been breached.

Blankly Mrs. Faleswell said, "Did I ask for comments? I thought I said pass your papers, did that not make *sense*?"

Her lips curled back from her teeth in a distinctively canine snarl. Dumbfounded everyone took their assignments and passed them to their neighbors numbly.

"Number 1..." Mrs. Faleswell droned all the way through "Number 45. Now add up the number correct and write it in large print on the top of the paper, then circle it. When you're done with that, pass them to the front."

Marty's brain revolted but he couldn't get his mouth to respond, how were they supposed to learn what they did wrong or even how to do the assignment if they corrected their assignments and turned them in *before* having the lesson taught? Mrs. Faleswell waddled along the front of the room gathering the assignments smugly, knowing that more of her students would fail this way, *that* would teach them!

Stupid kids! She thought, *I should have gone into research. Rats don't talk back.* None of these thoughts crossed her blank stare to be read by the students as she deposited the work on her desk and took her seat again at the front of the class. The mixture of confused stares, hurt looks, and sheer frustration made her smile inwardly, *The school will learn to pay me what I'm worth, so help me!*

Flipping to the assignment they had just completed she proceeded to read the instructions aloud and give the same vague examples that were in the book. Seconds seemed like hours in this class and Marty said a silent prayer of thanks as the bell sounded and he got ready to go. The class was frozen in midair as Mrs. Faleswell's voice rose, "The assignment for tomorrow... is pages 10 – 15. *Due tomorrow.*"

The groans were silenced by her icy stare. Everyone wrote the assignment quickly and dashed from the room now running behind to make it to their next classes on time. Making a mental note to bring his Spanish book to math class from now on, Marty charged to his locker, and as if it were a relay, changed books and was off again. Nick's movements were an exact duplicate of Marty's and they were inside the door of Mr. Wolden's class as the bell rang. Winded, they sat down heavily, not noticing the board until they did so.

Clearly printed were the words: *Hola! ¿Como estas? ¿Como se llama? Yo me llamo Senor Wolden.*

Noticing the upside down question marks first Marty commented, "How do we ask an upside down question?"

"*Hola?*" pronouncing the 'h' Nick's question was heard by a few others, who giggled.

Another student somewhere in the class asked, "We're learning about llamas?"

One final smart remark came from the rear, "Yo, me want llama too."

Swiveling in their seats every student turned to see Mr.

Wolden behind his desk at the back. This final comment had come from him. Quick with a smile Mr. Wolden eased the class. This sandy-haired, relatively young, teacher had seemed pretty laid-back since Marty first saw him. Moving to the front of the room he brought each student's focus with him. A maroon polo shirt, tan slacks and brown wing tips showed this twenty-something teacher had taste and style. There was more than one dreamy eyed girl in the room swooning over *this* teacher. He began, "'Hola clase ¿como estas?' Means 'Hello class, how are you?' 'Yo me llamo Senor Wolden.' Means, 'My name is Mr. Wolden', finally '¿Como se llama?' Is 'What is your name?'"

Cool! Marty thought, *I'm about to become bilingual!*

Chanting as Mr. Wolden pointed to the words, the class got quite proficient at these first phrases. He then had them all copy them in their notes. Struggling Marty finally got an upside down question mark on his fourth try. Nick, who was having much more success than Marty, had already completed the notes and was now watching Marty struggle along. Feeling Nick's eyes on him he looked up and Nick gave him a quick smile of encouragement, this helped him complete the notes with a bit of added assurance that he was doing fine. Then the bell sounded releasing them from their best class so far. At their lockers Marty and Nick prepared for science with Miss Baumer, probably the most different teacher of their day, and *that* was saying a lot!

In her early thirties her straight brunette hair hung to her shoulders, she had a slight over-bite so her front teeth protruded a bit giving her the look of a mouse. Lab goggles were part of her daily wardrobe along with a white lab coat that was buttoned up all the way from her knees to her throat. The only things anyone ever saw of her outfits were her black nylons and black slip-on shoes. Being very petite she could have easily been lost in the halls except for the lab coat and goggles, not one of the students at Rosewood would have risked the ridicule that *this* fashion statement might bring. Science class passed without any mishaps and it was again lunchtime.

Today Marty had remembered to bring a sack lunch so he and Nick returned to their lockers and retrieved their lunches. At the table in the lunchroom they talked quietly about their plans on how to obtain the key. His dream kept bothering Marty, *where have I seen that cottage before? It was not that long ago, but I can't place it.* After contemplating it, Marty finally decided *I'll have to think about it later.*

Choir class was interesting, Mr. Bachenheim gave them sheet music and announced the musical that the school would be doing was *Peter Pan*! There was excited chatter that buzzed around the room until, calling for quiet, Mr. Bachenheim continued, "Now class, for your audition you need to have a prepared solo from a musical. The auditions will be held three weeks from today on September 12. They will be immediately after school on the stage so let your parents know that you will need a ride if you usually ride the bus. If you don't ride the bus still let your parents know where you are so the school doesn't get a lot of worried phone calls. Mrs. Pinch in the office would *not* be happy with us if that happened. Oh, you can sign up for an audition time on the list outside of Mr. Wright's room. That's room 305 for those of you who don't know. Okay, let's pull out *For the Beauty of the Earth* and go through your parts."

Floating on the air, music caught Marty's heart and he realized that he was filling a void he had had for a long time but hadn't known it. Like all euphoric things, choir had to end and Nick and Marty trudged to *Ms.* Culbreth's class dreading every step that took them closer to the inevitable end.

Surprisingly they survived and because they had done their homework, they could follow Ms. Culbreth's monotone lecture and only had to battle falling asleep once, each.

Like sunshine on a cloudy day, Mrs. Penn's class was a

wonderful gift. Stepping inside the door was a totally fulfilling experience, they were entering a 'safe zone' and could feel it. The desks were still nowhere to be found but now a circle of thin pillows was formed on the floor. Taking the clue Marty and Nick seated themselves on two adjacent pillows and waited for the rest of the class to arrive. Obvious changes came over the students as they entered, it was fascinating to watch. Everyone seemed to leave their load of cares at the door and enter as a new person. Class started with Mrs. Penn standing in the center of the circle and explaining how today's presentation would commence.

"Each person will rise and come to the center of the circle, then amidst a circle of friends you will share your sounds of pain, happiness, joy, or whatever feeling you have chosen. To start with I'd like to share with you *my* choice."
This brought looks from several pupils that said, *She does the homework too? This woman is incredible!*

Quietly Mrs. Penn continued, "My feeling is loneliness," she reached in her salmon colored polyester pants pocket and brought out a neatly folded paper.

As everyone watched intently, she unfolded it and read, "Raindrops, teardrops, mix in puddles, swirl round not making bubbles, wind whistles lonely, howling, broken windows, cracked and scowling. Walking hollow footsteps fall, no one hears the teardrops fall," pausing, she dropped her hands to her sides, "Okay, now, who is next?"

No one dared to follow that! Without warning she said, "Mr. Whimpel, let's hear your feeling."

Standing slowly Marty made it to the center, he didn't know how, but he made it. Slightly crumpled his paper was raised and before he could start he looked over at Mrs. Penn. Her face was alight. She looked so eager, a faint smile of encouragement on her lips. Squaring his shoulders Marty stood to his full height, he would do his best because Mrs. Penn needed him to.

Glancing at his paper the title came into focus, he started, "Sunshine. Solo. Lost. Thick. Alone. Gone. Nothing. Dying. I return to sunshine, the clouds thin, joy and laughter pours in. Warmth and love felt in the night. Night-light, shining bright. Lighthouse find your way. Sunshine at mid-day."

The clapping that erupted was something Marty wasn't expecting and he blushed profusely as he walked back to his cushion.

"Next," Mrs. Penn's voice quieted the applause.

Soon the whole class was through and only a few minutes were remaining, Mrs. Penn stood again looking around at the whole class, "You are all so gifted, how did I get such a great class?"

She continued, "As you leave please make sure your name is on your paper and place them in the 7th period bin on my table. Thank you again. I know we have all learned today."

The bell rang and like the day before, everyone hesitated to move. Slowly they left, still hearing the sounds of the feelings that were shared. At their lockers they paused only momentarily to load up their homework then they were on their way. Walking in the sunshine made them both slow down, enjoying the fresh air after a long stuffy day at Rosewood. Talking even stopped as their thoughts took over. Marty fell back into visualizing his dream and went over the trail once more, still unable to place the woods, cottage, or pink blur. Lost in Qualf, Nick was reliving his awesome experience of the day previous, anxious to have another adventure.

Chapter 15
The Acne Pimple Strikes

Even with their ambling they arrived at Grandma Pentel's house within a few minutes of their leaving school. Today she was standing in the front room watching through the large window; as she saw them approaching a smile spread on her aged face and she lifted her arm in an excited wave. For Grandma Pentel an excited wave was more the speed of a parade wave, you know the one that beauty queens use?

Well there stood Grandma Pen excitement written all over her face at seeing them. She met them at the door and so did fresh baked smells. Each, in turn, hugged her and was welcomed home from the day of school. Quickly Nick asked, "May I use the phone to call my mom please?"

Pearl smiled at this well-mannered young man, "You certainly may Nick, it's on the wall in the kitchen."

Since the kitchen was their next destination anyway, they all moved there in a cluster. Nick used the phone to obtain permission to stay, which was quickly granted. He turned and was waved to a chair with a plate already stacked with three large cookies accompanied by a tall glass of cold milk. Before he began scarfing the cookies he said politely, "Thank you for the use of the phone and the cookies Grandma Pen."

Then, transforming back into a pre-teenage boy, he devoured the cookies in a race with Marty who had an unfair lead. Polishing off the last of the cookie crumbs and washing them down with the remainder of the milk only took a matter of minutes. Grandma Pentel then peppered them with questions about their second day and how their homework had fared. After hearing about math class she shook her head and clucked her tongue, "She could use a sound spanking! Shame on her for making school so confusing."

Stifling giggles at the mental image of Mrs. Faleswell

doubled over someone's knee receiving a spanking; they finished with the rest of the day taking turns to get the full narrative. Pearl interjected her feelings briefly about each teacher's approach to education and when they finished they were free to retreat to the basement and tackle their homework. They finished their homework more speedily today so that they could peruse their adventure book to see if anything else was there. Indeed there was, the discovery of the page, the mirror incident, and the alternate poem.

This book was truly incredible!

To their surprise there was even an illustration of Zanth. They studied this closely and tried to imagine the best way to get in. At dinner they separated and this time stayed separated 'til the next day. As Marty drifted off to sleep he began to dream about trying out for the play. How would his adventures help him with that?

"I want to see the picture of Zanth," Nisha pushed her way into the narrative again.

"Yes, me too, since we're stopped," agreed Alden.

Nick took the old volume and turned it to face the up-turned gazes of the youth and watched as each visibly leaned forward and took an audible breath of surprise.

"You went in *there*?" Menalee's concern was evident.

"They survived, didn't they?" Nisha turned and reassured her.

"Yes, we did, but that was the first of many times when I didn't know if I was going to," Nick grimaced remembering the frequent close calls that he experienced during his friendship with Marty, then a slow smile creased his careworn face, "But I wouldn't trade any of them, for all the safe hours reading in my house."

"Can we return to the story?" Billy asked with a slight annoyance tainting his tone.

"Billy, are you okay?" Menalee's concern now transferred to her peer.

"Yeah, I'm *danderific*, I'd just like to keep the story moving… that's all."

Zanth

Nick could tell that Billy was becoming impatient with all of the detours, and agreed to continue with the story.

Wednesday, September 12, 1990

Despite the dangers that awaited them in Qualf and the mysteries of Zanth that remained unknown Marty and Nick got distracted with the excitement of auditions for the play and the next three weeks passed quickly. Marty's dreams had passed into his waking hours as well; they had even helped him choose his selection for his audition piece. *Some Enchanted Evening* from Rogers and Hammerstein's **South Pacific** fit well because Grandma Pentel had the sheet music and it really showed off his voice range. *Trouble In River City* from Meredith Willson's **The Music Man** was what Nick had chosen. Practices had been held everyday after school in Marty's room. They had obtained a cassette of each musical soundtrack and found themselves not only singing their solos but learning *all* the songs from both musicals. Trading off the solos and harmonizing on the duets became a daily activity.

The week before tryouts they had focused on their solos again and were pretty sure of the selected songs; as a result it was with great excitement that Marty rolled out of bed that morning. He stumbled into the bathroom, flipped on the light, and quickly showered. As he was washing his face he felt a tender spot on his forehead, had he bruised himself somehow in his sleep? Climbing out of the shower he dried off and approached the mirror. Wiping away the steam with his hand Marty gasped, there was a reddish mound on his forehead, right smack between his eyes!

In reality it wasn't really *that* big, but to Marty it seemed the size of Bismorda's castle hill. *What could it be? Am I developing some strange disease? This isn't fair! On the day of auditions I, Marty Whimpel get struck with an incurable plague!*

He dressed slowly and trudged up the stairs. Charlotte and Pearl's smiles were quickly replaced with looks of concern at his solemn face.

Charlotte spoke first, "Sweetheart, what's wrong?"

Pointing silently at his forehead Pearl and Charlotte drew in closer to inspect where he was indicating, Marty awaited Pearl's diagnosis, "It's acne."

Wow!

This news hit Marty like a ton of bricks, *my Grandmother has seen this affliction before, it must be terrible if she knew it right away.*

Charlotte's mood was lighter, "Marty, it's a zit, a *pimple.*"

Soothing tones wouldn't help, *they both know I am a dead man and they were trying to let my last hours be filled with comfort.*

Resigned to enjoy his brief remaining time, he smiled weakly, "Oh, well if that's all it is, okay."

He would play the martyr, maybe by acting so well they would give him a part in the play out of pity. *When they find out I won't live to the night of the performance tears will be shed and it will be an absolute tragedy for all of Rosewood.* The misery of this scene actually brightened his mood a little. *If I can die a hero, why not? I didn't stop when I was facing the possibility of being eaten by Bismorda, this 'Acne Pimple' illness won't get me down either.*

All day at school Marty played bravely and only when he had confided in Nick as they walked to school had he been choked up. Nick's eyes were on Marty whenever he looked, *maybe I shouldn't have told Nick.* The look of worry in Nick's eyes made him long to comfort his friend.

As school finished and they moved to the stage, he laid out his plan to take it like a hero. This brightened Nick's mood somewhat so when they got to tryouts and sat down the anticipation of auditioning covered other cares. Mr. Wright came in with a portable cassette player, placed it on the top step then arranged the piano so any mothers who had come to play would have a place to put their music. As he went about these preparations Marty had a chance to look Mr. Wright over. He had dark blonde hair, parted on the left side, it was short and fit his face well. Gold-rimmed glasses framed his smiling eyes. As if he realized Marty's observations he smiled to himself. Deep creases along his mouth and eyes along with dimples appeared, he had definitely smiled a lot over the years. He looked older than Marty's mom, but he could tell they were close to the same age. As always he was in a white shirt and tie and nice dress slacks. *This guy is well put together!*

Mr. Wright would have been great for his mom! *Why had they not married?*

Nick began fidgeting at Marty's side and it brought him out of his thoughts. A group of people had gathered and was now waiting for tryouts to start. Mr. Wright stood, "Welcome everyone, I'm very excited with the response we have had for the musical. I know it will be a great success. If you could each fill out two audition forms and then bring them to Mr. Bachenheim and myself we can get underway. As you come to audition, please state your name and what song you will be singing. Thank you for coming today and break a leg!"

A few concerned looks from the non-drama students made Mr. Wright add, "That means good luck!"

Nodding, now relieved, the students stood, picked up two forms and quickly filled them out. Piles in front of Mr. Bachenheim and Mr. Wright soon appeared and electrified silence settled over the crowd of students.

"Marty Whimpel!" Mr. Wright's clear voice cut the silence and all eyes searched to find Marty Whimpel, few recognized this tall skinny kid as he stood.

Was he a new 8th grader or maybe a smaller than average 9th grader?

Only the few seventh graders in the crowd knew him. Nick's encouraging glance gave Marty strength. He stood, placed his tape in the hand of the DCPP (Designated Cassette Player Person) and took his place at center stage.

"My name is Marty Whimpel and I will be singing *Some Enchanted Evening.*"

The music started and Marty's voice rang through the multi-purpose room. No one stirred, he was really good, as the song finished the applause rang out. Seating himself, Marty heaved a sigh of relief. Many eyes were still trying to analyze this unknown face he was now *competition!*

Nick's turn came three people later; he also stood, scrutinized beneath the stare of the older students. *Trouble In River City* created a stir as well and the murmurs immediately following had to be shushed by Mr. Bachenheim. Shortly after Nick's audition they exited the school and headed home. "Acne Pimple" for the moment had been pushed to the back of Marty's mind as the two of them congratulated each other on their shining auditions. Arriving at Grandma Pentel's house they were surprised to not see her waiting in the window, sensing something amiss they hurried inside and began calling for her.

Her voice called from the small room, "I'm in here boys."

It was a bit muffled so they still worried, they rounded the corner and saw Grandma Pen seated on the sofa with the large story books stacked around her, she was crying! Marty and Nick came further into the room and knelt down in front of her on the carpet, "What's wrong Grandma?" Marty asked.

Wiping her eyes, "Nothing dear, I've just been remembering all of the fun times I had with your mom. There are so many happy memories with these books."

She ran her wrinkled hand lovingly over the faded cover of *The Three Dogs,* her eyes smiling at the times gone by.

"Grandma?" spontaneously Marty thought of something.

"Yes, dear?" her eyes sparkled as she locked gazes with Marty.

"Want to read *us* a story?" Then as explanation, "Nick hasn't ever heard you before, I think he'd like it."

Agreeing readily Nick nodded, "Yes, I'd love to hear a story, I *love* stories."

Pearl's smile was warm and gracious, how she loved her grandson and his friend. Sometimes she even forgot that they were just friends and treated them both as her grandsons.

"I'd love to read you a story, which one would you like to hear?"

At this she spread the books for them to see the titles.

"*The Three Dogs!*" Nick and Marty amazingly spoke at the same time and had selected the same story.

Exchanging surprised looks they then laughed and looked back at Grandma Pentel.

She chuckled, "Okay, well that was unanimous! *The Three Dogs* it is!"

Stacking the other books carefully at her side she held the lime colored book away from her and opened the cover.

"Once upon a time an old shepherd who had come to the end of a long and hard working life called his children to him one last time... After leaving all he had to his son and daughter he passed away. The two decided to part and the son would go out to seek his fortune."

Fortune? The word struck Marty suddenly; he remembered where the cottage was, in the story of *The Three Brothers*!

He struggled to pay attention to the rest of the story as Fetch Me Food, Eat 'em Up, and Shatter Iron helped Brendon to win his fortune and marry the princess.

"That was *great!*" Nick had been completely enthralled during the tale.

"Yeah Grandma, thanks, I like that story, but I think I like the story of *The Three Brothers* better."

Marty admitted, speaking truthfully because he really hadn't paid that much attention to *The Three Dogs*, but at this moment *The Three Brothers* was his favorite book in the world!

"Could I take *The Three Brothers* down to my room and share it with Nick?"

Nick almost said he would rather hear Grandma Pen read it, but Marty's look silenced him.

"Okay, dear, just be careful with it, it's quite old."

Marty grabbed the oversized book, put it under his arm, and stood, "Thanks again Grandma that was great."

"Yeah Grandma Pen, I hope we can do that again," Nick was sincere.

Pearl smiled; these boys had helped her to create even more fond memories with the treasured books. Her hand ran softly over the cover of *The Three Dogs* and she smiled, she, Pearl Pentel, was a very lucky woman! She had her family around her and that was a great blessing in her old age. She was getting a chance to finally leave her legacy with her grandson. Pearl could tell he was going to be someone great! People would really look up to him, and not just because he would be tall, he was going to make something of himself. She was sure.

Chapter 16
Tickled Pink

If Pearl only knew what was going on in her basement at that moment her feelings would have been confirmed. Upon reaching Marty's room Nick's curiosity got the best of him, he burst out, "So, what is so important that Grandma Pen couldn't read us the story?"

When they weren't in her company they both referred to her as Grandma Pen. Nick would have used the term with her as well, but he didn't realize that he could.

"Remember my dream, the one about the cottage and the bobbing pink thing?"

Before Nick could respond Marty had flipped open the book and was pointing to a picture of a cottage nestled in a forest.

"That's it?" Nick said in wonder.

"Yes it is! Now we have to find out how to get inside the book."

Marty's eyes were scouring the page as Nick asked, "Inside the book? Don't we just go through the door?"

"Yes. But we have to have a have a key to get in. Each place needs a different key."

As he explained this, the full meaning of his title hit him. He said, "That's what I do, I'm the key gatherer…"

"Yulesaychaater," Nick corrected.

"Yes, the Yulesaychaater."

Scouring the page he couldn't see any sign of a compartment that held a key. He turned back a few pages and there were two pages stuck together. His pulse rushing Marty recognized the sign. Prying gently at the pages, they finally separated. The scene with the little man on the stump had come alive, the leaves were blowing on the trees, but the stump was empty.

"The little man must have gone home," Marty commented.

Craning his neck Nick replied, "No he didn't, he's right there."

Nick pointed at the empty stump.

Marty looked at Nick, "Do you see him?"

"Yeah, why wouldn't he be there? The picture says 'The little man in a bright pink hat.' Doesn't it?"

"Do the leaves move in the picture?" Marty asked, trying to act uninterested.

"Of course they don't, it's just an illustration!" Nick responded.

The weight of what Nick was saying struck Marty, "You mean this picture doesn't move?"

Startled Nick looked at Marty, "No, should it?"

"It does for me..." Marty said softly.

"Really?"

Nick was squinting his eyes trying to see how the picture could move, then his eyes flew open, "Of course!"

"Of course, *what*?"

Marty was now worried he was totally crazy.

"You would see it different, if you're a Yulesaychaater you have to find the key, no one else *can* see what you do. That's why you're so special."

Taking this information at face value Marty replied, "Maybe, let's see..."

Scanning the opposite page he found a small door in the left hand corner accompanied by the words:

Look inside
You've got to think
To make it to the man in pink.

Running his finger along the door, he could feel the rough-hewn lumber and the small bump of the knob.

He mumbled, "I need my tweezers..."

Nick watched the next few minutes pass as Marty did

some very interesting and unusual things. One minute he was huddled over the book muttering to himself, then taking a pair of tweezers he removed something Nick couldn't see from the book. Placing it with a look of triumph on his finger Marty looked up at Nick and waited for his approval. Nick leaned forward and squinted hard at the tip of Marty's finger but couldn't see anything.

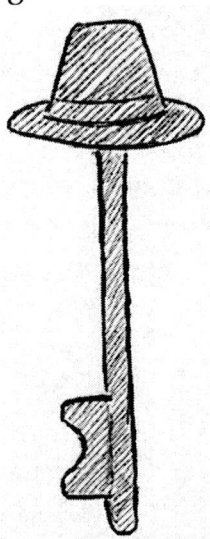

Then came the strangest part, he blinked, and there was a key. How it got there Nick could not tell, but he saw it sure enough. The head of the key was a type of pilgrim hat with the big buckle on the front, while the teeth portion was a rounded iron pipe with a simple two-prong piece jutting out close to the end. It was another old-fashioned key similar in age to Bismorda's. Marty made a few more movements over the page, studying the landscape, Nick guessed, then he set the book aside.

"Okay, let's go!" Marty stood, grasping the key in his fist, and approached the door.

Nick joined him and watched as the new hole opened; the doorknob took on a slightly greenish color, the click sounded, and the door opened to reveal a forest path a few feet in front of them. Marty led out leaving Nick to close the door. They turned back to see a giant tree that had a door knob sticking out of the bark, the only sign that it was a door back to their world.

Trotting lightly along the path they came to the fork where the stump sat. The little man was just returning to his customary position atop the stump as they approached, "Oh!" he let out, and stood at attention, "The Yulesaychaater! Welcome!"

Swiping the pink hat off of his head he bowed deeply revealing a horseshoe of white hair and the rest of his fleshy bald pate. Noticing this funny man's clothes took just a moment, he had on an olive green coat with black breeches, a white ruffle at his throat, white and red striped stockings and shiny black shoes with big gold buckles. He stood up straight again and spoke with his funny accent, "Follow me sir. I have what you want at my cottage."

Nick was impressed, he thought, *This is so cool, I could really get used to being treated like this.*

After a brief walk on the winding path a cottage came into view, it was the cottage from the book. At Nick's gasp Marty looked at him, smiled as if to say, *See? This is what it is like.*

Nodding in agreement Nick followed closely, not wanting to miss one single thing. The door to the cottage opened, a small round woman with a kind smile stood there in her patched dress and white apron, the man addressed her, "Wife, the Yulesaychaater is here! He's come for the key!"

Hearing this, the rotund woman curtsied, her head bowed, "Welcome to our humble cottage, sir."

She withdrew from the doorway so they could enter. The little man fairly danced down the hall as Marty and Nick followed. Turning into a back room they all pulled up in front of a large wardrobe. Flinging the doors open the man knelt down to where a small drawer was all but hidden in the wood grains. He pulled it open and retrieved the key from Marty's dream. It was presented as if it were the crown jewels into Marty's palm. He tried to receive it with the solemnity that it was offered, but couldn't help smiling at this funny little man and all of his idiosyncrasies.

Turning down the offer for dinner, Nick and Marty made their way back to the woods and the door back home. Safe in Marty's room they both examined the key closely. It was very detailed; at the head there was a sort of mask with limbs of some kind branching off of it. The teeth area was four pieces one sticking out of each side, creating an X shape if you looked at it directly from the end. Marty took the key and stowed it in his pocket for safe keeping. They both went to work. He retrieved the bag from under his bed with the mirror, spell book, and the book of light inside. Meanwhile Nick cleared a spot on the carpet to open the spell book. Their school textbooks were now all neatly stacked to one side.

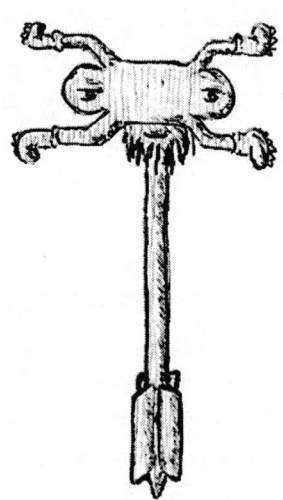

The stage was set.

Plopping down next to the bed Marty pulled out the spell book and placed it between them on the floor. The key was then extracted from Marty's pocket ready for the upcoming adventure. As the key drew closer to the lock a feeling began to creep up Marty's neck. It was sort of like when you're watching a scary movie and the bad guy is hiding in one room and you want to yell at the good guy to stay out or run away.

Now you can understand why Marty was a little hesitant to place the key into the lock. Only when the key finally made it into the lock did anything *truly* happen. The book began to shake, and suddenly flew open with a huge sigh.

"My goodness that does feel nice!" The book was talking!

"The book said that?" Billy interjected.

Nick looked up from his reading and glanced over his glasses at the youth who had spoken. He was one of the leaders of his group of friends, Nick could tell, but he also sensed he did not have the faith necessary to continue on the journey with them. From the few interactions he had had Nick knew that after today Billy and possibly others would never return again.

"Yes, the book was speaking," Nick replied matter-of-factly.

"Why shouldn't the book speak?" Menalee asked defiantly. "*I* would have said something if I had been closed up for a long time too."

Smiling at the girl who was so much like her namesake, Nick continued, "There are so many things that you may find unbelievable in the world of books…"

"But that's what makes it so great!" Weston exclaimed, "It's like a place made up of all of my dreams!"

"Yeah I love that they could, I mean, you could just escape to Qualf or someplace else anytime. Even though your life sounds wonderful to me, I would give anything to have a Grandma like Grandma Pen," Nisha said dreamily.

"What about school?" asked Wendy, "I think it sounds delumptious! I would love to have a live teacher like, well like *any of them* really even the horrid ones sound better than the best day with a droid."

Alden was so happy to see that he had not been the only one who had become so involved in the story, "What about after school cookies? I don't know what they are, but they sound amazing!"

"Much better than the tableteals I get, that's for sure," Saul compared.

"What are tableteals?" Nick wondered aloud.

"It's a pill that has all of the vitamins and nutrients your body requires instead of actually eating the food," informed Wendy. "It's your meal in a tablet, a *tableteal*, they're awful! But I really don't have anything to compare it to; I've never had anything different."

"Hearing about eating makes me want to try it," Menalee explored, "My dad said it was too much wasted time chewing everything, but *I* think it sounds worth it."

"Me too," chimed many of the others.

Nick looked around at these bright-eyed youngsters and couldn't believe how many differences there were in just a few generations since his own adolescence. Science had definitely taken great strides by the sounds of it, but so many of the joys of life had been lost by the greed of man.

Clearing his throat he quieted them, "May I continue?"

They all gave their consent and Nick again found his place in the old volume:

"Looking down at the open book they saw a woman who was rubbing her limbs and grimacing, she was quite beautifully dressed in a lavender gown that brushed the floor of the room she was in. Golden hair that shined when she moved was held upon her head in an impossible bun. On top of her hair she had a long pointed hat with a veil flowing from the tip that fluttered down her back. She smiled and her white teeth sparkled in her child-like face. Overall she was just breath-taking.

"I've been trying to get this book open for ever-so-long. The Zanth sisters locked me in here and wouldn't let me out." Then she paused, her hands flew to her mouth as she fell into a low curtsy, "Oh, I'm sorry sir, I didn't realize it was *you*."

Nick and Marty exchanged glances. Which one was she talking to?

"To be in the presence of the Yulesaychaater is indeed humbling. Please forgive my earlier grumblings. They come from a poor upbringing."

Finally Marty found his voice, turned to Nick and asked, "Do *you* see her? Can you *hear* her?"

He wanted to make sure this time. Nodding, Nick showed that he too had seen and heard the beautiful woman in the book. Not quite understanding why Nick couldn't see the pictures move in one book but he could in another Marty turned his attention to the maiden, "I'm sorry you have been cramped in there, I have been looking for the key for quite a while."

There he went again, sounding much more mature than twelve.

"May I ask your name?"

She blushed promptly but responded, "Misselthorn, sir, at your service."

"Okay, Misselthorn, can you help us get to Zanth?"

Her color drained and she looked instantly terrified. She stammered, "S-s-sir, you d-don't w-want to g-go there."

"But I *do*," Marty insisted, "The Zanth sisters have kidnapped Bismorda and her entire kingdom!"

Again Misselthorn's hands flew to cover her mouth, "They *didn't!*"

"Oh, they did, and they left this," Marty pulled out the note the Zanth sisters had left and held it so that Misselthorn could read it.

"Oooh those *two!* They just think because they got cursed they can wreak havoc on everyone else!"

Misselthorn stamped her tiny foot in anger.

This was news to Marty, "What? The *Zanth sisters* are cursed?"

"Of course silly, how else do you think they got so ugly

and mean?" Misselthorn giggled at Marty's naiveté.

"Well, I just thought that witches were supposed to be that way," Marty answered simply.

"No, only ones with curses on them are ugly and mean. Didn't you know that Bismorda and I are witches too?"

"I thought you were a princess!" Nick blurted.

"No! *Princesses* are worse than any cursed witch; they're spoiled and rotten on the inside with a candy-coated shell. They may look pretty but it's what's on the inside that counts. Honestly if you're to be an Eyahge'er you better get the story right!"

Marty and Nick gasped, "You know what an Eyahge'er is?"

"Yes, afterall *I* know the language of books, don't I?" Misselthorn taunted.

She was teasing them!

"Misselthorn!"

Marty spoke a little more sternly than he had planned to. The girl was instantly contrite.

"I'm sorry, sir, it's just been such a long time since I got to talk to anyone. I was just having a little fun."

Coming to her rescue Nick said, "It's ok, Marty, I don't mind."

Misselthorn gave a gasp she had been unaware that the Eyahge'er and Yulesaychaater were on such close terms.

She was even more humbled, "I'm sorry I did not know that you were equals, sir. I will not be so cheeky with the Eyahge'er again."

"It's okay Misselthorn, we *are* friends, but we can take a joke too!"

Marty's frankness took Misselthorn's admiration to an even higher plane.

"Oh, that's ever so nice," Misselthorn bubbled, "No one will believe I've spoken with both the Yulesaychaater *and* the Eyahge'er!"

Nick couldn't stand it any longer, "What exactly *is* an Eyahge'er anyway?"

This caught both Misselthorn and Marty off guard. They looked at Nick while Misselthorn answered, "It's a story teller."

"A *story teller*?" Nick wasn't very impressed, "just a story teller?"

"It's attitudes like that, that have pushed our world to the brink of extinction!" Misselthorn bristled. "*If* there aren't any story tellers there is no need for stories."

She twirled around and gazed out the window of her portrait, her shoulders slightly hunched.

Marty could sense her feelings had been hurt, he glared at Nick, who was repentant instantly, "I'm sorry I didn't mean it, I just thought..." Nick floundered, "I don't know what I thought."

This finish sounded lame even to his ears.

She spoke without turning around, "Well maybe you *should* think," turning toward them she continued, "Think what would happen to us if no one shared *our* story."

The gravity of this hit both Nick and Marty, what *would* happen? They didn't want to find out.

"Misselthorn?" Marty ventured, "Can you help us?"

Considering, she replied, "I may be able to, but I'm not sure."

"I meant, can you tell us about the Zanth sisters?"

In response Misselthorn drew a chair to the foreground of her picture and sat down, "Grisele and Mopel are twins, they have always lived together, because they got along so well. Many people get confused which one is which but they don't even look like each other, it's just that they act so similarly. They were always the belles of the balls," she sighed remembering the better times.

"The one who put the curse on them was very clever, by cursing two witches that were that close it merged them along with their powers. It also doubled their evil so more destruction could occur.

"With two as one now a very powerful spell would have to be used to save them, but none of us have that much power. It would require outside help."

The tale seemed to be over so Marty asked, "Can you help us understand this?"

He now took out the page with the poem on it from the book and showed it to her.

"It means you need a mirror to fight the OhRa."

This confirmed Nick and Marty's guess.

"There's another poem when you look at it in a mirror," Marty attempted, before he could retrieve the mirror Misselthorn spoke again, "It talks of giving the sisters a way to help and that will break the spell."

"Yes, that's right!" Marty and Nick answered together.

"What can we ask them to help us with?" Marty wondered, "It says it has to be something they can't fail at. What would that be?"

"Do you have a cold?" Misselthorn tried.

"No," Marty turned to Nick, he too shook his head.

"A headache, backache, sore tooth?" Misselthorn listed more mortal ailments.

Then Marty's plague popped out of Nick's mouth, "What about *Acne Pimple?*"

Marty glared at Nick that had been their secret! Misselthorn's voice made Marty forget his betrayal, "That might work, I myself have never heard of it, but I'm sure they have. It might just do the trick!"

Excitement flowed from Misselthorn as she rose out of her chair. "Let me tell you how to approach the sisters."

A hush fell over Nick and Marty, neither dared breathe; this was what they had hoped for.

"You must find their main chamber in the skull of the Chukaht; they will be there among their books and potions.

As soon as you get close the OhRa will sense your presence so you must walk backwards towards them. With the mirror shining over your shoulder you should be able to guide yourselves without injury. Once you have the OhRa in your mirror, you must lock eyes with it, by doing this you cause it to go into a trance. Then you are in direct communication with Grisele and Mopel. You must ask your question only after the OhRa is in a trance, otherwise it will make the sisters curse you."

"How do we know when it is in a trance?" Marty was taking mental notes on all of these instructions.

"The eyes of the OhRa are usually wide open, however, when they droop to being half closed, it is in a trance."

"Where *is* the OhRa?" Nick asked.

Marty was glad he had Nick here; he had forgotten to ask that one.

"Did I forget that? Oh well, I need to tell you first what happened to the Zanth sisters, then you will know what to expect," she took a deep breath and plunged into the narrative.

"Mopel was the taller of the two so she was chosen as the carrier of the OhRa. They were turned into one form with two heads, four arms with claws for hands, and they glide along on a type of slimy mussel, so you can't hear them coming. They are covered in stitches, over their eyes and mouths, their clothes, or covering, has patches all over it as well."

Shivering at this mental image both Marty and Nick braced themselves for any more horrors.

"The OhRa itself isn't a frightening sight, it's just unusual. It is attached to Mopel's head by a membrane that extends into a neck. Around that neck it wears a ring with a seed of evil embedded on it. The mouth is covered in a hanging mass of fur; the face has four antennae, two extending from each side, one above, one below the eye."

"Your description has been most…descriptive, thank you." Marty swallowed over the lump that had formed in his throat. Then he stopped, "Wait, look at this key, is this the OhRa on the top?"

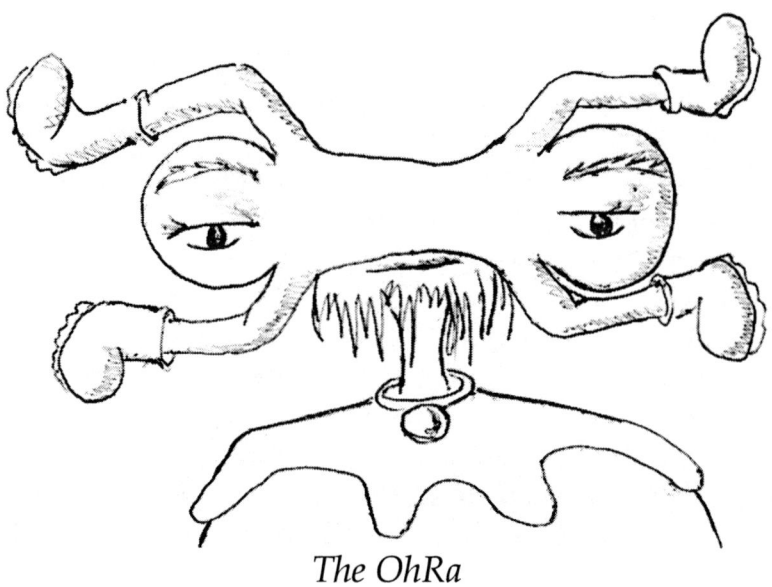

The OhRa

Holding up the key for Misselthorn to see, she nodded, "Yes, that's it, is that the key you used to free me?"

Nick answered, "Yeah, that's the one we got from the little man in the pink hat."

"Misselthorn, I was just wondering what I might use this for," Marty held up the book of maps.

She looked at the cover, "*Future* adventures! That book contains maps and information about 1,400 different destinations, quite a good start I'd say."

"*1,400!*" caught off guard by this large sum Nick was now quite attentive. "Cool!"

"That's only one book, there are many more filled with other lands too, but right now you two need to help Bismorda's kingdom."

You're right Misselthorn, thank you so much for your help. We'll have to talk again soon," with this Marty closed the book as Misselthorn curtsied her farewell.

"Whew!" Nick whistled, "Sounds like quite an adventure! When do we go?"

"Right now!" Marty was determined to face the Zanth sisters before any more time went by.

"Let's go!"

They both stood, packing the few things they thought they would need, the mirror, and the book of light, leaving everything else stacked by Marty's bed. Getting the key that they had received from the little man in the pink hat, they changed Marty's door into a portal and Marty crossed his fingers that it would take them to Zanth.

Chapter 17
Zanth Awaits

The simple clicks that brought about the portals would never cease to amaze Marty or Nick, such a simple sound, but such a drastic change. Peeking around the door brought a pungent smell of wet dirt and something long since dead. A quick flash of Ms. Culbreth's face made Marty pause. Hey if he could handle Killbreath, that meant he *had* to be brave right?

They moved into the darkness and pulled the door closed behind them, flipping off the light-switch as they did so. Marty put the key in his pocket, then fumbled in the bag for the book of light. Once he found it he held the book as he had on the way back from Bismorda's castle, vertically in front of him, but this time he barely cracked the cover not wanting to forewarn the Zanth sisters of their arrival. Then he pulled out the mirror handing it to Nick.

The thin beam of light hit a dull grayish wall that was rough to the touch. Where were they? Nick's gasp behind him made Marty glance back. Reading his lips was difficult in the dim light, but he finally made out, "*The skull.*"

They were inside the skull of the chukaht! That meant the sisters were close. Muffled sounds in the distance made them move cautiously. The light hit the path and it looked like they would be going downhill for a bit to start. So Marty led out with the light in front. A turn in the road brought Nick forward to test it with the mirror. Faint flickers could be seen in the reflection and both of their hearts began beating uncontrollably. Cautiously they proceeded toward the far off light.

Marty stowed the book of light in the bag and Nick took the lead armed with the mirror. As the flickers grew into a stronger orange glow Nick slowed, then stopped. They stood for a few moments mustering courage, finally Nick handed the mirror to Marty and they proceeded to the final corner. From their vantage point they could see directly out of the eye sockets of the chukaht's skull. Ever so slowly the sky was lightening with the coming of dawn. It struck Marty, the poem had said that they had to come during the day and they had completely forgotten that warning.

If they had arrived any earlier they would not have survived this first encounter. Raising the mirror to look around the corner it caught the glow of a fire crackling about twenty feet from where they stood. It was close to the center of the main chamber. He scanned for the sisters and then he saw it.

Huddled on the floor, a mass was sitting or crouching by the fire its arms folded on each side of its enormous figure, the heads rested at odd angles, the OhRa stuck out of the top of the tallest head. It was asleep! But even as he thought that, the eyes of the OhRa shot wide open and the figure stood, it's arms sticking out in four directions, claws clicking menacingly as their metallic sheen caught the glow of the fire.

It began to glide forward as Marty gulped and stepped out from behind the wall, his back to the creature, Nick quickly followed stepping past Marty so they now had the mirror between them pointing over Marty's right shoulder and Nick's left. This sudden movement stunned the creature into a silent hover, the claws continued to click but it was no longer advancing.

The incessant clicking reminded Marty of a fleet of cockroaches that he had once seen in a movie, it gave him the shivers. Taking advantage of this pause, Marty and Nick began walking backward toward the stationary figure. They both had their eyes locked on the mirror and were each trying to gain eye contact with the OhRa. Finally it was into Nick's eyes that it stared.

They had backed to within ten feet of the creature and Nick's arm came up to motion for Marty to stop. The wide-eyed creature stared at Nick's reflection daring him to blink or look away. Suddenly Nick's eyes began to burn, he had to blink...they were so dry...it was going to blind him if he didn't blink soon. He could feel his eyes beginning to water, but it wasn't enough, it felt like he were looking into the sun. The feeling was penetrating into his sinuses and his head was ready to explode, he just knew it. That's when the unthinkable happened...he *blinked*.

In that brief instant it advanced fully prepared for the kill and feast on fresh meat, but Marty's gaze froze it within just a few feet of their position. This time the staring contest continued until the breathing of the sisters slowed and the four menacing arms relaxed to the sides of their monstrous form. Only then did the eyes droop to half open.

Marty had done it!

Speaking clearly he quickly posed the question, "Can you help to cure *Acne Pimple*?"

In the vacuous cavern his voice echoed almost tauntingly as they waited for the answer. He held his breath as suddenly two voices spoke out of the single mouth on the OhRa, "Grisele, do you remember that spell?"

"Oh, Mopel, you know I have an atrocious memory! You're the one who always remembers everyone's birthdays."

"Ok let's see," the slightly higher head bent in thought, the claws came up and clicked together, then suddenly, "Oh yes, I remember I wrote that one down it was a particularly strange one that not many people ask for."

She rummaged through the contents on a nearby stack, slashing pages with her razor sharp claws. "Oh blast these stupid claws they make a mess of all my best spells!"

It was then that Marty realized these witches didn't want to be like this, they wanted to be free, his fears were wiped away. However, he still kept eye contact with the OhRa, he wasn't *that* carefree.

"Here it is..." the spell had been located and placed on the top of the stack closest to Nick.

After placing it there the Zanth sisters backed off and began to chant the spell. As they chanted in their rhythmic singsong, Nick and Marty inched closer to the pile until Nick had the paper in his hands. Then they moved slowly toward the exit. All the time Marty kept eye contact watching their strange gyrations as they chanted. As the sisters intoned it together, it went like this:

The Cure of the Acne Pimple

Ingredients listed here in order
Fresh wax from and Irish Gorder,
The eye of one Snoth, crumbled,
Mixed together never tumbled.
Wrinkles of a Batwort's ear
The acid of a Nighten's tear.
Next comes three hairs of a Garth
You know they wander back and forth.
Add these three to your concoction
Steady now, it's time for action.
Tines of three one-eyed Screms
Then five different kinds of Phlems.
Add to this one horn-tailed Speakur
Apply heat under your beaker
Let it simmer, bubble, boil
Then pour it in some old tin foil.
Let it cool, set, and congeal
And when it's rubbery to the feel
Spread it over all your skin
Wait thirty seconds, soak it in.
Wash completely in warm water
Then you'll be fair as Pharaoh's daughter.

Then their voices changed and became one gravelly growl:

Go now, leave us, question not,
Do not look back, no matter what.
Peace and quiet we desire
Don't make us set you on fire....

This last comment caught Marty off guard and he realized that as the voice had begun to change the droopiness in the eyes had started to lift. They had to get out of here and fast! Thinking quickly he slid the bag off his shoulder and whispered out the side of his mouth, "Nick, take the book of light and blind it so we can get away!"

Quick as a flash, Nick had the book out and opened fully over his shoulder, blasting the OhRa with a full ray of brilliant sunlight. The claws and arms came up to shield the eyes of the OhRa, but the damage had been done, it was blinded, but only momentarily. It shrieked with pain, a strange unearthly sound similar to nails on a chalkboard but magnified in the empty cove.

Nick snapped the book shut, shoved it and the spell under his arm and headed for the exit. Marty was close on his heels holding the mirror with the canvas bag clutched in his other hand. As they ran Marty fumbled with the mirror getting it back in the bag as he reached in his pocket and retrieved the key. They rounded the corner as they heard the shrieking die away, which meant the creature would be fast approaching.

Running up the incline to the door they threw it open. Rushing into Marty's dark room they slammed the door and threw themselves against it. Marty inserted the key and the click sounded.

They were safe!

Sliding to the floor they both let their breathing slow down and their pulses return to normal. Sitting there in Marty's room Nick started berating himself, "I can't believe I blinked! I almost got us killed! I'm so stupid..."

Marty waited for the tirade to calm down and then said in a calming manner, "But you *tried* that's the main thing. I'm just glad we went together I wouldn't have had enough arms to do everything myself and neither would you. Bismorda was right, together we *are* unstoppable!"

The smile that he offered Nick was lost in the darkness of the room, but the comfort in his voice had seemingly cheered Nick because he pulled out the ingredients to the spell, flipped on the light and began reading them aloud, "Irish Gorder, Snoth, and Batwort? Where are we going to find all of these things?"

"Misselthorn can help us, and then we have the book of maps, we should be able to put this together in no time," Marty replied optimistically.

"Okay, but I think we better get our homework done or our moms are going to skin us alive!" Nick had reverted back to reality.

"Yeah, they're much scarier than the OhRa!" Marty joked.

Nick laughed too.

At the mention of real life again Marty wondered aloud, "How do you think we did at try-outs today?"

Nick shrugged, "Don't know, Mr. Wright said that the call-back sheet would be posted first thing tomorrow. After call-backs the final lists will be posted Friday."

"Well, I hope we made call-backs," Marty confided.

"Me too, the musical would be a lot of fun," Nick agreed.

After their homework was done they parted for the evening. As Nick got ready for bed that night the scene kept playing through his mind, he was looking in the mirror at the weird mussel-like OhRa, their eyes locked, they glared at each other, the burning in his eyes, and then that cursed blink! No matter how many times it replayed it always ended in disappointment. *I could have cost us our lives; I wouldn't blame*

Marty if he never invited me on another adventure. Afterall I turned out to be a complete failure. Before Nick closed his eyes and finally drifted off to sleep, he made a commitment to himself, if Marty let him go on another adventure, *I will never let him down again!*

"*Did* he let you go on any more adventures?" Menalee was full of concern.

Nick looked up from his reading and his eyes smiled down at her, "Bless you, of course he did, that's why the book is titled *Adventures of Marty and Nick* if I had only gone on a few it would read *Adventures of Marty and a few with Nick.*

Menalee pondered this for a moment, "I guess that would make sense."

"Of course it does," Billy said, "why else would he want to share the adventures if they weren't his."

The note of condescension in his tone bothered Nick, would this boy try to lead the others away?

He could not let that happen.

"Shall we continue?" he asked in an overly cheerful tone cutting off any further comments before they could be made.

Most of the heads nodded, so Nick proceeded to re-open the book and began reading again.

"About the same time Marty was already well into a horrifying dream. There was a huge red mass growing on his forehead. As he went from day to day it got bigger and bigger until he was confined to his bed where he had to lay on his side with the red growth propped on pillows next to him. The excruciating pain was so realistic he woke up drenched in sweat.

Looking around wildly in the darkness Marty felt his forehead. There was a small tender spot with a slight bump, it *had* started growing! Groping for the bedside lamp he flipped it on, slid out of bed, and rushed to the bathroom. After turning on the light he scrutinized his face in the mirror, sure enough the bump *was* bigger.

He had to do something and quick. As he was fumbling around with the bump in the mirror, it blew up! Some icky white gunk followed by a touch of blood was all over his fingers.

Marty froze.

What have I done?

Terrified he took a quick inventory, tenderly he reached up to his forehead, no pain. *Am I cured? No, how could that be? Maybe it burst in preparation to grow a larger one. Yes, that must be it.* Staring cross-eyed at himself in the mirror he could almost feel the second poisonous wave of Acne Pimple seize him. He felt sick, he needed to lie down. Staggering back to his bed he dropped onto the haphazard sheets, pulling them up around him.

Only when he was sufficiently wrapped up did he notice he had left the bathroom light on. Mustering all of his remaining strength he feebly hobbled to the bathroom. As he did so he remembered how his mom had used a wet washcloth to soothe his face when he had been sick. Preparing the washcloth took all of Marty's extra reserve energy. He was dying, he knew it, but he might as well do all he could to ease his suffering. Hands shaking he wrung out the washcloth. Somehow he turned off the light, and made it back into bed. When he was there he draped the wet washcloth over his forehead kind of like the headband worn by students in the *Karate Kid*. That image made him smile weakly *he* was like Daniel fighting the enemy.

Drained of all energy Marty drifted off to sleep.

Chapter 18
A Call To Play

Thursday, September 13, 1990

Somehow Marty made it through the night and when he woke felt surprisingly better. His hand flew to his forehead the moist washcloth had been discarded sometime during the night. The bump was definitely gone; for now anyway. Climbing out of bed he got ready for school, halfway through his preparations it hit him, the callback list would be posted this morning!

The only thing he could think of now was getting to school and finding out if he was on it. Getting to school had never taken so long! Breakfast, gathering homework, kissing mom, and Grandma, Marty finally left. Hustling up Farnsworth to the corner he saw Nick already waiting at the corner.

Looking closely at Nick he could tell he hadn't slept very well, "What's wrong?"

"Nothing," was the evasive reply.

"You don't look like you slept well," Marty tested.

"I slept well enough," apparently this conversation was over.

Switching gears Marty ventured, "I wonder if we made the call back list."

Something changed in Nick as he smiled longingly, "Yeah I wonder, that would be fun to be in *Peter Pan*."

"Let's go find out!" Marty punched the air and led them toward Rosewood.

Upon arriving they found an anxious group of students huddled around Mr. Wright's door, the list hadn't been posted yet. Joining the group they waited. The energy in the crowd was unbearable, finally the door cracked, an arm appeared, the paper was attached to the wall, and the arm retreated. A mass of pushing bodies strained to see if their names were on the coveted list. It wasn't alphabetical so Marty had to read the whole thing, Nick's was right close to the top, he was excited for Nick, but kept reading.

There.

His name was halfway down, *I made the first cut!* Withdrawing from the crowd he found Nick against the wall with a huge smile on his face.

"I got called back as Peter Pan!! Can you believe it?"

"Wait! How do you know what part you got called back for?"

"I read the left hand column. Your name is grouped with those who got called back for the same part," Nick rolled his eyes as if to say, *Amateurs!*

Marty again approached the wall, found his name and to the left…Captain Hook!

Turning he shouted to Nick, "I'm going for Captain Hook!"

Nick was joyous, "We could play opposite each other that would be awesome."

"But we'll be enemies," Marty realized.

"Yeah, but what better people than best friends to play enemies? Then nobody really gets hurt," Nick reasoned.

Flying by in a blur the day was done and they found themselves again at Mr. Wright's room for the cold-reading portion of the try-out. Nick read for Peter Pan quite a few times one of them was opposite Marty. By the time they headed home Nick had some of the script already memorized, and was quoting some lines to Marty. Since Marty only read twice for Captain Hook he had to make up his lines, but they had a fine duel anyway.

They arrived at Grandma Pentel's out of breath and excited, luckily both Marty and Nick had warned everyone they may have to stay after school, so when they saw Nick's mom over at Grandma Pen's they weren't *that* surprised.

Janet's shoulder length brunette hair was pulled back

in a ponytail and her long legs were curled up under her on the couch as they entered. She stood quickly wanting to hear how it had gone. Close behind her was Grandma Pentel in today's choice of pastel green housecoat.

Marty and Nick shared their experiences Marty told them he was jealous that Nick had been able to read so many times, but he was also excited at having been chosen too. After they were congratulated they all had cookies and milk in the kitchen, and Marty and Nick went downstairs to attack their homework.

Once they were in Marty's room, he had to share his dream with Nick. After the full tale Nick was shaking his head, "That's not good Marty especially since *your* dreams come true."

Marty agreed, "I know, that's why I got so worried."

Nick reassured him, "Hey, I'm sure we'll get the cure together before anything real bad happens," he hesitated, "that is, if you still want my help."

Taken aback Marty exclaimed, "*Want* your help?! I *need* your help! Together we are unstoppable remember?"

Marty's energetic response spoke volumes to Nick and he felt safely included in any adventures that lay ahead. With that business aside they began reading aloud from the map book about the different lands. They made it through thirty without finding one of the ingredients mentioned in the spell's recipe. Luckily the book included information about all of the kinds of creatures found in each destination, but at this rate it would take them a month and a half if they read about thirty lands every single day! It was going to be a lot of work but they would do it. Patience would pay off they were sure of it.

They did their homework and separated for the night after wishing each other luck on being chosen for the show. Even with the excitement of the musical both Marty and Nick fell asleep quickly and slept through the night.

Friday, September 14, 1990

Meeting breathlessly at the corner Nick and Marty rushed to school to join the smaller, but infinitely more excited cluster of students. After what seemed like forever, the door creaked open, the arm appeared, the list was posted, and the door swung shut. The group became a frenzy of arms and pulsating bodies trying to see over each other.

Somehow Nick made it to the front without Marty but quickly he turned and barreled toward him shouting, "We *both* made it! I'm Peter Pan and you're Captain Hook! We did it!"

They were thumping each other on the back not caring about the sidelong glances of disgust they were getting from those who had been given the various chorus parts instead of the leads. The most venomous looks came from the ninth graders, they had lost over these seventh graders?

Oh the injustice! They huffed off in alternate directions throwing back spiteful glances at the two still rejoicing in the hall.

Suddenly Nick stopped, "Hey! This is our first adventure together in *our* world!"

If anyone had heard this comment they would have surely thought they were crazy, but luckily the hall was now deserted.

Marty agreed, "Yeah, you're right, our team has triumphed again!"

They punched the air, gave each other high fives and did a spontaneous little victory dance. Sailing through their classes Marty and Nick couldn't wait to share the joyous news with those at home. Throughout the day they received awed congratulations or dirty looks in the halls. Both of these looks were received with the same cheerful smiles, they were on top of the world *nothing* could affect them today!

Tuesday, October 2, 1990

A little less than three weeks later the practices for the play were well under way.

This particular morning though, could change the course of history forever, so it was worth mentioning. Marty rolled out of bed and bleary-eyed made it to the shower.

Again he was washing his face and the tenderness he had felt before was *back*! He jumped out of the shower, didn't bother to dry off and stood staring at his forehead in the mirror. The red bump in the middle of his forehead *was* bigger, he knew it, the plague had returned! But he would not let it get him down he now had the antidote, or spell, to cure himself. Only problem, the ingredients he had no clue about yet, and he and Nick's diligent study of the map book had died off with the excitement of the musical.

This new scare would have to be thwarted by vigilant study and determination. It was not a time for slackers! With added zeal Marty prepared for school and when he met Nick at the corner he was ready with a game plan. Every day after play practice one of them would work on homework, the other would study the map book, when one of the ingredients was discovered, they would both stop, and go find it. After retrieving it, they would return, then take the ingredient to Bismorda's palace, they couldn't risk having this project discovered. With ingredients such as those listed they were sure to arouse suspicion if they were to keep them under his bed.

Nick readily agreed and the day at school stoked their fires of preparation. Each assignment was gladly stacked onto their homework. The more homework they received, the more time they had to study in the map book without detection. Upon arrival at Grandma Pentel's house that afternoon they devoured their after school snack for one purpose only, the sheer energy it would provide for their quest. Mumbling thanks they descended to their war camp, or in other words, Marty's room. Nick was selected to do homework first, since

Marty could not focus on anything but the enemy at hand.

Mere moments later, with no warning, Marty stumbled across their first clue. Marty's excited whisper had to be repeated three times before Nick understood him, he had found the Phlems! They were a strange root-like plant harvested from the sands of Tarbath in the early part of October, it was perfect. The timing was just right and they would be gathering the rest of the ingredients in no time. Marty retrieved his tweezers and began scouring the book for the door.

The next two pages were predictably sealed and after prying them open the blowing sands of Tarbath greeted Marty's view. Nick's eyes grew wide, he could see the picture moving too and tapping Marty on the shoulder he revealed this wonder. Acting as if this were nothing special Marty replied, "I knew it would happen sooner or later."

"What?" Nick was a little miffed at Marty's nonchalance.

"I knew you would see the things I do," he was fiddling with a small area on the page and Nick craned to see what he was doing.

Curious he questioned, "What are you playing with over there?"

"Can't you *see* it?" Marty's tone suddenly changed.

"No, if I could I wouldn't have asked," Nick was slightly put out.

"It's a door made of driftwood, it reads:
This door leads to the banks of the Sems
As close as you'll get to the harvest of Phlems."

"Really?" Nick moved Marty's hand and glanced at the page, "Nothing is there! Are you joking?"

This remark puzzled Marty; he began to mutter, "Why didn't the book's illustrations move for him? Now when they do he can't see the door? Am *I* crazy?"

Then it hit him, he jumped up, grabbed his history

book, and the book of spells, and sat back down. Flipping open the history book he found two pages that stuck together, pried them apart, and found a picture of New York in 1920 moving along at full tilt, he pointed at it, "Do you see *this*?"

Nick leaned forward, "Yeah, it's a picture of New York in 1920. It says so along the side of the picture."

"Is it moving for you?" this theory of Marty's was making him excited.

"Of *course* not!" Nick looked at Marty like he'd lost it, "that's our history book!"

"But, see, it moves for *me*!" Marty flipped open the spell book to Misselthorn's page, she wasn't there, but the room was, in fact they caught a mouse scavenging for crumbs, it squeaked and ran out of sight.

"You see *this* one move right?"

"Yes, that's Misselthorn's room, I *talked* to her, remember?"

"So you see the pictures move if the books are from the land of stories, but if they are from our world you see nothing. Although you see the pictures move, you don't see the door that holds the key or the instructions in either, right?"

"Right!" Nick was picking up on this theory. "So what you're saying is I can only see the pictures move if it is from the world of books, otherwise I see nothing. But I never see the area that the key is, because I am not the Yulesaychaater?"

"One hundred percent correct!" Marty was beaming. "We figured out another one of our personal gifts. You see the story, because you're the Eyahge'er or storyteller, I see both the story and the key because I'm the Yulesaychaater or key gatherer. We see what we need to see to do our jobs."

"Cool!" Nick was impressed that he understood this thread of reasoning.

"Let me get this key to Tarbath, then we'll head to get the Phlems," Marty decided.

"Okay, I still want to watch, even though I can't see

anything, 'til you have the key."

The history book and spell book were closed and moved off to the side as Marty again took up the tweezers, opened the minute door, extracted the key and let it swell on his index finger.

"I will never get tired of watching the key appear like that, it's like *magic!*"

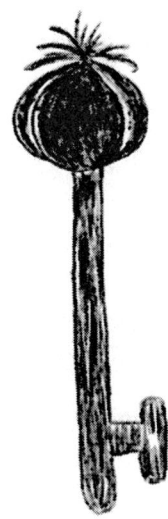

Tarbathian keys were apparently black because this one looked like it had been retrieved from a fire, the only thing was it gleamed in the light and looked like a jewel. The head of the key was an onion-like form and the area for the teeth jutted out to the side in a T-shape.

Marty and Nick looked at the blowing sands of Tarbath. Without thinking anymore about it they shut the book and approached the door. Turning the key brought a howling wind on the opposite side of the portal. Peeking out, they saw the clear waters of the river Sems being rippled heavily. The leaves on the foreign trees were whipping around like fan blades, and the sand was being sent in little spinning funnels every which way. Observing the landscape for a moment before they headed out into it, Marty turned and retrieved two t-shirts from his bureau to tie around their faces for protection and the canvas bag to carry the Phlems.

As they exited the room, they pulled the door shut behind them.

Chapter 19
The Smell of a Fresh Phlem

Tarbath

Leading down to the river was a narrow overgrown path. Marty and Nick picked their way along it briefly looking back, a driftwood shack stood where they had just entered Tarbath. These doors had a way of camouflaging themselves that left Marty and Nick wondering who was in charge of keeping their way home hidden.

At the river's edge they took long drinks of the cool refreshing water. When he was finished Nick leaned back from the river, noticed something a little ways down the bank, stood, and approached the object cautiously as it stood there protruding from the weeds.

It was a pick!

Retrieving the slightly rusted pick he turned and retraced his steps to Marty's side.

Marty looked up, his eyes widening as he saw what Nick was carrying, "Great! We can use that to dig for the Phlems."

Now that they had both been refreshed by the water, they tied the t-shirts across their noses and mouths making them look like robbers in an old western. Then turning toward the never-ending sands they set off to find the Phlems. Still wondering how they would be able to tell the difference between the Phlems in order to collect five different kinds of them a spot in the distance caught their attention. Blackened by the produce apparently, a round spot of ground stood twenty feet away. As they approached it, the strong scent of peppermint filled the air.

Looking down at the dark earth they could see purple tufts poking out, proving there *was* life. Squatting near the edge of the field they each reached out for the same plant, stopped, looked at each other, and laughed. They really had too many things in common right down to their thoughts! Marty finally extracted the first Phlem, it was round, about the size of a peach and covered with stripes. They weren't solid stripes like a candy cane, instead they were like those of a tiger starting out skinny, growing fatter and then tapering off to nothing again.

The root was a cream color and the stripes were a deep purple almost black.

Holding the Phlem in his hand Marty smiled at Nick, they had found the first ingredient!

He could almost feel the poisons of the Acne Pimple leaving his body as he dropped the Phlem into the bag with a smile.

"One down, four to go," Nick reminded just to keep their mission in perspective.

"Where to next, navigator?" Marty turned to Nick for suggestions.

"Let's try over that next dune." Their conversation was muffled slightly by the t-shirts over their mouths, but it was better than getting their mouths and noses full of sand. As a result the protective t-shirts stayed in place.

Squinting off to the left where Nick was currently pointing, Marty could see the tops of some type of vegetation. Nodding in agreement, Marty rose and they headed in that direction. From the top of the rise they looked down at a new landscape. No longer was the sand moving with the wind, it was a solid blanket before them punctuated with waving silver plants that glinted in the sunlight. These plants ranged in height from a few inches to as much as a foot.

Kneeling next to the nearest of these, Nick tried to pull it from the ground, but the ground proved unforgiving, and the Phlem didn't budge. Since his bare hands hadn't succeeded he decided to try the pick, using the point he tried to scrape away some of the cement-like sand, still no luck. Taking hold of the handle like a baseball bat, Nick aimed the point as close as he could to the Phlem and swung with all of his might. The point sunk into the ground, but only an inch, he would have to keep working at the soil to try and loosen the Phlem from captivity. A second time Nick swung and sunk the pick into the sand, this time a large chunk of the sand broke free and Nick was able to pry the plant out by it's silver leaves. Surprisingly the Phlem came out with no earth clinging to its layered skin.

Marty drew closer and they examined their newest Phlem. This Phlem was the size of a large banana, but looked like a piece of shrimp with it's jointed body glistening in the sun. It, like it's leaves, was a metallic silver but it was not cold like metal instead it was warm and smooth to the touch. Nick handed the second Phlem to Marty who added it to the now growing collection of roots in the canvas bag draped over his shoulder.

"Your turn, Marty," Nick now passed the baton of navigation off to his friend.

Marty looked further along this new terrain and saw the vegetation he had seen from their first discovery spot. A type of tree or something as large as a tree was now only about fifty feet away from where they stood. He pointed toward it and started walking Nick fell in step behind him. Upon arriving at the large growth they discovered it was not in fact a tree at all, it was a type of planter device that had circular holes all the way up the length of what would have been the trunk. Overhead there were large palm frond shaped pieces of metal providing shade from the direct light of the scorching Tarbathian sun. The tufts of growth coming from the holes were a golden yellow, a little like corn silk. For some reason Marty reached forward and poked at the top of one of the tufts with his forefinger. It retreated quickly from Marty touch, almost as if it were trying to escape human contact.

"It's coming out the other side!" Nick shouted.

Marty quickly moved to the opposite side of the planter and, sure enough, there was a Phlem sticking out a good finger's length from the side of the planter.

Again reaching forward Marty grasped the root and pulled it free from the planter with very little effort. Gazing down at the Phlem that lay in Marty's palm they saw a deep brown root similar in texture to a metal file it had criss-crosses along the full length of it and was about a foot long. It was rounded on both ends and from these rounded ends the golden tufts were growing. It looked a little like a handle grip from a bicycle because it had bumps on one side as if it were grown so you could take hold and pull it out by it's own grip. Marty added it to their increasingly strange collection of Phlems in the bag.

"Two left," Nick chirped, he was loving every minute of this.

Truthfully, so was Marty, but he was on constant lookout for life forms of any kind. So far they hadn't seen any other than the Phlems and it was beginning to make Marty a little uneasy. As if his thoughts had been heard, off to their right Marty saw a movement but when he turned to look nothing was there.

"Did you just see something?" Marty asked Nick.

"Yeah, what was it?"

"I'm not sure but it moved fast."

"Where did it go?"

As they spoke they walked toward the place where they had seen the movement.

Without warning the sand under Nick's feet gave way and he landed flat on his back with a loud thud. If Marty hadn't been watching he wouldn't have believed what happened next. The sand where Nick had been standing was moving!

Right before his eyes the sand took shape and stood up. The creature was about three feet tall and was the color of tar along its front, but its face, neck, and the backs of its arms, legs, hands, and feet were the same color and texture of the sand. It had a flat head that only had two bumps for eyes at the top. There actually wasn't much depth to any of its frame except from the front or back. It was almost two-dimensional. The flattened gumdrop head was attached to an extremely thin, long neck. Its body was the shape of a tear drop and its arms and legs jutted out from it like toothpicks. There were three fingers on each hand and flat, webbed feet. What *was* this thing?

It made a deep bow and fell into a groveling position speaking with a muffled voice since his face was pointed toward the ground, "I'm sorry, sir, I was trying to stay out of your way but we San Dovers do have to tend the Phlems. It is a great pleasure to meet you, Yulesaychaater, sir. My family will not believe my extraordinary luck. I can't wait to share the pleasing tale that I was actually *walked on* by the Eyahge'er! They will be so proud."

At this Nick was a little defensive, "I didn't mean to, but you were right under my feet!"

"Oh no, sir, it is a great compliment to be walked on, it means we are very brave and do not give away our identity to anyone. Usually I would have moved away after you fell down, not letting myself be seen, but when I realized it was the Yulesaychaater, I had to stop and express my humble gratitude and the love of my people for your great sacrifice."

"*My* sacrifice?" Marty was thrown off balance.

San Dover

"Why, saving Bismorda from the curse! She had preyed on our people as the great invisible flying serpent, but when she was free of her curse she returned and brought many wonderful gifts to beg our forgiveness. She is now one of our closest allies."

Marty hesitated, but Nick blurted out, "So you haven't heard?"

"Heard *what*?" the San Dover's gravelly voice was concerned.

"Bismorda's whole kingdom has been taken captive!"

"Oh no! By whom?"

Rising to a kneeling position the San Dover was wringing his hands and looking anxiously from one to the other of them. It was a pitiful scene to watch him.

Marty spoke, "I'm... I mean, *we're* trying to do everything we can. We're on a quest right now that should save Bismorda's kingdom and the Zanth sisters."

"Oh kind sirs, you are truly of noble blood to sacrifice yourselves for others. Thank you."

Marty leaned down and helped the San Dover to his feet. "Can you help us?"

"Oh sir, I would be most delighted if I could."

"Can you help us find two more kinds of Phlems?"

The San Dover thought for a moment then replied, "Which ones do you have?"

Taking the canvas bag off his shoulder Marty showed the three previously harvested Phlems to the San Dover.

As he turned the Phlems over in his hands he kept nodding and finally spoke, "Well you now have the mintus, fruitus, and metallus genus' you still don't have the nutus or the gellataneous forms. You'll want to head in that direction," here the San Dover pointed to the right, "to find the nutus, and you'll have to return to the river to find the gellataneous one."

Thanking the San Dover they left him and headed to find the nutus Phlem in the direction he had pointed. The land slanted downward suddenly and Marty and Nick found themselves sliding in the loosened sand until they were at the bottom of a rather deep hole.

Directly in front of them was a large bushy plant sticking out of the center of a pool of water. Nick and Marty circled the pool trying to figure a way to cross the water, get to the tree and get back again. Testing the pond, Marty's fingers hit solid, not liquid water. The pool was not wet or cold; it was under some type of glass plate or something like that. He could see the water moving under the surface and turning to Nick said, "We can walk on it, it's solid!"

Approaching Marty, Nick looked down as Marty knocked on the solid covering, his eyebrows raised, "Why do you think there is a lid on the water?"

"To avoid spills?" Marty joked.

Laughing Nick rolled his eyes and stepped out onto the

pond, "Come on, I think you're *turning into* the nutus genus!"

The 'bush' was about ten feet tall and covered from top to bottom with three-foot long, dark green leaves.

They couldn't see the trunk at all. Actually, Marty thought, it looks like the top of a pineapple sticking out of the ground. Nick grabbed one of the leaves and lifted it up, a sudden flash of electric blue grass caught them off guard. When they paused to look closer they could see row after row of unusual fruit clinging onto the under-side of the leaf. Reaching forward Nick plucked a fist-sized Phlem and showed it to Marty. Now that the Phlem had been picked they studied it. The nutus Phlem had bright blue strands growing out of the top, the part that would have been a fruit was covered by a dark grey-blue shell, and there was a swirling pattern that covered the whole of it.

"One left," Nick said triumphantly as the nutus Phlem was deposited in the bag with the others.

Marty turned to the walls of sand that were surrounding them and looked at Nick, "Yeah, but how do we get out of here?"

For the first time on this adventure they started to panic. The sand would only slide under their feet not allowing them to get far up the steep incline, they couldn't get out! Sitting down at the water's edge they gazed alternately at the gurgling pond and the impossible face of the sand walls. Suddenly Marty stood up, looked at the tree, then back at the wall of sand, "There has to be a path that the harvesters use. The San Dovers probably can't climb walls of sand any better than we can."

They now started looking for a path instead of just climbing where they had come down. A sudden wind made them squint their eyes to avoid getting sand in them, it started at the top of the hole and the howling grew to a loud echo where they sat. It felt as though they were going to be shaken to pieces by the reverberating wind. They watched as a funnel of wind came to the edge and traveled down toward them skimming the surface of the sand wall on its way. Its speed and intensity dissipated as it lost the force of the additional winds. It petered out to nothing before it reached the spot where they were and only then did Nick and Marty see the amazing treasure that had been uncovered, STAIRS!

There were stairs sticking out of the steep incline of sand leading right up to freedom! In their excited state Marty and Nick stood and began racing up the stairs, halfway up they were winded and had to stop, these stairs were much steeper than they looked. After a brief rest, they started again, this time at a much slower pace. They soon were out of the hole and on their way back to the river Sems. Thirty minutes later after much trudging in the sometimes-blinding sand filled winds, they came over the dune directly west of the river and again descended to the banks of the clear, refreshing Sems.

After reviving themselves with lots of cool water they looked around to see where the final genus of Phlem could be. Nothing among the plant-life on the banks looked anything like the tufts of the various Phlems they had already gathered. Then, almost by accident, Nick looked *into* the river and exclaimed, "Hey, Marty! Look at those orange things along the bottom! Don't they look like the same kind of plant?"

Peering into the water Marty watched as the fibrous tufts swayed in the current.

"Yeah, they *do* look a lot like the ones we have, let's try them."

With that, he lay down on his belly, extended his arms into the gurgling waters of the Sems, and grasped one of the orange plants. With a slight tug it came free of the sandy bottoms giving off a small cloud that washed downstream like an ephemeral dancer in the waves. This final Phlem was by far the most interesting. Damp orange fibers from the top now plastered themselves to the skin of the six-inch-long root.

The root itself had the feel of a water balloon, its shape changed with the slightest movement and it was pale peach in color with random dark orange spots on it, like paint splatters. They quickly understood why this was a gellataneous Phlem, it was very close to the consistency of gellatin. Placing this final Phlem in the bag, carefully so as not to rupture it, brought a feeling of great satisfaction to Marty and Nick.

They had completed the first of *eight* tasks.

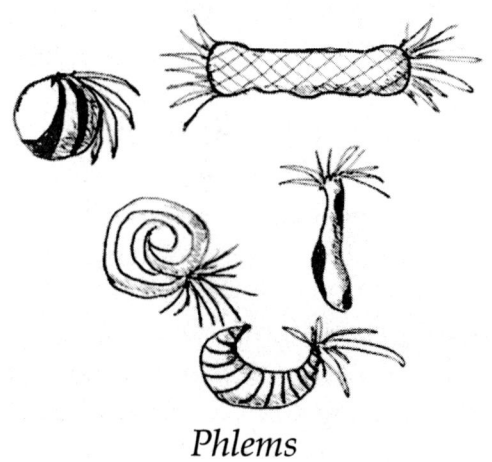

Phlems

With the canvas bag full of the five different Phlems now they could take them to Bismorda's castle to store them until they could gather the remainder of the ingredients. Nick and Marty climbed the overgrown path again toward the hidden door in the driftwood shack. Upon entering Marty's room Marty turned the key as Nick retrieved Bismorda's key from the drawer. Swapping keys, Marty changed the door again into the entrance under the bridge of Qualf.

By the time Nick and Marty had reached Bismorda's castle they were dragging, it had been a very long day and they weren't done yet. The sun was low on the horizon but they didn't even notice. Entering the now familiar entrance hall they moved toward the lab, inside they looked around for something to store the Phlems in but couldn't find anything big enough. It was time to go exploring again. Even in their exhausted state this change in scenery revived them and they were ready for another adventure.

They left the lab and moved toward where Marty had been put in bed in the long wing of rooms. Turning right they walked past the storage room and bedroom and walked headlong into a huge mirror! It ran from floor to ceiling and made the hall look much longer than it really was. After recovering from the collision they picked themselves up off the floor and headed in the opposite direction.

Again passing the bedroom, storage room, and entrance hall they entered a new and unexplored area of the castle. Opening the first door on their left revealed a large ballroom, the floor was a glossy wood and an enormous chandelier hung over the center of the room. The walls were draped thickly in deep green and gold velvet. It was exquisite, but this was not what they were looking for, not right now anyway.

Pulling the door shut they continued on down the hall. The next door opened onto an oversized dining hall with a long table running the full length of the room surrounded by high-backed chairs. A tablecloth covering the table must have been placed the day of the attack. The only thing that showed the absence of people was a thick coat of dust over everything in sight. Again the door was pulled shut and they continued to the next door. Surprisingly this opened onto a large winding stone staircase that led up and down.

Instead of investigating the stairs they chose to stay on this level for the time being. As they closed this door they looked toward the end of the hall and saw themselves in another full-length mirror, it was another optical illusion game! So, if that were the case there was only one room left on this level, they held their breath as the last door opened onto a spacious kitchen.

Pots, pans, spoons, knives, and forks were piled up on

counters or hanging from hooks around the room, there were even many stacked on the floor. This was just what they were looking for. They walked further into the room; Marty grabbed a large saucepan off of one counter, and with a clang set it down on the big center preparation table.

Now, how to keep the Phlems fresh?

Nick was poking around and opened a small door off of the kitchen, he exclaimed, "Hey Marty I think I found their fridge!"

Indeed, what he had discovered was the larder, a place that was used to store dry goods, meats, cheeses, and other foods. It was cooler than the castle itself and might just work to satisfy their needs. Plopping the Phlems into the saucepan Marty brought them over to Nick who had cleared a place on one of the shelves. As he did so, the smell of meats and cheeses hit Marty's nostrils, his stomach growled hungrily in response to the savory scents followed closely by Nick's.

It had been hours since they had eaten their after-school snack; maybe a *little* cheese wouldn't spoil their appetites for dinner. Retrieving a large knife from the cutting board Marty returned to the larder where Nick had selected a cheese and placed it on the sideboard in preparation. Marty cut two thick slices off of the orange block, Nick replaced the cheese and Marty washed off the knife. There was no running water so he had to pour water from a pitcher that was standing near the sink.

Much of what Marty did was so different in this world compared with home, but somehow he didn't mind the adjustments. Returning to the slices of cheese they began to nibble as they exited the larder, shut the door, and continued out of the kitchen. The cheese was rich and flavorful. As they ate it seemed to melt like chocolate in their mouths, leaving a creamy texture on their tongues that they enjoyed until the next bite. It was different from any cheese they had eaten before and they liked it.

The descent off of Bismorda's hill was an exultant one, they chattered about Tarbath and the various Phlems that were now awaiting the other vital ingredients.

The cheese lasted until they arrived at the doorway back to Marty's room. In Marty's room the turn of the key brought them back to Grandma Pen's house. Marty's hand was still on the knob when it turned in his hand and came open.

Charlotte's face startled them and theirs startled her, as a result they all three flinched. After recovering, Charlotte saw the mostly eaten pieces of cheese in their hands, "Couldn't wait for dinner?"

Her reproach was not unkind, "Two growing boys, we'll soon need an extra refrigerator! Oh, Nick, your mom just called, dinner's ready. Same for you young man," at this she reached out and tousled Marty's hair.

"Okay, thanks Mom! We were just headed up," hoping his tone wasn't too forced.

He waited until the door was closed and looked at Nick, "That was *close!*"

"Do you think she noticed these?"

Nick was holding up the t-shirt that was still hanging around his neck, they had been in such a rush they hadn't removed them after returning from Tarbath.

"I hope not!" Marty said, "And I hope she doesn't ask Grandma about the cheese!"

Nick nodded emphatically, "I still can't believe we were that close to getting caught!"

They were still shaking a bit from the scare of reality as they removed the t-shirts, ate the rest of the cheese, gathered and stowed the books and keys, and left Marty's room.

Chapter 20
Hallowe'en Treats Can Be Tricky

Wednesday, October 31, 1990

Hallowe'en in Junior High is a totally different experience from Elementary, and Marty quickly found this out. To start with, there was to be a costume contest during school for those who were dressed during the school day and there would be a costume party or dance that night in the gymnasium. This would be Nick and Marty's first school dance; well first dance that mattered. They had worried about it for weeks since they had heard the announcement. Since the play was only one week away and they had both learned their lines and characterizations so well, they decided to go as Peter Pan and Captain Hook.

Marty woke up early to get everything on with time to spare. He had on a long black wig with curls that hung down his back and over his shoulders. A wide brimmed hat with a huge white plume was perched on his head. He had drawn the wrinkles on his face and shaded in stubble with make-up and the black curly moustache was in place. His costume was made up of a white ruffled shirt with a form fitting blue vest adorned with gold buttons, a red waistcoat with tails trimmed in gold brocade that flared out behind when he walked, black knickers buttoned at the waist and knee, and long white socks that started somewhere above the knee under the hem of the knickers and traveled down his legs to disappear into black leather slip-ons that were topped with large gold buckles. All that was left was the hook, which he would hold in his hand after breakfast. It had a handle similar to a sword with a rounded piece that covered the hand and was then concealed under the lace of the sleeve, revealing only the menacing hook and rounded silver plate.

Voila! His transformation was complete! He smiled into the mirror, and Captain Hook smiled back, he looked really good! His heart raced with excitement as he gathered his books for school, but *what about the dance tonight?* This thought made him stop.

What about it? He asked himself. *You don't know how to dance! You'll look stupid! People will laugh at you!* That blasted inner voice seemed to be taunting him again.

Ignoring the pessimistic views of his psyche he brushed these thoughts aside and then Marty thought the only comforting thing he could think of, *"At least the Acne Pimple disease has slowed down! So, there!"*

It didn't really address the issue at hand, but it did make him feel better for the moment. Shortly after returning with the Phlems the newest lump had disappeared without a trace. *It's scared! I know it, it can sense that I have the cure so it is not going to do anything to me now.* At least that's what he kept telling himself.

After breakfast he completed his costume with the hook, posed for Grandma Pentel and mom to take pictures and admire him; then he headed to school.

From a distance Marty could see a form dressed in shades of green waiting at the stop sign on the corner, as he got closer Nick's details filled in. He had a pointed Robin Hood style hat on with a sleek red feather poking out from the brim. His green outfit had ragged short sleeves and along the bottom it was also uneven. The collar was neat and folded precisely to frame his neck with exactness. The shorts were tattered appropriately and his leather belt at the waist carried his dagger in its sheath. Leather moccasin-like slippers with flaps in front and in back of where his foot went in were worn proudly as the chilly wind blew against Nick's bare legs and arms. He had an almost purple tint to him, but he was still smiling from excitement.

"We'll win for sure, we look awesome together!"

With that, they were on their way to school. Not many were surprised at their choice of costumes, but they were shocked at how good they looked. Comments floated behind them, "Man, I wish *my* costume was that cool!"

"Look at them, they look so *real!*"

"They really do look just like Peter Pan and Captain Hook!"

Some of these comments came from the ninth graders who had been so put out by Marty and Nick's placement in the school play these, most of all, were nice to hear. It was soon evident that most of the school day would be basically one long party because of the holiday. P.E. was spent helping to decorate the gymnasium for the dance. Math and Science were spent in doing strange problems that made words or different answers to Hallowe'en centered questions. Not surprisingly Mrs. Faleswell had a set of cat ears on with a tail pinned behind her, and Miss Baumer was a mad scientist. This was hard to guess because all she had done differently was to make her hair a little frizzy.

In Spanish they learned Hallowe'en is different in other places and some countries don't celebrate it at all. Senór Wolden wore a colorful woven poncho and a sombrero so he looked traditionally Spanish. In choir Mr. Bachenheim let them watch an old black and white version of Phantom of the Opera, it was pretty cheesy, but made them all grateful for colored T.V. The biggest surprise of the day came when they arrived in Ms. Culbreth's class, she was sitting behind her desk dressed as usual but she had a simple sign hanging around her neck, written in large black letters it said, WICKED WITCH. Marty and Nick had to fake like they had been seized by coughing fits to hide their laughter. Ms. Culbreth had a sense of *humor?*

They proceeded to hear historical horror stories many of which were still unsolved mysteries.

At Mrs. Penn's classroom door they were greeted by an elegantly dressed Mrs. Penn. She had fixed her hair up and had a tiara placed, like Miss America, among her curls.

Dressed in a floor-length, blue-beaded, sequin covered dress she was a knock-out. Long white gloves that went up to her elbows accentuated the white sash draped across from her right shoulder, it read TEACHER and that was it. She welcomed them all in and as class started she turned to write on the board the back of her sash came into view for the first time. The rest of her sash read, IN DENIAL.

The class roared with laughter and started clapping. Mrs. Penn turned around, feigned surprise, and began doing a parade wave as the applause settled down. Finally she spoke, "It's funny but all of my classes have done the same thing, I'm so glad that you all love it when I write on the board."

Her eyes twinkled with her little joke and the chuckles rolled through the students. Suddenly Mrs. Penn's face grew dark and she began speaking in an eerie voice, "Once upon a midnight dreary, while I pondered, weak and weary, over a many quaint and curious volume of forgotten love – while I nodded, nearly napping, rapping at my chamber door – 'Tis some visitor,' I muttered, 'tapping at my chamber door – only this and nothing more.'"

The tale continued as the man sat and a raven came in by the window causing the man to go mad with its constant ridicule.

She finished with "And my soul from out that shadow that lies floating on the floor shall be lifted – nevermore!" Here her head dropped so her chin was on her chest, after a pause, it popped back up and she said, "That was a poem called *The Raven* by Edgar Allen Poe. He was an author who began writing at the age of eighteen, or that was when he was first published, in 1827.

"When he died in 1849 he left a legacy of ironic, dark, even sinister poems and tales, many of which are only used around Hallowe'en because of their scary qualities.

"We're now going to watch a movie that was made from one of his short stories entitled *The Pit and the*

Pendulum, don't anyone lose your heads!" She cackled like the wicked witch of the West in *The Wizard of Oz* and turned on the movie as the lights flipped off.

After the movie finished Marty and Nick went to Grandma Pentel's house where she was putting on the finishing touches to her front window. Cobwebs had been hung to make the house look older, a large black spider hung on a string was frozen on it's descent in the center of the window, and a small cauldron that would have dry ice smoke pouring out of it later was in place on a small three legged stool visible from outside.

Grandma Pen paused when she saw the boys approaching and waved them inside. The smell of Grandma's chili met their nostrils as they opened the door. According to her it was to be a new tradition on Hallowe'en. She had invited Thomas and Janet Chrismon over for dinner so Nick wouldn't have to leave tonight.

As an afternoon snack Grandma Pentel had made orange pumpkin cookies so, after downing a few each, they retreated to the basement to study more from the map book. This was the first day they had not had play practice *and* homework, so they were going to take advantage of it, they did promise however, if they found anything they would go on the adventure the next day when they didn't have to risk their costumes getting dirty.

Since their adventure to find the Phlems they had had to lie low, that close call made them quite nervous. Still, they would have to continue their adventures so that they could save Bismorda's kingdom and Marty from the dreaded Acne Pimple.

In the section called Quixant they found one important word, *Nighten*!

"Hey Marty, here's the Nighten!" Nick was overly excited over finding the coveted bit of information. "Let's read about it."

Marty looked at where Nick's finger was pointing and began reading, "The Quixant Nighten is a beautiful but heart-rending creature. The luxurious plumage of its head ranges in color from a blinding white to light blue, its beak is similar to that of the Mazurnit, but the tip has a dark red spot to mark the leader. The flock only gathers at mating season and then separates for the remainder of the year. Its body is a membrane that is easily seen through but impossible to penetrate. Fins with webbed front sections and armed with a thorn-like claw located mid-way up, these along with its beak are used to protect its young and scavenge for the insects and small roots that it eats. Their three toed feet are useless for anything except walking. Nightens are non-migratory birds they simply walk to their own territory on the island of Quixant and exist there peacefully. When the Nighten consumes any food it is instantly turned into a very powerful acid that is excreted through tears. This brings us back to our first description, it is beautiful because of its exotic characteristics, but heart-rending when found alone excreting large acidic magenta tears."

"Wow, that's quite the bird!" Nick acknowledged.

"Yeah, let's see if there's a picture," Marty tried to turn the page but the next two were stuck together.

Being quite used to this by now, he separated the pages patiently to reveal a brightly lit scene of far-off Quixant. Waddling along the coast was one of the colorful Nightens, they could tell from the description.

Seeing the tears sliding down its face was pitiful Marty had to agree, his eyes skipped to the opposite page and scanned for the door to the Quixant key. Up in the center of the first paragraph was a door that looked like a raft, complete with a rope handle,

Nick jumped up, retrieved the tweezers, and handed them to Marty. Even though Nick couldn't see what was happening he knew this was the time for tweezers so he was doing his part. Once again with the fine-tuned precision of a surgeon Marty went to work, Nick clearing his throat made him look up, "You okay, Nick?"

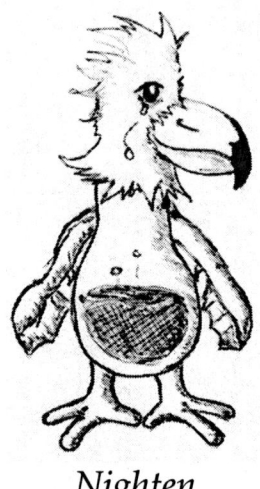

Nighten

"Yeah, I was just curious what the door said," smiling faintly he continued, "after all since I can't see it, it makes me wonder what they say."

"Oh, I keep forgetting," Marty apologized, "it says:

'Through this door you'll find the key,
Go to Quixant then you'll see,
Though it's acid the Nighten's tear,
Will not strike your heart with fear.'

So it sounds like we have nothing to worry about here either."

Nick sighed, he was happy there was no danger, but he secretly wanted a chance to prove himself again. Suddenly there was another full-sized key balanced on Marty's forefinger, and they leaned forward to scrutinize it. This key was clear, well, kind of, it was a *little* cloudy; it had a hoop-like head with a magenta teardrop dangling in the center of the vertical hoop. Further down the length were two teeth on opposite sides and at two different heights.

Nick liked this key the best so far it looked like glass and was the least like any key he had ever heard of or seen before. Stowing the key in the drawer with the others they were just going to talk to Misselthorn when Charlotte called down that Nick's parents had arrived. They made their way upstairs in their full costumes and were greeted by motherly gasps of delight. Charlotte admired Nick's costume and Janet admired Marty's, then Nick and Marty posed in a dueling stance for Thomas to take pictures of them in all their finery.

After dinner Marty and Nick went back to the school leaving all the adults at Grandma Pen's to handout candy to Trick-or-Treaters and discuss how much their little boys had grown up. When they arrived at Rosewood the teachers were there and waiting in the front hall as well as in the gymnasium. Music was floating out into and through the mostly empty halls, it was a little spooky, but Marty and Nick were so nervous they were barely walking let alone paying attention to their surroundings. On the way to the school they had discussed what they would do, any fast songs they would just stick together, move to the beat and mingle, the moment a slow song came on they would make themselves scarce. With this plan in place they entered the dimly lit gym.

The decorations that they had done in P.E. had been added to apparently because there were many more balloons than they had blown up and the streamers had not been hung by their class. With the overall effect in place it was quite nice, in the subdued lighting anyway. Someone had assembled a large amount of balloons into an overwhelming spider that hung from the ceiling with its legs reaching all over the room.

White streamers had been arranged into a pair of spider webs extending over two of the four doors so the remaining two doors were used to enter and exit the dance. Haunting melodies were playing as they entered and they could see Mr. Bachenheim behind two large amplifiers with a pile of large cardboard squares stacked in front of him, he was playing *records*! Then Marty remembered what they had learned in music class, the fibers used on records recorded a much richer sound than cassettes, so it made sense that Mr. Bachenheim would use his preferred method of music.

Crowd control was not an issue yet, there were only about twenty people that had shown up, most lived in the surrounding neighborhood and had walked, but soon there should be a large crowd of excited students so the teachers were prepping themselves in their assigned positions. Within thirty minutes the crowd had increased ten times and doubled again within the hour. Marty and Nick only had to act thoroughly interested in the refreshments for one song so far, the rest had been fast paced and everyone interacted freely.

The throng of students suddenly parted and a fairy princess with golden ringlets came into Marty's view. It was Sara Matticen one of the seventh grade officers that Marty kind of liked. His heart stopped and his mouth went dry, she looked *amazing!*

The light caught her porcelain complexion, she positively glowed, her wings were sparkling in all their glory, and Marty almost wet himself with nervousness. After praying all evening that there wouldn't be a slow song Marty found himself now praying that there would be one, and quick, before he lost his nerve.

The muses of Rosewood were listening because a slow song started and, like magic, Marty floated to her side. He had practiced the words a million times just in case by some sheer chance he would ever have an opportunity like the one that now presented itself.

He opened his mouth and "Dancing you, huh?" came out.

Oh if only his sword was real, he could end the embarrassment quickly right here on the dance floor.

Sara looked at him with her gorgeous azure eyes, blinked once as if clearing sleep from them, and said, "What?"

Another chance! I won't screw up this time. He took a deep breath and, "Me dance you, huh?"

Somehow in her utter perfection Sara understood and agreed to dance. Marty was elated! Taking her to the center of the floor his hands moved to her waist, hers went to his shoulders and the ADSRC (amazingly difficult slowly rotating circle) dance began.

Marty could hardly take his eyes off of her stunning beauty which was okay she was looking off in every direction but at him so he couldn't be caught staring. The super-stupendous miraculous occurrence had to end sometime and unfortunately it did all too soon.

Marty called after her, "Thanks...nice...bye," as she disappeared into the pulsing waves of humanity that were the students of Rosewood.

Somewhere back on the planet earth Nick poked him in the back and hissed, "You didn't tell me you were gonna ask

Sara Matticen to dance! I was standing there and suddenly you weren't. When I found you, you were out in the middle of the dance floor. Did she say anything to you?"

Marty thought for a moment, even though he knew the answer he didn't want to sound pathetic, "No, we just enjoyed the dance."

Actually he couldn't speak for her, but he could die in the next few seconds and be completely content. He snapped back to reality as Nick continued, "So are you gonna ask her again?"

Shrugging, Marty blushed, luckily he had Captain Hook's make-up to hide behind, and he answered in his suave couldn't care less attitude "I don't know, maybe, if I feel like it."

Secretly, Nick was jealous that Marty had beat him to building up enough courage to ask Sara, he had been planning to ask Monica Brussard from their science class, but he hadn't done it yet. Now there was a personal goal set *I have to ask Monica, because if I don't Marty's more brave than me, I can't and won't back down from the challenge!* Marty was still floating blissfully in his dream of Sara, when Nick saw Monica.

She was in a long Shakespearean gown of deep maroon, and she was about ten feet away. A slow song followed *The Monster Mash.* Nick saw his chance and took it.

Coming up alongside her he bowed, "M' lady, I would be honored if I could have this dance."

He'd heard that line in a movie once and it had worked then so he had memorized it, just in case he ever found himself in a situation like this. Excited that he had actually pulled off the line he tuned back in as she shrugged, "Sure, why not?"

Nick had to struggle not to giggle excitedly. Walking to an open spot they took up the same stance that every other dancer was in and began the rotating circle of song. Unlike Marty, Nick actually talked to Monica. He started, "So, what do you think about Miss Baumer's class?"

"It's okay, but I like Mr. Bachenheim's better."

Nick was surprised, "Are you in the choir?"

"No, I have Mr. Bachenheim for band."

"*Oh*? What instrument do you play?"

"The flute."

"Cool, do you like it?"

"Yeah, it's okay, it just takes a ton of breath support to play correctly."

"Really? Singing is the same," Nick confided.

"So, are you getting nervous for the play?" she seemed genuinely interested.

"A little, but I think by the time we perform I should be ready."

"Well, I'm going to be there opening night," she said it so naturally that Nick had to look at her closely to see that *she* was blushing and averting her eyes. Nick was stunned, she was flirting with him!

Picking up her cue he said, just as naturally, "That'll be great! I hope you stay for autographs after."

Monica looked up at this comment, met Nick's eyes, blushed deeper still, and looked down at the floor. Suddenly Nick realized the music had stopped and a faster song had come on, how long had they been standing like this? Pulling slowly out of the dance position he said, "Thank you for the dance, I think I have a new favorite song."

Monica stood and watched as Nick disappeared back into the mass of bodies. Sighing deeply she began quietly planning how she would ask for his autograph the night of the show. Soon after Nick and Monica's dance the whole Hallowe'en dance came to a screeching halt with an announcement, the costume contest winners were about to be announced.

Mrs. Drindle, the vice principal, stepped to the microphone and her voice came over the sound system sounding distant and fuzzy, "I'm so pleased with the turnout tonight," she oozed.

In her mid-forties she was dressed in her usual business suit coat with matching skirt, the only difference was she had a badge that said, UNDERCOVER MOM on it pinned to her lapel. Continuing she said, "The costumes this year are very impressive and it has been extremely difficult to choose the winners."

In front of Marty a couple ninth graders leaned closer together and spoke loud enough for him to hear, "I bet it goes to the officers, like it does every year."

Refocusing on Mrs. Drindle Marty caught her explanation, "We have chosen a boy and girl from each grade and then a boy and girl over all. So, all together that makes eight winners tonight. The winners are..." she proceeded to name one boy and girl from the ninth and eighth grade officers, now it was seventh grade, "Sara Matticen and Brett Colter," these two were officers.

Marty didn't care though, this gave him another chance to gaze at his beloved Sara. In fact, when he heard, "Marty Whimpel" it didn't register until Nick poked him in the back and whispered, "Marty, you won best over all! Get up there!"

Tripping over his feet, but not too much, he made it to the raised platform amidst the applause, accepted his prize, a certificate and candy bar, and took his place next to Sara, he almost fainted but held onto consciousness valiantly.

The dance was now officially over and he again tried to speak to Sara, to congratulate her on winning, "Candy nice huh?" was all that came out followed by a goofy snort that was supposed to be a laugh, she looked at him and without so much as a comment left the gym as quickly as her fairy legs would flutter.

Gazing longingly after her Marty was still standing there when Nick found him, "Hey Marty, congrats that's so cool. Did you say anything to Sara?"

Marty finally snapped out of his trance, "Yeah, I sounded like a two year old, I can't even say two words to her without stumbling over myself."

Nick was now curious, "What *did* you say?"

"I don't know, I know what I wanted to say, but like one word from each sentence makes it out and then runs together so I sound like an idiot!"

With all of his dating experience consisting of the single dance with Monica under his belt Nick felt quite sure that his advice would be useful, "Just relax Marty, be yourself, she'll see the light."

Marty looked doubtful so with added emphasis Nick reassured, "Really!"

That said, they headed home to get any leftover Hallowe'en candy for their sweet stashes.

Chapter 21
Reality Bites and Sometimes Melts Plastic

Friday, November 2, 1990

After the thrills of Hallowe'en the return to reality was a major let down. School was just school again, but play practice revived some of the excitement. There was exactly one week left until they performed. Tech rehearsal would be Monday, dress rehearsal on Tuesday, matinee and opening night Wednesday, then run Thursday and Friday. But Marty and Nick were excited for a totally different reason, they would be going to Quixant tonight, in fact they were planning to ask if Nick could spend the night then they would be safer against further discovery.

Arriving at Grandma Pentel's house they found her in the window taking down the spider webs and other decorations, they offered to help her get the higher corners because they could reach higher than she could. It was then that Marty realized what Grandma Pentel had gone through to hang up the decorations for Hallowe'en, he turned to her, and she smiled, her eyes twinkling, telling him without words that it had been worth it whatever the sacrifice.

How he had grown to love her over the last few months. Their friendship was something he would always treasure. His thoughts floated back to Rousy, she wasn't anywhere near Grandma's age, but he realized that she had been put into his life to help him prepare to have a lasting relationship with his own grandmother, and he was grateful for that. After packing the decorations away they all sat down to enjoy cookies and milk, Marty spoke, "Grandma what did you used to do for Hallowe'en when you were a kid?"

"Well, we didn't have all these candies like you have today, that's for sure," Pearl began, "In fact we didn't have much of anything, but we sure had fun. We would go to the city hall where there was a costume gala. I remember the first year I got to go, I had dressed like a fairy princess, I was in my best dress and I had found a long, straight stick that was my wand. My mother had helped me starch some muslin wings and we pinned them on my back. I was quite a looker in those days," she smiled at them, "my dance card was all filled up just after I arrived."

"Dance card, what's that?" this came from Nick, but Marty wondered the same thing.

"Oh they were little cards that we had so that young men could sign up to dance with us it was like an appointment card. Well just after I arrived someone took my card and I guess it was passed around quickly because when I got it back, it had been completely filled!" Her pleasure was evident on her face and in her voice. "By the end of the evening I was quite worn out, even my wings hurt," she joked, "but it was so enjoyable I have never forgotten it."

"That sounds really cool, Grandma!" Marty responded.

"Yeah thanks for sharing that story with us Grandma Pen," Nick didn't realize his slip.

Pearl let it pass with a simple comment, "Anytime sweetheart, I love sharing history with *my* boys!"

She winked and only then did it register what he had said. Pearl saw it register and held up her hand, "Nick, I don't mind at all if you want to call me Grandma Pen, if I had known you were comfortable with that I would have insisted on it *long* before now!"

She chuckled at both Nick and Marty's faces, their evident shock at her being so open with them left them speechless. "Hadn't you better give your mother a call, Nick?" Pearl re-routed their thoughts.

"Oh, yes, I do need to, thanks for reminding me," then he added with emphasis, "*Grandma* Pen."

"I like the sound of that," Pearl mused as she gathered the plates and glasses with Marty's help.

Moments later, permission for the sleep-over granted,

Marty and Nick were again in Marty's room planning how to successfully retrieve some of the Nighten's tears from Quixant.

"We need something to hold them in," Marty was saying, "but what?"

"How are we going to catch the bird first?" Nick wondered.

This stopped Marty in his thoughts, "Well can't we just ask him to stop?"

"Suppose he's different from the San Dover?"

"Hmmm, I hadn't thought of that," Marty admitted sheepishly then added, "Boy, am I glad I have you here, I'd be lost completely."

Nick was pleased by Marty's acknowledgement. He had been studying the ingredients again and said, "Isn't a beaker one of those glass things we've seen in Miss Baumer's class?"

"Yeah I think so, why?" wondered Marty.

"It says here 'apply heat under beaker' maybe we could use one to catch some acid tears."

"That's right!" snapping his fingers Marty continued, "Miss Baumer said that beakers can resist most acids because they're made so strong. *Great thinking!*"

Nick was thoroughly pleased at being complimented two times in such quick succession. He was going to try for a third.

"Did Bismorda's lab have any of them in it?"

Marty's face scrunched up in thought, "I'm not sure, do you remember seeing any?"

"I'm not sure either, but it would be a good place to start looking."

"We might even find a net or something we could use to catch the Nighten!" Marty added, "Okay, let's get going."

With this decision made they gathered the things they would need, the key to Quixant, the key to Qualf, and the book of light. Placing them all in the canvas bag, they were ready to go. The key was inserted for Qualf, the click sounded and they were on their way to their next adventure. Back at Bismorda's castle they quickly found a beaker in the lab. Looking at it closely Nick observed, "This looks a little like the San Dover's head! Well if he were doing a weird head stand."

Marty looked at it, the glass vase-like beaker *did* look a little like a San Dover, but he commented, "I think it looks like a San Dover's head with a tube coming out the top."

Nick looked at it again, "Yeah I guess that is more what it looks like."

This settled, they put the beaker in the bag and began a search for a net of some kind. After thumbing through a few books each and being attacked by a small storm cloud, and a gust of wind, they decided to try another route; they would scan the bindings for the books' contents. Some books had nothing written on them, others were written in strange foreign writings, and the rest were very intriguing like *Spells for the Fungi* by Finda Little, *Rooting for Riches* by Cannie Diggit, *Money Can Grow on Trees* by Rich Planter, *Special People Come in Ordinary Packages* by Ima Okey, and *How Long Is Human Life?* by Mathew Usala.

There were no signs of nets anywhere when Nick spoke, "Wait! I think there was a net-bag in the kitchen."

Marty looked at Nick, "I don't remember seeing one."

"I saw it in that closet thing we put the Phlems in, I had to move a bag of roots off the shelf. The bag was like a net, it just might work."

Trusting Nick's memory they moved to the kitchen, opened the larder, and Nick produced a fishnet-like bag containing roots that looked a little like the nutus Phlems, but they were bright green. After dumping these onto the preparation table, they put it with the other items in the canvas bag.

"Should we have some kind of gloves?" Nick asked.

"*Gloves*? What for?" wondered Marty.

"Miss Baumer taught us you're supposed to wear protective covering if you're going to handle strong chemicals like acid."

Grateful that Nick paid attention in Miss Baumer's class, they looked around in the kitchen for something that they could use. Settling on some oven mitts they put them in the bag and were now fully prepared for their quest.

When they reached the door under the bridge Marty thought aloud, "I wonder if the door would work to go straight to Quixant from here."

"Let's not try it, I'd like to not get stuck in another land forever," Nick reasoned.

Clearly this thought hadn't occurred to Marty who opened the door and led the way back into his room. After clicking back he swapped keys and clicked again.

When the door opened a warm tropical breeze blew into the room and enticed them to enter Quixant. There were many new sights that vied for their attention as they entered the land of Quixant. Between the strange vegetation, the brightly colored flowers and birds, and the lapping violet waves of the ocean they almost got whiplash turning their heads so quickly.

Eyes wide, they tried to drink in all of their surroundings, when the piercing shriek at their feet almost made them jump out of their skins. Jumping back they both looked down, there between their feet was a Nighten. They had almost walked right on it.

It was thoroughly put out apparently and was letting them know it. Squawking and flapping its fin arms it was preparing to charge them, like an angry bull. They weren't particularly scared, after all, it was only six inches high, but if they acted quickly they could catch it right now. Whipping out the beaker and net, Marty set the beaker down in the powdery sand as Nick whispered urgently, "the oven mitts!"

Again Marty reached into the bag, grabbed frantically for the oven mitts, but dropped the net. It was quite a sight really, these quick movements actually frightened the Nighten, and it burrowed back into the sand, leaving a simple lump.

Nick, who had watched this now understood what to look for in the sand and explained this, "Marty, they dig a hole and bury themselves in the sand, that's why we didn't see it before," he then pointed at the lump, "see, it looks like a simple pile of sand, but it's really a Nighten's burrow."

Marty scanned the beach, there were hundreds of places that could have held Nightens but since they were sure there was one here, they would use this Nighten for it's tears. Handing one set of oven mitts to Nick and donning the other himself Marty picked up the net. Nick retrieved the beaker from the sand and they approached the lump of sand. Taking careful aim, Marty tossed the net. It landed spread open over the mound, instantly, the Nighten was out of the sand, fighting the net for freedom.

Marty and Nick rushed forward, Marty snatched the net and gathered the Nighten up in the folds of mesh, Nick held out the beaker to catch the magenta tears that were pouring out of its eyes. Catching about one out of every ten left the beaker relatively empty, but Nick's oven mitts were emitting clouds where the acidic tears had hit and begun eating their way through.

Finally, deciding they had gathered enough, Marty let the Nighten out, it promptly began a sort of distress call or something because hundreds of Nightens began emerging from the sand and coming straight at them.

One Nighten alone wasn't scary but hundreds of angry Nightens was truly bone-chilling. Taking this as their cue to leave, Nick and Marty started backing up toward the door. Luckily the door was standing right at the edge of the beach so they reached it just as the Nightens combined into a mob that were all shedding magenta acid tears menacingly.

Slipping through the door they slammed it shut and could hear the pelting of the Nightens flinging themselves against the wood as Marty inserted the key.

The click sounded and silence.

Sitting there on Marty's bedroom carpet it was hard to believe what they had just been through, but the beaker with magenta liquid, oven mitts with burn holes in them, and the seriously damaged net all bore witness that their visit to Quixant had indeed occurred.

They waited for their breathing to slow back down to normal then Nick quipped, "Lucky we didn't need five different Nightens!"

Appreciating Nick's humor, Marty laughed. It helped to ease the shock of the Nighten attack.

"Let's go back to Bismorda's later tonight, I'm pooped," Marty suggested.

"Sounds like a plan," Nick agreed, "Where do you want to stash this stuff?" He held up the beaker and oven mitts riddled with holes.

"Under the bed!" the universal teenage answer.

So they piled all of their loot under the bed and sat back down on the floor to relax until dinner.

After dinner they returned to Marty's room and gathered their provisions for their excursion to Qualf. The canvas bag was loaded with the book of light, the remaining pieces of net, and one set of the oven mitts. Nick donned the second pair to carry the beaker of Nighten's tears and Marty shouldered the bag. They were ready to go. Inserting the key transported them back to Qualf; this was becoming quite a familiar route for them. A short time later after depositing the beaker of tears in the larder they were back in front of the door to the stairs.

Marty took a penny from his pocket in fact it was the

same penny that he had used on his first adventure he considered it his lucky penny now and said, "heads we go up, tails we go down."

"Okay, deal."

The small copper disc flew end over end and suddenly a thought hit Marty out of nowhere, *Why did we run headlong into the mirror on one end of the hall, but we saw our reflection in the other?*

This thought made him gasp and he completely missed the penny as it plinked onto the ground. Nick, who couldn't hear Marty's thoughts, wondered how Marty could miss a simple coin toss.

He spoke, "Are you okay Marty? That wasn't *that* hard to catch." Bending down Nick retrieved the coin and was about to flip it himself when Marty caught his arm. The look on his face frightened Nick a little, "Are you seeing a vision or something? You look kind of spooky."

"Why did we not see our reflection in the mirror?"

This question threw Nick a curveball, "*What*? What mirror?"

"The one at the end of the hall, remember when we were here looking for a pot? We ran right into *that* mirror," he pointed to the far end of the hall, "Why?"

"Because we weren't paying attention," Nick reasoned.

"Look," Marty pointed at the full-length mirror closest to them, his reflection pointed back. "You can see us, right?"

"Yeah, that's what mirrors do."

"Watch," Marty withdrew the book of light from the bag and cracked the cover in the opposite direction. The hallway was still light enough to see by, but the bright stream of light shot to the end of the hall, and didn't come back in the form of a reflection.

Nick stared, comprehension dawning, he turned to Marty. "Is it a window?"

"I'm not sure what it is, but it's *not* a mirror, I know

that for sure."

"Let's go check it out," Nick suggested.

"Yes, let's."

Turning toward the opposite end of the hall they approached the curious non-mirror. As they drew closer, Marty thought of another experiment he could try, he stopped at the bedroom and opened the door. Eerily the door in the mirror opened without anyone there.

So the non-mirror reflected some things but not others.

Marty's theory was shattered.

Or maybe not.

Once they were close to the mirror they both stood facing it and Marty knocked on it. A hollow reverberation echoed somewhere deep behind it.

They looked at each other, "There's some kind of passage behind this, how do we get in?" Marty wondered aloud.

"Let's find a candle!" Nick suggested.

"A *candle*? What for?"

"I read once in a mystery novel that they used a candle and could see air moving by holding the flame up by a solid wall and the flame flickered. Then they found that it was a secret passage."

"We already know it's a secret passage," Marty reasoned.

"Okay, then let's look for a secret lever somewhere."

"What objects are usually secret levers in those books you read?"

"Books!" Even as he said it a thought hit him, which he voiced, "That's what the Zanth sisters were looking for in the lab, they weren't trying to find the spell book. They were trying to open *this* wall!"

"Then there must be something really important in there!" Marty's brain was now racing.

Nick's face was clouded for a moment and then it

cleared, "Of course, Snow White!"

"Snow White, what has *she* got to do with this?" Marty was having a hard time keeping up with Nick's thoughts.

"A magic mirror! One that only responds to specific words or spells."

"Like, 'mirror, mirror on the wall…'" As Marty spoke a large purple cloud formed in the center of the huge mirror.

"Keep going, Marty," Nick urged out the side of his mouth.

"Please let us into the secret hall," Marty tried to make it sound a little more like a spell by rhyming it.

A long low creaking began and the mirror slowly split, right up the center, from floor to ceiling and began opening until there was a path wide enough to enter, then all movement stopped. Once they had recovered from the shock Nick and Marty looked at each other. Without speaking Marty opened the book of light and led the way into the passage. Not even a second after they had cleared the opening the walls creaked again and slowly closed behind them with a deep clang.

Chapter 22
A Hidden Wonder

Luckily the book of light could be adjusted to increase the amount of light provided. Marty opened the cover half way and the passage was bathed in light, revealing an ancient stone corridor leading down a spiral staircase. Each step they took echoed off the heavy stone walls and the light raced just ahead of them disappearing around each turn. When they finally reached the bottom of the stairs they could tell they were deep underground. A cavern opened up in front of them and the light was swallowed in the vastness of it. About twenty-five paces in front of them something reflected the light, not like a mirror, but it lit up in the thick darkness. As they approached it cautiously they had a chance to see it in detail.

Whatever it was, it was set up on a wooden table off of the stone floor. The object looked like a jewelry chest or something similar. It was covered by hundreds of little doors at least they looked like doors, they were fit together closely with little handles. At first glance it looked like a puzzle of some kind, but there was no pattern whatsoever, no picture, just all the colors and shades you could ever imagine all stuck together in this unbelievable cubic tower. Some areas looked like precious jewels that sparkled in the light others looked like rusted metal. It was definitely a curious work of art, if nothing else.

Unable to resist Marty reached out and ran his fingers over the top of it. It was smooth and cool but had the texture of wood. Then he tried one of the panels and the handle instead of opening a tiny door brought out a type of drawer.

He wondered, *what is so special about this thing that it's hidden clear down here?*

When Nick saw the drawer come out he gasped, then muttered, "I wonder…"

Letting Marty hold the light he leaned forward and

looked very closely at the shapes, in miniscule writing, just as he thought, were names, *Reinstalled, Poisentre, Qualf,* and many more.

"Hey Marty, look at this," he pointed at the drawer marked Qualf. "Try putting the key to Qualf in this drawer," he then reached out toward the drawer and received a jolt of electricity.

"*OW*! Hey! What's wrong with this thing?"

"What happened, Nick?"

"It shocked me!"

"Really? Why didn't it do anything to *me*?"

They stood gazing at this strange contraption and wondering why it shocked one but not the other. Finally Nick repeated, without touching it this time, "Try putting the key to Qualf in this drawer."

Marty retrieved the key from the bag, pulled out the drawer marked Qualf, and placed the key inside. Sliding the drawer closed they watched to see what would happen. The knob of the drawer began to glow, a faint green color, but that was it.

"Interesting," Marty commented.

"I wonder if the other keys we have would do anything different," Nick ventured.

"We'll have to bring them next time and see what they do," Marty said as he retrieved the key from the drawer, "Until then I guess we won't know any more about it."

Nick agreed and they turned to leave. Climbing the stairs in silence they realized they were still thinking about the strange collection of drawers. Maybe Misselthorn could help them figure out what it was, but that would have to wait, right now they were going to explore more of the castle. As they reached the top of the stairs the deep creaking sounded and the mirror-door opened once again.

Apparently if you made it in it knew you and you could get out with no problems. They headed back to the stairs and heard the clang behind them of the door closing. Without flipping the coin they mounted the stairs and started upwards. When they came out on the first landing they entered the door and found themselves again in a large hall lined with doors. A quick examination revealed many more elaborate bedroom suites, nothing of real interest to a couple of teenage boys. Re-entering the stairwell they continued climbing up. It took a while to reach another landing. This level took them onto the outer walls of the castle where they could overlook the entire kingdom of Qualf.

They need only to ascend to the turrets, but only one was straight off of the stairs, how would they get to the others? With this question still unanswered they again took to the stairs. After climbing only ten or fifteen stairs they came to another landing. This time as they went out they found themselves on the opposite side of the castle, looking down on the landscape from one of the lower turrets.

How did *that* happen? This castle really *was* magic. They had to keep reminding themselves but it certainly was confusing. As they continued their search they found that every turret in the castle emerged from the same staircase, impossible to believe, but true nonetheless! The top turret brought them to a dizzying height, and they felt giddy looking down, this would be such a cool castle to live in!

Watching the sun set from this height was exhilarating and probably a once in a lifetime event so they enjoyed every minute of it. Once the horizon had blurred to a deep purple they decided to descend to the lower areas of the castle. Marty took out the light book and led the way back down to the main level.

Nick spoke, "I'm hungry, can we eat something before we continue?"

Marty's stomach growled in response, "Sure, let's see what they've got!"

Upon entering the kitchen the light hit the preparation table first, they could see the bright green nutus roots.

"Let's try one of those," Marty suggested.

Nick was game, so they tried to figure how to open it. They settled on smashing it with a mallet they had found hanging on a hook with the other utensils. Peeling the shell away they revealed the juicy center, it was a deep green, had a chewy texture, and it tasted like lime candy. After consuming that, they opened the larder, sliced off a few pieces from various cheeses and meats, and sat down for their feast. Tasting these foreign foods was quite an experience. Even though they looked like regular meats and cheeses, the tastes were vastly different from what the boys were used to. Some of the cheeses squeaked in their teeth, others tasted of fruit; it was a rare occasion when they found a cheese that *tasted* like any cheese they had eaten before. The cured meats were similar to the cheeses in the fact that they were each exotic, but with the meats there wasn't a single one that tasted familiar in any way.

Once they were full they picked up the book of light and the canvas bag and were on the trail of exploration again. Going downstairs was stranger than going upstairs, maybe it was because it was dark, but the castle seemed to echo more. Turning the last time around the central pillar they came out onto the single lower landing. A corridor that was already well lit extended out in front of them. Marty closed the book of light and they stepped further into the basement of the castle.

Lining the walls in rainbows of color they could see the bindings of an enormous collection of books. Walking slowly along Marty and Nick were overwhelmed with the sheer number of volumes, they hadn't even looked at the subjects they contained. Marty glanced toward the end of the hall and noticed there was a door. As he approached it he could see it was a very modern door to be found in this castle out of the medieval time. It was made of metal, he turned and called to Nick who was studying the shelves, "Hey come here quick, let's see where this door leads."

Nick hustled toward Marty as he turned the knob. The scene that greeted them neither teen expected. A boat was tied to a simple pier jutting out from the door. They stepped onto the wooden pier, followed closely by the creaking of planks, and made their way to the waiting boat. It was then that they noticed they were under the stars not under the castle. Brushing this aside they climbed into the boat, untied it from the pier, and pushed off. Suddenly a heavy fog rolled in around them and Marty remembered, this was from his dream!

They rowed for a long while, not exactly sure where they were going, when off in the distance a light flickered into view.

"Let's go toward that light!" Nick hollered, his voice trotting off into the darkness.

Marty sat still, not trusting himself to speak; he was having another of his dreams come true. In the back of his mind the Acne Pimple dream was roaring, if his other dreams came true *that* one had to too, right? The fog parted just then to reveal the large candle on the island of Bicolotern.

Marty had to tell Nick, "Nick, *this is from my dream!*"

Thinking for a minute Nick paused, "Wait, you mean *that's* the Checkpohmer?"

Marty nodded.

"See, I told you your dreams come true!" Nick was convinced, and suddenly he too felt the foreboding of the Acne Pimple dream.

They refocused their energy on their current situation and rowed to the shore. As they landed they congratulated each other, pulled the boat a safe distance onto the shore, and walked the short distance to where the towering candle stood overlooking the island. The plants they passed, like the ones in his dream, were growing books, as they got closer the voice came over them in a soothing wave, *"Don't pick the red, pick the blue."*

Nick froze, "That voice sounds so familiar!"

Marty smiled, nodding, he would let him figure it out himself, but he re-emphasized the warning they had just heard, "Stay away from the red ones Nick, just trust me."

Then he turned his attention to the lime green books of his dream. A growling sound behind him made Marty turn around as he did he flashed back, a true déjà vu. Nick was poking at a bush of red books and suddenly it snapped at him. He fell back, scuttling with his hands and feet somewhat like a crab.

Marty ran to his side to help him up, "Why didn't you listen?" was all Marty got out.

The look on Nick's face was enough to say he didn't need any reprimand, muttering to himself, "What's *wrong* with me? I can't seem to follow simple instructions!"

Marty overheard him and broke in, "I should have stayed with you, I knew you would do that, maybe I could have stopped you."

"I don't need a baby-sitter!" Nick snapped.

"Sorry," Marty retreated then paused, mustered a little anger of his own and said, "fine, you do as you like, I'll be over here when you're done pouting."

Leaving Nick sitting in the sand Marty walked back to where he had been before all of the chaos with the plant had so rudely interrupted him. The lime green books ranged in subject matter from fairy tails to philosophy this surprised Marty for some reason. He had expected these books to all be on exotic topics, but now that he found they weren't, he accepted that too.

Marty had moved on to a flowering yellow plant, he could see random illustrations taking shape in the folds, he had always wondered if the writing came first or if it was the pictures, this was his answer.

As he was admiring the beauty of this plant Nick's voice sounded from behind him, "I'm sorry Marty..."

For a minute Marty thought that was it then Nick continued, "I should have listened, I don't know why I don't pay attention when other people tell me stuff, maybe I just have to find out for myself," Nick mused.

Marty shrugged and added softly so as not to offend, "This time it wasn't *that* important, I guess the bush probably wouldn't have killed you, but I hope when it comes to more important things you *will* listen, that's all."

On that note they decided to head back, they had now seen Bicolotern, the garden of books, and the final mystery of Bismorda's castle, it was time for sleep. Boarding the skiff they pushed off and began rowing back toward the pier where they had started. The fog had dissipated and it was now a clear beautiful night, allowing for an amazing boat ride. Mirror-like, the water spread out in front of them, reflecting the stars and moon, making it seem like they were in space.

Miraculously the pier materialized, only when it did did they notice anything unusual, there was no land in sight, just the pier and a door, out in the middle of this body of water whatever it was. This was truly an amazing and confusing world. It sure kept you on your toes! After Marty and Nick re-secured the boat to the pier they entered the door back into the basement hallway of Bismorda's castle.

On their return trip through the cavernous room they saw a sign engraved over the door, the first half was in the same ancient slashes as on the spell book, the other was written in English it said, *"Checksuejeeper's Lair."*

Exchanging questioning glances as they both wondered what a Checksuejeeper finally they decided they would have to ask Misselthorn. Retracing their way through the castle with the use of the book of light they headed home. Outside again the moon was high and Marty and Nick could tell it was late. Upon arriving at the door under the bridge weariness finally settled in, it had been a long day and they wanted only to sleep.

The key was inserted, the click sounded, and they were back in Marty's room. Grabbing a pillow and a few blankets each, they curled up on the floor and were asleep without another word.

Chapter 23
Lights, Camera, Anxiety!

Wednesday, November 7, 1990

Following their adventurous Friday the weekend went by peacefully. Monday and Tuesday were busy with the technical rehearsal and dress rehearsal, the cast was now primed and ready for their four performance run. Today's matinee was to be for the elementary schools of the area and tonight's show would be their first real performance with a paying crowd.

Excitement was flowing through the whole student body to the point of distraction, even though the cast consisted of less than fifty, they were going to have a lot of guests today so they had to show off how grown-up they were. Elementary students began arriving in their school groups rosy and windswept from the chilly November outside. Filing through the hallways their eyes grew wide at the large halls and the lockers, they would whisper until their teachers would shush them. The parade of children continued into the multi-purpose room where chairs were set up to accommodate the more than five-hundred young audience members. Backstage the hushed frenzy had been underway for more than an hour, but the news that their audience was filing in added fuel to the fire. Running through silent warm-ups Marty and Nick were both suffering from an acute case of butterflies in their stomachs. The cast gathered for one last round of encouragement and then separated to their positions in the wings.

The curtains raised and the show proceeded, the Darling family said good-bye to mother and father as they left for the evening, Peter Pan entered, enticed the children to come to Never Land and they all flew out the window to follow him. Flying was achieved with harnesses and wires, but the elementary children were left in awe, each one wishing that they could be the ones flying along with Peter.

The remainder of the show went very well and the cast was rightfully excited for the evening production.

Hours passed like minutes, the show for the second time that day had been completed successfully this time to a sold out crowd of eight hundred.

Nick and Marty congratulated each other as the curtains closed and they moved out with the rest of the cast to thank the audience members for coming. Charlotte and Pearl found Marty and Janet and Thomas found Nick, after expressing congratulations they went home leaving the boys with the rest of the cast.

As soon as the parents were gone a notepad and pen were shoved under Nick's nose. He lowered the pad and found Monica standing there with a smile on her face, "Can I have your autograph? I lost mine..." she said sweetly.

The meaning was lost on Nick who was already scribbling a note as he stared at Monica, then he handed the pad back.

She glanced at it quickly, in his scrawling teenage penmanship, he had written, "I may be the star, but I'm *your* biggest fan."

Blushing she looked back at him, he smiled and found a spot on his costume that was needing some serious attention, so he stared at it, not daring to meet her eyes again. By the time he looked up, she was gone, he hoped this would be the start of a good friendship, but he would have to wait and see.

Wednesday, December 5, 1990

Before they knew it the run of the show was over. It had been a huge success, but it left a void for those who had been in the cast and schoolwork was just not the same. They had been bitten by the bug of show business, Nick and Marty knew they could never go back to normal. It wasn't even the fame that the show had caused, it was the excitement of the delivery, the build up and release of that excitement, it was…a completed mission.

With the completion of one mission their minds turned back to a much larger and more important one, to save Bismorda's kingdom. The successful collection of the Phlems and Nighten tears had propelled them to continue searching for other ingredients albeit half-heartedly during the musical. Here they were in the beginning of December, and they had only found two; when suddenly they stumbled on a third quite by accident.

Scanning through the beginning of the map book Marty was surprised when two pages stuck together. This clue wasn't lost on Marty and he quickly scanned down the page's contents and found what he was seeking…the three-toed Garth! Reading aloud he continued, "The Garth is found in the jungles of Poisentre. This monkey-like creature is cross-eyed so it frequently becomes lost and therefore is perpetually seeking a home. Making nests out of long jungle grasses, the Garth is prone to sleep at the base of tall trees nestled among the roots. Known by its distinct coloring and unusual wanderings the Garth has become a much sought after creature. Once a thriving population existed, but because of outside forces it has become endangered and now fewer than five hundred exist worldwide."

Here Marty opened the stuck pages revealing a scene that had patches of light in a deep green backdrop. Suddenly the shadows began moving at the base of a large tree and they saw a flash of pink, and then the shadow was still once more. So, the Garth was pink, or some part of the Garth was pink they would have to look closely at the roots of the trees when they arrived in Poisentre. The opposite page contained some very strange writing, even more so than the scratches of the spell book.

Marty and Nick were wondering what language it might be when out of the corner of his eye Marty caught sight of the door in the top left corner of the page. This one was made of reeds or bamboo tied together like a raft Marty looked up as Nick returned to his side with the tweezers, he had sensed Marty would need them and had silently gone to find them in the drawer. Marty's motions were fascinating to Nick who watched intently, until the full-sized key appeared on Marty's outstretched finger.

This key was shiny brass with a flat head, shaped like a coin. Engraved on the face of it was the head of a Garth, at least they assumed it was a Garth they had yet to see a picture of one, but the engraving was cross-eyed and looked something like a monkey so it fit the description. The key had three teeth at the end, two on one side one on the opposite; all of them were small and flat. Glancing again at the picture Marty tried to guess what the weather would be like. Since it was a jungle it *should* be warm, right?

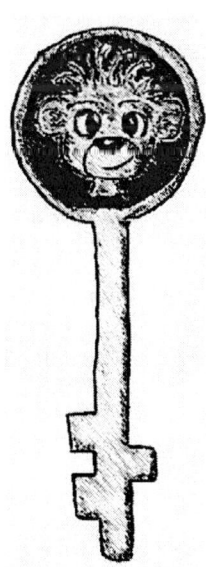

He looked at Nick who was deep in thought, "What do you think we'll need?"

The question brought Nick back to reality as he remembered, "Poisentre has a scope at Bismorda's, that's one of the names you read out when we were there. I was just trying to remember where I had heard that name before, and it just came to me."

Marty smiled, "Good thinking, or should I say remembering, I hadn't even thought of that, but now that you mention it, you're right there is one there. Let's go back to Qualf and see what the weather is like in Poisentre."

With the mention of Qualf Nick's hand came up, "Wait, I just remembered something else, we never asked Misselthorn about the sign at Bismorda's."

"Right again, let's do that quickly, then we can be on our way."

Nick fished the spell book out from under the bed and flipped it open. Misselthorn wasn't there again and upon further inspection they could see dust and cobwebs lining her room.

Misselthorn was missing!

Chapter 24
A Furry Close Escape

Misselthorn's disappearance added a new problem, where had she gone? Or worse, who had kidnapped her? Closing the book Nick looked at Marty, they agreed silently to set off for Bismorda's castle. Coming to the top of the hill as the sun stroked the castle they were again hit with a sense of foreboding. Had they left the door open when they left the last time? No, they were sure they hadn't, yet it stood slightly open, which could only mean one thing, *intruders*!

Since no one else was left in the kingdom their thoughts immediately went to the Zanth sisters, were they still inside? They hadn't brought the mirror! They would be defenseless against the OhRa! Despite their fear they mounted the stairs silently and crept to the front door.

Marty whispered, "Squint your eyes, if you see them, close your eyes tight! Don't open them for any reason!"

Nick nodded and they both narrowed their eyes to mere slits. Having reached the door, they entered cautiously. No sound met their ears, but they couldn't be too careful. On their mucous membrane, the Zanth sisters made no sound anyway. Quickly they went to the sitting room, peeked in and retrieved another small mirror that Marty remembered seeing in the drawer of the side table.

Now that they were armed they felt safer but they wouldn't feel completely safe until they were done with the Zanth sisters entirely! Their next destination was the observatory, so they went there without delay. They found the telescope for Poisentre and froze mid-stride, hanging from the eyepiece was a note. It had been attached somehow but as Marty took hold of it there was no resistance as it came free in his hand. Swallowing over the lump in his throat he read aloud:

"Two ingredients you have found, the third is on its way,

To gather all successfully we can't await the day.
Since Misselthorn couldn't stop blabbing to you,
We were forced to take her don't cry, "boo hoo".
You see we know you won't succeed
Dark forces will stop the will to read.
You might be infected still, with it's simple charm
But others now succumb to us without a slight alarm.
Reading was meant for those
Who had a will to think,
But you see the world today
Would rather sit and stink.
The library is a place
Where no one wants to go
Anything that requires thought
Is not allowed to grow.
Sit down with your computer or your TV screen
Let us take from you the books you'll soon forget you've seen.
They're old and smelly no one likes to have them in their house,
In fact they're like vermin now like rats or the small mouse.
The truth of the matter is it takes up too much time
To sit with children and to read a simple nursery rhyme.
It's much more fun to watch a show or play computer games
The world won't need the books they cannot spell their names!
You have probably figured out that once a month is all,
The adventures you're allowed are far between and small.
So turn away, forget this quest, leave well enough alone,
No one will know the difference if this is never done.
But if you decide to proceed the harder tasks will come
The dangers multiply for you and you won't know where from.
Good-bye Nick and Marty, until we meet again
That is if you still hope you have something else to gain.

Signed,
The OhRa

Down at the bottom scrawled in a hurried hand it said,
"Help us, only you can save us now, the OhRa is gaining strength."

The Zanth sisters were now calling out for help!

This newest message was very threatening almost like a challenge to keep them from going on, but with renewed determination they agreed that they would not give up.

"That sounds *scary*," Nisha lamented, "I think *I* would have given up after getting that letter."

Nicholas Chrismon looked over the book that he was reading and into the frightened, but sincere eyes of the spunky brunette. "Do you really feel we *could* give up?"

"Of course they couldn't," Saul confirmed, "Bismorda's kingdom needed them."

"Not to mention the Zanth sisters," Menalee replied softly, "they're calling out for help in that letter, they really don't want to be under the OhRa's spell."

"You're right Menalee, Grisele and Mopel didn't want to be cursing everyone all the time, they had started out just wanting more power and that power overtook them."

"Did they get free of the spell?" Wendy inquired.

"Well, that part comes later, we'll have to wait and see," Weston reasoned, "that would ruin the rest of the story, right Mr. Chrismon?"

"Call me Nick, please, and yes, it would definitely spoil the remainder of the story if you knew the outcome now," Nick agreed.

"Can we get back to the story then?" Alden requested, "I don't know about you guys, but I really want to hear more about Marty and Nick's adventures."

"Me too," agreed a chorus of voices, everyone, in fact, except Kimber and Billy.

Nick noted the lack of enthusiasm in these two youth and wanted to comment on it, however majority rules and so he picked up the book and began reading again.

"So *that's* why we only find one adventure at a time, and they're spaced a month apart!" Nick was studying the note again, "The OhRa wants us to get bored and give up the search for ingredients. I wonder if the spell is more than just to cure the Acne Pimple. What do *you* think Marty?"

"Even if it only works for the Acne Pimple it would be worth it to me," Marty explained matter-of-factly.

"Yeah, you're right, let's get to Poisentre!"

"Let's look at it first," Marty reminded him.

Glancing into the telescope a beautiful tropic green jungle met Marty's eye, the sun was high and it looked very warm compared to the snow-covered ground back in Scat-town. With this in mind they set off for Poisentre, and they wouldn't return without the hairs of the Garth. Under the bridge again Marty thought aloud, "With both keys here do you think we could get to Poisentre, return directly here, and then get back home?"

Nick shrugged, "I guess we can try it, the Garth doesn't look nearly as scary as the Nighten turned out to be."

Marty didn't mention that the Nighten hadn't *looked* scary at all, but boy had looks been deceiving! Instead he inserted the key to Poisentre and turned it with a soft click. Now instead of entering his room they stepped out into patchy shade under the heavy jungle canopy.

Exotic sounds quickly enveloped them, a strange call from overhead made them look up just in time to see a multi-colored bird with an enormous beak take flight. It surprised them both when it fell from the sky with a thud and looking toward the ground they found a large reptile crawling along slowly. Had this monster thing *eaten* that beautiful bird?

They continued to watch the slithery walk of the lizard and right before their eyes the short and stubby legs of the lizard grew long and sleek and covered in fur and the tail quickly elongated and also became furry. The scales turned into spotted fur and Marty and Nick became frozen as they were caught in the yellowish gaze of a jungle cat! With fluid movements the cat began to circle the boys causing them to back up into each other seeking refuge.

However, all they found was another trembling body

pressed close to their own. At the completion of its third circle the cat crouched and with a low menacing growl, pounced. Quickly closing their eyes the boys prayed for a miracle.

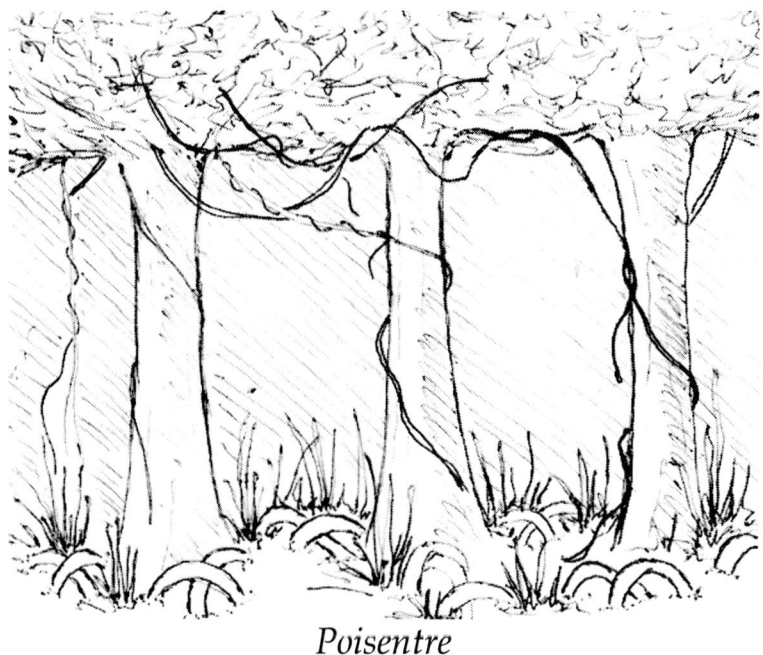

Poisentre

Instead of feeling the heavy body of the cat land on them they heard a flutter of wings. Again opening their eyes they saw the same multi-colored bird making its way deeper into the jungle on its rainbow plumage.

Slowly turning to face each other Nick and Marty questioned what had just happened with only their eyes as the speakers.

They had indeed been lucky.

Shaking off the shock of the last few minutes they both became aware of their surroundings once more. Various shapes began to move among the deep purple-blue shadows and they were sure they could make out what must be at least one Garth, but they couldn't be positive until they got closer.

As they walked along, picking a path carefully through

the thick undergrowth, they kept hearing new sounds some of which made them look at each other in alarm.

Drawing closer to the trees they were surprised when a pair of eyes suddenly appeared and began following their every movement. Stopping in their tracks Marty whispered to Nick out the side of his mouth, "Do you see what I see?"

Nick whispered in return, "Yeah, it's cross-eyed!"

They had almost stumbled onto another of their ingredients! Edging nearer to the shadows cautiously they could finally make out a shape, it was covered in a dark blue-purple fur that matched the shadows precisely, it did have the form of a monkey, but no tail and it had two fingers and a thumb on each hand and three toes on each foot. The Garth slowly sat up, and a bright flash of pink flared from the shadows, Marty realized that the fur on its belly was the color and texture of pink cotton candy. Marty found himself fighting the urge to reach out and tickle it's tummy it was extremely cute and the fact that it was cross-eyed only added to its irresistible charm. Apparently it couldn't see very clearly because they had come within three feet of it without a look of fear crossing its face. It sat up like a human almost, it was squatted with its knees pulled up to it's chest and it's hands rested on the fur covered knees.

The Garth

It looked regal, as if they should bow. Long hairs poked out of its head begging to be felt so Marty reached out and stroked the Garth's head. It turned its face to him affectionately and gave out something like a purr that Marty could feel from his finger tips all the way down to his feet. Nick approached on the opposite side and switched off with Marty feeling the soft fur of its head run through their fingers, the purring increased in volume. Before they realized it they were completely surrounded by wide-eyed Garths all wanting the same attention.

Each one was petted in turn, but they began to push in closer begging to be chosen again, Marty finally realized they had to try and get out of there as quickly as they could or they would literally be smothered with love. Grabbing Nick's hand he motioned with his head for them to pull slowly away, Nick followed still patting heads along the way. The crowd of Garths followed along beside them brushing up against their newfound friends. As the bamboo door came back into view they made a run for it, this quick movement startled the Garths.

Looking over their shoulders Nick and Marty saw the Garths wandering back and forth blindly seeking the loving pats. It was kind of pitiful to watch them collide with each other, but before Marty and Nick could be drawn back to comfort them they remembered their close escape from their furry hug with death.

Through the bamboo door they stopped on the banks of the river and combed their clothes free of the purple and pink hairs of the Garth colony. Before they headed up to the castle again, Marty re-inserted the key to Qualf and with the soft click again peered into his bedroom with a sigh of relief. No matter how much he wanted to crawl into bed and fall asleep he realized he had more important things he had to do first. The Garth hair had to be stored at Bismorda's castle with the other ingredients. A quick trip to and from Bismorda's castle had them back in Marty's room in less than an hour and now instead of falling asleep they had to focus on homework for the following day.

It was getting close to Christmas and Santa Claus didn't give cool presents to kids with bad grades!

Chapter 25
The True Christmas Spirit

Friday, December 21, 1990

The two weeks prior to Christmas break flew by and now as Nick and Marty made their way to Grandma Pentel's house they could feel the two weeks of freedom spread out before them like a great beacon of light. Like a Checkpohmer! As they entered Grandma Pentel's front room they were greeted by piles of Christmas decorations.

"Hello, Grandma, we're home!" Marty called.

Pearl materialized from behind one of the stacks. Today she was wearing a festive red and green plaid housecoat with matching slippers. "Hi boys, come give Grandma Pen a squeeze!" She threw her arms wide and hugged them both. Then she explained, "I thought we could decorate for the holiday, since it's next week and I can't do it alone. We'll get everything ready and then tonight we can go get a tree with your mom. What do you think?"

Nick was secretly jealous that his family wasn't like this, his mom always decorated on December first and never let anyone else help. Their tree was artificial and it remained decorated year round, they just put a bag over it and put it in the back room. The only time they had to take apart the tree was when they moved. Nick was sick of the fake limbs and unrealistic metal stump; he wanted a real tree just like in the old movies. He tuned back in to Grandma Pentel's instructions of where she wanted which decorations. For the next few hours they were happy to help hang lights in the window, garlands on the fireplace, paper snowflakes, and set out the porcelain nativity set. They also took care to choose the colors they were going to decorate the tree in.

Charlotte arrived home to find the halls thoroughly decked indeed. They all went to a nearby tree lot, Nick included, selected a beautiful pine tree and after the employees that were dressed as elves finished tying it to the Tercel headed home to decorate it singing Christmas carols at the top of their lungs to the radio.

Monday, December 24, 1990

'Twas the day before Christmas at Grandma Pen's house,
The air was smelling of pie and roast grouse.
Marty and Nick were restless with glee
The presents were stacked 'neath the 'real' Christmas tree.
Grandma was bustlin' in a festive housecoat
Nick dreamed of a car with remote.
Marty expected some books filled with tales
Their thoughts were far from witches or scales.
Then evening came with a knock at the door
The Chrismon's were here and the kids on the floor.
All gathered around Grandma Pen and the Bible,
If strangers looked in this might look quite tribal.
But Pearl opened to the Gospel of Luke
Then told of the angel, it wasn't a fluke.
Jesus was born and the star it appeared
This was where all of their eyes filled with tears.
The thoughts of their presents flew far away
As they heard of the babe asleep on the hay.
The circle was whole, would never be broken
No word was said, not whispered or spoken.
Twinkling lights on the tree they did glow
And outside the ground all covered with snow
Was far removed from the babe and the stable
But quietly they all kneeled round the table
Gave thanks to God for the star, His own Son,
And vowed to remember how it all had begun.
They quietly rose and hugged one another
This circle was close like sister and brother.
Next day they would meet, share what they'd been given

But now by a glow they were secretly driven.
This small group of six would bundle up warm
Then go out to carol and bring Christmas charm.
With things said, for the night they were parted
So on the morrow they could get started.
Marty fell to sleep with a dream
It wasn't about cakes covered with cream
Instead he saw on the edge of Scat-town
A small apartment all old and run-down
Inside was a boy dressed in black clothes
He had nothing new to wear except those.
A sound made him rise and go to the door
His eyes dropped down and looked at the floor,
There piled neatly in boxes and bags
Were colorful clothes, not old black rags.
His smile was warm and his face was light
With this good dream Marty slept through the night.

Tuesday, December 25, 1990

Christmas morning dawned and Marty leaped out of his bed. Unlike other children around the world on this morning he was excited to see which presents he could give away. In his mind he could still see Ben Wildern the big kid from Mrs. Penn's class. His smile drove Marty upstairs with gusto; there had to be *something* he could give him.

Usually Marty hated getting clothes for Christmas, but he found himself hoping that he *did* get clothes and they were too big for him so he could give them to Ben. As Marty got to the top of the stairs the soft glow of the Christmas tree lights warmed the scene. There were boxes covered in festive paper piled all over, the stockings were brimming with trinkets and fruit, and Marty noticed that there were six stockings.

The Chrismon's stuff was over here! Santa sure was a very smart man, he knew that they would be coming over first thing, so he just delivered everything to Grandma Pentel's.

As he sat on the floor looking at all the splendid gifts a soft voice behind him made him turn around, "Merry Christmas, Marty."

"Merry Christmas, Mom!"

He stood up, went to her, they hugged, and then they stood looking at the quiet glow together.

"It's been a major change for you to come here, I hope you're doing okay with it."

Marty looked up and could see his mom's eyes were glistening, he reassured her, "Mom, I *love* it here. I've got Nick and you and Grandma Pen and all my new teachers. I don't know why, but I have a feeling I wouldn't be doing this well if I had gone to Central."

"Honest?" Charlotte turned to face him.

"Honest!" He hugged her again, he didn't say his next thoughts, *I wonder how dad is doing.*

As if hearing his thoughts Charlotte spoke, "I hope he's half as happy with his new life as I am with *mine.*"

"Dad?" Marty asked the question even though it was obvious who she was talking about.

She nodded quietly, Marty could tell, it still hurt, but there was something else, a sparkle that was back in her eye. He hadn't seen her eyes sparkle, really sparkle, since he was very young, and he realized that it had been smothered in the failing marriage with his father. But now that Samuel Whimpel was out of her life the spark had been re-ignited.

For some reason Marty's thoughts went to Mr. Candletier and the large candle on Bicolotern. That was one of the things that had started the flame for Marty, that and Bismorda. His thoughts reached out to her, *I'm trying. I haven't given up. I haven't stopped. I just can't fight the OhRa's spell. I can only get one ingredient at a time and soon Nick and I will go after the fourth one. Don't lose hope!*

Then suddenly he spoke the next thought, "I love you."

"I love you too, sweetheart," Charlotte gave him one

more squeeze.

Marty hadn't meant to say that out loud, but he let his mom believe it had been meant for her. He *did* love his mom after all. The thing that surprised Marty was that he loved Bismorda too, not in a romantic way, but they had a special bond and it was more than plain friendship because it was different than how he felt towards Nick.

With these thoughts tumbling around in his head he turned as Grandma Pentel came into the room, "Merry Christmas, Grandma."

Charlotte echoed, "Merry Christmas, Mom."

"Merry Christmas you two, come give Grandma Pen a Christmas squeeze!" Pearl bubbled.

Before any presents were opened the three of them moved into the kitchen and started getting Christmas breakfast ready. Marty had just finished setting the table when there was a knock at the door. Racing to the front of the house assured Marty would get to see Nick's face when he saw the lights and presents.

He opened the door, "Merry Christmas, Chrismons!"

This was the first time Marty had used those two words in the same sentence so close to together and he realized they were very similar.

They all called back, "Merry Christmas, Marty!" as they stepped in out of the cold.

Pink cheeks and rosy noses testified how chilly it had gotten during the night.

Glancing out on the fresh coat of snow Marty realized they had all walked. They didn't live far it was true, but it was *really* cold!

Janet followed Marty's eyes, "We didn't drive because the snow was so beautiful. We didn't want to be the ones to ruin it."

Behind her back Thomas rolled his eyes but smiled down at her, Marty could tell Nick's parents were still very much in love. They took a quick peek in the back living room where the presents were piled high and then made their way into the kitchen to be welcomed and again wished 'Merry Christmas' by Charlotte and Pearl.

Over breakfast Marty asked, "So, who are we going to carol to today?"

This wasn't expected so early, but it was welcomed anyway, "Did you have someone in mind, Marty?" Charlotte wondered aloud.

Taking a large forkful of hash browns he nodded.

"Oh, *who*?" Pearl was now openly curious.

Marty swallowed, "The Wilderns."

"You mean Ben from Mrs. Penn's class?" Nick volunteered.

"Is that Bruce Wildern's son?" Charlotte asked Pearl.

Surprisingly Pearl nodded, "Don't know of any other, that family has been through so much, first Cathy was lost to cancer, then Bruce went to the bottle. Thank goodness he's on the mend, but heaven knows what that poor boy of his has been through."

"I was thinking," this brought the attention back to Marty, "instead of caroling to them we could leave presents, but we won't let them know who did it so they can't say no to our gifts."

"That sounds like a very Christian thing to do," Pearl agreed.

Around the table all heads were nodding, Marty's idea was accepted unanimously. Finishing breakfast took only a few more minutes then they adjourned to the living room to open their gifts. The whole time they opened gifts they were on the lookout for things they could each give to the Wilderns. Marty had received one green and one red long sleeved t-shirt that would have been huge on him but looked to be perfect for Ben's large frame. Thomas Chrismon had been given pants that were much too short for him, but in measuring them against Marty's frame it was discovered they would be almost perfect for Ben.

Charlotte would give them her new toaster, Janet would give her new salad bowl, and Grandma Pentel gave up her new frying pan. Quietly Nick's new remote control car was placed on the growing pile of gifts. They all knew how much of a sacrifice this was for him, but he insisted that Ben get something fun to play with. With the presents all unwrapped and stacked neatly in piles the group now set to the task of re-wrapping the gifts for the Wildern's. New paper was retrieved from the small room and while Marty, Nick, and Thomas wrapped, Janet, Charlotte, and Pearl went and gathered canned items and some of Pearl's home-bottled food to make up a care package.

Such a care package wouldn't be the same without some of Grandma Pentel's homemade rolls so Pearl took out a fresh dishtowel and wrapped a dozen rolls in it. This was the finishing touch, now they were ready to go. Luckily Pearl knew where they lived so they all bundled up, each taking an armful, and they made a quick path to the apartments just two blocks up Farnsworth.

It was still early so they were quite sure they would be able to do this undetected. Once they arrived at the apartment building they stood huddled together as Nick and Marty made silent trips up to the second story where the Wildern's apartment was located. As soon as all the gifts were in place Marty and Nick high-tailed it back to their families and they all headed home to get ready for their morning caroling to the neighbors.

Snow began falling on their return trip and quickly covered any tracks that they had left so a few hours later when Ben and his father found the gifts and looked for any clues as to who might have left them, there were no signs anywhere. Grandma Pentel had prepared some 'goodie plates' as she called them and they delivered these to the houses around the neighborhood while singing favorites like *Jingle Bells* and *Silent Night*.

A few hours later they returned once again rosy cheeked and chilled through, but with warm hearts. They gathered around the kitchen table for hot cocoa and spiced apple cider and reveled in the memories they had just created. When asked, Nick only had one regret about giving Ben his car, he would have loved to see his face when he opened it. This had truly been a Christmas that none of them would *ever* forget.

A few days after Christmas, Marty was out shoveling snow when he saw Ben walking with his father. They waved and smiled at each other. Marty felt a rush of warmth inside, he had been a good influence in the life of one of his peers. He hoped he would get to know Ben better in the coming months. He seemed like a very genuine person, but he had had to deal with so many difficult things at such a young age it had made him seem older. Marty couldn't wait to see him at school in one of his new shirts.

Monday, December 31, 1990

The last day of the year was a mixture of joy and pain, joy because they were going to start a fresh new year, but pain because of all the changes that had taken place over the last year. One thing was for sure, some of the pain would not be repeated; at least they hoped not. The divorce papers had finally been sent and were now processed, Charlotte and Samuel Whimpel were now *officially* divorced.

Interestingly enough Marty was happy for his mom and felt bad for his father, because he no longer had any claim to their happiness. One day, somewhere in the future, he might look his father up again, but for now he would not worry about it, he would just be grateful for a loving mother and grandmother. They gave him the affection he needed.

Tonight they would gather again, the six of them, to

ring in the New Year together. Nick had already received permission to sleep over after the festivities. They had discussed in detail what they would do in the remaining six days of vacation. Their fourth hunt for the vital ingredients needed to cure Marty and save the ever diminishing population of the land of books was their first priority.

Charlotte had purchased some simple noise makers and they gathered around the T.V. watching New York City's Time Square where the large apple had begun it's descent with the crowd cheering and the countdown going.

They joined in on the final, "ten...nine...eight..." 1990 was fading fast, "four...three...two...one...*Happy New Year!!!*"

Cheering and blowing or twirling their noisemakers the small group at 5443 S. Farnsworth Avenue welcomed the New Year with open arms as if to say, *Give us a squeeze 1991!*

Chapter 26
Oh Yeah? Well, **Cotolspik** *to You TOO!*

Thursday, January 3, 1991

Three days into the New Year Marty and Nick found two more pages in the map book stuck together, that's when they knew their next adventure was about to start. Before Marty pried the pages apart he turned to read about where they would be going and what ingredient they were about to find.

Nick scanned the page faster and whispered, "The Batwort!"

Sure enough, the section was on the Cotolspikian Batwort. Marty started at the top of the page and began reading aloud, "Cotolspik is a sparsely forested region near the human land of Bulgaria it is the nesting spot of the Batwort and has been declared a safe zone in all three worlds."

"*Three* worlds?" Nick interrupted.

"That's what it says," Marty answered, "I wonder what it means?"

"Well ours is one," Nick reasoned.

"And the world of books is another," Marty calculated.

"What could be the *third* world?" They both asked aloud.

With this question still unanswered Marty began reading aloud again to try and refocus on the current situation, "The Batwort is a furry mammal, with a brownish grey coat and green, scaly wing-like ears. Each winter it grows a thick coat of fur and sheds the skin on its ears, similar to a snake. Instinctively the Batwort never leaves Cotolspik."

He took a breath and continued, "Its main sources of food are the mossy lichens that grow on the trees, and the acorn-like nuts of the tickelink bush. The Batwort nests high in the native Cotolspik Permet tree and only descends at night to gather food. Being an incredibly clean creature the Batwort buries the shells, shed skin from its ears, and any other of its waste products using its webbed feet."

"That sounds like quite a cool creature!" Nick commented; he too had re-routed his brain to the problem at hand.

"Let's check its picture out," Marty began prying even as he spoke.

The pages separated and a scene with some trunks of trees and small shrubs appeared. As they watched the page objects began fluttering to the ground, they looked closer and could see nut shells and something like a see-through sandwich bag crumpled in a pile at the base of the tree. Marty scoured the opposite page and found a wooden door caked over with dirt and leaves in the center of the page. Working with the tweezers he soon had the door open and a new key growing on his finger.

The newest key was a shiny silver white, the head was O-shaped with small wings sticking out from the sides, and the teeth area was shaped like a shovel. These keys just kept getting more unusual, but each one was fascinating to look at, Marty and Nick took turns studying it, and then Nick spoke, "So when do we go?"

This time Marty thought ahead, "What are we going to need to get some of those skins?"

"Isn't Bulgaria somewhere in Europe?" Nick questioned.

"I think so, why?"

"If it is, then it's covered in snow there right now, like it is here, so we would need a shovel and warm clothes." Nick reasoned sensibly.

"Okay, we can't exactly go get a shovel from outside and bring it down here, do you think there might be one at Bismorda's palace?"

"Probably not, but one of the farmhouses might have a

shovel of some kind," Nick suggested.

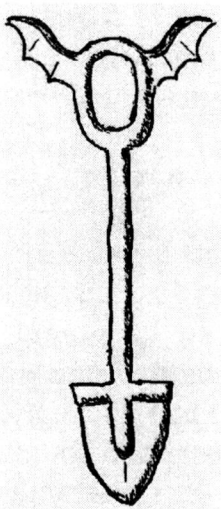

"We haven't gone to any of the other homes in Qualf, maybe you're right. We'll need to borrow a shovel and some blankets to wrap up in, then we won't need to get our coats either, agreed?"

"I think the people or creatures will understand if we're using their property to save them. Yeah, let's go round up the supplies."

Marty retrieved the key to Qualf from the ever-growing pile in his dresser drawer and returned to the door where Nick was waiting with the handy canvas bag and the key to Cotolspik.

Marty said, "Go ahead Nick you can open the door to Qualf," as he handed the key to Nick.

Accepting the key Nick approached the door, but nothing happened, the key to Qualf just hit the doorknob with a metallic chink, no keyhole opened. This was strange, Marty took the key and tried, the knob glowed, the hole opened, and he turned the key, making the clicking sound. Only then did Marty turn to look at Nick. The disappointment was clear on his face, they hadn't thought that Nick would be unable to access the portals himself. This new revelation was more than they had planned for, what if something happened to Marty? Nick could be stuck somewhere forever, or if Nick tried to help on his own, he would be unable to.

"I guess that's one of the gifts of the Yulesaychaater," Nick said resignedly.

Marty was forced to agree, but he felt bad that there was yet one more thing that Nick couldn't do. If it had been up to Marty, he would have split all of the gifts evenly so they had the same number or shared all the same ones, but he was unable to do that, so he had to accept it. Opening the door they exited Marty's room and came out under the bridge.

Once they were on the path they looked for branches off of the trail for the first time ever. Forks in the road are not something you usually focus on when you have a specific goal in mind. Not far from the bridge they found a small side trail they decided to follow. It wound in and out of the trees and opened onto a small farm and a building that would have been considered a shack. Squinting, Nick pointed into the center of the plot where an object was protruding from the tangle of weeds. Marty looked closer and began walking toward it, the object happened to be a shovel.

After getting the shovel loosened from the weeds they realized it was quite rusty from exposure to the elements, but still it was usable. Realizing that the shovel had been in the middle of digging a trench made Marty stop, "Whatever was using this shovel disappeared right in the middle of digging."

"Bet it was surprised," Nick reasoned.

Leaving the field they moved toward the shack-like shelter and walked right in. It was very dim compared to the sun outside, so they had to pause to let their eyes adjust. There, in the gloom, was a stack of blankets, apparently these were the only type of bedding used and they were ragged, but they would do the job. Piling on blankets to provide some protective covering they headed back outside and were on their way to Cotolspik. Back under the bridge Marty inserted the key to Cotolspik and the click brought a cold that almost froze Marty's hand to the knob.

Taking out the key and throwing the door open they were greeted by a snow-covered foreign landscape. Exiting the relative warmth of Qualf, Nick and Marty entered the small stand of Permet trees in Cotolspik. The sun was just setting along the horizon and they realized they might just get to see a Batwort! This way they wouldn't have to dig all over in the snow they might get a chance to watch it bury the skins and shells and then retrieve them with little trouble.

Permet trees were very interesting; they looked like large stalks of broccoli sticking out of the snow. The trunks were a deep green and as Marty and Nick got closer they realized that they were covered with a thick moss, "this must be the stuff that the Batworts eat," Marty said.

I wonder where the tickelink bushes are," Nick looked around as he spoke and his eyes fell on a small lavender shrub that was near the edge of the enclosure of trees.

Looking closer he could see a small ring of nuts lying on the ground around the tree, "Hey Marty, let's go check that bush out," Nick was already on his way toward it and Marty joined him.

The tickelink bush was a plant like they had never seen before; it was about four feet tall and covered with lavender puffballs. Marty thought they looked like purple cheese puffs on sticks. Piled beneath it were dozens of the acorn-like nuts.

As Nick and Marty were studying the tickelink bush a sound of crunching snow made them turn and look behind them. Walking toward them was obviously a Batwort.

They were frozen in place, if they moved they might frighten it away.

The creature was about two and a half feet tall and covered with a thick brown-grey fur, its wing-like ears were folded against its body making a sharp color contrast. The Batwort had not been fully described in the book, it had no nose, two round bulbous eyes, and a wide mouth, it looked something like a furry earplug with wings and legs. Still holding their breath, so as not to frighten the Batwort away, Nick and Marty looked a little like two patchwork pillows thrown on a white carpet.

Proceeding without acknowledging them at all, the Batwort walked right under the tickelink bush, opened its mouth wide and with a long serpentine tongue licked up a whole pile of tickelink nuts. Apparently it was only holding the nuts in its mouth because they couldn't hear any crunching.

All of a sudden its wing-ears stood straight on end and began a light waving motion. It raised off the ground a small distance and its wings then began to caress the underside of the tickelink bush. The tickelink bush began to shake and suddenly a couple dozen purple cheese puffs extended at odd angles on their own individual branches.

Batwort and a Permet Tree

It looked like the bush had grown hair. Without

looking back the Batwort turned, walked slowly toward its tree, then lifting off the ground gracefully it floated into the unseasonably green leafy branches and disappeared. Not two minutes had passed before another Batwort glided down from a different Permet, landed, and made its way toward them.

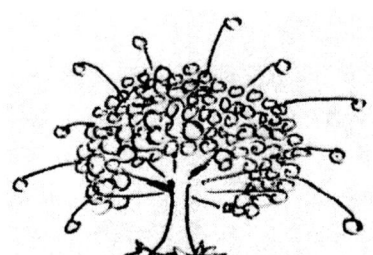

Tickelink Bush

While Nick and Marty weren't watching the tickelink bush had dropped more nuts, apparently from the extended limbs because they had retracted into the main part of the bush once more. This Batwort's wings looked flaky and as it extended them over its head to do its wave, the left wing shed it's covering, which fluttered quietly to the ground. In turn it was on its way back to its nest, when Nick ran forward and snatched the skin from the ground.

The quick movement was heard by the Batwort, it turned and lifted off quickly, thinking it was being pursued. Marty and Nick began retracing their steps to the still open door when a third Batwort descended right in front of them. It froze and so did they, the three of them locked eyes and, without warning, it turned and ran, quite quickly, for such and oddly shaped creature, straight out the door and into Qualf!

A loud splashing followed quickly after its exit and Marty realized it had fallen into the river. He raced forward and through the door. Marty's movement brought Nick back to awareness and he followed closely behind. Dropping the shovel, bag, and ear-skin on the bank they threw the blankets off and both waded into the shallow river where the Batwort was floundering.

Its wings were wet and stuck down to its matted fur and it was sputtering on a mouthful of water. Approaching the Batwort from opposite directions they snatched it up and were able to hold the struggling creature between them as they stepped from the flow of the stream. Once on the bank Nick grabbed one of the cast-off blankets and began trying to dry the Batwort. Because he had let go so suddenly Marty lost control of it and the Batwort was now racing toward the sunshine-covered banks and out from under the bridge.

As Marty and Nick watched open-mouthed the Batwort stopped, shook off the water, and lay down in the sun drenched grass. They looked at each other and had to stifle their laughs, they were drenched from battling in the river and both of them looked like soaked cats. Following the Batwort's lead they came out from under the bridge into the sunshine and lay down in the soft grass.

Soon, all three had dried off and having spent such an enjoyably quiet time together had now gained a mutual respect for one another. Before anything else was done the Batwort stood, gave a type of bow, extended it's ears, and flew back under the bridge and through the still open door back to Cotolspik.

Struggling to their feet they went back beneath the bridge, Marty closed the door, retrieved the key to Qualf, and changed the portal back to his own room. Nick gathered the blankets, shovel, ear-skin, and bag and they trooped back across the bridge to return the items they had borrowed. After depositing the blankets and shovel at the small rundown farmhouse they turned their sights to their final destination of the day, the castle.

Walking once more into the clearing on the top of the hill brought a sense of fear to Marty and Nick. It was hard to explain this time, but the hair on the backs of their necks stood up and they knew at the same time that something just wasn't right.

Instinctively they walked quietly up the stairs to the front doors and there, posted where they could not miss it, was this note:

> *Congratulations on your fourth stunning finish*
> *We were quite sure that your zeal would diminish,*
> *But since it hasn't, the tasks, they get harder*
> *In fact the next three are under the water.*
> *We've taken the liberty to help you out*
> *Since we don't want you to scream and shout.*
> *You'll find inside of Bismorda's castle*
> *Lined up quite nicely and without hassle,*
> *Gear you will need to breathe on each mission,*
> *Please keep in mind this is not simple fishin'!*
> *You'll figure out which things you will need*
> *When each task arrives since you know how to read.*
> *The one thing we forgot to mention*
> *Is the widespread, heart-felt contention,*
> *That's brewing right now with those down in the depths,*
> *See, we've stirred it up, yes, taken the steps*
> *To make it more difficult to brew*
> *Your Acne potion and Pimple stuff too.*
> *So good luck, au revoir, see you later this year*
> *But if we don't we might shed a tear*
> *We've never been challenged by such a smarty*
> *As the Eyahge'er and you Mr. Marty.*

> *Again signed,*
> ### The Zanth Sisters

"Are they getting stronger? Why do the signatures keep changing?" Nick voiced the same concern Marty had.

"I don't know it seems that they gain some control to help us, then the OhRa stirs up problems with our next ingredients. I don't know what is going on except that they need help."

With that Marty took the paper off the door and pushed it open. A single light in the chandelier glowed down on the massive entrance hall, leaving a kind of eerie glow over everything, but it was more light than had been there for months and for that they were grateful. Lined up along the wall on the right side of the entry way were what looked like scuba tanks, next to these they found two sets of snorkels and flippers, a bunch of glass fish bowls were stacked at the end. Then they noticed there was a line of objects on the opposite wall that were much more unusual. There were two sets of everything, but they didn't know what the objects were.

After exchanging questioning glances Marty spoke up, "I guess we'll have to find out what all this stuff is later."

He set a pair of tongs down and eyed some mysterious looking slime in a bag. Turning away from all of these new objects Nick and Marty made their way to the kitchen. Once they were in the larder they checked on the Phlems, they were still doing fine, the acidic Nighten's tears were still bubbling menacingly, and the ball of Garth hair hadn't gone anywhere. Nick laid the wrinkly ear-skin of the Batwort on the shelf with reverence; they were now half done with their tasks.

"It's hard to believe that we have collected all of this stuff," Nick marveled, "Five months ago I didn't have any idea what a Batwort or a Phlem was."

Nodding Marty added, "Yeah the same time last year I was barely reading, had no clue about Qualf, and my best friend was Rousy."

"Rousy? Who's that?" Nick questioned a note of jealousy creeping into his voice.

"My librarian back in Wisconsin." Marty hadn't talked about Rousy to Nick, he wasn't sure why he hadn't but he figured now he could share Rousy with his *new* best friend.

"Her name was Mrs. Rousekewitz, she was funny, and

old, and just...amazing!" All of his memories came flooding back and he found himself near tears.

Now he knew why he hadn't shared Rousy with Nick, because he missed her so much it made him cry still and that wasn't very cool. Nick sensing emotions were close to the surface said, "It's okay Marty, you can tell me about Rousy another time."

Marty swallowed over the lump in his throat, and managed to say, "Thanks."

Taking one last look at their stash of odd objects Nick and Marty walked out of the larder and Nick shut the door behind them. On their way back down the hill Marty re-read the note from the Zanth sisters, "What do you think they mean by 'those down in the depths'?" He asked aloud.

"My guess is the creatures of the sea," Nick offered.

Then suddenly Marty shot in the dark, "Maybe that's the third world that we heard about!"

Nick nodded, "It's sure possible."

"What do you think we'll have to do to make friends with them?"

This time Nick shrugged, "We don't even know if the creatures are human-like, I'm guessing they're not, but we never know here."

"I guess you're right, we'll just have to wait and see," then after a minute's pause he spoke almost to himself, "I really *hate* waiting."

Chapter 27
Love Is... A Swamp?
Thursday, February 14, 1991

On Valentine's Day, that day when Cupid works overtime, Nick could finally restrain himself no longer; he had to ask Monica to "go out" with him. In Science the fateful note was passed with those immortal words:

WILL YOU GO WITH ME? CHECK A BOX

□ YES □ NO □ MAYBE

Holding his breath while she read it, he analyzed her reaction, was it pleasure or guilt that he read on her face? He couldn't tell! Marking her answer and refolding the note she passed it back under the table. Gripping the paper 'til it was drenched with sweat Nick finally worked up the courage to read it. In her hot pink pen she had marked...

YES!

And not with just a mundane X but she had drawn a beautiful heart. It *was* true love! Nick could barely contain his joy. He'd have to start planning his new routine of getting her to class and carrying her books. After all that was *the* major point of going together right? It wasn't like dating, they didn't go anywhere or do anything except the outward show of undying affection *at school.* Hand holding was the biggest of the advantages, but Nick would have to get some extra practice carrying lots of books and having an extra hand to hold his beloved Monica's.

It seemed hours 'til the end of class when Nick and Monica's romance could begin officially. Marty eyed Nick with a sidelong glance, *There is only one thing that could have been in that note that would make Nick this happy,* Marty thought and he was jealous that she had responded positively.

Months ago, just after the Hallowe'en dance, he had

tracked down Sara's locker in The Officer's Hall and poured his entire twelve-year old heart out into that same meaningful note that Nick had just written Monica.

Later that day Sara had bumped into him in the hallway on purpose so she could drop the note without being seen handing it back. His poor heart broke as he had opened the neatly folded square and in bold black she had X'ed in the NO box! Sometimes life just wasn't fair and on that Valentine's morning Marty knew this without a doubt. The bell rang and Nick floated to Monica's side, as he took her books and they walked together, the whispers started.

All suspicions on the latest "couple" were confirmed when at lunch she joined the table where Nick and Marty usually sat. Her friends watched enviously, they hadn't been asked to "go" with anyone yet and each dreamed of that special day. In each of their teenage lovesick minds they made note of Nick's romantic way of asking her on the "National Day of Love," they all hoped that their future boyfriends were as sweet. By the time they walked home Marty was in quite a state, he didn't want to breach the topic with Nick, but Nick couldn't stop talking about how pretty Monica was.

He called her his *only one* the *love to end all loves* and kept saying they were *meant to be together.* Marty felt nauseated, would he have to listen to this *all* day? If so, he would rather Nick go home than come back to Grandma Pen's, but he didn't say anything, he just stewed in his jealousy until they were sitting down together with the map book open between them, then he blew up.

"I really don't care that you're going with Monica, it's a stupid, mindless thing that goes on only at school!"

Before Nick could pipe in that he planned to call her that night too Marty charged on, "and if you're not going to focus on the next task, then I wish you would just go home."

Nick looked at Marty, saw that he was serious, and clamped his mouth shut.

Marty watched Nick, *Good,* he thought, *That should keep him quiet for a while.*

After a few minutes of uncomfortable silence they came across two pages in the book stuck together and all of their squabbles were forgotten. Leaning forward they saw their next target, the Snoth of Debocket. They read together anxiously, "Found in the swampy marsh of Debocket, the Snoth, known for its rather distinctive pungent odor and glue-like mucous, thrives on a water-bound sludge. All Snoths live in a shell like a snail. This shell is called 'the eye' of the Snoth because it is the center of a Snoth's life, without its 'eye' the Snoth will dry up, curl in upon itself, and die. The 'eye' of the Snoth is common in many cosmetics that are found in a powdered form."

The book continued: "If you are thinking of capturing some of these interesting little guys, be sure to have a supply of *Debocket Bog Sludge* for them to live on, otherwise things could get nasty! When handling the Snoth you will want to use some Snoth-resistant tongs otherwise you'll ruin your hot-dog tongs and destroy a perfectly good Snoth. Because of the glue-like secretion the Snoth needs to be kept submersed in a swamp-like setting until you are ready to extract the Snoth from it's eye, otherwise the Snoth will curl up inside of the eye, rendering it useless." They were almost through the article when one last thing caught their eye, "You will need smackelarf skin gloves and ipsidian boots to venture into the swamp of Debocket, otherwise you will be sucked into the depths of the swamp and be lost."

"*Smackelarf skin* gloves?" Nick repeated.

"And ipsidian boots…where are we supposed to find those?"

Marty wondered for a moment then spoke again, "Did you see any gloves or boots at the castle?"

"I don't remember any, but I do remember a bunch of really strange stuff on that left wall. Maybe in that mess there might be some smackelarf skin gloves..."

"And ipsidian boots," Marty finished with a smile, "Let's go find out."

Before they left, Marty extracted the key to Debocket from a lichen covered door on the sealed page. Looking it over they were surprised to see nothing like a normal key's teeth on it, instead there were two squiggly prongs sticking out, making it look somewhat like a solid worm impaled on the end of the key.

The key itself was a mossy green colored metal and attached to the head of the key was a four-legged snail creature they assumed was a Snoth. Marty pocketed the key and went to get the key to Qualf.

As he did, he thought of something, "Hey let's take these other keys and put them in their drawers in that box thing in the secret chamber."

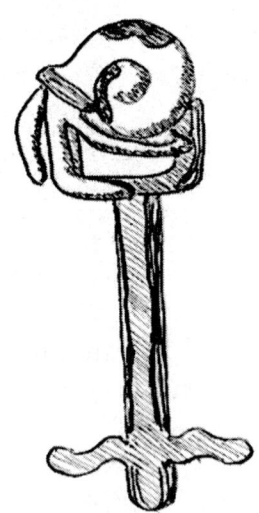

"Okay, sounds like a plan," Nick conceded.

Grabbing the canvas bag Marty removed the pile of keys from the drawer and dropped them with metallic plinks as they ricocheted off each other on their descent into the bag. Nick had retrieved the book of light from under the bed and it joined the keys in the bag. They were now ready to go to Qualf, gather the necessary tools, and retrieve a Snoth or two from the bog of Debocket.

Within minutes they were on the path up to Bismorda's castle when Marty spoke, they had been traveling in silence so it caught Nick off guard, "Let's wait 'til we're back with the Snoth, then we can put the key to Debocket in its drawer too."

This sounded logical, so Nick simply shrugged and said, "Okay."

Since there was nothing to impede their progress Nick and Marty arrived at the top of the hill, where the castle stood, within thirty minutes as usual. Unlike last time there was no threatening note and they were in the entrance hall trading the canvas bag of keys for two of the glass fish bowls, the bag of slime, it was the only thing that they could assume was from a swamp, and now they had to find the smackelarf gloves and ipsidian boots. Sifting through the strange pile of odds and ends on the left side of the entrance corridor Nick found some long boots that looked like patent-leather; they were jade green and were rubbery to the touch.

"These must be the ipsidian boots," he speculated as he held them up for Marty to see.

At the same time Marty was holding up some scaly grey gloves and he replied with, "And these must be made of smackelarf, they feel like a fish skin."

Indeed they were slippery and thin, but sturdily built. They decided to exchange the canvas bag for something bigger so they stacked all of their supplies together and went into the lab on a search.

In a low cabinet they found a large woven bag that would easily hold everything they would need. Stopping to check the list of things that were required they discovered they still needed to get the Snoth-resistant tongs. Returning to the entrance hall they quickly located the tongs and deposited them in the larger bag. The tongs were quickly followed by the bag of bog sludge, two pairs of smackelarf gloves, and two pairs of ipsidian boots. They each took a fish bowl and were again on their way.

Under the bridge they donned their gloves and boots, since they didn't know what the land would be like when they stepped out into Debocket, they wanted to be prepared. When they were dressed they looked at each other and couldn't help but laugh, the bright green boots were thigh high on each of them and then the gloves went just beyond their elbows. This made it look like they had begun transforming into some strange creature with green legs and scaly arms. Marty tried to retrieve the key from his pocket but found the smackelarf gloves were so stick-resistant he couldn't take hold of it. Removing one glove he was able to get the key, turn it in the lock, and return it to his pocket.

Thinking quickly, he also threw the door open before putting the glove back on.

If you were to bottle the smell of the bog of Debocket, a simple mention of it to your future children would make them cry. Marty and Nick's noses wrinkled in disgust, and would have run for cover if they hadn't been fastened to their faces, as they stepped out the door and into the fetid waters of the swamp. At the door they had to sit down to put their legs into the water, when they pushed off from the ground in Qualf, instead of having to swim, they kind of bobbed where they stood.

Surprised that they didn't feel solid ground under their feet they realized the ipsidian boots were keeping them afloat. The book had said without the boots they would be lost, what a scary thought! There was no way to know how deep this bog really was. In order to move in the moss-covered water they had to shuffle their feet and legs, this propelled them slowly forward and they soon were about twenty feet from the door.

Their torsos and upper thighs were out of the water,

but from the thigh down they were under the opaque waters of Debocket. Only about an inch of their bright green boots were revealed above the murky sludge. Looking over their shoulders they saw the door hovering a foot above the putrid water.

The Bog of Debocket

These portals were quite fascinating in where they chose to pop up. Brushing something small, but solid with his leg Nick took his fish bowl and tried to scoop it up.

The second the bowl hit the water there was a tremendous sucking sound and Nick found himself empty-handed and the bowl nowhere in sight. It had been lost to the swamp!

Luckily Marty had brought another bowl passing it to Nick he reached into the bag, opened the packet of bog sludge and carefully poured it into the extended bowl. Taking out the tongs in preparation for another solid object they shuffled along in the relative silence.

Relative silence because there was a strange unearthly hum that seemed to vibrate the very air around them, but where it came from they could not begin to guess. Marty felt the next one brush his leg and he stopped. Stopping is easier said than done when you're bobbing mostly out of the water. He managed to come to a slower glide while prepping himself to snatch the Snoth.

Dipping the Snoth-resistant tongs into the thick ooze he felt them close around an object. Extracting it from the thick dredge was not easy, but he didn't lose the tongs. Holding the golf-ball sized shell over the fish tank he let it drop into the freshly poured sludge. "One more," he mouthed not wanting to risk taking a lungful of stench. They had kept their breathing shallow so as to not make themselves puke.

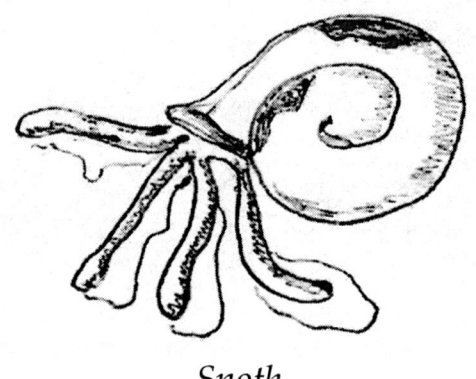

Snoth

Shuffle-kicking once more took them forward and Nick stopped this time, whispering, "I've got another one on my right side."

Marty turned so he could use the tongs properly. He dipped them into the goo once more, clamped onto another Snoth, and brought it out wiggling four mucous covered legs wildly. With a plop, it too was added to the dredge in the fish bowl, and it was finally time to return to the living air of Qualf.

Turning in the bog was difficult, they had to shuffle in a kind of circle, it was a bit like dancing, *shuffle ball change* they kept thinking until they had changed directions and were again pointed at the door. Moving forward, they were back at the door within minutes, probably encouraged by the soft gurgle of the river and the clean fresh air they knew awaited them in Qualf.

Nick leaned through the door to place the fish bowl safely onto the banks of the river before he pulled himself out of the slime. Once he was out he turned to Marty and took the tongs and bag so that Marty could step free of the ooze too. As the door was pulled shut, cutting off the unbearable reeky ripeness of the swamp, Marty and Nick breathed deeply the sweet clean air of Qualf.

Stepping out of the ipsidian boots Marty collected the two pairs and stowed them in the bag over Nick's shoulder. Keeping on the smackelarf gloves Marty picked up the fish bowl of Snoths and they were again on the trail to Bismorda's castle. Amazingly the gloves held onto the glass, but they wouldn't work on the keys. Marty tried to peek into the noxious mass of putrescence to see if he could make out either of the Snoths he was unable to identify anything but the deep green color and floating particles of stinky refuse.

Giving up on sighting the Snoth for now they traipsed up the path and were grateful for the solid ground beneath their feet and the freely flowing pure air that filled their lungs. In the larder at Bismorda's castle Marty placed the bowl of Snoths on the shelf with their increasingly odd assortment of ingredients. Number five had been successfully collected and they both heaved a sigh of relief as their smackelarf gloves were stacked together, laying the tongs on top of them.

When it was time to put these ingredients together in the fateful Acne Pimple recipe they would need both the gloves and tongs, but they were going to remove the boots in the bag so they wouldn't stink up the larder. Going back to the entrance hall they swapped bags again; their next destination was to the box of drawers in the hidden cavern far below where they now stood.

"Mirror, Mirror, on the wall, please let us into the secret

hall," Marty spoke clearly the words he knew would open the mirror's secret.

Slowly the full-length mirror split in response to his plea. Pulling out the book of light they descended into the secret cove under the castle. Echoing off the stone walls each step boomed away from them just one step ahead. Once again, as they stood in the cavern-like room, the ordinary wooden table stood in a puddle of light.

Perched on the flat table top was the curious box of drawers which seemed even more unusual than before. Some of the drawers reflected the light simply making it glow; others refracted the beam and sent rainbows dancing on the stone walls. Remembering how it had shocked him before Nick lingered back a few steps. It hadn't been a simple static shock, it was a full current of electricity as if it had been plugged into some unseen outlet and was protected by an electric force field.

Marty stepped up to the box, extended his hand, and ran it along the smooth surface of the top as if it were some kind of beloved pet.

Was Nick hearing things, or did it purr? *No*, he had to be imagining it, *boxes don't purr!* And yet, Nick could have sworn the box had given off a sound of contented release, a sigh if you will, as Marty touched it, as if it were, indeed, a living thing.

Almost instantly Marty found a drawer and opened it, "Which one is that?" Nick wondered aloud.

"Qualf," Marty replied.

Since Nick wouldn't, or in reality couldn't, come any closer Marty decided to read the rest aloud as he came to them. Making a small pile of keys on the table with some metallic clings and plunks Marty began to search for each drawer. Nick noted the echoes reverberated around until they disappeared close to where they had begun.

There didn't seem to be any sense of order to the

drawers because after Marty called out "Qualf," he searched for some moments in silence, then, "Poisentre," which in turn slowly rolled away into nothingness.

Nick realized that Marty was merely opening the drawers; he had yet to insert any of the keys. Apparently his plan was to open all the applicable drawers and then sort out their keys. Nick watched in an anticipatory silence, as Marty's search continued.

The oppressive quiet was only punctuated by Marty's call as he pulled out a moldy green drawer for Debocket, a dust colored one for Cotolspik, a magenta drawer for Quixant, and a textured drawer that looked like sand-paper for Tarbath. These had joined the simple wood drawer of Qualf, and the dark purplish blue drawer of Poisentre.

Mentally Nick was keeping track of how many keys were left, if his tally was correct the only ones remaining were Zanth and the key to the little man with the pink hat, what was that one called?

He almost asked Marty when, "Zanth," was announced and a black jewel-like drawer was pulled out.

Then Marty voiced the question that had been burning inside of Nick, "What was *that one* called?"

Nick of course knew exactly which *one* Marty was talking about, but he had no clue what it was called, so he answered honestly, "I don't know."

Mumbling off some possible names that he had read one struck Nick, "Wait repeat that last one."

"Which one? *Treasure Quest?*"

"Yeah, that one! I bet it's *that* one. Wasn't the story about finding your fortune, or in other words, *treasure?*" his pulse pounding, Nick was positive it was the right one, but why was he so sure? That was what he couldn't explain.

Finding the *Treasure Quest* drawer again Marty pulled out a pink drawer that looked like it was made from the material of the little man's hat. Now Marty was positive too, he smiled at Nick as if to say, *Good thinkin'!*

His face, shadowed in the limited light, was a bit eerie, but Nick knew it was a look of gratitude. Now came the sorting of the keys.

Laying all of the keys out in a line, Marty picked up the black shiny key of Tarbath first, and placed it in the sandpaper textured drawer. As he slid the drawer shut, a slight glow started around the knob, and Nick exclaimed, "Wow! That's cool!"

Curious, Marty turned to look at Nick and question what was so cool, but as he turned he noticed Nick was facing the wall of the cave and pointing. Following the indicative finger Marty saw what was *so cool*, an image of Tarbath had appeared on the wall, it was projecting from the handle of the drawer. As each subsequent key was inserted into its proper drawer a moving picture was thrown somewhere onto the wall. When all of the keys were inside, seven scenes were displayed on the walls of the cave each one casting more light into the dark abyss of the quarry.

Reluctantly Marty withdrew the key to Qualf, the only one that was absolutely necessary right now, and announced it was time to head back. This was not welcome news, but it was necessary that they get back home, so they pulled themselves away from the enchanting cove. Marty grabbed the canvas bag and book of light that they had actually shut and laid on the table to better see the 'magic slide show.'

Pocketing the key and opening the book of light they used it to illuminate their path back upstairs. Marty and Nick looked longingly back twice until the turn in the staircase obstructed their view. Exiting the underground cave of wonders Nick and Marty realized they had changed in some way, it wasn't a huge, noticeable change, but they could feel it nonetheless.

Soon they were back under the bridge and a click was all that stood between them and reality. Hovering with indecision Marty's hand was poised, but hesitating to insert the key. *What was so difficult?* They could always come back.

Somewhere inside them they both knew for the first time that it wouldn't always be true, but for now they accepted it and stepped back into Marty's room.

Chapter 28
An Ictat In Gwimmet

Friday, March 15, 1991

Exactly one month from the note Nick and Monica broke up. In a simple, yet complex, note she explained that he wasn't giving her enough attention, but later that day Nick found that she had been asked out by Brett Colter, the seventh grade class president. This didn't sit well with Nick and he was moody all day. At lunch he avoided looking in the direction of the officers' table, because he didn't want to see Monica with Brett; that would have been too much.

Marty tried to comfort him, but had to give up because Nick needed to mourn his lost love. After a painfully long day for Nick he agreed solemnly to go to Marty's and maybe even spend the night if they found anything interesting in the map book. At Grandma Pentel's, Nick put on a mask of false happiness to avoid any further questioning by adults who just didn't understand young love.

Finally down in Marty's room the gloom was dispelled as they were flipping through the map book and two pages stuck together. This time the place identified Gwimmet held the vital ingredient, the one-eyed Screm.

Reading aloud, Marty soothed Nick's spirit, "Gwimmet is a submersed 'sea state' populated by several species of exclusive origin."

"Sounds stuck up," Nick interjected still stinging from his recent separation.

Marty nodded and continued, "One of the more unusual specimens is the one-eyed Screm. When fully mature they are a bright pink color and their single eye is a startling blue in contrast. They are the size of a Scrimmit and are easily seen with the naked eye. Tines or spikes protrude from the suction cups on each of the Screm's six legs. These tines are used in the ancient art of acklink and are a precious commodity to the Carbono people of Gwimmet.

"Extracting the tines is a painstakingly difficult task and can only be done effectively using plungie-tweezlins. A vital part of proper tine removal is keeping the Screm alive; if death occurs the tines collected from that unfortunate Screm will dissolve and become useless.

One-Eyed Screm

"The atmosphere of Gwimmet, as stated before, is that of a fully submersed 'sea state.' It is covered by the Carbono waters, which bubble incessantly, similar to carbonated water used by humans in their soft drinks. Using a tank of klinx and a suit of plastordim will ensure safe passage into Gwimmet; however, something is needed to barter with the Carbono people to obtain the Screms.

"The Carbonic people enjoy many hobbies one of which is a rare form of squilling. Using beads baked in the ovens of Tillan they stack them carefully into ilfonic patterns, creating beautiful show pieces for friends and family. You need only find the right family and they will trade *anything* you want for the coveted beads."

"Okay," Nick said looking up from the list he had written, "Is that *everything*?"

After Marty agreed that that was definitely everything, Nick read back, "We need a tank of klinx, a suit of plastordim, and something to trade, the beads from Tillan would be the best thing, and the plungie-tweezlins, so we can get the tines."

This certainly sounded like an overwhelming list considering they didn't know what any of the items were, but they had confidence that they could find the needed things in the entrance hall of Bismorda's castle.

Marty was retrieving the key to Qualf when Nick reminded him, "Don't we need a key to get to Gwimmet?"

Again grateful Nick was there to keep him in line he sat down with the key to Qualf in one hand and his trusty pair of tweezers in the other. After separating the pages, Nick gazed at the bubbling view of Gwimmet as Marty did his intricate surgery-like movements on the opposite page.

Nick said absently, still looking at Gwimmet through the turquoise bubbles, "What does this door say? You haven't read the last few aloud to me."

Marty squinted at the page, the minute writing surrounding the seaweed-covered gate read:

> Enter in the Carbonic's lair,
> Don't mind the Screm's one-eyed stare,
> Take this key and go therein,
> The Carbono people's hearts you'll win.

An object flashed quickly across the opposite page, it looked pink, but it moved so quickly they weren't sure.

If that was a Screm, how in the world would they catch one?

Together they scrutinized the distant scene of Gwimmet. From their vantage point they were looking at the gate located on the edge of town. If it hadn't been for the constant rising bubbles it might have been a town from anywhere in the human world. At least from where they sat it looked like that.

Refocusing on the retrieval of the key Marty used the tweezers deftly and in another moment a fleshy-pink-tinted key had appeared full-size on his outstretched finger.

Straddling the rectangular head of the key was a six-legged octopus-like creature with a single central eye fixed open in a blank stare. The teeth of the key looked like a stop sign that had been shrunken to minute proportions. Taking this key in one hand, the Qualf key in the other and the canvas bag over his shoulder Marty approached the door.

Nick stood, folded the list of items, and shoved it in his pocket. They were back in Qualf with the turn and click of the key. As they walked up the path Nick took out the list and consulted it with an occasional clicking of his tongue.

Finally Marty couldn't stand it any longer, "What is *wrong* Nick?"

"Nothing," his answer came too quickly and sounded evasive.

"Why do you keep clicking your tongue like that?"

"Was I clicking?" now stalling Nick tried to think of a way to re-route the conversation.

"Yes, you were clicking, and you only do that when you're upset or confused about something," Marty observed.

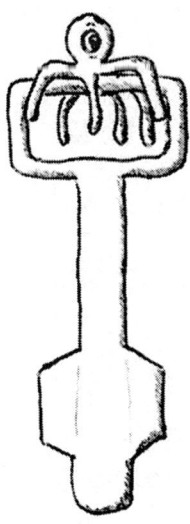

Shocked at how well Marty knew him he decided to

come clean, "I was just wondering how we were supposed to keep the Screms from swimming out of the fish tank."

Pausing, Marty looked at Nick, *how does he do that? He always looks and searches and finds every little detail that I myself would have overlooked and under-searched and lost.* Shaking his head he began searching for a solution as well.

Now with both of them contemplating this conundrum they walked out onto the top of the hill. Soon, as they stood in the entrance hall they were looking at the tanks of klinx closely, attached to the tops were tubes that extended until they came to nozzles that they assumed they had to put in their mouths and to finish off the ensemble there were also masks attached. These were so similar to scuba tanks that even an expert would probably have been confused.

Moving across the hall they rummaged through the remaining items and found what had to be two suits of plastordim. They looked like a type of metal, in fish scale patterns, but they felt like spandex rubber. Adding these to the tanks in the center of the floor they moved back to the odds and ends on the left side. In the area where they had found the bag of bog sludge two bags of exotic looking carved items were propped against the wall.

"These must be the Tillanian beads," Nick whispered.

There was no reason to whisper, but he did it anyway. Consulting the list one last time they saw that they needed plungie-tweezlins, but not until they were going to remove the tines, so they were technically done for now. Returning to the stack of fish bowls they each grabbed one, still unsure how they would keep the Screms inside but willing to trust the list of requirements.

Quickly changing into their plastordim suits, they donned their shoes for the walk, and divided the remaining supplies between them. Each one now had a klinx tank strapped on like a backpack, a bowl, and a bag of beads under their arm. Marty had one more item, the key to Gwimmet, an essential part of this journey. Hiking down the hill with all of their gear had them sweating by the time they arrived under the bridge.

Tillanian Beads

Fishing the key out of his bowl Marty inscrtcd it in the doorknob. The click brought a loud bubbling sound on the far side of the door, and when Marty tried to push the door open as usual from this side, he couldn't get it to budge. So instead he tried to pull it open, logically this wouldn't work on the single direction hinges, but it swung towards him easily, revealing a wall of water somehow not spilling out on top of them completely defying all laws of gravity and reason. The bubbling view was quite an unusual one compared to Marty's room that they were so used to seeing.

As a result they kept one eye fixed on the foreign landscape and helped each other with their nozzles and masks. Fully prepared they looked into the fizzy world of Gwimmet unflinchingly and stepped through the door. Becoming engulfed instantly was very strange and all Marty and Nick could do was flail their legs until they had gained control of how to maneuver around in their new surroundings. When they finally became mobile they propelled themselves in the direction of the town of Gwimmet.

Since the water was constantly bubbling it was similar to swimming in a Jacuzzi, but much deeper. The air bubbles tickled through the plastordim and occasionally lifted them unexpectedly so they were constantly on their guard for the unexpected. The floor of their current environment was so far away it faded into darkness except for the raised area where Gwimmet stood.

Built on what looked like coral, the homes were on several different levels. From a distance they had looked similar to human homes, but now that Nick and Marty were at a closer range they could see they looked very different. The roofs were made of cast-off ship lumber and the walls, though white, were full of holes like Swiss cheese. Through these holes could be seen the eyes of small children, or what looked like children, while Nick and Marty passed slowly by with their fish bowls and bags of beads. They didn't realize how very unusual *they* must look to the citizens of Gwimmet. It suddenly hit Marty that the homes were actually part of the coral and differed only by coloring.

As they floated through the town the curious eyes watched them closely, but did nothing to impede their progress. When they had been in the town for approximately twenty minutes they were suddenly grabbed from behind by two large creatures. Not being able to turn and see behind them Nick and Marty could only make out the muscular webbed hands that held their arms to their sides rendering them useless except for holding onto their fishbowls and beads.

Now moving swiftly through the effervescent water they were being pushed to some destination, they knew not where, by some force they knew not what. Stopping abruptly in front of one of the larger dwellings they were greeted by a strange creature indeed. It was a female, they guessed by her long greenish-yellow hair, and she had some sort of control in this town because she spoke and Marty and Nick could feel the vice-like grips loosen on their arms. This left their hands tingling and somewhat painful as the blood rushed back into them.

Looking at the face of the creature Marty noticed she had human-like eyes but they were a glossy black instead of having a colored iris; her nose, or where there should be a nose, was two snake-like slits that bubbled occasionally. Her mouth was similar to a human one when closed, but when opened it looked like a goldfish's. In place of ears were fins that twitched occasionally in the mass of flowing curls. Her skin was scaly and reflected bits of light and while it lacked any specific color it continued to shimmer as if it had a secret. At her throat she wore a string of extraordinarily large pearls with a shell pendant dangling from the center. Around her shoulders in a type of wrap were lengths of seaweed. Her arms were quite muscular probably from using them to swim. Between her fingers were flaps of skin that made them webbed. At her chest started a slick white muscle-membrane, similar to the tentacle of an octopus. In three alternating lines ran suction cups and at the end of her body it rounded becoming a mass of fibrous material similar to an anemone.

She was speaking, they thought, because her mouth was moving, but nothing was making it to their ears. Then as her mouth stopped moving her voice reverberated inside their heads in a high-nasally voice, "It is a great honor to have the Yulesaychaater come to visit us here in Gwimmet. I am what s known as the Leading Lady, my name is Gratzwinda. You were brought here by Terpen and Scrit, two of my loyal subjects." She went on to state, "A message arrived that strangers had entered the village carrying a large quantity of Tillanian beads and the villagers were frightened that you were robbers coming to loot us of ours as well."

Her dialogue stopped there and her mouth opened again, moments passed, her mouth closed, and the voice again permeated Nick and Marty's thinking cores, "Unfortunately my people do not know you by sight, but they are very familiar with your tale. You are truly legendary in the whole of our world." There was a slight pause and then, "Please, come inside."

Moving to the side, Gratzwinda motioned them in, and they followed where she was indicating. Inside the dwelling was lighter than outside of it, it had a phosphorescent glow that dispelled the shadows, and actually made Marty and Nick forget they were so far under the water. The first room must have been the parlor because it had half a dozen sizes of chair or sofa formations protruding from the porous floor. There was a fireplace with a glowing ball of greenish light in the grate. Above the mantel was a portrait of Gratzwinda poised at the shoulder of an aged looking couple, obviously her parents.

Looking again they realized that in the portrait was a much younger Gratzwinda, it must have been painted many years previous her parents may even be deceased by now. As Nick and Marty were gazing at the portrait Gratzwinda perched herself gracefully on the coral ottoman and opened her mouth to begin speaking, her voice startled Nick and Marty moments later when it hit them because they had been unaware that she had begun speaking.

"That was when I was just older than a hatchling," a watery sigh punctuated her speech, "My father and mother were the Grand Duke and Dame of all Gwimmet when the dreadful war started."

War? Marty and Nick exchanged glances.

"In fact, that painting was just before it broke out. Three ictats later I was left without parents and became Gwimmet's Leading Lady at a mere ninety-five. Dealings of all governmental issues pass through me, so you see why you were brought to me first. Please sit down so we can chat awhile."

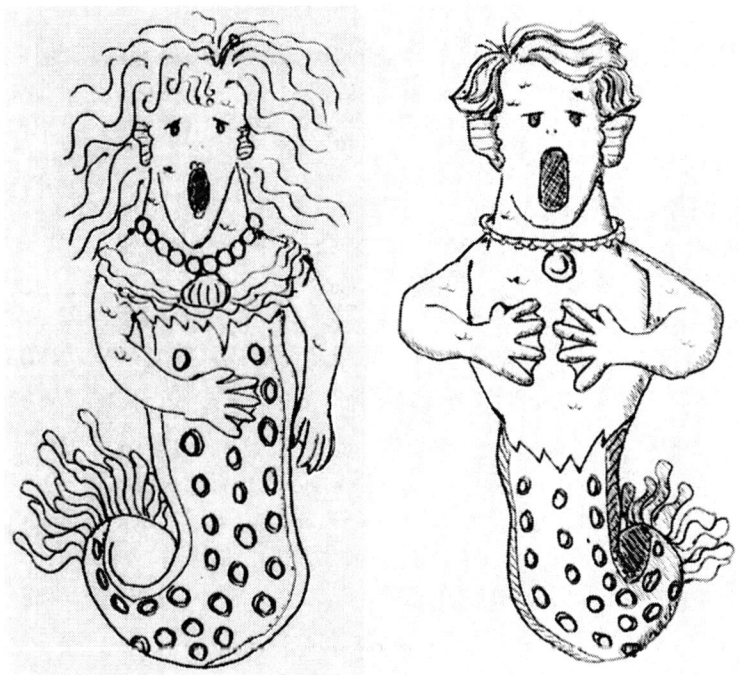

Gratzwinda & Guard

Nick and Marty were both bursting with questions so they eagerly sat on the prickly coral easy chairs. *Now, how to speak under water?* They decided to just try talking with their mouth pieces in and see if they could be understood.

Nick started, "Who did you have a war with?"

"What is an ictat?" Marty quickly followed.

After a moment's relay time Gratzwinda began to answer Marty's question first, because it was the easier of the two, "An ictat is similar to an eon in human time."

An eon? Again Marty and Nick exchanged glances, *wasn't that a really long time?* She had said it like ictats were days or years, but eons?

Then she started answering Nick's question, "We went

to war with the Aquiestrans, they came upon us so suddenly our whole village was destroyed before we knew it. When the water settled we were left homeless and had to start all over again. Once our village was rebuilt we went and sought revenge upon them. So, it was back and forth until this coral plateau we live on is the only one left for miles around, the whole land of Gwimmet has fallen piece by piece into the depths of the ocean.

"Robberies, plunders, and mass chaos were everyday events for us for so long that the people are still shaken by any change however small. That is why your appearance has startled them so."

Here Gratzwinda's eyes moved to the fish bowls and bags of Tillanian beads which Marty and Nick were still holding. A twinkle passed her glossy black eyes and she spoke again, "Were you coming with a specific purpose in mind? You've brought quite a collection of the marvelous beads from Tillan, and since you're not here to steal *our* Tillanian beads I can only suppose you're selling yours, am I correct?"

Marty and Nick nodded, and spoke together, "Screms."

It took a moment for their answer to reach each other and Gratzwinda. When it did they looked at each other and giggling, which is difficult to do under carbonic water, Marty continued, "We need three one-eyed Screms."

"We need as many one-eyed Screms as this will buy," Nick amended offering the bag of intricate beads.

Gratzwinda's face clouded in thought for a moment. Apparently she was converting the ratio of Screms to beads because, when she spoke all that came out was, "Four, and some sealer."

Before Marty could ask what *sealer* was Nick said, "Done."

Standing, or actually floating, up from her seat she disappeared and was back in a moment with two items, one was a large jar of squirming pink legs and bright blue eyes, and the other a long container that looked to Marty like plastic-wrap. Setting the jar down on the ottoman she put out her hand gesturing that she wanted something, Marty ventured forward with the beads, she shook her head and her hair floated up in a cloud around her face.

As her hair began to settle back around her shoulders he offered the fish bowl and she took it. Setting it down beside the large jar she began making a series of quick movements. She had removed something that looked like a long bubble from the box and had it fastened over the fish bowl's opening. Dipping her webbed fingers into the large jar she removed a muscle with a single eye and six flailing legs then putting her hand through the bubble thing on the fish bowl she released the first Screm.

One more time she repeated this and there were two Screms zooming around in their new environment trying to get out with no success. How was she able to keep them in the bowl? They noticed how tightly packed the jar was too, how did she stop them from escaping? Marty's questioning look caught Gratzwinda's eye and she held up the long container, clearly printed on the side the label read:

SCREM SEALER – Keep those speedy Screms under wraps for all your household needs. Tine proof, puncture proof, semi-permeable.

Semi-permeable? Looking to Nick for an answer all he got was a glazed look and a shrug.

Again Gratzwinda saw the question pass between them and, being perceptive, guessed that they wanted to know what semi-permeable meant so she said, "It means you can access it one way, but it is unbreakable the other." When that left a couple of confused blank stares she decided to show them.

Taking Nick's bowl, she put another piece of sealer on

it, this time she set it down and tried to put her hand into the bowl, but it wouldn't go in. Before she spoke again she re-inserted her hand into the first bowl, through the sealer and again extracted it. This is when Nick's eyes shot wide open, he understood. Now in an excited frenzy he explained to Marty as Gratzwinda rewrapped the sealer on the second bowl and retrieved two more Screms.

After the delayed dialogue took place Marty wanted to confirm that he understood the concept so he repeated slowly, "Okay, the sealer can hold one thing in, while it lets something else in, but it won't let the first thing out?"

Nick and Gratzwinda nodded. Marty understood but it was still confusing how it actually worked. With the Screms sealed in their new bowls they each handed their bags of Tillanian beads over to Gratzwinda who promptly accepted one as if the beads were made of gold. She gave a questioning glance to Marty about the second bag, "But I only figured the cost from one bag, I didn't realize you wanted *two* bags of Tillanian beads to be spent all in the same place."

Marty looked at Nick and, as a smile spread across Nick's face, he asked, "What else can we buy with Tillanian beads?"

Gratzwinda again became the perfect hostess, "Well you can goo-gyoung and see what you like."

"Goo-gyoung?"

Marty and Nick looked at each other as Gratzwinda explained, "It means to 'look around' in your language. Feel free to float around for a while."

Nick was excited for this new opportunity to explore an exciting foreign place.

Unfortunately Marty looked at the gauge on his klinx tank and realized it was close to being empty, they had to get home and fast! Noticing his worried expression Gratzwinda hurried into the other room and within seconds returned with a large bag of odds and ends that she offered, "This amounts to another bag of Tillanian beads," she explained.

Trading the small bag of beads for the much larger mesh bag they waited while Gratzwinda stashed the sealer, jar of Screms, and two bags of beads. As she emerged she escorted them out the front door. For the first time Nick and Marty saw the muscular guards that had brought them. One had short greenish-yellow hair, the other had muddy brown hair, in all other aspects they were almost identical. Each had a pendant necklace around his beefy neck and brawny arms were hanging peacefully at their sides. Massive chests tapered down to impossibly thin waists and then the tentacle-muscle started just below where a human's belly-button would be. The major difference between the women and men was that the tentacle was placed at the level of their chest on women and men's was at their waist.

Having made this observation Nick and Marty thanked Gratzwinda and bid her good-bye. Swimming back past the rest of the villagers Marty and Nick saw that the Carbono people had come out of their dwellings and were playing with their children. As Nick and Marty got closer the Carbonians lined up and bowed respectfully as if it were a royal procession passing. Kicking against the carbonic waters they were back at the door to Qualf within minutes and none too soon.

They hovered in the water looking out at the door, they could see the world outside through a fizzy film of water and it made it look quite strange. Grasping the bowl in front of him and the large bag behind Marty decided to step out the door sideways, or at least at an angle, right foot first. He settled his foot on the ground and pulled the rest of his body out slowly. Feeling his full-body weight again was almost overwhelming added to that was the large bag of items he now had to lug at their actual weight and a bowl of Screms.

He managed to step out of the way so that Nick could come through as well before they closed the door. They had to sidle along under the bridge until they had come out onto the sun-soaked banks of the river Sems where they collapsed in a pile of shiny, slippery, dripping wet exhaustion. Removing the tanks and nozzles and masks so slowly you wouldn't have known they were moving unless you stared at them for any length of time, they settled in to enjoy the warmth of the sun.

When they finally became aware of their surroundings again they looked at their equipment and remembered the fish bowls. They each brought one closer to study the Screms in action. Floating gracefully through the water the Screms actually slowed down in the sun, as if they sensed the warmth and were basking in it too. Before they knew it, both Marty and Nick had fallen asleep.

A few hours later as the sun was setting Marty awoke with a start, looking around wildly, trying to remember where he was. Smacking his lips he could taste a strong flavor of bubble gum, it must be the after-taste of the klinx, that's probably what made it different than regular oxygen. Marty smiled at the unusually subtle difference.

Nick sat up slowly and he too noticed the taste, "My mouth tastes like bubble gum."

"It's the klinx," Marty informed him knowledgeably.

"That makes sense since it caused bubbles why shouldn't it taste like 'bubble' gum?" Nick smiled slyly.

Taking their equipment and a fish bowl each, they decided to leave the large mesh bag on the banks and take it back home with them to explore what they had received. They began their return to Bismorda's castle and even though they had taken a nap they were still worn out by the time they reached the top of the hill. They stumbled into the corridor, piled their equipment haphazardly, and changed back into their human clothes.

Only then did they take the Screms to add them to their collection. Standing in the larder door they looked over their menagerie with a kind of satisfaction, they had now filled two shelves and were going to need to get two more items into the larder before they could do their experimental spell to ward off the menacing Acne Pimple.

Marty had had only two other feeble brushes with the dreaded disease, but neither had exceeded the beginning size, he was sure they had frightened it into submission. Sleep became a very high priority just at that moment and both of them started to nod off while standing. They needed to get home as quickly as possible. Nick closed the door to the larder, and they retreated back through the entrance hall.

Marty grabbed the canvas bag with the key to Qualf and retrieved the Gwimmet key as well from his plastordim suit pocket, and they were on their way back to Marty's room. Back on the banks they grabbed the bag of Gwimmetian artifacts and retreated under the bridge for the fourth time that day.

Marty inserted the key to Qualf and returned them to his own room. Once they stepped onto the plush carpet their legs gave way and they literally collapsed. Somehow managing to raise his arm to the keyhole Marty returned them with the simple click of the key and then his hand slid slowly down the door to rest near his already sleeping body.

They slept late into the next morning their minds were almost at ease, they had two more tasks and they would be sure to save Bismorda, the Zanth sisters, and Marty. If they only knew what the next two tasks would bring they probably would not have slept so soundly that night.

"What's going to *happen* to them?" Menalee suddenly burst out a look of extreme worry on her young face.

"Yeah, you can't stop there," Nisha demanded, "You have to tell us that they got through."

"Of course we got through," Nick's sparkling eyes looked down at Menalee, Nisha, and the other concerned youth surrounding his knees, "I'm *here* aren't I?"

Weston let out a nervous laugh, "I guess you are, so you *did* survive, but what did you have to go through?"

"I can see you have really begun to sense the importance of Marty's mission, I hope that you will all continue to feel that all of your lives," Nick looked over the others heads directly at Billy and Kimber, "I know *I* have."

"Can we get on with it?" Billy fidgeted under Nick's unwavering stare.

"Yes, *we* can," Nick refocused back on the others who were indeed wrapped up in the story.

Chapter 29
A Love Note Leads To Capture!

Upon opening the net bag, handfuls of pearls and precious stones tumbled out, then the really strange stuff began to surface. A reflective pool hovering in a ball that looked like a snow-globe, but little live fairies were flitting back and forth inside, a hook made from some kind of bone, a purple metal dagger with a jewel encrusted handle, and a mirror that didn't reflect anything. After sifting through the odd assortment of items from Gwimmet they put the sack of artifacts at the farmhouse that they had borrowed the blankets from. The farmhouse was chosen because of its location, it was closer than the palace, and they could move the sack later. It turned into a quick visit and then they had to return to complete their homework.

Friday, April 12, 1991

Another month took all of Rosewood into the center of spring and the season of new beginnings hit the seventh grade hard. Nick and Marty were moony-eyed over their lost loves, and then the unexpected happened. An anonymous note was slipped into both of their lockers. The notes were identical in wording but the handwriting was different on each.

Being quite undecipherable they had to work together to try and make out the workings of the teenage girl's mind that found itself scrawled onto paper in front of them. They had to wait until they were safe at Grandma Pen's to decode the unusual letters, and that took all the patience they had combined. When they finally spread the two notes out in front of them on the floor this is what they read:

Since the night you took the stage
My heart has been in a rage
You pass me by, I don't exist

Why can't I ever **make** your list?
You seem so nice I want to cry,
Why can't I ever catch your eye?
I've loved you a long time,
Can **you** understand my rhyme?

-     **N. A.** (on Nick's)
-     **C. T.** (on Marty's)

They were left with some major questions following their readings:

1. Why would two girls write the same poem?
2. Who did they know with the initials N.A. or C.T.?
3. Who had seen them perform and had followed them ever since?

After these major questions there were hundreds of minor ones that pelted them, there had to be a type of code to it, but what was it?

Nick noticed something strange. There were letters that had been retraced so they were darker, he began writing these down as he read them out loud, "S...E...E...M... E...A...T...A...G...A...M...E...?...W...I...L...L...Y...O...U...? ...N.A.C.T.," he paused to study them and asked aloud, "What does *that* spell?"

They put their heads together over the paper and Marty used his pen to draw lines where there should be breaks, it now read: SEE/ME/AT/A/GAME?/WILL/YOU? and the initials.

He wondered aloud, "How do *you* sign your initials?"

"What?"

"Do you write your initials in print or do you do them in cursive?" Marty clarified his question.

"Cursive, why?" wondered Nick.

"Most people do, I think, so why are these initials in

print and punctuated with periods?"

Nick caught his implication, "You mean these are more words, *not* initials?"

Marty nodded, then his face clouded over, "But *what* do they stand for?"

"*Girls are stupid!!*" Nick exclaimed in exasperation.

Without thinking Marty said matter-of-factly, "No those aren't the right letters."

Nick laughed, "I didn't mean that's what it stood for, I just meant it would be easier to write out a simple note than go through all of these moronic codes."

Marty could tell by Nick's tone he wasn't *really* upset, he was actually really excited but he was putting on a front to pretend he wasn't interested. You see, boys are quite complicated too. Marty found that he too was intrigued. These girls had gone to a lot of trouble to convey their sincere admiration for them. Reading some more words into the message he summarized, "So, basically they want us to meet them at a game, when is the next game?"

"Today at 4:30," Nick answered quickly after a mental review of the announcements at school.

"Okay, so they want us to meet them tonight. How do we find them?"

"That must be what the letters tell us, let's think."

Acting offended Marty said, "That's what I *have* been doing, thank you very much."

"Sorry, how 'bout *I* think, you just sit and look pretty?" Nick joked.

Marty slugged Nick in the shoulder, but not too hard, "Hey now, them's fightin' words!"

Nick sat up suddenly as if struck by an electric current, "Wait, don't they have letters on the sections of the bleachers?"

"Yeah, why?" Marty wondered.

"Maybe they're giving us a placement in the

bleachers," Nick explained.

"There aren't enough sections that go up to N," Marty reasoned.

"But there is an *A*, possibly N means 'Near'."

"Okay, so we meet them 'Near A' what does C.T. mean?"

"Maybe, come together?" Nick surprised himself with his sleuthing capabilities.

"'Near A, Come Together, Will you meet me at a game?'" Marty re-ordered the message and it made more sense, he nodded, "That just might be it. So, what time is it anyway?"

"Almost 4:00," Nick checked Marty's bedside clock.

"4:30." A smile spread over Nick's face and then slowly over Marty's.

"Let's go meet our *fans*, shall we Peter?" Marty had slipped into his Captain Hook accent.

"Should we take pens for autographs?" Nick asked in his impish Peter Pan dialect.

They stood together and left Marty's room, their moony-eyed love-sickness gone and their teenage rush of spring fever taking over. By the time they were to the top of the stairs they were in a fit of giggles so that Grandma Pentel's voice had to rise a bit to make herself heard over them, "What *is* so funny?"

A splash of cold reality sobered them from their momentary drunken giddiness, "Nothing, Grandma Pen," they said in unison, only to have the mere fact that they had spoken together catch their funny bones and set them off again.

Finally Marty choked out, "We're going to go to the game over at the school, it starts at 4:30."

"Okay, do you know when it will be over?" Pearl asked.

"About 6:00, I think," Marty managed as they went out

the front door.

"Teenagers," Pearl sighed, shaking her head, but even as she did a smile spread across her lips as she quoted softly, "'It was the best of times, it was the worst of times,' Dickens certainly knew the tale of two boys."

Still smiling she went into the kitchen to start dinner. At 4:15 Marty and Nick were scanning the crowd of people as they marched past from their lookout point 'Near Section A' of the bleachers. At 4:30 the scoreboard lit up and the baseball teams took the field. Just as they were about to give up, they felt movement close behind them.

Swinging around they found Monica Brussard and Amy Tillart, the girl with braids from choir that had laughed so hysterically on the first day of school. Well, you could have knocked either one of the boys over with a feather.

Nick's thoughts were racing, *How could she like me, if she broke up with me?*

Marty's mind was also racing, *Has Amy ever given me looks or any other sign of her secret love for me?* Secret smiles flashed in his memory, he had never really noticed her because he was always trying to get Sara to notice him. He felt a wave of guilt wash over him for having been so rude and thoughtless.

Monica finally broke the awkward silence, "So, you got our notes?"

Amy giggled, "Of course they got our notes, why else would they be at a baseball game?"

Marty found he really liked the sound of Amy's giggle. He studied her for the first time, she was kinda short, well, shorter than Monica anyway, her hair was long, down to the middle of her back, it was a light mousy brown, and it glistened in the sun. Her nose was pointed and freckles danced along the bridge of it as well as on her cheeks. She smiled easily and her eyes were framed by long lashes that cast shadows onto her cheeks. As she looked up at Marty her green eyes pierced him to his very center. *So, why haven't I noticed her before?* Only one answer, *I've been blind!*

Marty hadn't noticed but Nick and Monica had moved a few steps away and were now talking quietly. When he realized he was alone with Amy he didn't start floundering, he actually felt very natural, even in the silence.

Finally he spoke, "So, do *you* like baseball?"

Amy blushed, "No," she admitted honestly.

"Then, why the game?" Marty wondered aloud, "Why not some *other* time and place?"

"Do you know of any other big events that are coming up where we could meet you without drawing a ton of attention to ourselves? Besides you're guys and guys like the all-American pastime don't they?"

Man, she had really thought this thing out, Marty was impressed. There was only one other question he wanted to know, well, only one that puzzled him at the moment, "Who wrote that poem?"

"We both did," Amy admitted, "We've spent almost two months perfecting it."

Apparently she felt she needed to explain, so she began at the beginning, "Monica and I are in math together, and we've been friends since like the first day of school."

Marty liked the way she talked with her hands.

"So we decided to go to the play together, I mean, do you know how long it's been since seventh graders got a lead in the school play?"

His curiosity was piqued so he asked, "No, how long?"

"Well, Monica's older sister is at Lockhurst and she told us it's been like ten years!"

Marty was impressed with her extensive research.

Continuing she asked, "Do you know how long it's been since *two* leads were seventh graders?"

Dumbfounded with her interest he fed the fire, "I have no clue."

"Almost seventy years!" Amy said triumphantly.

"*No way!* How did you know that? How *could* you know that?"

Blushing even deeper she confessed, "I'm on the yearbook staff and I researched all the way back to the start of the school."

"How old *is* Rosewood anyway?" Marty was fascinated with how much Amy knew.

"Almost a hundred years old. To be exact it wasn't a junior high school all of those years though," deliberately leaving bait to test his interest level she waited for him to bite.

"What was it before?"

Amy smiled, her ploy was working, "A carriage factory."

"Really?" the history of Scat-town was truly diverse.

"Yeah, it opened just after Scat-town was settled in 1890, but it was much smaller back then."

"So, is there any of the building that is that old?"

"No, it actually caught fire and burned to the ground in 1906, but when the company sold the property to the state in 1917 the first school was built and was named Rosewood after the carriage company."

"Man, you really know your history!"

Pleased at his response Amy confessed, "I've always loved history."

Unable to let the opportunity go by Marty said, "So you must not have Culbreth for history."

"Oh, Marty, that wasn't *nice!*" but her eyes twinkled with laughter, "Actually I've learned as much as I can about Scat-town."

"You would get along great with my Grandma."

"Oh, who is she? I've studied up on most of the people around here," she said modestly, "I might know something about her."

"Pearl Pentel," Marty answered.

"*The* Pearl Pentel?"

Clearly Amy *had* studied about Grandma Pen, she began to bubble, "She was a teacher, here at Rosewood actually, she was one of the first students here too. Rufus Pentel met her at their first faculty meeting, you see, he worked here too."

This was crazy; Amy knew more than he did about his own grandparents!

"How do you know all of this?"

"I told you, I love history, I also love to read and your Grandpa Rufus' history is in the library," she stated this bit of information as if it were a well known fact to everyone.

"I didn't know that," Marty felt a little foolish admitting this, after all they were *his* grandparents.

"So, what do *you* like to do?"

The abrupt change in conversation threw Marty off guard, "I, uh, I like to read too."

"What was the last book you read?"

Without thinking he answered, "A book on Gwimmet."

"*What?*"

Realizing his mistake, but too late, he tried to make some sort of cover up without much success, "I was just kidding."

"How did you come up with such a weird name if you were just kidding?"

Amy certainly was perceptive!

"I meant, swimming, but sometimes my words get all mixed up."

This seemed to be an effective excuse and it covered up his blunder quite well, she smiled, "I do that all the time, especially when I start talking too fast."

Safe, at least for the time being Marty asked her the same question, "What was the last book *you* read?"

This made her brow furrow, "Well, let's see, I finished *Pride and Prejudice* last week and *Little Women* on Tuesday, so I guess it would be *Little Women*."

"Wow, you really *do* read a lot!" Marty was pleasantly surprised.

"Well, I'm reading *A Tale of Two Cities*, *The Adventures of Huckleberry Finn*, and *Les Miserables* right now, I usually have four books going at once but I figured since *Les Miserables* is over two thousand pages it counted for two," she smiled shyly, "You did it again!"

"What?" Marty was confused.

"You got me talking again, and I had tried to get you to tell me more about yourself."

"I don't mind, you're really smart, I like listening to you."

Amy blushed deeply for the third time, "Well, you're a very good listener."

Here it was Marty's turn to blush, "Really? I guess it's cause I was interested in what you were saying."

This was only partly true, he enjoyed watching her speak too, but he didn't dare tell *her* that.

They were standing with their heads huddled together when Nick and Monica returned, she spoke first, "How are you two doing?"

Apparently the discussion had softened Nick because he was holding her hand.

He threw a look to Marty that said, *I'll tell you about it later.*

Amy answered for them, "Did you know Marty's Grandma is *the* Pearl Pentel?"

This apparently meant nothing to Monica but Nick was surprised, "How do you know Grandma Pen?"

"Is she *your* grandma too?"

This hit Monica.

Nick shook his head, "No, I just call her that."

"Oh," Amy and Monica said together.

"So, do you guys want to stay here at the game?" Nick

asked.

"No!" Marty, Amy, and Monica said with such force that they all looked at each other and burst out laughing.

"Do you know where the park is?" Nick asked.

"Uh, yeah, it's right over there," Monica answered thinking Nick was serious, she also asked, "Haven't you ever been there?"

Marty started laughing, "Monica, he's teasing you, he is just hinting that he wants to go to the park. That's how he does things."

Hearing this explanation Monica nodded as comprehension dawned, "Oh, okay, I get it. Yeah, let's go to the park and swing on the swings."

"Sounds like fun," Amy agreed.

Nick and Marty exchanged glances that showed their surprise at such an easy compromise. With that they were off to the park that was adjacent to the baseball diamond. They all enjoyed their time in the park and said good-bye for the weekend as they heard the crowd breaking up at the end of the game.

Back at Grandma Pentel's Marty and Nick started sharing their individual stories, Marty told his first then he asked Nick, "So, what happened with Monica and *Mr. Officer?*"

"I guess he flattered her at first, but then he just kept trying to buy her off and she didn't like it. So she told him to take a hike. Monica had been helping Amy to make up the note to you, so she decided she would copy it and give one to me too."

"So, does she like you again or what?" Marty was curious.

"She said she never stopped liking me, in fact, that was one of the things that made her want to break-up with him. After comparing him to me she realized she had liked me all along, she had just been confused by a fast talker."

"It sounds a little like a soap opera," Marty confessed.

"I agree, but the crazy thing is, I believe her, and I think that is exactly what happened."

"Well, it's good she came to her senses," Marty joked.

"That's actually what I told her," Nick admitted.

They both laughed at that. After their discussion about Amy and Monica they decided to look in the map book to see if it was time for the next ingredient. Knowing that they only needed to flip through the pages was useful because they knew as soon as two stuck together they would have their next adventure. Nick and Marty sat down with the book between them and began flipping, but not one time did they find two pages stuck together. Marty was about to put the book away when he thought aloud, "It's been a long time since we looked at our adventure book, want to do that for a while?"

"Sure, that would be cool," Nick hadn't been thinking of their book either, in fact the miracle of finding it had almost been lost in his mind among all of their other awesome adventures.

Marty turned and reached under the bed, the spell book came out first, then on the second try the red-backed book came out, it was quite dusty from non-use. He brushed it off and cracked it open. They started reading and relived the adventures of all of the ingredients, the Phlems, Garths, Snoths, Nightens, Batworts, and last of all the Screms.

Each of the stories was accompanied by illustrations of the keys, characters they had encountered, and the actual ingredients. Turning the last page they were surprised to see something they hadn't seen before, another poem, printed clearly inside the book.

You're already proving us right
Why do you put up a fight?
This book has lain unused so long,

You thought that you weren't of the throng,
The ones who get all too busy,
Running 'round 'til they get dizzy.
But this gift you have been given,
Lay under your bed for months hidden.
You're also becoming lazy
The thrill of study has grown hazy.
You think by flipping through the book
The things you need to find and cook
Will leap out, grab you, pull you in,
You better listen up my friend.
If you as the Yulesaychaater,
Think to teach a son or daughter
Of mankind the joy of reading
You can't cut through books blindly speeding.
The next two tasks you'll find through learning
Then maybe you'll keep the candle burning
Of the books through all the ages
Fill shelves with volumes and with pages
Not just dusty smelly ones
Some that you may read to sons
Or Daughters who love a fairytale,
If you'll study you'll not fail.

By the time they got to the end, they both felt extremely guilty because it was *all* true. The thoughts of just a moment ago melted and they set to really reading the map book as they had started that very first day. By the time Nick had to leave, they had only gone through fifteen lands, it seemed that it had become more difficult to find information in the book.

Maybe that was part of the challenging and humbling lesson.

Chapter 30
Just What I've Always Wanted, A Phlicksplaat!

Friday, April 19, 1991

After a full week of studying from the spell book they came across two pages that stuck together, they had at last proven themselves worthy by their diligent study!

Poring over the passage inscribed they read aloud, Marty acting as voice, "Jasquint is a shallow sea village populated by mussel men and women. The unusual Phlicksplaat is also found floating around in the waters of Jasquint. If, by chance, you're able to catch a phlicksplaat you might find somewhere on its body the parasitic horn-tailed Speakur. Phlicksplaats are a fish-type creature with an uncharacteristically long tongue with which it searches the sands of Jasquint for its food. The tongues of the phlicksplaat have combed over every inch of Jasquint, but it is through their thorough searching that the sandy soil is aerated and cultivated allowing the lush underwater plant life to thrive and flourish. In turn the thnats which the Phlicksplaats eat swarm around the vegetation and the food chain completes itself. Phlicksplaats range between two-and-a-half to five feet in length depending on their age. The larger the phlicksplaat you find, the larger the Speakur will be that's attached. Horn-tailed Speakurs are a worm-like parasite with a suction cup mouth through which it feeds on the host Phlicksplaat. For defense the Speakur has a bulbous tail with sharp horns or spikes protruding from it similar to the prehistoric Ankylosaur.

Jasquintians are a Victorian-style people who are mussels. Along the sandy bottoms you will see hundreds of shells, all closed during the day, but at night they open and inside the lid you can see the owner of the shell. Reminiscent of the Victorian era cameo or locket, the circular lid frames the mussel people ever so well. Their community is extremely social and they thrive on classical music. You may even get them to peek out of their shells during the day if you were to play a little Bach or Beethoven."

Here Nick interrupted, "So, the mussel men and women look like *real* people?"

"It sounds like they live in the lid of a clam or something like that," Marty tried, "I remember seeing an old locket of Grandma Pen's."

He continued, "It's a necklace that you can open and it has small pictures in it," then he picked up in the reading, "'*Underwater music*?' You may ask, well it's not as difficult as you might think. Using the trillo wing's special quality of recording sound and its resistance to water, you can save enough music to attract the attention of the Jasquintians."

"Why do we need to talk to the Jasquintians?" Nick broke in again.

Marty shrugged, "Let's see if it says...where was I...oh here it is... 'Funny you should ask that, the Jasquintians are the only ones who know how to catch the Phlicksplaats. Even though I as the author tried to entice it out of them, they wouldn't budge. I guess that's what I get for trying to move a mussel."

"The person who wrote this is pretty funny!" Nick commented amid his giggles.

Without stopping Marty read on, "Why, thank you, young man. Now, shall we continue?"

Nick froze and slowly nodded his head as Marty continued the article, "You'll need a smirkle, that is similar to the human snorkel, but you can be understood much better with a smirkle in your mouth than with a snorkel. Say that five times fast, ha, ha, oh I say, the Eyahge'er was right, I *am* quite funny."

At this Marty stopped, looked up at Nick who hadn't moved and said, "This book can hear us, and knows us, and it's *talking* to us," he finished with awe in his voice.

Looking back down at the book he scanned through the printed page and found where he had just read, and opened his mouth but his eyes moved quickly to the next sentence and he closed his mouth again.

Sensing something was wrong Nick asked, "Are you, *Okay*, Marty?"

Marty nodded and read feebly the next words, "Well, what did you think I was doing? Of course I'm talking to you! This is the chance of a life time I get to help the Yulesaychaater fight the witches of Zanth. Unfortunately they have me under a curse too, so I can only do what they tell me, when they tell me, but once you start reading I'm allowed to tell what I know, so this is part of what I know, I can talk with the reader of this book through print. I haven't dared 'til now because I thought you would give up after the sisters threatened you, I know *I* would have, but I'm not nearly as brave as you. I only have a spine, not a backbone.

"Well, let me finish the information about Jasquint before the Zanth sister catch on to my deception. You will need some scrimlets for you feet, made from the hide of the blomb they keep you afloat, a little like an inner tube, but are shaped like a flipper. For your body you'll want a dry suit, it helps to keep you from getting your clothes all wet, these are commonly constructed of slipmank skin. They look like silk, but feel like rubber, and they button like pajamas. For your eyes you'll need bandis glocks they're like swimming goggles that don't fog up. Well that's all from my end. Good luck and see you next month."

Marty sighed as he looked at Nick, "The surprising thing is, I've almost expected the book to talk to us, but now that it has, I'm curious how it was done."

"Should we get the key and be on our way?" Nick reminded.

Marty agreed and pried the next two pages apart. A beautiful top view of Jasquint was shown, the vegetation growing around some shells in the near-white sand. A flash crossed the page and they had to assume it had been a Phlicksplaat since that was the only animal they had read about.

In the page opposite a shimmery shell-like door was imbedded it said:

"Jasquint is behind this door
Mussel men and what is more,
The Phlicksplaat if you catch it will
Help you to complete the bill."

Marty finished reading this out loud and then worked on the door, it was difficult because it was a totally different type than he had had to work with as of yet. Finally by wedging one prong of the tweezers under the edge he was able to lift the hatch-like door away from in front of the key.

The full-sized key, when it appeared, was interesting to say the least. At the head it was the shape of a school crossing sign, turned upside down. In the center was a circular hole with a spiky baseball bat-like appendage hanging down. The tip of the key was pointed and the teeth area held a single simple rectangular piece. It was tinted a sky blue and it glistened like glass.

"We need to go to Bismorda's and collect all the stuff, did you write it all down?" Marty asked as he stood.

Holding up a folded paper, Nick nodded, then spoke, "Don't forget the trillo wing! We need it to record some classical music."

Retrieving the key to Qualf and the trillo wing Marty met Nick at the door. Nick had remembered the canvas bag and had it over his shoulder, ready to fill it with the needed supplies. After the key was inserted and the click sounded, Nick and Marty stepped out onto the banks of the River Sems.

Making good time, since they weren't weighed down

by anything, they crested the hill and were moving into Bismorda's castle within twenty minutes, a new record.

Looking at the remaining objects in the hall, they were able to find the smirkles and scrimlets rather quickly, they were all that was left with the remaining fish bowl on the right hand side of the hall.

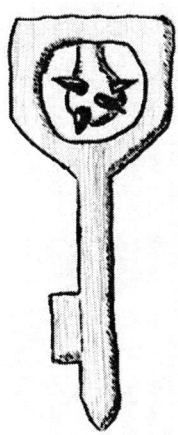

Crossing to the left they sorted through the clothes there until the silky-looking, rubbery feeling dry suits of slipmank skin were rolled up and stowed in the bag. Two pairs of the bandis glocks went into the bag as well. Further along the wall they found a record of Chopin, and a small packet of something oily. Reading the tiny printing on one side of the packet it said, "Phlicksplaat essence, food for your pet Speakur. One month supply."

"Man, those Zanth sisters thought of *everything*!" Nick exclaimed.

"Yeah, we'll have to ask them where they got it all," Marty thought aloud, "I've been wondering, remember Gwimmet?"

Nick nodded with a puzzled look, "Yeah, why?"

"Remember what Gratzwinda said about the Tillanian beads?"

"She thought we stole them, or her people did," this

statement brought a look of comprehension on Nick's face.

Marty agreed, "See, I hope that the Zanth sisters haven't *stolen* all of these things."

"That would not be cool," Nick responded.

"Let's hope not, but I still want to ask them when we get the chance," Marty finished as he picked up the record, "Now, where would we find a record player?"

"Do you think they would listen to music in the sitting room?" Nick tried to think logically.

"Maybe, let's check in there first."

After a quick search of the sitting room brought nothing that resembled a record player they had to think of another possibility.

"Is there anywhere that they store things in this place? A closet maybe?" Nick contemplated out loud.

"The storage room!" Marty almost shouted, "The first door on the right side of the main hall."

"Oh yeah, we didn't look in there during our first search since you knew what was there," recalled Nick.

"Well, let's go check in there," Marty led the way after a quick deposit of all the other items except the record and trillo wing onto the entrance hall floor.

Turning into the hallway, they took their first right. As the door swung open so did Marty's jaw. When Marty gasped it caused Nick to assume this room had changed since Marty had seen it last. It was now an elegant and spacious music room.

There was a harp in one corner that glittered as the light reflected off of its gilt surface. It was paired with a delicate brocade stool that just begged for someone to seat themselves and begin a haunting melody on the strings. In the far corner stood a grand piano, its ebony aloofness allowing it to look arrogant and elegant all at once.

The remaining instruments were either hanging from pegs on the wall opposite them or laying in repose against one cushioned chair or another in various parts of the room. The room's instruments were an amazing collection ranging from a pan-pipe made from simple swamp reeds, to an electric guitar plugged into a very expensive looking amplifier.

Bismorda must *really* like music! She had items from all over the world and from the beginning of time, or so it seemed. In the corner behind the door sat an upright phonograph with a huge flower-like funnel speaker on the top. Nick recognized it from one of his trips to some museum or other, "This is a really old record player, but it should do the trick."

When they approached it they realized that someone had updated it, because it was plugged into an outlet in a power generator, "Bismorda doesn't use electricity in the house, except for things she has acquired from the human world," Marty observed.

Removing the record from its cardboard jacket Marty placed it on the center post inside the box of the record player, fitting the hole onto it. Lifting the arm he placed the needle into the record's grooves and searched for the power switch.

It was to the right of the turn-table by the volume and speed controls. Flipping the switch brought the turn-table to life. As it slowly started rotating the record crackled to life. Before long, Chopin's *Polonaise* was playing, and now for the hard part, how to record with the trillo wing?

The wing lay in Marty's palm and both he and Nick tried pushing it across his palm, then speaking to it, finally Nick had an idea, he stroked it gently with his index finger. It quivered, started to hum, then rose off of Marty's palm, just in time to catch the closing bars of *Polonaise* and as the record went on to play one of Chopin's concertos it continued, catching every note.

Music lilted through the air and the boys began to really like the sound of it when the humming slowed and the trillo wing came back to rest on Marty's outstretched palm again. Turning off the record player they left the record of Chopin in place, just in case they wanted to listen to it later, and departed the music room.

Back in the entrance hall they loaded themselves up, each taking a smirkle and pair of scrimlets, Nick took the canvas bag with their dry suits and bandis glocks inside while Marty got the fish bowl and Speakur food. Double checking that he had the trillo wing in his shirt pocket and the key to Jasquint in his hip pocket Marty gave the order, "Let's move out," as if they were cowboys on a cattle rustling spree in the old west.

Back under the bridge they decided it would be best to see where the door took them first then, they would prepare themselves accordingly. Marty inserted the key and the click that followed took them to Jasquint, at least it did behind the door. Turning the knob, Marty swung open the door, revealing a large body of water that stretched out farther than his imagination with no sign of dry land anywhere. Cautiously they leaned out of the door far enough so they were peering down into the water.

It was clearer than *any* explanation given by Ms. Culbreth, and they could see a large quantity of clam-like shells in clusters on the near-white sand surrounded by sea plants. The entire landscape of Jasquint was four feet under the water. They retreated back into Qualf and decided to put on their dry suits here and take the smirkles and scrimlets with them. Pulling out the silky, rubbery garments from the bag they each took a pair of the pajama-like outfits. Marty donned a dark blue set and Nick slid into his black one. This unusual getup made them feel like they were getting ready forbed, but they now had layered their clothes so it was weirder than usual.

Marty sat down on the bank, dangling his feet into the waters of Jasquint through the open door, and then slipped into the chest-high water. Being careful not to step on anything he turned back to Nick, who was still standing above him in Qualf, "Hand me the smirkles, bandis glocks, and scrimlets. You should jump in, this is *so* strange. I can feel the pressure of the water, but I'm completely dry, I don't even feel the water on my skin, except on my feet and arms."

Musselman & Woman in Jasquint

Nick leaned down, delivered the equipment to Marty then he too slipped into the water, being careful not to tread on the shells or plants. Placing the smirkles in their mouths they talked just to test it out, and it was true, you couldn't tell that anything was in their mouths at all just like the mouthpieces on the klinx tanks. Next they put on the bandis glocks and leaning down into the water they put the scrimlets on their feet. Immediately their feet pulled out from under them and they were face down in the water. The scrimlets held their feet afloat, but in order to talk to or reach the Jasquintians they would really have to fight against them. They swam a distance into the open water near the largest cluster of shells to play the music.

Marty retrieved the trillo wing and holding it in both hands he was able to get the music to start. The wing fluttered violently against Marty's palms until he let it float freely. Spiraling in the water it created a small funnel of bubbles and the sound grew louder. Chopin was even better underwater it felt like the *music* was making them float! Marty was so taken by the sound that Nick had to poke him in the side to get him to notice that the mussels were stirring. Bubbles began forming around the lips of the shells before they separated and floated to the surface.

Slowly the first shells began to open. A cultured English accent broke through the water and could be heard over the music, it was the voice of a man, "Oh, I say, Beatrice, do you hear that? It's Chopin, I haven't heard Chopin in ages. It's been simply ages!"

Marty and Nick located the face that belonged to the voice and were able to study him, his slick black hair was combed straight back from his face, he had a black moustache that twirled slightly on the ends, he had a monocle fixed over one eye, and was peering through the water to see who had brought the wonderful music. His high collared shirt with neck tie was definitely old fashioned.

The voice of a woman answered in rapture, "Oh, John, it *is* wonderful isn't it?"

It was easy to locate the woman, she was in the shell right next to the one she called John. Beatrice was a serious looking woman with her hair pulled back into a bun on the crown of her head leaving small wisps of curls around her face, her high collared dress had a fringe of lace and she looked less excited than her voice sounded, but Marty and Nick reasoned it was probably from having her hair so tight. As the boys looked around they realized that most all of the shells were now open revealing women and men from a by-gone era. Some women were fanning themselves lightly with lacy plumes, others were chatting together, the men were all dressed nicely too and all of the mussel people of Jasquint were looking at Marty and Nick, the carriers of this beautiful change of music. The trillo wing stopped and drifted down through the water until it came to rest back in Marty's open palm.

He pocketed it, cleared his throat and addressed the now captive audience, "Good afternoon, people of Jasquint, I hope you enjoyed the music of Frederic Chopin we brought with us," Marty pronounced it correctly *Show-pan* after hearing John say it just moments previous.

Back in Bismorda's castle when he read the label on the record he thought it was pronounced choppin', like *choppin'* wood. He went on, "I am Marty Whimpel and this is my best friend Nicholas Chrismon," at this everyone began chattering.

"It's the Yulesaychaater!"

"The Eyahge'er *here*?"

"Together, they come together to bring music to *us*!"

"They truly *are* great."

These responses made both Nick and Marty blush, which is a little strange when you're face down in water. Just then Nick remembered something, they had forgotten the fishbowl! He tried to get Marty's attention, but he was talking again to the crowd.

"We've come to get a horn-tailed Speakur off of one of your Phlicksplaats, but we were told you were the only ones who could help us to catch one…"

"Excuse us for just a moment," Nick burst in.

Pulling Marty over a few feet he then whispered, "We forgot the fishbowl, what are we going to do?"

"You go get it, I'll stall so they don't go back inside their shells, okay?"

Marty went back to share small talk with the Jasquintians as Nick swam as quickly as he could back toward the door to Qualf. Without removing the scrimlets, Nick managed to stand up in the water, in fact, he was basically walking on water, only his feet were still submerged. Luckily he had had practice with something like this with the bog of Debocket, now by slow shuffle steps he could keep himself stationary on the ever-moving water. In this position he could easily reach back through the door to get the fishbowl on the river bank. In his haste he dropped the food packet out of the bowl and had to finagle his way around the doorframe until he could reach the small parcel. Once he had the food back in his possession he started back for the group of Jasquintians.

Somehow he maneuvered around so that he was facedown in the water again, this time holding the fishbowl in one arm under the surface and propelling himself back to Marty's side with his free arm and legs. As he swam up to join them he heard, "Oh, here comes the Eyahge'er now."

There was a round of applause.

Marty turned and said, "I was just telling them how you help keep me on task and focus on these adventures."

Nick appreciated the compliment, especially in front of such a large gathering, all he could think to say was, "Did you find out how to get the Speakur?"

"*See*, what did I tell you?" Marty had proved his point amply and the Jasquintians applauded again.

As the noise died down John spoke up, "To get a Speakur you say?"

Nick nodded.

John raised his voice and called, "Andromeda! Come here girl!"

It sounded like he was calling to a dog, but in an instant a large fish that could only be a Phlicksplaat was hovering next to Marty and Nick, but giving full attention to John.

"Stay girl, good girl," John spoke to her soothingly.

Andromeda was a fine specimen of Phlicksplaat indeed, she was about four feet long and had a set of sleek silvery scales. Her fins were iridescent and her mouth puckered, it looked like she could start whistling on command.

Nick and Marty moved to opposite sides of her to scan for the Speakur, Nick spotted one first, "Over her right fin Marty, I found one!"

Reaching forward slowly Nick took hold of the glossy green Speakur along its middle, luckily it was about six inches long, because when he had grabbed the mid-section the tail started flailing, trying to hit Nick with its spiky ball, but it was unable to bend that sharply.

Phlicksplaat

Pulling the Speakur free let a thin cloud of blood ooze from where it had been attached to the Phlicksplaat.

Andromeda let out a kind of hum. She was purring

because they had removed the Speakur, it must have been quite a nuisance to her. Placing the Speakur in the fishbowl, Nick held the bowl so that the rim was above the level of the water to prevent the Speakur's escape, and thanked Andromeda with a quick pat along her side.

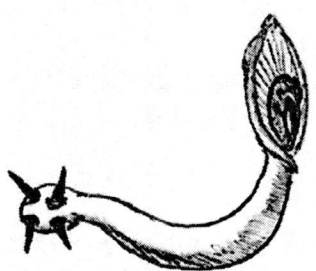

Horn-tailed Speakur

John spoke up again, "Thanks girl, good girl, daddy loves his Andromeda, go play!"

Quicker than time travel, Andromeda was gone again. Marty turned to John, "Thank you so much sir, we are *forever* in your debt."

To this John replied, "No, no, Yulesaychaater sir, it is *we* who will forever be in the minds of young and old because of your great sacrifice and you too noble Nicholas, Eyahge'er, sir! Good show boys, jolly good show." With that he gave a mighty yawn, "Well, ta-ta. I'm dreadfully sleepy, I can barely keep my lid open. Give our best to Bismorda when you see her next."

When the shell had closed completely the sound of snores quickly filled the water surrounding them. Marty and Nick turned in the water and swam back toward the door, all the while Nick made sure to keep the rim of the bowl out of the water.

At the door Nick demonstrated how to get out, he gave the bowl to Marty and stuck his arms up to grasp the doorframe. Using the frame as a brace he pulled himself upright, then standing on his scrimlets he was able to step up over the doorframe and back into Qualf onto the banks of the Sems. Getting the bowl from Marty, Nick placed the bowl to the side and then helped Marty out of Jasquint. Gazing back along the beautiful horizon of blue they pulled the door shut.

Peeling off the sopping wet dry suits they were amazed to find their clothes were completely dry underneath, except where Marty had put the trillo wing while he was swimming. Wringing the water from their dry suits they put them back into the canvas bag. Nick found the Speakur food packet, which had somehow remained plastered to the side of the fishbowl as they transported it back to Qualf, and after opening the plastic-like bag emptied it into the water.

It clouded the water, but settled along the bottom surface of the bowl quite quickly. Happily the Speakur attached itself to the glass and began feeding. With the extra items packed into the canvas bag or in hand, the boys went once more to Bismorda's castle, weary, yet triumphant. The space they had cleared for the Speakur's bowl on the shelf in the larder was perfect.

They checked on the Screms in the fizzy water, apparently they lived off of the bubbles, because they were swimming around oblivious to anything around them except their bubbly paradise.

Gazing into the murky bog sludge they tried once more to check on the Snoths, but were unsuccessful, they could only hope that they were doing well in their putrid home. After checking that the other items were still in order Nick and Marty swung the larder door closed anxious for their final adventure.

On their way back through the entrance hall they froze, the hair on the back of each of their necks stood up. Fastened to the back of the front door was a paper that rustled in the stillness of the cavernous entry. Had it been there when they returned?

Or had the Zanth sisters come and left as they made

their trip to the larder? Automatically their eyes narrowed to slits and their other senses intensified seeking any foreign sounds or movements. Inching forward they got to the door without interference.

Marty reached forward, removed the note, cleared his suddenly choked up throat, and read:

"One left now, that's all to do
We both doubt you'll make it through
The bear-like people of Phason Wil Blanch,
Love to eat humans with a side of ranch.
The Irish Gorder is kinda harmful,
It has spikes, don't get an armful.
Keep your flesh well undercover,
With the clothes of ottis lauver.
Take a lure for the Whears,
Those are the human-like bears.
In a vase of pilsmot clearly,
Gather the wax you want so dearly.
Use a siglen, but be wary,
Of the leaves, they're sharpish very.
The Gorder grows out of the trunk
Of a rare tree called a skrunk.
This last time our words if heeded
Will get you the item needed."

Taking a deep breath they both blew out slowly.

Obviously if the Zanth sisters had entered while they were there, they hadn't been discovered, or the note truly had been left earlier and they just hadn't noticed it, but Marty couldn't shake a bad feeling he had in his gut. Brushing it aside as best he could he spoke with a forced carefree air, "Well, let's go home, shall we?"

Nick noticed the false air, but said nothing as they dumped the wet clothes out of the bag, picked up the key to

Qualf and left as quickly as they could. The folded paper was stored in Marty's back pocket and felt like a hot coal to his conscience, why was he getting this feeling?

Under the bridge the key was turned in the lock and its click sounded, bringing Marty's room back, without hesitation they entered. Immediately they both tensed, something was different, taking a quick look over everything, they couldn't tell what was missing, but *something* was gone, they could sense it. The key was turned again to return them to Grandma Pentel's and they went on an in-depth search.

"The *map* book!" It was Nick who realized first, "I put it on the floor, right here by the bed, but it's gone!"

Marty bent to check under the bed to see if maybe it had slid under somehow, but he knew it hadn't before he looked. As they stood there in disbelief the paper in Marty's pocket gave him a jolt, he jumped, and pulled it out quickly. Unfolding it he realized there was more writing on the back of the page. Reading out loud once more:

"Thank you for leaving the key, we only could use once
So we've waited, watched, and prayed that you might prove the dunce.
Left, it was, inside Bismorda's castle
We returned and used it, without a hassle.
The map book seemed to want to talk, we needed it to stop
So while you were at the bottom, we were at the top.
We only had the power to use the key twice,
But twice is all we needed it worked ever so nice.
We left the clues to get you to your next station,
The time for that mission will be near your break, or vacation.
Thanks again, for careless use of the key you found,
But don't worry we can't come to your world, we're bound.
Take heed boys the key you need will come to you in May,
All we give is the month, you must await the day.
Take care and we hope to see you soon,

Better hope your job is done, by the month of June!

The OhRa

    Letting the paper lower until it was at his side Marty spoke so quietly Nick had to lean forward to hear him, "I failed, I'm not good enough to be the Yulesaychaater, I let the book down."

    "No, Marty, we'll be fine, the Zanth sisters made sure we got the clues, and they said they'll give us the key. I'm not sure how they'll do it, but they want us to win too. They'll get us the key."

    Marty said one more time, "but *I* failed..."

    Then like a gaping mouth the silence swallowed them.

Chapter 31
Seeing Is Believing, Well, Sort Of

Monday, April 22, 1991

The news of Marty and Amy and Nick and Monica was common knowledge around Rosewood by Monday at 8:00 a.m. Nick had an advantage to Marty because he already had Monica's schedule memorized, but Marty stayed up late Sunday night going through Amy's schedule and his plan of getting around the school.

When Monday came it was with confidence that they walked into the school. It seemed there were nine hundred pairs of eyes glued to Marty and Nick as they walked to their lockers. Within minutes they were prepared for first period and split up to escort their respective female counterparts to their classes and rejoin in P.E.

The only time during the day they were all together was at lunch so they took advantage of this time and planned another "outing" for the four of them. It was to be on Saturday the 27th, Monica would come over to Amy's which happened to be two blocks away from the school too, but in the opposite direction. Marty was enraptured that his house was only four blocks away from Amy's!

They would get together at the park for a picnic and then go from there. Amy had expressed interest in meeting Grandma Pentel so they could possibly visit Marty's home afterwards, the bell that signaled the end of lunch came far too soon and they promised to discuss the details on the following day. After school Marty and Nick returned to Grandma Pentel's to study and the subject of the girls came up, so they decided to run an idea past each other.

"I was just thinking," Nick began.

"About Monica?" Marty guessed.

"*And* Amy," Nick continued.

"Why both of them?" Marty could feel his face become

hot with jealousy.

"Not in that way Marty," soothed Nick. "I was just thinking how much fun it would be to take them on an adventure."

"You thought about that too?" Marty was not only surprised, he was dumbfounded, "I was thinking how I could ask you what you thought about it, but I guess you beat me to it."

"Cool, so you think we could do it?" Nick asked hopefully.

"Do you think they'll believe we *can* take them on an adventure?" Marty wondered.

"Hmmm, I hadn't thought of that," Nick replied and got that look on his face that he always did when he was deep in contemplation.

Marty thought for a moment then spoke, "How 'bout if we kind of test the water on Saturday?"

"How?" Nick mused.

Again Marty fell silent, his brow furrowed, then he spoke, "What if I tell them the story of Bismorda, but make it sound like *just* a story?"

"Then what?" Nick wondered.

"Well, if they seem really interested, or ask questions about it, we could tell them a little more."

"What if they guess that it's *not* a story?"

"Then we can tell them that it is real, and swear them to secrecy," Marty concluded.

Nodding Nick agreed, "Sounds good, we'll give it a try."

Dreamily Marty continued, "I'd love to show Qualf to Amy."

"I want to show it to Monica too," Nick admitted.

With that agreed upon they finished their homework thinking of their ladies fair and dreamed of the adventures they could go on together.

Saturday, April 27, 1991

In anticipation of their picnic Marty and Nick enlisted the help of their moms and Grandma Pen. All of the women were practically in hysterics, their 'little boys' were growing up! They helped prepare picnic style food on Friday night and Saturday morning so that when the appointed time arrived there was a picnic basket full of food, a blanket, and even a portable radio to play some music on. Pearl, Charlotte, and Janet stood arm in arm at Pearl's large window watching their boys make their way toward the school and the adjacent park where the girls would be waiting.

They all sighed collectively. To say that the girls were impressed would be an understatement, they were *floored*. Nick and Marty were honest and said they had only helped with some of the food, but Monica and Amy were still full of compliments. They actually chose classical music on a majority vote. Monica was the only one not in favor, but she seemed to get used to it after a few minutes of listening. After the food had been consumed except for a few pieces of fried chicken and a little potato salad, they all sat back to relax and talk.

Marty took this as his cue, "Do you guys want to hear a story?"

Amy and Monica traded glances coyly and giggled.

"Sure, daddy, tell us a story," Amy said in a teasing tone.

"*Okay,*" suddenly a little embarrassed Marty began, "Once upon a time in a town called Broomstick, there was a boy named Bartholomew," he had to think quickly to change the name of his hometown and his name as well, but the rest of the story came out quite smoothly and his audience was leaning forward in anticipation by the end of it.

"Oh, that was a *great* story!" Amy sighed.

"Too bad there isn't *really* a door where we could go

into a different world," Monica added sadly.

"That would be a little like *The Lion, the Witch, and the Wardrobe* by C.S. Lewis," noted Amy, "Except in your story it's just a door and not a wardrobe of course."

By this time Marty and Nick were wriggling with excitement themselves.

They had been carefully evaluating the comments when the final cue fell from Monica's lips, "I wish *we* could go on an adventure like that."

Amy began to nod in agreement when suddenly Nick and Marty burst out together, "But you *can!*"

Staring at them in disbelief Amy and Monica began to protest, but Marty cut them off.

"Bartholomew is *me*! *I* helped to save Bismorda and Nick and I are trying to save her and her kingdom again *right now.*"

Nick jumped in enthusiastically, "Yeah we've been on some awesome adventures to Debocket and Gwimmet."

"*Gwimmet?*" Amy asked suspiciously and turning to Marty she asked pointedly, "But that's what you told me that first day, a week ago, was that for real? You really *did* read a book about Gwimmet didn't you?" She was now fully facing Marty.

He nodded.

"Why didn't you tell me about all of this *then?*" Amy was a little injured at his lack of trust.

"Right, on the first day we actually talk to one another I tell you all about how I find keys and go into foreign places through my bedroom door. You can't tell me that you would have believed me. You would seriously have thought I had lost it and walked away," Marty explained defensively.

Amy was silent for a moment and she replied, "Yeah, you're probably right," she giggled then added, "It's still pretty hard to believe, but since both of you *can't* by crazy I guess I'll have to accept it."

Marty looked at Nick, was she mocking them or was she being completely genuine? Then he turned and looked at her again, her eyes were twinkling as she spoke anew this time in a whisper, "I would *love* to go, it's like a dream come true for me," the next thing caught them all off guard, "I wish it had been me…" and they could tell she meant it.

For the next few moments they sat in silent contemplation and then Marty's brain clicked almost audibly, "Since you liked my story so much, how 'bout we have Grandma Pen tell us another one?"

"Oh, *would* she?" Amy was rapturous.

"Does she tell them as good as you?" Monica asked, this was quickly followed by a deep crimson blush.

"Better," Nick interjected.

"If we're all in agreement, let's clean up and head over there," Marty suggested.

If you had all seen the four of them from a distance you would have been reminded of ants bustling quickly along, packing things away, and then each taking something to carry they left the park.

On the brief walk back to Grandma Pentel's Amy adjusted her load so she had a free hand and could quietly slide it into Marty's. He almost tripped and fell over his feet right there on the sidewalk, but recovered nicely so that no one would have known this was his first time ever holding a girl's hand. Except for the huge amount of sweat that was now pouring between his palm and Amy's it was an exceedingly pleasurable experience. Marty was ultra self-conscious about the added wetness, but as they got to Grandma Pentel's porch Amy withdrew her hand and nonchalantly wiped it on her shorts.

When he threw a glance at her she smiled back as if to say, *Sweaty palms are a part of the territory, it's okay.*

He breathed a sigh of relief as they entered the house and called, "We're home, and we brought some *visitors!*"

Some muffled talking ceased and three very excited women entered, Charlotte, followed by Janet with Pearl bringing up the rear.

After brief introductions of the girls to Charlotte and Janet, Pearl pushed forward and said, "Come give Grandma Pen a squeeze!"

Amy about burst with joy at this prospect and Monica hesitated only slightly before she too gave a big hug to Pearl. After Marty and Nick received their dose as well Amy spoke, "Mrs. Pentel, I have read your husband's history and know *all* about you. I admire you a great deal. It's a great pleasure to finally meet you."

Flattered Pearl colored slightly, "My dear, I didn't know I would have such a distinguished guest coming to visit or I would have gussied up."

"Oh no! I love you just the way you are, it's very close to the way I pictured you," Amy consoled.

"What's missing?" Pearl wondered curiously.

Amy hesitated just a moment under the scrutiny of everyone present then said shyly, "Actually I pictured you sitting down with a big plate of chocolate chip cookies and glasses of milk for everyone."

Pearl chuckled, then grew a little serious, "Well, will you forgive me if the cookies are *oatmeal*?"

Amy's eyes grew wide, "Did you bake cookies *today*?"

"Most every day there's something to be baked," Pearl said, "but today I was just showing Janet, I mean Nick's mother how I make my oatmeal cookies, she really liked them the last time she was here."

"I *knew* it!" Amy said triumphantly.

At everyone's questioning glances she explained, "I knew she would share her recipes, in your husband's history he said it was like pulling teeth to get you to share your recipes, but that just didn't sound like how I imagined you."

"You really *do* know me pretty well," Pearl mused, her

eyes twinkling at this young girl with the long braids, and seeing herself so many years ago. "Do you like reading everything or just *ancient* history?" Pearl joked.

Everyone laughed at that, but Amy responded, "I love reading everything, but I *really* like history, especially the history of Scat-town."

"Grandma, we were wondering if we could hear a story, would you read us one?" Marty asked.

"Do you all like fairytales?" Pearl gathered them all in a sweeping glance, "*Grown-ups* included."

Looking at one another they all nodded.

"Okay, Marty go get the books and everyone else gather round the couch here."

With that Pearl seated herself and everyone but Marty crowded in closer, Janet and Charlotte sat on opposite sides of Pearl on the couch while the kids sat on the floor in front of her. Marty brought the books from the side room and handed them to Grandma Pentel who carefully looked through the pile until she decided instead to share the choice with them. Turning the six books so they could all see the titles each person selected a different one, but Amy's choice, *Puss In Boots*, was heard first, so that was the one agreed upon.

Settling in to hear the story they quieted and Pearl's voice rose as she took center stage:

"Once upon a time a poor miller had come to the end of a hard-working life and gathered his three sons around him to bid them each farewell. Rewarding each son according to their age the oldest got the mill, the second the donkey and the youngest was bequeathed the cat. The two oldest decided to continue doing business together while the youngest was left to fend for himself with only his cat..."

Pearl's audience was wrapped up in the story as Puss with his master's boots set out to impress the king, then after eating the ogre whom he had tricked into turning himself to a mouse Puss rewarded his master with a whole kingdom.

"And Puss retired, only hunting mice for fun."

The group sat in silent awe as the story closed. No one dared to break the spell that Pearl had cast over them.

Finally Pearl herself asked, "So, who wants some cookies and milk?"

Standing the seven of them filed into the kitchen to sit around the kitchen table and enjoy some of Grandma Pentel's homemade oatmeal cookies and ice-cold milk. Excusing himself, Marty slipped downstairs to straighten up his room so that if the girls wanted to go on a tour they wouldn't see his unmade bed or clothes all over the floor. After a quick cleaning spree he again appeared upstairs to pose the offer to Monica and Amy. They agreed to a tour, but they said after the tour they would have to go.

Making their way down to Marty's room they stopped at the wall of toilet paper and Amy spoke, "So, it's *true!*"

"What?" Monica asked.

"The promise that Mr. and Mrs. Pentel made to each other after the Depression. They vowed they would never again be without toilet paper. Now I see it's here, it's like a story coming true," Amy's tone was reverent.

She took books very seriously; this was one of her topics of study coming to life in front of them. As they entered Marty's room he moved to his dresser drawer and pulled out the key to Qualf. Holding it out on his open palm Amy and Monica both leaned forward to get a better view. Amy's hand reached forward tentatively and her fingers closed around the key. She giggled nervously as she felt the cold metal key and intricately formed creature on the key head. Examining it closely she held it up to her eyes as if she were a jeweler viewing a precious stone to verify if it were genuine.

Marty almost expected her to pull out a jeweler's scope and give it the once over, but she had evidently had her fill because she handed it back to Marty with a mischievous smile, "Thanks, that *is* really neat. I sure would love to see it at work."

This little bit of encouragement was all that Marty needed, he shut the bedroom door and motioned for Monica and Amy to draw closer. Nick, who already knew what was going to happen had come up beside Marty and now moved to make room for the girls to see. In a sort of ceremony Marty held the key in his hand and moved it toward the doorknob which in turn glowed, a keyhole opened and the key was pushed into place.

Following the turn of the key and clicking sound Monica spoke, a little disappointed, "Is that *all*?"

"Shh..." Amy reprimanded, she was staring at every movement respectfully.

Marty didn't speak, he turned the knob and threw open the door. The river Sems was burbling softly along at their feet, and Amy ooed as Monica sucked in her breath with surprise.

Sweeping his arm graciously in front of them, Marty spoke, "Welcome to Qualf."

"Let's give them a tour!" Nick said emphatically.

"Do you *want* a tour?" Marty asked, already knowing the answer.

"Yes!" both girls replied simultaneously.

"We'll show you the village today and then show you the castle next time, okay?" Marty offered.

After only a moment of contemplation the girls both nodded excitedly. They weren't going to say anything now, but Marty had just made a commitment to bring them to Qualf again, they had both heard him and they were going to hold him to it. Touring the village was an adventure that Nick and Marty had not done yet so they were in for a few surprises as they set out to show the girls a good time.

Chapter 32
The Town Holds A Secret

As they stepped onto the banks in single file Marty grabbed the key and took it with them, he was *not* going to be responsible for another abduction by the Zanth sisters. The path on this side of the bridge meandered lazily in and out along the dotted countryside. They stopped and gazed at a few small farms similar to the one Marty and Nick had visited.

As they got closer to the main town there were still no signs of life and the girls began to wonder where everything and everyone had gone. It was time to tell them about Bismorda's second disappearance, this time a complete abduction and not just a simple three hundred year curse.

"We were challenged to help Bismorda and her kingdom but the only way we could help them was to go to Zanth and ask the witches to help us," Marty related.

Nick continued, "So, we went to ask them to help us cure Marty's Acne Pimple disease."

Monica broke in, "You asked the Zanth witches to help you cure *zits*?"

Being girls Monica and Amy had matured faster than Nick or Marty and had already been battling acne for a few years.

"But, you can't fight zits with magic! You need acne treatment that you buy at the store," Monica reasoned.

Amy was willing to believe in the magic, "So, you went to the witches, what did they give you?"

Nick, who was now hesitant under Monica's questioning held back and let Marty continue.

Gladly, Marty resumed the tale, "Grisele and Mopel Zanth have a creature called the OhRa attached to their head and we had to win a staring contest with it. Once we did we got a list of ingredients that we have to find and then mix together to make the Acne Pimple potion that will cure me of the disease."

Amy had only one question, "A staring contest, *how* did you win?"

"Well, the OhRa can freeze you with its stare so we had to approach it with a mirror over our shoulder, the reflection can't hurt you it's just the actual eyes of the OhRa that can," Marty explained.

"Just like Medusa in Greek mythology," breathed Amy.

"Except I don't know if it turns you to stone," Marty ventured, "For some reason I just thought it froze the people it caught."

"Maybe it does," Amy reasoned, "Have you found *any* of its victims?"

"No," Marty found he was actually disappointed he couldn't show Amy the results of a failed battle with the OhRa.

"So, they're not all placed around the castle? That's where they all were in *The Lion, The Witch, and The Wardrobe*," Amy tried.

"No, nothing is anywhere near the castle, Nick and I have been all the way through it and we've gone up to it about a dozen times since the beginning of the school year with the different ingredients we have gathered."

"Oh, tell me all about the ingredients," Amy was giddy with excitement.

"Well, there's the wrinkles of a Batwort, tears of a Nighten, hairs of a Garth," Marty recalled fondly.

Nick wasn't about to let Marty take all of the credit so he spoke up again, "The Snoth of Debocket, one-eyed Screms, five Phlems..."

"And a horn-tailed Speakur!" they finished in unison.

Monica, still unbelieving, held back while Amy was bursting with more questions, "So, what's left, where do you keep them, what do they all look like, and how do you know where to find them?"

The entire time they had been talking they were getting closer to the town square and as these four questions fell from Amy's lips they caught their first awful glimpse of the OhRa's wrath.

They had just stepped into the village proper and were met with all different sizes of blocks. At first it looked like a large child's forgotten toys until they realized the blocks were see-through, like glass, solid as ice, and inside of each a shocked and motionless creature that had at one time occupied a home in Qualf staring in horror at their last sight, the OhRa. It was a strange menagerie indeed, creatures they had never seen before, now preserved as if they were museum displays.

Reaching out his hand Marty expected to feel a frigid block under his fingers, instead it was lukewarm, smooth as a finely polished piece of furniture, but a little springy to the touch like gelatin. Evidently it was a very strong substance, because no one had moved for over six months.

All four of them picked their way through the crowded square until Nick's voice broke the stillness, "Marty, it's *Misselthorn!*"

Marty broke into a run weaving in and out of the forms until he reached Nick's side. Within seconds Monica and Amy had joined them drawn by the worry in Nick's voice. In the sunlit square they stood in a semi-circle in front of a form, frozen in the position of begging. She was on her knees looking up, her hands clasped in front of her. Misselthorn's long blond hair was in two braids, swaying, yet still. For the first time Marty and Nick noticed how young she was, or how young she *looked* anyway.

After the shock of finding Misselthorn wore off, they realized that this collection of people and creatures weren't all from Qualf, these were prisoners from many different lands, but why were they all gathered here in Qualf? This question couldn't be answered yet, and while they awaited an answer they split up again to search among the victims.

Marty made the next discovery, "Hey you guys, the map book is over here!"

Monica and Nick were there with haste to see the book, it was hovering in its own cube of gelatin. After gazing at the book for a moment, they realized Amy had not joined them. A sudden panic seized the group, where could she *be*?

They split up to find her. When they finally did locate her she was standing stock-still in front of a tall block, her eyes fixed wide in a stare, their approach finally roused her and she slowly raised her hand to point with a shaky finger at a paper she had been studying. Reaching forward, Marty pulled the paper free and then it was his turn to freeze, his arm still extended, the paper went limp in his grip.

He was staring at the frozen gaze of Bismorda! His knees went weak and he had to sit down right there in the dirt. The others crowded around him.

When he finally spoke his voice trembled slightly, "That's Bismorda," he gestured at the figure suspended in the gel.

Nick, Monica, and Amy turned to stare open-mouthed at this witch they had heard so much about but had not laid eyes on before. Lavender hair streamed down her back and over one shoulder like a waterfall over a protruding rock on its descent down a cliff. She was twisted at the waist, as if something had tapped her on the shoulder unexpectedly and she had whirled around in surprise. Her youthful face was caught in a mixture of surprise and terror. Marty's shock wore off, and he glanced down at the paper in his hand. After a preliminary glimpse he started at the top and read aloud, his voice startled the other three who turned around to focus on what he was reading:

"Don't you like our gift for you?

Some from far and near ones too.
Floating for your eye to see,
Trapped, unless you can set free.
Prisoners kept, can prove a bother,
But since they helped one another
Their strength enough to cast a spell,
I was forced to help as well.
Now from their spell I am released,
Don't you worry just movement ceased.
Thelfix only holds them still,
I do not really wish *them* ill.
Storyland has become weak,
You will not hear one still voice speak.
As the Eyahge'er and Yulesaychaater,
You've survived under the water,
As a team gone to Debocket,
You'd succeed inside a rocket,
But you'll have to study deeply
The last task will not come cheaply.
In the world where you're from,
Can you find two more so dumb?
Willing to give and fight their all,
Perhaps for others take a fall.
If your force you can double,
For us you may make some trouble,
But if not, just give up now,
You can't win, no way, no how.
As you see we keep collectin'
Pesky pests in thick clear pectin.
There is only one small way,
Your team of four could save the day.
Fearless, faithful, brave, and true
In short Marty, a lot like you.
Choose your team "Marty's elite,"
They can't be bums off of the street.

If they prove true loyalty,
One day you may be royalty.
We hope you're equal to this test,
If not, we're sure you'll do your best.
Take one last look around,
All these figures on this ground
Will not be here to stay
In fact, they'll disappear later today.
Once you finish your concoction,
We will start a precious auction,
For these friends who stand here now,
You must figure out somehow
To buy their lives from our grasp
Or on June eighth they'll start to gasp.
Lungs will fill with Thelfix 'til,
All their forms have grown quite still.
While they're in this frozen state,
You are free to contemplate,
But from death no more to wake,
And *that* spell you cannot break.
So go quickly, choose your group
For the last task train your troop,
To fight the Whears of Phaeson Wil Blanch,
You'll be like a U.S. Army branch.
Fight for what you know is good,
If you think you'll win, you *could*.

Signed,
The OhRa

"Who *is* the OhRa?" Amy managed.

"A creature, or curse, that has control of the Zanth sisters," Marty spoke automatically not really looking at anyone. He was trying to put this note into his brain and figure out what it meant.

The group of four stood, transfixed as a slow sizzling sound started at the edge of the clearing. Turning, they watched as the forms began to evaporate into thin air. Soon they were staring at an empty clearing and they had not moved a muscle.

After an eternity of silence Marty spoke in a hushed tone, "Will you girls go with us on this last adventure?"

Amy and Monica still had thousands of questions, but they nodded slowly and Amy's voice spoke for the both of them, "Yes, Marty, we *will*."

Instead of continuing their tour they all moved back to the banks of the river Sems and sat down in the soft grass. They had to decipher the full meaning of this note, then plan their attack.

After re-reading the note four times through Monica spoke first, "So on June 8th those creatures will drown in that Thelfix stuff?"

"That's what it sounds like, Monica," Marty agreed, "So we have to solve this thing before that happens!"

"What kind of training do we need?" Amy said unexpectedly.

"I'm not sure, but all I can think of is that you have to *believe* in what we are doing. If you start to doubt the project or don't believe we are actually in a different place, we *could* fail," Marty reasoned.

"We don't know where Phaeson Wil Blanch is, but it has to be near Ireland," Nick explained.

"*Ireland*?" Monica was shocked.

Marty and Nick both nodded their heads.

Knowing this needed more explanation Marty continued, "The last ingredient is wax from an Irish Gorder, its a plant of some kind. Because of the name we have to assume it's somewhere near Ireland."

"*Cool!*" Amy exclaimed, she was definitely sold on the idea.

"We need to get home," Monica suddenly became aware of the passage of time.

"Yeah, we do, Marty let us know if we can do anything to prepare," Amy said sincerely.

"Keep your schedules open after school, we may be going before the end of next week," Marty advised.

"Aye, aye captain," Amy saluted.

They all stood and walked under the bridge again. Returning to Marty's room was a definite let down for Amy, but Monica seemed relieved. They led the girls back upstairs where they said their good-byes and were on their way back to Amy's. Janet commented about the time and she and Nick followed closely behind.

Marty claimed he was sleepy and he escaped back down to his room to think about what they could do. He laid down on his bed after putting away the newest note and the key to Qualf, and surprisingly fell right to sleep.

Looking around he found Amy on one side and Nick on the other, Monica was nowhere to be found.

What had happened to her?

Marty opened his mouth to ask, when a movement made him look up quickly, too late.

Next second he was rolling blindly with some creature on him.

Its grip was tightening and he could feel himself gasping for breath.

Suddenly he was awake and try as he might he couldn't sit up, what was *wrong*?

As he lay there and let his mind clear he realized he had rolled himself up tightly in the sheets of his bed. He tried to laugh at himself, but the coverings were too tight, he had to unroll himself before he could laugh at his folly. Rolling slowly, opposite to the way the sheets were wrapped, had him wriggling soon and completely free within minutes.

Now he could think about his dream. Where was Monica? Had she been *attacked* by the weird creature that got him? What was the creature that was all over him? Only putting together what he knew of the next adventure, he assumed it was a Whear, but he now knew no more about what they looked like than before, he just knew they moved quickly. Understanding that he would now have to let the others know to be very careful on their mission and be ready to move quickly he got up to prepare for bed. The mystery of what happened to Monica would have to wait, but he would give her special warnings to be alert.

"I'll let Nick know too, then there will be three of us watching out for Monica," Marty spoke aloud and nodded into the darkness, his mind grasping his latest plan.

After brushing his teeth and changing his clothes he again crawled into bed and fell back to sleep without any further dreams of pending attacks.

Chapter 33
A Trip to Whear? I Don't Know

Friday, May 10, 1991

After almost two weeks of being ready Marty woke and had a feeling that *today* was the day. He slipped out of bed and went to his bedroom door, throwing it open he stepped into some damp grass. Surprised he became quickly aware and looked around him. He wasn't under the bridge, where was he?

A tree off to his right caught his attention it looked like it had fallen over and was laying on its side, but there were two tops and a big hole in the side. Compelled to look into this hole, Marty walked over to the tree in his bare fee, and reached inside. Closing his hand over something wooden he drew out his hand and caught sight of a key. This must be the key to Phaeson Wil Blanch!

As this thought crossed his mind he sat up in bed.

It had been a dream!

But it was so real! There was even wet grass that he had stepped on, how could it have been a dream? In his hand he could feel something, it was wood. Sliding out of his bed he made his way to the light-switch and flipped it on. In the flood of electric light Marty examined the newest key.

It was carved from a very dark wood the head was adorned with a flower that Marty guessed was the Irish Gorder. The teeth area had a single triangular piece jutting from the side. Placing the key in his drawer Marty prepared for school. Filled with excitement he couldn't wait to tell the others that their adventure to find the final ingredient would be either today or tomorrow, depending on when they could get all of them together. At the corner he told Nick the great news and they both rejoiced on the short walk to school.

Marty told Amy as he was walking her to first period and she had to clamp her hand over her mouth as she squealed with delight. Nick shared the news but received a totally different response from Monica, "So, why didn't we find the key *together*?"

She questioned, "If we're so important to the 'mission' why does Marty get to find everything, and we just go along to carry it? I'm not a pack mule, Nick, and neither are you!"

Nick was surprised with her hostile feelings and hesitated to speak, this hesitation was what Monica was waiting for, "You don't want to go on this *thing* do you Nick?"

"Yeah, I do Monica, I've been waiting for this adventure all year long, I wouldn't miss it for anything."

After a moment of silence she cleared her throat.

"Okay, if that's the way you feel, I guess I'll go too," Monica said resignedly, the pout clear on her face.

"We'll find out if Amy can go today after school, and plan from there," Nick concluded.

At the lunch table they huddled with their heads drawn close together, even Monica caught the excitement, at least for now. The plan was to tell parents they were studying for their math finals and would be at Marty's house after school. In fact they could call all of their parents from Marty's and save them gas. Then Monica could spend the night at Amy's and Nick could stay at Marty's. With this plan in mind they were all excited to go as soon as school was over.

Just to spite them, because of their excitement for the end of school, the day dragged and seconds were like hours. Even so, school did finally end and they walked together to Grandma Pentel's.

When the group walked into the house Grandma Pentel was there with open arms.

She hadn't planned on four but that was easily remedied by putting out two more glasses of milk. They all gathered around the table and Nick, Amy, and Monica in turn used the phone to call their parents. Permission granted they all sat together eating fresh baked cookies and chatting easily about school and trivial things, not willing to let slip any hint of the adventure that awaited them.

Amy was in a deep conversation with Pearl as the others finished and stood. She looked up and realized she needed to make an excuse to continue later, "Grandma Pen, I have *so* enjoyed our conversation, can I take a rain-check to continue it later? I have to go study."

Flashing her winning smile put on the finishing touch and Pearl agreed willingly. After excusing themselves they trooped downstairs to "study." In the safety of Marty's room they pulled out the first poem Nick and Marty had received from the witches of Zanth about Phaeson Wil Blanch. After studying it, Amy taking notes this time, they consulted their list.

"Clothes of ottis lauver, a lure for the Whears, a vase of clear pilsmot, and a siglen," Amy read back for all to hear.

"Sounds like gibberish to *me*," Monica grumbled.

Nick, who had taken the job of quieting her qualms,

spoke, "That's what I thought at first too, but there really are things up at the castle that fit this list. It's part of the adventure to pick out the supplies."

This seemed to appease Monica for a few more minutes and Marty took advantage of the timing. Putting the key into the door, collecting the canvas bag and the key to Phaeson Wil Blanch, he grabbed Amy's hand and rushed out the door. Monica was lead through the door by Nick and they were on their way. As they walked up the path Nick asked to see the key and this diverted Monica from complaining about the walk. Amy still hadn't seen the key either, but she allowed Nick and Monica to ogle over it, she was starting to be embarrassed by Monica's outbursts and this new item seemed to be keeping her from whining she would let it be.

Marty and Amy spoke quietly, "So, Marty what do you think ottis lauver cloth looks like?"

"I don't have a clue, but I'm sure it won't be like slipmank skin, or I mean, a dry suit."

"*Slipmank skin?*" Amy wrinkled her nose, "That sounds a little gross, what did it *feel* like?"

"It's actually pretty neat stuff, it looks like silk, but it feels like rubber. The dry suits we wore into Jasquint were made of slipmank skin. They keep your clothes totally dry even when you're under water."

"Wow, that must have been cool," Amy was in awe.

The path ended at the top of the hill where the castle leaped into view and both Amy and Monica stopped in their tracks. Their mouths fell open with the sight of Bismorda's palace and only when the boys jolted them back to reality did they close them.

"Okay, let's go inside, get the equipment, and get *going!*" Marty sounded like a tour guide and in tour guide fashion he led the way up the steps pointing out various interesting points about the structure they were about to enter. Inside the grand entrance hall they had to pause for their eyes to adjust to the dim light. Then they made their way to the left side of the hall, the only remaining objects being lined up there. A pile of four outfits was the first thing they encountered.

"These must be made of ottis lauver," Amy surmised. Feeling the clothes she spoke again, "They feel like corduroy!"

Sure enough the suits had the distinct look of corduroy, too. A dark brown, they had slots for their feet, but there were full hoods and gloves sewn in place.

"They look like snow suits for little kids!" Monica exclaimed with distaste.

Clearly wearing this would go against *all* of her fashion rules. Marty had moved further along the wall and came back with a package of some strange mix of stuff floating in it.

Reading from the label, "Effective for all your Whear luring needs, contains a strong sleeping drought, timperslungs, and spindle-biths. Covers the scent of ordinary humans."

"*Timperslungs?*" Monica wrinkled her nose.

"Spindle-biths?" Amy was amazed at the variety of new objects she had already encountered in such a short time.

"This has to be the vase of clear pilsmot!" Nick declared as he picked up a small container that looked like an oversized glass pinto bean.

As he brought it up from the ground the top fell open, "Well, at least I know that there's an opening, for a moment there I didn't know how we were going to do anything with a glass bean."

"That leaves the siglen," Amy commented, checking off her list.

"Is *this* it?" Monica asked tentatively as she held up something that looked like a bizarre set of salad tongs with a trigger in the handle and small suction cups along the inside.

"I think she found the plungie-tweezlins!" Nick exclaimed.

"The *plungly-duckings*?" Monica tried weakly.

"No the *plungie-tweezlins*," Nick said slowly, "They are used to extract the tines of the one-eyed Screms."

"Oh," Monica was still confused, but she figured a simple response might stop adding more confusion to her already over-stuffed brain.

"*This* has to be a siglen!" Amy held up a tube with a syringe-type handle.

Looking around they had to agree with her because that was the last thing in the hall that they could see. Well, except for the furniture that is.

Putting the siglen, vase of pilsmot, and the whear lure into the canvas bag Marty passed them each a suit of ottis lauver for them to carry. Holding out his hand toward Nick he was presented with the key to Phaeson Wil Blanch, "Shall we go?" he asked the others.

"*Yes!*" came from all three, Monica's was noticeably less enthusiastic than either Nick or Amy, but they headed out anyway.

Back beneath the bridge Marty remembered, "Hey, we could put the other keys into that box in the secret cavern when we're done in Phaeson Wil Blanch."

Not waiting for a response he went back into his room, retrieved the keys, and was back with them in a matter of minutes. Turning the Phaeson Wil Blanch key in the knob the door was opened onto the grass and simple view of Marty's dream.

"Okay, let's get ready," Marty pulled on his suit of ottis lauver and zipped it shut.

Placing the hood over his head Marty adjusted his hands to the strange gloves and was finally situated into the outfit. Checking on the others verified that they were prepared as well. Amy and Nick had a glow of excitement coloring their cheeks while Monica was clearly having an inner struggle with this huge fashion faux pas. Marty picked up the canvas bag and led the way through the door. Amy was close behind with Nick hot on her heels, a sound behind them made them turn around.

Monica was still on the grass under the bridge. She was pounding on the entrance as if there were a window that had suddenly closed and wouldn't let her across the threshold. Doubling back they stood looking at Monica as she attempted to get through the door, but repeatedly failed. Nick finally stepped forward, back through the doorway and into Qualf. Taking Monica's hand he began to lead her through, but his hand was the only thing that couldn't make it through until he let go of Monica's hand again.

"What is going on here?" Monica was distraught, her voice muffled on the other side of the force field.

Suddenly Amy stepped forward, through the door, and took Monica back toward the sun-covered banks of the river Sems. Nick and Marty exchanged questioning glances, what could they be talking about? Just a moment later Amy was back beside them and Monica had not moved from the side of the river.

"What did you *tell* her?" Nick asked in an accusatory tone.

"I just asked her if she believed anything that was going on here," Amy explained, "She said 'No, it's too hard to believe it.'"

Her explanation stopped there and Nick had to prod again, "So, she said she didn't believe it, what has *that* got to do with anything?"

Here Marty took over, "Nick, if you don't believe in the cause, in saving Bismorda or her kingdom, you aren't allowed into the land of books. I was actually surprised Monica made it to Qualf again."

Nick stared in unbelief, "You mean, just because she has had a hard time *believing* in these adventures she can't go on them?"

Marty and Amy's heads went up and down, nodding in unison, "How can you go on an adventure that you don't think possible in the first place?" Marty posed.

The sound of a twig snapping close behind them caused them all to freeze and fall silent, their senses becoming overly aware of the creatures they had completely forgotten about. Only shadows met their eyes as they slowly rotated in a circle but their neck hairs were all bristling in anticipation.

Where were the Whears? Hands shaking Marty reached into the bag over his shoulder and pulled out the bag of bait. Pulling it open he poured the chunky liquid to form a small puddle on the thick grass. Folding the bait bag and returning it to the canvas one on his shoulder Marty started to step away from the trap.

Nick and Amy taking his lead also began moving out of the clearing and into the shadows, to watch the action. A low growl came from the opposite side of the clearing and a bear walked out into the clearing, just like a person would, on two legs. It had on torn shorts and swung its arms just like a person.

Suddenly it fell into a crouch like a cave man, hands or paws on the ground, legs pulled up to its chest, it began sniffing the air. Three more Whears came out of various parts of the forest and joined the first one. All four of them appeared to be male at least they were all wearing shorts in a variety of colors and stages of disrepair. Crouching in a circle they began to snuffle in patterns, they were talking! Finally a small breeze blew from where the bait was set in the direction of the Whears.

Quickly the four of them turned and pounced on the puddle in the grass. Their movements were faster than comprehension; it made Marty flash back to his dream and the unseen attacker that got him in such a tight grip. Refocusing on the group of terrifying Whears he saw that each had apparently obtained some of the bait because, within seconds, they were all laying on the ground snoring.

Whatever was in the bait sure was strong, but because they didn't know how long it would last the needed to get going and fast. Marty began searching for the skrunk tree from his dream. Nick and Amy followed his example, but weren't quite sure what they were looking for.

A short distance from the clearing stood, or should I say lay, the skrunk tree. It looked like a normal enough tree, at first glance.

Amy actually commented, "Who cut it down do you think?"

A Whear

"No one, look, the roots of the tree grow from the side where it meets the ground, and there are *two* tops."

Sure enough, there, on each end were large branches covered in leaves and looking like two large shrubs attached by a huge trunk in between. A large knothole in the trunk was hollowed out and looked peculiarly inviting. Just in case, Marty passed the siglen to Amy and the pilsmot vase to Nick.

Skrunk Tree

"Follow my lead," Marty instructed, "I think that the Gorder is inside of that hole, I'll grab it, Amy, you get some of the wax, and Nick you have the vase ready to catch the wax, okay?"

Simply nodding, the three of them approached the trunk. As they drew up alongside the hole, Marty took a deep breath and reached into the hole. Something hit his hand, hard, and he withdrew it, to reveal a handful of three-inch-long spikes imbedded into the glove of his right hand. Lucky that he had on his ottis lauver outfit or Marty would have been in a whole lot of pain.

The spikes glinted in the sun, they were a metallic green, upon inspection they resembled large sewing needles without the eye for the thread. Marty plucked out the spikes, six in all, and discarded them in the grass.

"Okay, I'm going to go around the other side of the skrunk, I'll grab the Gorder, hold down its spiky limbs and you get the wax, agreed?"

Somewhat more hesitant now that they had seen the result of touching the Gorder, Amy and Nick nodded, swallowing over the newly formed lumps in their throats. Marty made his way around to the far side of the tree, coming up opposite the other two with only the trunk between them. Amy quickly familiarized herself with the siglen, it was just like a syringe minus the needle and tapered end.

Marty again approached the hole but this time put *both* hands into the black recess. They closed around a very wiggly and skinny something, Marty fought with it, but he had its limbs pinned to its sides as planned.

Finally pulling it into view they saw a wildly struggling…flower!

The Gorder

Its four enormous petals were gleaming white and brushed with a bright orange-red that faded into a dark purple as it entered the mouth of the flower. The pistons extended out of the mouth, wriggling wildly, like several unruly tongues on a two year old. Indeed, as if it had been a child, the flower was turning its head as if it were not anxious to take its medicine.

Marty's face was growing red with the struggle, "Hurry, get the wax!" he managed through clenched teeth.

Up until he spoke Nick and Amy stood slack-jawed staring at the unbelievable encounter they were having with a "wild" flower. At Marty's words they leaped into action, Nick held the vase open in one hand, and reached forward to hold the head of the flower still with the other. Amy shoved the siglen into the mouth of the flower and pulled out the syringe lever. A thick greenish-black liquid filled the siglen almost completely. Extracting the tube from its mouth made the flower cough mightily, then it sneezed.

Nick let go of its head as Amy put the siglen into the pilsmot vase complete with wax in the tube and she and Nick backed away from the skrunk tree. Exhausted, Marty jumped back from the tree as he released the panting Gorder. For only a second the Gorder remained within view and then sank back into its knothole with a slight whimper.

"Man!" Marty wheezed as he tried to catch his breath, "*That* is one active flower!"

Nick and Amy were looking at the pilsmot vase and the siglen that stood in it. Marty rejoined them on their side of the tree and also began watching the now dark purple wax ooze from the tip of the siglen. It reminded them of grape jelly as it filled the vase and engulfed the end of the siglen. To speed up the oozing process and to save the siglen, in case they needed it again, Amy reached forward and took hold of the siglen again, as she pushed the syringe lever all the way back into the base of the siglen forcing the remaining wax into the vase, a slight fizz began to cover the wax. She then withdrew the siglen, Nick snapped the lid closed and they were ready to go back to Qualf.

Back in the clearing they were greeted by an unusual surprise, as they stepped out of the shadows they found that the bait had continued to work after their departure. Now over a hundred Whears lay in a crowded haphazard mass between them and the door back, how were they going to tip-toe their way through?

Ranging in size and shape the Whears actually looked like so many over-sized teddy bears scattered by a thoughtless child, but the three youth knew better. Taking every precaution possible they inched along, passing outstretched paws that had deadly claws concealed just beneath the surface hair and gaping jaws that they knew had menacingly sharp teeth. When they were right in the middle of the clearing Amy began to make a concentrated grunting…she was fighting a cough!

Holding their breath they continued to slowly pick their way across when suddenly Amy began an uncontrollable coughing fit. They were torn between running for the door and freezing so they wouldn't attract attention if the Whears woke up. After pausing long enough to make eye contact they finally decided to make a run for it.

As they reached the door, exited into Qualf, and Marty was pulling the door closed behind them he saw the first twitches of the Whears. Finding the key to Qualf quickly in his inner clothes he changed the door back so that it led to his room again and then joined Nick and Amy as they approached Monica.

She sat on the banks glaring into the rippling water, the only thing that was different from the last time they saw her was she had taken off the ottis lauver suit and it was laying limp in the grass some distance behind her looking broken and discarded.

"We're back," Amy said as she came up beside her and knelt down in the grass.

If Monica heard, she didn't register the comment, she only blinked.

Nick knelt down in the grass on her other side and made his attempt, "Will you come up to the castle with us?"

Again no response from Monica, not even a blink this time. Amy and Nick stood, shrugged, and started to move away, Marty bent down, picked up the suit off of the grass, and slung it over his shoulder. The three of them left Monica again sitting by the Sems, and walked up to Bismorda's castle in silence.

Upon entering the castle they slipped out of their ottis lauver suits and took the Gorder wax to the larder. As they opened the door and stepped in Amy took it all in eagerly. Shelves of unusual things surrounded her and she forgot Monica, asking what each item was and where they had come from, she touched the Garth's fur, gazed into the bubbling Nighten acid and stagnant bog sludge, watched for a moment as the Screms swam around in their fizzy tank, ran her fingers over the scaly skin of the Batwort's ear, poked at the Phlems, and watched with interest as the Speakur inched along the bottom of its bowl feeding on its powdery food.

Longingly she gazed at the vase of wax in Nick's hands, he read her look, Amy wanted to place the final ingredient on the shelf to complete the collection. Reaching forward the vase changed hands somewhat like the passing of the torch and she placed the vase reverently onto the lowest shelf by the bowl with the Speakur. A collective sigh escaped them as they looked once more on the peculiar, but vital ingredients that stood before them.

Shutting the larder door their unspoken decision was made, they would return another day to combine all of these ingredients and create the most needed Acne Pimple potion. They couldn't leave Monica sulking on the side of the river indefinitely or she would never speak to any of them ever again, even now they weren't sure that she ever would anyway. This also meant a postponement of the placement of the keys, they would take the trip to the secret cavern before they mixed the potion on their next visit.

Quietly they descended the mountain again. A sense of

triumph already permeated their small group, all that was left was mixing the ingredients and the captives would be free, Marty would be cured, and the Zanth sisters would be released from their curse. As they came over the bridge Monica stood wordlessly, disappeared under the bridge, and crossed back into Marty's room.

Exchanging glances Nick, Amy, and Marty knew this was the last time Monica would step beyond the realm of the human world, she may even be a completely different person now because of this change, they would have to wait and see.

Chapter 34
At Last, A Curse! I Mean, Cure!

Saturday, May 11, 1991

After returning Friday night, they studied in their math books, because they really would be having their math final in a few weeks and this task actually had Monica back to her old self, well almost, she had lost something, a spark in her eye or something just as subtle. Sadly, Marty and Nick talked about her lack of belief and the result well into the night after the girls had gone home. Monica would never be allowed back into the land of books, except as a simple reader, and even that desire may fizzle out over time.

Amy's phone call caused Charlotte to wake Marty and Nick, it wasn't early, but they *had* stayed up late.

"Monica's gone home, can we go back today?" then she added because her parents could hear, "I still get stuck on the stuff from chapter sixteen and twenty-two."

"Yeah, sure, how 'bout in an hour? Is that cool?" Marty checked the clock, it was 10 now, 11:00 would be perfect.

"Okay, I'll see you then, do you want me to bring anything to snack on?"

Boy, she was good! This way they could be in Qualf without stopping for lunch.

"Uh, yeah bring some apples," he spoke into the phone, "I'll get some cheese from our fridge and we've got milk too, so we'll be set."

"Okay, I'll be there soon, bye."

"Bye," Marty hung up the phone.

Charlotte and Pearl were sitting at the kitchen table and had been listening to the one side of the call, "Are you going to study some more today?" Charlotte guessed.

"Yeah, Monica went home, but Amy is still having problems with a couple chapters, is it okay if we study through lunch?"

Before either Pearl or Charlotte objected, he spoke again, "Amy's bringing apples and with some cheese and milk we should be good for a few more hours."

"Okay, but plan on a late lunch then," Pearl conceded. "Sounds great, Grandma! Amy will be pleased to talk some more with you. Thanks."

Marty and Nick rushed downstairs, cleaned up, showered, and ate some toast before Amy showed up. Quick hugs were shared with Pearl and Charlotte and the three of them descended into Marty's room armed with chunks of cheese, glasses of milk and two apples apiece.

Gathering all the notes that had been taken, the letters from the Zanth sisters, the list of ingredients, the remaining keys, and a square of tin foil Marty had managed to save off of a baked potato that he had eaten months ago, he filled the canvas bag and they were off on the adventure they had been anticipating for almost a year. Amy put the apples and cheese in the bag just in case, but they left the milk on the dresser they would drink that when they returned.

Charged with the excitement of this final test, they almost ran up the incline to the castle. Bursting into the clearing and racing each other up the steps, they were in the entrance hall within minutes. Quickly Marty led Amy to the laboratory where the potion would be mixed and showed her around.

Leaving the canvas bag there they made their way to the larder, Amy was handed the Garth hairs and pan of Phlems, Nick donned the smackelarf skin gloves, took the Snoth-resistant tongs in one hand and the bowl of sludge in the other, Marty picked up the bowl of Screms and their first load was delivered to the countertop in the lab.

The second load brought the Nighten tears, the horn-tailed Speakur and the Batwort skin. Marty stayed in the lab arranging ingredients as Nick and Amy went to retrieve the Gorder wax and the second bowl of Screms. When the ingredients were all in place Marty read through the potion again, speaking as he walked along pointing to each item, "crumbled Snoth eye, mixed with Gorder wax, then add Batwort wrinkles, and Nighten's tears, Garth hairs, Screm tines, Phlems, and Speakur, add heat, pour in foil, cool and apply to face, wait thirty seconds, wash with warm water, and we should be done."

Amy read it over his shoulder for the first time, "It sounds like the witches in Macbeth! 'Bubble, bubble, toil and trouble,'" she mimicked in a haggard voice.

Once again Nick and Marty were amazed at how much Amy had read, but since it wasn't the time for a book report Marty asked, "Where did we put the plungie-tweezlins?"

In response Nick disappeared into the hall, reappeared with the odd contraption, and placed it on the counter. Marty surveyed the odd display and momentarily was overcome with emotion. Blinking twice to clear his brain and his clouded eyes he began spouting instructions to Nick and Amy who jumped into action, "We need to extract the tines of three Screms using the plungie-tweezlins, get the Snoth out of its eye, and a clean beaker."

Rushing to the cupboard, Nick retrieved a clean beaker and Amy stood like a deer, trapped in the headlights of an oncoming car, unsure whether to run.

Smiling at her Marty patted her shoulder, "Okay, now that we have a clean beaker, can you help me with the Snoth?"

Amy's trance was broken, she smiled weakly, "Yes, I think so, tell me what to do," her voice was eager.

"Put on one of the smackelarf gloves, I'll put on the other one," they each slid a glove on as Nick watched. "Okay now use those tongs to pull a Snoth out of the sludge," Marty pointed at the green murky bowl.

Eager to please Amy clicked the tongs and fished into the bowl, they closed around something almost instantly, her eyes grew wide and she pulled it out. If smells could be classified on a putrid scale the stench that grabbed at their nostrils would have been off the charts. They all winced with the pain and shock of the smell. Looking quickly at the shell they could tell something was wrong, there was no Snoth protruding from it and they realized that this Snoth had died.

The potion was not able to use a dead Snoth in its shell. Marty reached out and pushed the Snoth eye back into the liquid. Instantly the smell began to dissipate. Shaking the tongs to drop the Snoth Amy fished again shakily to find the second, hopefully living, Snoth. Within seconds she again pulled a Snoth from the goo, this one was wiggling its four legs wildly. Marty sighed with relief that the second Snoth had survived. It too gave off a strong smell, but nothing compared to the dead one they had discarded.

Holding the Snoth in the tongs, Amy now had no idea what to do so she looked blankly back at Marty. He reached forward with his gloved hand and pulled on the mussel of the Snoth until it came free of the eye, then he tried to drop the wriggling mass into the bowl, but his glove was hopelessly congealed to the mucous-covered tentacles.

Slipping his hand out of the glove he dropped the glove and attached Snoth into the bowl where it slowly sank into the thick ooze.

"Okay, Amy, can you hold that for another minute?"

Nodding, she just stood there with the eye of the Snoth clamped in the tongs eagerly awaiting orders. Marty took the pilsmot vase and poured some of the Gorder wax into the clean beaker coating the sides with the thick purple liquid, this took a few minutes because it was now quite thick. When there was about an inch of the almost black slimy wax settled in the bottom of the beaker he snapped the lid back onto the vase.

"Can you crush the eye of the Snoth with the tongs?" Marty asked Amy.

"I...I think so, I can try at least," she ventured.

"Good, aim it over the mouth of the beaker," Marty instructed as he stepped to one side.

A cracking sound filled the stillness of the lab, looking at Amy's scrunched up face they could see this was taking quite a bit of effort. Suddenly the whole eye just crumbled and most of it made it into the beaker landing in the wax. The concoction changed colors slowly where the eye of the Snoth had made contact it became a bright orange.

Without thinking, Marty began to brush the stray pieces of the eye out of the way as he watched the reaction of the two ingredients. When he realized what he was doing, he stopped; he could have been plastered to the counter forever! Evidently, though, after the Snoth is removed from the eye, the eye loses its glue-like properties, because he remained free and the counter even came clean.

With the area around the beaker now free of anything but the required ingredients Marty wondered what to mix the wax and Snoth eye with. Luckily Nick had been thinking ahead, while Amy was busy crumbling the Snoth eye, he had found a glass wand like what Miss Baumer used in science to stir chemicals. Nick presented this to Marty who smiled and thanked him. Slowly mixing the two ingredients Marty noticed that the ooze was turning into small clumps of purplish dough with orange spots.

Marty grabbed the Batwort skin and, because it was brittle already, he only had to pull at it slightly and it came apart with a crackle. He dropped the piece into the beaker. It floated down to rest on the clumps of combined ingredients and sat there, waiting for something more to happen. Next, for the Nighten's tears, Nick had put on the trusty oven mitts and was holding the beaker of bubbling magenta liquid.

Ever so carefully he poured a small amount into the other beaker. As the acid hit the mixture already present it sizzled and popped again liquefying the clumps and turning the piece of Batwort skin into a blackened thread-like twist that disappeared into the ooze.

Now a grayish-purple, the concoction was strange to watch, it seemed to be almost alive. Amy was combing through the Garth hair trying to get three perfect specimens. When she did, she presented them to Marty. Dropping the hairs into the beaker they slowly melted into the thick mess intensifying the color only slightly…it was now a bit more grey.

"Now, we need tines from the Screms."

This task was peculiarly daunting because it had to be done with such precision and, as a result, they were all hesitant. Finally Amy grabbed the bowl of Screms, "Where are the plungie-tweezlins?"

Nick came forward with them, but continued to hold onto them, showing that he would be the one doing the work.

Marty joined them and spoke, "What can we use to hold them?"

Without hesitation Amy said, "The Snoth tongs should work."

Retrieving the tongs he realized that indeed the size of the groove in the tongs matched the head of the Screms precisely. Placing the tips into the bubbling water Marty held the tongs open, ready to catch one of the swimming Screms. After three misses, he finally caught a Screm by the head and pulled it out of the bowl. Holding it so Nick could aim the plungie-tweezlins, Marty averted his eyes not sure he wanted to see what would happen. As he did so he saw Amy's face, bright with interest, and decided that he too could watch.

A sharp *sproing* sounded and the wiggling Screm stopped, Marty had missed the action! He caught sight of the plungie-tweezlins re-opening and the wiggling Screm being released but he hadn't seen the tweezlins in action, they had been so fast. Nick shook the plungie-tweezlins over the mouth of the beaker and small tines sprinkled into the dark liquid. Marty dropped the still wiggling Screm back into the bowl with a plop and was able to catch the second Screm on the first try.

With new determination he watched as Nick aimed the plungie-tweezlins at the convulsing legs of the Screm. There was no warning, just the loud *sproing* sound and the jaws of the tweezlins had a hold of the legs of the Screm. Marty became aware of a small sucking noise coming from the plungie-tweezlins, this must be the sound of the tines being extracted. Dropping the second Screm back into the glass bowl as Nick deposited the tines in the beaker made Marty smile, they were almost done!

Amy removed the bowl of de-tined Screms from the counter and brought up the second bowl to replace it. After catching the third Screm Marty was confident they wouldn't even need the fourth one as he turned back to Nick. As the plungie-tweezlins came open after the tine removal the Screm jerked free of the tongs and landed with a sickening squish on the hard floor.

A black oily liquid dripped out of the plungie-tweezlins. The extracted tines had melted, because the Screm had died just like Gratzwinda had said. Taking extra care with the fourth and final Screm they got the tines and returned it safely to its bowl. Only when they deposited the newly extracted tines into the mixture did they heave a sigh of relief. Watching the combination closely a few sparks shot from the last set of tines as they melted into the gooey gunk in the bottom of the beaker but the color remained the same.

Speaking aloud Marty reassured himself as well as the others that the end was near, "Just the Phlems and Speakur left!"

"How are we going to fit the Phlems into the beaker?" Amy wondered aloud.

"By cutting them up," Marty had already thought about this part, "We need to go to the kitchen and find something that will cut into all five kinds of Phlems. I think we can shatter the mintus and nutus Phlems with the same mallet, but the metallus, gellataneous, and fruitus Phlems will need different utensils."

With this new idea in mind they all went to the kitchen to find the needed instruments. Marty found the mallet he had used on the lime-flavored Phlems and then a cheese grater caught his eye, he grabbed that too. Amy found a small paring knife and Nick found a vice grip that could prove useful. Now prepared, they returned to the lab.

Marty attacked the mintus and nutus Phlems with the mallet, breaking them open, Amy grabbed the fruitus Phlem and began cutting it into slices, Nick tried the vice grip on the metallus Phlem, when that didn't work he decided to try the grater Marty had found. Surprisingly the metallus Phlem grated easily into shiny shavings. Amy reached for the gellataneous Phlem and decided to keep it in the pan, sliding the whole pan in front of herself she poked the Phlem with the knife blade and then squeezed it. With a light pop its skin disappeared and the jelly insides hit the sides of the pan some splashing onto the counter and covering Amy's hands.

A smell of cream filling hit her nostrils and Amy licked her hand clean.

"This is *delicious!*" her voice brought Marty and Nick around to look at her.

"Hey!" Marty said in a mock scolding tone, "Don't lick the bowl until the mix is done!"

"You sound like my mother," Amy said jokingly.

"Okay, let's get some of each of these Phlems into the beaker. Then we can eat what's left," Marty said with a smile at Amy.

Dropping some of the shavings of the metallus Phlem in, Nick stepped aside, Amy came forward, deposited two slices of the fruitus Phlem and a glob of the gellataneous one, Marty dropped in some splinters of the mintus and some of the meat of the nutus then stepped back to watch what would happen. The pieces of the different Phlems just settled into the goop as if waiting for the final steps to be carried out.

Using the tongs again, for safety reasons, Marty retrieved the horn-tailed Speakur. As he pulled it from the water, it squirmed uncontrollably, and like the Screm, slipped from the tongs. With a splat the Speakur hit the hard floor, mortally wounding itself with the spikes of its own tail. It was dead before Marty got to it, but luckily the spell didn't care if the Speakur was alive or dead. Scooping it up with the tongs he dropped the remains of the slug-like Speakur into the beaker, now for the heat! Having located a Bunsen burner in a corner of the lab Nick brought it to the counter and lit it. A tripod was retrieved and the beaker was placed over the low flame.

It was a good thing they had seen Miss Baumer do this so many times in class or they would have had no idea what to do. Now, the worst ingredient of all, *patience*. As the heat increased, the liquid became more runny and started changing colors. Streaks of yellow appeared in the purple-grey mass and then bright blue joined in the swirl. Marty began stirring again with the glass chemist's wand. Soon a full rainbow of colors was swirling in the beaker, as they watched in amazement. Marty stopped stirring as the heat built up and the colorful liquid began bubbling. Changing from the multiple colors to pitch-black the liquid began to give off a smell like burnt fruit.

They wrinkled their noses in response and Marty motioned for Nick to remove it from the heat with the oven mitt. Nick picked up the beaker and Marty spread out the tin foil, as he did so, it tore in half.

"Blast!" he took the two pieces and set them side by side on the counter.

Carefully Nick poured two equal portions of the ebony ooze onto the pieces of tin foil, and set the now empty beaker onto the counter. Drawing in closer to the two puddles the three of them watched and waited as the pools first steamed, and then slowly cooled before their eyes. The potion took on a shiny rubber look after about ten minutes and Marty finally poked it with a tentative finger. It jiggled, silently laughing at these mere mortals as they attempted to perform a magic spell.

Taking a deep breath Marty was about to spread the goop on his face when he realized, he had no warm water to wash it off with after thirty seconds of application so he spoke, "Let's go to the kitchen to get some water, there's a sink in there."

Once again they all trooped into the kitchen. Marty carried one of the pieces of foil with the precious Acne Pimple potion on it and Nick had grabbed a hand mirror from the hall table on a whim, maybe the potion would change how Marty looked, he didn't know. Taking a great big handful of the pudding-like blob Marty smeared it on his face.

Wow, this stuff tingles!" he declared.

"You look like you're spreading tar on your face," Nick commented.

"Shh," warned Amy, she was anxious to see the result.

"Start counting," Marty instructed as he finished the application of the cream.

Thirty seconds never lasted so long. Finally Nick motioned that the time was done and Marty quickly washed off his face in the kitchen sink. As he came up out of the stream of water Amy gasped, Nick's eyes bulged and Marty knew instantly that something had gone very wrong.

Chapter 35
Battle of the Cursed

Passing the hand mirror to Marty, Nick couldn't help but stare at him again. Gulping over the sudden lump in his throat Marty brought the mirror up in front of his face. The reflection in the mirror showed him his own face, but it had a shiny look to it, along with a strange blue tint and as if having a blue face weren't enough, scales were beginning to form as he watched in horror. His face was turning into some type of reptile he had never seen before.

After the scales Marty was actually surprised that the transformation stopped there. Looking back at Marty from the mirror was a scaly, blue-faced Marty, it was surreal, but by touching his face he could verify that it had actually happened. *How could he go home? How could he ever leave Qualf again?*

Suddenly Marty realized his only way out of this fix, "The Zanth sisters! We have to go and visit them again!"

"Can *they* help you?" Amy wondered aloud.

"They are the only ones left to help me!" Marty said in desperation, "Nick, get the keys!"

Obediently Nick raced to the lab got the bag with the keys and brought them to Marty.

"What are we going to do?" the note of concern was clear in his voice.

"Go down, get the key to Zanth and pay a visit to those, *witches*!" Marty couldn't keep the contempt out of his voice.

"Did they do this on *purpose*?" Amy couldn't help but wonder.

"They were the ones who gave us the potion they had to know what would happen!" Marty said vehemently.

Amy wasn't going to stop being the voice of reason, "What if they gave you the ingredients that might help *them*?"

Marty stopped fuming instantly, and Nick said, "You

think that might be it?"

"It may be, from reading through these letters and messages left by the OhRa and the Zanth sisters, it appears that sometimes they have to outwit the OhRa, so that they can get things done."

"I think you're onto something there," Marty agreed. "Nick, remember how that last one said that the OhRa was back in control, there had been some spell cast by the prisoners or something?" Marty questioned.

"Yeah," Nick nodded, "So you think that somehow, when we went to them the first time, Grisele and Mopel tricked the OhRa into believing this was a simple spell?"

"It has strange results on humans, but maybe not on witches," Amy reasoned.

"Maybe they convinced the OhRa that this spell would maim me and then it really *could* take over the land of books," Marty guessed.

With these new possibilities in mind Marty looked for the light book, but they had forgotten to bring it. Returning to the lab they scoured the shelves for something else similar, Marty ran across a book with a star on the binding, cracking it open a pale bluish-white light poured out, "Well, it's not as strong, but it should do the trick," he decided.

Leaving the lab again they went to the hall mirror. Amy stood in wonder as the magic mirror opened and the secret passage was revealed. By the pale light of the star book they descended to the cave of images.

This whole new part of their adventure had overwhelmed Amy so that she finally asked, "Are there any *other* big surprises you want to throw at me today? I'd like a little time to prepare if there are."

Marty smiled at her, "Well, enjoy the view down here, it's probably the most peace you'll get for a while."

Watching the images dance on the walls they stood in silence for a few moments.

Marty broke the silence as he withdrew the keys to Gwimmet, Jasquint, and Phaeson Wil Blanch from the bag on his shoulder. Metallic plinks echoed through the cave as Marty fumbled with the keys on his approach to the box of drawers.

To start with, Marty pulled out the key to Zanth from its drawer and then he began locating the other drawers, dropping the corresponding key into place as he found them. Without the image of Zanth but now with the scenes of Gwimmet, Phaeson Wil Blanch, and Jasquint the look of the cave had changed. The keys were beginning to light up the cave on their own. Going back up the winding stairs they re-emerged in the hall of the castle. Stopping only to retrieve the remaining black glob of goo on the foil and the hand mirror Marty led the small group back along the now familiar path to get to the bridge.

"Okay, Amy, the Zanth sisters are a pretty frightening sight, they are joined as a single creature. Waving four arms, clicking claws, it has two heads, the faces are stitched up and the OhRa is attached to the head of the tallest one. It moves around on a weird snail-like mussel so you won't hear footsteps, just close your eyes when I say, don't look. *No matter what!*" Marty instructed.

"Okay, are we ready?"

"Yes," Nick and Amy spoke together.

"Let's go," Nick said, swallowing the fear that had begun to creep up his throat.

Marty used the key to Zanth on the door to transport them to the inside of the chuckaht's skull. Pushing the door open quietly Marty stepped onto the packed dirt and waited for Nick and Amy to join him.

He realized that they were avoiding directly looking at his strange face, he couldn't blame them it *was* freaky. Nick took the mirror as he passed. Moving along the blackened corridor without the aid of light had them all feeling along the rough boney interior of the skull. Arriving at the first corner Marty used his free hand to let Nick know he needed the mirror.

Instead of handing over the mirror, Nick moved beyond Marty and became the leader of the small team. Using the mirror to see around the corner, Nick moved them closer to the flickering light that was the witches' lair. Without being told, Amy narrowed her eyes to mere slits in anticipation of the encounter with the Zanth sisters.

At the final turn they could hear the clicking of the sisters' claws and realized, it was still night!

There was no faint gleam of gray along the horizon, it wouldn't be light for hours, but they *had* to confront the OhRa now, Marty had to be restored to normal. Nick looked through the mirror to see around the corner and saw that the Zanth sisters had their back to them. Stepping into the room Nick started moving backward toward where the sisters were by using the mirror to guide him over his shoulder. Marty almost called out to him, but realized if he did so the Zanth sisters would hear him, and it would surely be the end for all of them.

So instead, he stepped out with his back toward them and motioned for Amy to follow. Marty and Amy could only hope Nick would be able to get the OhRa into a trance. Nick had backed up to within six feet of the crouched figure; without making a sound he refocused the mirror so that he had a straight shot to make immediate eye contact with the OhRa when it turned toward him.

Then, he sneezed.

Marty and Amy almost exploded out of their skins, they couldn't turn to see what was happening, but they wanted to more than anything. Nick's sneeze had startled the Zanth sisters as well. The form spun around, the OhRa's eyes wide with shock, luckily Nick had recovered quickly following his sneeze, and he was able to lock gazes with the

OhRa immediately. Because it was still night their strength was at its peak but Nick was so determined he managed to send such a glare that the forward movement of the hulking mass was stopped and the OhRa became slack-eyed within seconds.

Without rejoicing over his triumph he called to Marty and Amy, "The OhRa is in a trance! What do you want to ask the Zanth sisters?"

Talking directly to the sisters Marty spoke, "Grisele and Mopel, you gave me an Acne Pimple potion that has turned my face blue and scaly. Why did you give me such a damaging spell?"

Grisele chuckled and Mopel spoke, "We knew we could count on you! Did you bring the leftover potion with you?"

"Yes, I have it here!" Marty held up the foil over his shoulder so that the sisters could see it.

"Oh, come to us quickly, *please*, before the OhRa awakens!" Grisele pleaded.

"How?" Marty asked, "We don't want to get jelled or frozen or whatever it is you do."

"Don't make eye contact, have the Eyahge'er give you directions so that you can get to us," Grisele suggested.

"Listen closely Marty, you must spread the potion onto the OhRa's eyes, then around the base of it and onto both of our faces too," Mopel instructed.

"Okay, I'll be there in just a minute," then quietly he spoke to Amy, "Close your eyes and take my hand we're going to take this adventure *together*."

Marty reached out his hand, Amy took it, and they clamped their eyes shut as they swung around so that they could move forward to Nick's instructions.

"Come forward three steps," Nick called.

Marty and Amy shuffled forward three steps in response. Following Nick's instructions Marty and Amy maneuvered awkwardly, but finally they successfully made it to the form of the sisters.

"Okay, take some of the goop in your hand," Nick instructed over his shoulder as he watched the action in the mirror.

Marty did as he was told, "Move your hand to the level of your face then straight out from you."

Doing this, Marty struggled with the temptation to look, but fought the desire and succeeded in coming in contact with the antennae on the right side of the OhRa. Pulling his hand back toward himself a bit he encountered the right eye of the OhRa.

It began writhing in pain.

You've never had such a difficult task as putting face cream on a wriggling person with your eyes closed, I'm sure, but if you could just image the difficulty that Marty was faced with. Marty had to reach out with the hand that held the foil, toward Amy. Bumping his left hand into her he spoke, "Take this, I need to hold its head still."

Watching these actions was almost humorous, like a game of pin the tail on the donkey, but infinitely more dangerous. Now with both hands free Marty located the OhRa that was twisting in place, trying to clear its eye by blinking.

Surprisingly it had not awakened from its trance; it must have been the added strength of the Zanth sisters holding it in this dazed state. Finally Marty found the left eye with his right hand and covered it with some of the cream that was now spread liberally over the entire creature because Marty was unable to guide his hand without spreading it.

Finding the base along Mopel's hairline the black mess was easily spread in place since it now covered both of Marty's hands up to the wrists. Amy had ventured with the remaining muck to help the process of spreading it over where the face of Grisele should be. Making contact, she covered the whole of Grisele's exposed flesh with the pitch-colored slop wrinkling her nose as she touched the stitches protruding from the disfigured face.

Marty had moved down the front of Mopel's face as well, he too became squeamish with the feel of the prickly stitches but continued the task until her face was completely covered. Stepping back from the mass of the Zanth sisters Amy and Marty waited with their breath held and eyes pinched even tighter shut.

Nick was the only one who got to watch the incredible transformation in the handheld mirror. A glowing shower of sparks shot out in an arch over the sisters, the arch turned into a glowing pair of scissors. They opened once at a side angle over Mopel's head and closed once menacingly to sever the OhRa from its position.

The pair of sparkling scissors flipped in the air so that its points fell between the two sisters' heads, the snipping action was repeated and the one form was now two. These separated figures began spinning slowly in place until they were two blurs of light. The OhRa was still floating in the air at this point and no one ventured near it. As the two balls of light continued spinning the entire room began to glow and change.

Sparks flew out from the two glowing spheres and wherever they hit the grisly skull melted away leaving purity and goodness. It was no longer dark and dingy, the gaping sockets elongated and filled with glass, the walls became gleaming white and the floor became glistening marble with flecks of silver swirling in it.

The only thing that remained even similar was the fireplace that still had a crackling fire in the grate. Now, lit up with an overhead chandelier the spinning balls of light came to rest, one was a beautiful woman in a flowy navy-blue organza-like dress and the other was stunning in a wispy blazing-red one. The one in the red whipped a bag out of nowhere and caught the OhRa as it fell out of the air.

"*Cool!*" was all Nick could manage to articulate.

He was still watching the reflection of everything in the mirror over his shoulder and Marty and Amy were still frozen in place, their eyes clamped shut.

The taller one in red stepped forward offering her hand to Marty, "I am Mopel Zanth…"

"And *I* am Grisele!" interjected the one in blue.

Then, realizing their audience was still unable to see them Mopel said, "You may open your eyes now and look at us, we won't hurt you."

She also motioned for Nick to turn around and approach. Because of the change in the voices Marty dared to open his eyes just a slit, then they flew open wide and bulged, "Amy, open your eyes, you won't *believe* this!"

Next to Marty, Amy's eyes opened, took a few seconds to adjust to the brilliance bouncing off the gleaming walls and floor, then she too stared around taking everything in slowly. The Zanth sisters stood close together, they were sisters you could tell, but they didn't look like twins. They both had long hair, Grisele's was dark-blonde, almost brown, and Mopel's was the shiny color of caramel.

There wasn't a huge height difference, but their faces differed in shape. Mopel's was long and slender with high cheek bones and Grisele's was fuller with a slightly pointed chin, her face almost looked like a heart. Both of their noses were slightly rounded and their cheeks were pink with excitement. They watched with their sparkling hazel eyes to see what these three humans might do next.

Nick joined Amy and Marty as they gazed at the sisters; completing the semi-circle of gawking awkward teens. After quite a time of silent staring Marty spoke as he looked at the sisters, "Pleased to meet you, finally," then speaking before he could stop himself, "You're both *beautiful!*"

Grisele and Mopel looked at each other and giggled, "Oh it is nice to be back isn't it?" Grisele said, Mopel nodded and they hugged each other.

"Oh, I've missed your hugs, I was always afraid of those horrible claws on your arms, I never asked for one," Mopel related with tears brimming in her eyes.

Amy couldn't help it she *had* to speak, "How long have you been like that?"

"Oh," the sisters pulled apart and thought, Grisele began, "Ever so long, I don't even remember."

"I *do*," Mopel interjected, "I remember the beautiful dances that we used to have, they were called balls, but that's been oh so many years ago."

Marty knew that Bismorda had been transformed for over three hundred years so he guessed, "About 1624?"

Both sisters stopped, looked at each other, "You know, that sounds just about right," Grisele admitted.

"How did you *know* that?" Mopel was curious.

"That was the year you cursed Bismorda to be that serpent-monster thing," Marty explained.

Both of the sisters flinched with the accusation.

"Oh, *that*," Grisele said guiltily.

"We were so angry about losing everything we took it out on one of our dearest friends, what were we thinking Mop?"

"We *weren't* thinking Gris, that's why we did it," Mopel said sadly, "'*Never do anything in haste, always think before you act*,' that's what mother always taught, but we sure didn't heed her warnings."

"Speaking of Bismorda," Nick finally broke his silence, "Shouldn't we be setting her and the others free?"

This got everyone's attention, and Marty finally remembered his own predicament. His hand came up to his face and he was surprised to find smooth skin.

Grisele saw his actions, "Yulesaychaater, when *our* curse was broken, so was yours. You're cured, but not from Acne Pimple."

"That's something all humans must live through on their own," Mopel explained.

"You mean *anyone* can get Acne Pimple? Is it deadly?" Marty was still worried.

"Heavens no!" Grisele chuckled, "It comes from clogged up pores in your skin, the best remedy really *is* warm water, but instead of all those other ingredients just use some soap."

Nick was slightly put out, "So we did all of this for *nothing*?"

"I wouldn't say for *nothing*," Amy chided softly, "We did just set Grisele and Mopel free."

Nick blushed, how easily he had forgotten the events he had just witnessed. Mopel held up the bag with the OhRa in it, "What would you say to a final adventure?"

"A *final* adventure?" Amy, Nick and Marty asked, startled.

"Well, a final one for *this* school year at least," Grisele smiled slyly.

With that, they all agreed that is was time to free Bismorda and the other captives.

Chapter 36
Free At Last!

Mopel led the procession holding the bag with the remains of the OhRa out at arm's length. Walking through the shining corridors of the transformed palace, Nick, Marty, and Amy's eyes caressed the extravagant interior. Tapestries hung from the walls and large oriental rugs splashed bright colors onto the gleaming whiteness. The transformed castle now resembled a well-preserved museum.

After traipsing through half a dozen hallways they were finally led to a large ornate room filled wall to wall with the masses of thelfix filled with hostages.

"This will probably take a while," Grisele noted.

"Let's get the smaller ones first," Mopel directed.

As they began focusing on individual blocks Marty recognized a few of them, "Here's the *San Dover*!"

Bending down in front of the sandy looking figure Marty requested, "Let's start with him!"

Mopel held the bag over the block and began chanting:

> "Anyone near us, used to fear us,
> Twins are free don't you fuss.
> Thelfix melt, make it clear
> Clear away, right now, right here."

As her words echoed around the hall the clear mass of gel dissipated, melting quickly away without even leaving a puddle.

The San Dover spoke, "Oh, you are *back*! Yulesaychaater, you truly *are* magnificent. You have saved us all!"

Grisele jumped in with another spell, "Let's see, what was it again? Oh, yes!

> You are off the beaten path

Return now to your own Tarbath!"

With a twinkle, the San Dover was gone.

"Where did he *go*?" Amy questioned.

"To Tarbath, dear, that's where he lives," Grisele spoke to Marty now, "At this rate we may be here all day!"

"It's okay Grisele, we've waited a long time for this, and so have the prisoners, a few more hours won't hurt any of us," as he spoke he checked with Nick and Amy who agreed emphatically.

"Okay, who's next?" Mopel inquired.

They released the creatures one by one and following their release each of them acknowledged Marty's greatness and heroism before they were "twinkled" back to their homes. When they got to the map book they were greeted with a most energetic paragraph:

"Oh, I say you have proven to be even more gallant than I planned. Amy, your courage was unsurpassed and the Eyahge'er, may I say, *Good show!* Don't forget to write down this adventure and your feelings, oh wait, that's all being done by your adventure book, but you must not forget the feelings you have had here. Keep the land of books alive within yourselves. And *never* forget the power of one voice."

Closing the book Marty looked up to find Amy distracted, "Amy, what's wrong?"

"Look over there," she pointed to a tall figure whose back was to them, "That figure looks familiar."

As she spoke, she walked over to the tall block of Thelfix and made her way around to the front of it.

"Oh, Mr. Candletier!" she exclaimed, tears filling her eyes, "I wondered why he had been gone from school."

Then she stopped, her eyes cleared and her hands came to her hips indignantly, "Why in the world is *he* here?"

Marty looked at Nick guiltily, they hadn't been back to the library for a few months so he hadn't noticed the disappearance, he hesitated then asked, "When did he start missing school?"

Amy thought a moment, "About two months ago."

Marty felt horrible, he hadn't even realized Mr. Candletier was gone! Well, now he needed to explain to Amy how Mr. Candletier was involved, "Amy, you've heard the creatures call me the Yulesaychaater and the book just called Nick the Eyahge'er..." Amy wasn't following this explanation and it was clear on her face. "Well, the Yulesaychaater, me, I am a key gatherer, and the Eyahge'er which is Nick is a story teller, Mr. Candletier is the Checkpohmer or the book watcher. He's one of us," here Marty motioned to Nick and then himself.

Amy finally registered understanding then disappointment, "You say, 'He's one of us' but you didn't point to me, so I'm not included?"

Before Marty could say anything Grisele stepped forward, "Oh, you *are* included, in fact you are a major piece in this puzzle. You see, you're a Shenahnger, one of the faithful."

"A *Shenahnger*, I like the sound of that," Amy conceded.

Nick and Marty were surprised that she had received a calling as well, but it *did* make sense. It was the reason she could come into Qualf or any of the other lands with them.

"Well, let's free the Checkpohmer," Amy refocused the group's attention.

Mopel stepped forward, held up the bag and chanted again. The thelfix melted and Mr. Candletier came out of his trance.

"Oh, Nick, Marty, how good to see you, we were beginning to lose hope," then he noticed Amy, "You must have been really worried about my absence from school. I'm sorry to have given you such a scare, you see, I didn't have much say in the matter."

He smiled down at Amy as he drew her close, "Marty,

Nick, I'm sure you've met Amy already, but you could learn a lot from her. She is in my library every day and reads like a ninorm."

"Don't you mean a *bookworm*?" Amy giggled.

"No, I don't. Bookworms *eat* books, ninorms study them," Mr. Candletier instructed.

"Oh, I'd *love* to meet one of those!" Amy said ecstatically.

"Well, you just might, sometime," Ignatius baited with an alluring smile. "*If* you stay close to these two," he pointed at Nick and Marty, "You could be a wonderful team together."

"We already are," Marty assured him.

At this comment Amy's eyes grew wide and she blushed.

"I mean it, there won't be adventures without *you* there," Marty pledged.

"*Promise*?" Amy asked skeptically.

"Promise!" Marty reassured.

Nick cleared his throat, "Shouldn't we get the rest of these…" here he motioned to the remaining blocks of thelfix, "home?"

Mopel and Grisele nodded and came forward again, "We've only got a few left, but they're quite important ones."

Stepping up to Misselthorn's kneeling figure Mopel chanted her spell and the thelfix melted faster, with all of them assembled, their strength was growing unstoppable. Misselthorn shook out of her trance and beamed, "I knew you would come through for us, I see you have a Shenahnger with you as well."

Amy was beaming, she *was* important to the mission after all.

Misselthorn stated, "And, she must be a very *strong* one."

Blushing quickly Amy's head bowed.

Continuing, Misselthorn encouraged, "You'll need more Shenahngers before you're through. It will be part of your mission just to find them."

With that she turned to Grisele, "Alright, I'm ready to go back now."

Grisele moved her hand and spoke:

> "Back to where you can be help,
> Back you go to the land of Felp.
> Be near when they are in need
> Help them always to succeed."

This was more than the others had received, but she *was* another witch, so maybe that had something to do with it. Also by the sound of things the adventures were *not* over, but only beginning. After setting three more witches free and sending them back to their homes, they got to Bismorda's block of thelfix, and made short order of releasing her as well. Standing, in all her majesty, the circle was finally completed.

Grisele and Mopel embraced Bismorda in turn. The three of them could easily have been beautiful blossoms in their cascading dresses Grisele in nighttime blue, Mopel in fiery red, and Bismorda in forest green. Amid the rustling floor-length dresses Nick, Marty, and Amy exchanged triumphant looks and the reunion was indeed complete when Marty got to introduce Nick and Amy to Bismorda.

"We must all stay in touch," Grisele said wistfully, "It would be such a pity to lose friends like you."

"Gris, don't, you'll make me *cry*," Mopel's bottom lip quivered and she bit it for control.

"Oh, we'll come visit next year for sure, won't we kids?" It was Mr. Candletier who spoke, surprising all present.

Obediently Amy, Nick, and Marty nodded.

"*I'm* ready to go home now," Ignatius smiled at Grisele,

who stepped forward, waved her hand and spoke:

"Checkpohmer may you long live
Happiness to children shall you give.
Go now and safely return
Back to the Isle of Bicolotern."

Mr. Candletier disappeared in the twinkle still waving to them all. Marty made a silent vow to visit the library first thing Monday morning to check that Mr. Candletier was doing okay still. Never again would he neglect the library or his friend the Checkpohmer.

"I think it's time to get you home," Bismorda looked at Marty, Nick, and Amy, then looking over at Grisele, "Did you modify time yet?"

Grisele nodded in the affirmative touching the tips of her forefingers together in some gesture of magical knowledge.

"*Modify* time?" Marty perked up, as did Nick and Amy. "Yes, Marty, have you not been aware that most of your adventures have been getting longer and longer?"

Nick, who *had* been keeping track, nodded. Marty just looked blankly back at her. "Do you remember when you first started coming to visit?" Bismorda attempted to explain, "How long did it take you? In your world I mean."

"An hour," Marty responded without hesitation.

"Correct, you should have noticed that each of your missions have been returning you later and later as the Zanth sisters became more controlled by the OhRa."

Nick jumped in, "I noticed, our last venture to the Gorder took almost three hours!"

"See," Bismorda said pointedly, "Grisele controls the interworld time clocks so that visitors are not kept more than thirty minutes in their own time."

"Well, *actually* it's twenty-nine minutes and thirty

seconds, if you really want to be precise," Grisele said proudly, then she shook her head and her face clouded, "That nasty OhRa had me pushed back only thirty minutes in over three hundred years and then in less than *one* year it gained enough power to make me slip two more hours!"

Mopel patted Grisele's shoulder reassuringly, "It's not your fault Gris. You'll get back up to speed soon enough."

Here she smiled to show off a dazzling set of teeth, "Why, let's check how you did," Mopel leaned over and peeked at Nick's wristwatch.

"See? It's already two hours ago! By the time they return it should be pretty near perfect timing!"

Nick studied his digital wristwatch and was amazed to watch as it reached sixty seconds, it jumped back three minutes. He showed Marty and Amy.

They then began their farewells to Bismorda, Grisele, and Mopel.

"Gris, we'll just go back by way of the portal, that way you two can catch up," Bismorda said thoughtfully.

"Oh, you *are* a dear, Bis you must come soon for tea!" Grisele invited.

"Wouldn't miss it!"

The small group turned to leave the now empty room and the lights dimmed automatically, the beauty of magic was overwhelming yet simple. Finding the portal was a slight challenge, but after peeking into a whole line of elegant rooms the very last door in the hall opened up on the burbling river Sems. Bismorda led the way, followed by Amy, Nick, and Marty in that order. Pulling the door closed behind him Marty turned the portal back into his bedroom door. Marty had planned to just return home, but then he remembered the mess up at the castle, the underground cavern, and the sign in the room of books. Turning to Bismorda she read his first concern before he spoke.

"Don't *worry*, the mess is already cleaned up. Scrimt

and Sayvd were among the first ones released remember?"

At the mention of the trillos Nick piped in, "Who sacrificed their wing for your recording?"

Amy wasn't following this line of conversation, but she was still paying very close attention to see what she might pick up.

"Yes," Marty agreed, "Nick and I were concerned about the wing."

"Well, do you remember the Batwort?" Bismorda questioned.

Surprised by the turn in questioning Nick and Marty looked blankly back at her.

"The Batwort sheds the skin on its wing-like ears, and the trillos do too. I have a whole drawer full of their cast-off wings. I use them to record my favorite songs," here Bismorda went into a fond memory for she began to hum.

Nick and Marty recognized it immediately, "Chopin's *Polonaise!*" Marty stated excitedly.

Bismorda's eyes came open, her cat-like pupils dilating, she smiled, "I'm so glad you were able to use my old gramophone record."

Here Amy finally understood something, "You have a record of Chopin? Is it a real recording of *him* playing?"

Bismorda chuckled, "No dear, it's another artist but they play it beautifully."

Remembering the year that Bismorda was changed Nick interrupted, "But Chopin wasn't around in 1624!"

"I know that, but I *did* have some time after Marty freed me to acquire some different likings. One is the whole collection of classical composers," Bismorda sighed.

Changing the subject Marty brought up his other two concerns, "What is written over the door in your room of books? It said 'Checksuejeeper's Lair,' what does *that* mean?"

Bismorda looked at them all slyly, "It means the Book Collector's Home."

At the questioning glances she explained, "That's why I have a door to Bicolotern and a small vessel to get me there and back, *I* collect all the ripe books. I can't even imagine how many spoiled books are littering the ground now."

She shook her head sadly, "The OhRa had one last triumph, a lost harvest of books."

Nick asked Marty's final question without realizing that he was, "What is that box that is down in your secret cavern?"

"Oh, you *found* it?" Bismorda was overjoyed, "I'm so glad, was it harmed in anyway?"

Marty and Nick shook their heads.

"Thank heavens," then noticing their questioning glances, "It's the Yulesay-cheekeygee."

"The *what*?" Marty asked.

Surprisingly Amy was the one who spoke, "The *Yulesay-cheekeygee*, you really must pay more attention," she scolded, then eagerly she asked, "What does that mean?"

"It means the key keeper," she expounded, "The origin of the box is quite extraordinary, it was about a year prior to my first transformation that it appeared unexpectedly on my front landing. I had no idea what it was but as I tried to touch it I felt a surge of energy rush through it and had to pull away."

"That happened to me too!" Nick interjected.

"Well, I didn't know what to do with it, but I couldn't very well leave it sitting there, so I floated it inside. I was going to put it in my sleeping chamber, but as I got near to my room I realized the long mirror had opened at the end of the hall."

"I saw that too, isn't it neat?" Amy interjected.

Bismorda smiled and nodded, "Well, I decided to take this box into the passage, since I had never seen the mirror open in that way before. I took the winding staircase, which lit up as I descended. At the ground level the cavern opened up and all that stood there was a simple wooden table."

"But how did you know what it was?" Marty wondered.

Continuing Bismorda related the story, "As I had the box hovering beside me I realized there was something engraved on the table it said, *'Yulesaycheekeygee yohgee nudushipshow'* which means *'Place the key keeper here'* and it had an inlaid square that fit the keeper precisely. After putting it in place I never moved it again. When I went back up the stairs the mirror opened, I stepped out and I haven't been able to enter the secret cavern again," here Bismorda's tale ended.

"Want to see it again?" Marty teased.

Bismorda's cat eyes glowed in response, "I'd *love* to, especially if you've figured out what to do with the keeper."

"Oh, I have, but I'll let you see *that* for yourself."

With that the group turned and moved quickly up the hill to the castle. Buzzing and chirping sounds again filled the air and reminded Marty that everything was back to how it should be. Inside the castle Marty took the lead and made a beeline for the hall mirror. Speaking the magic phrase, the mirror swung open, and they descended in the darkness until the cavern opened out in front of them, the various scenes lighting up the gloomy stone walls.

Marty went to the Yulesay-cheekeygee and re-inserted the key to Zanth, this time the image showed a scene reminiscent of a Bavarian Chalet, large and white in the plush green countryside near the water's edge. This brightened the room more and Bismorda stood in awe looking around at the walls. After a few moments of silence Bismorda spoke, she was choked up, "The Yulesay-cheekeygee shows our world at peace, but only you as the Yulesaychaater have control of that peace."

It was as if Nick and Amy had melted away, Bismorda turned to Marty, "Promise me you will keep our land safe."

"I *promise*," Marty managed under her watchful stare.

The glowing eyes next pinned Nick, "You must remember everything you see here. You have to remember, promise?"

"Yes," Nick agreed, "I promise, I'll never forget anything here."

"And as a Shenahnger, Amy," Bismorda turned at last to bring Amy into the glowing pools that were her eyes, "You *must* have the faith and keep believing that all of this is real. Can you promise me you'll do that?"

"Always!" Amy's emphatic answer echoed in the hall.

Bismorda seemed pleased with the responses she had received, so she turned to leave and the group followed her back up the darkened stairwell. In the main hall they bid farewell.

"Don't forget to come tell me of your adventures from summer break! Read lots of books and enjoy every minute of freedom, after more than three hundred years of captivity take it from me, *freedom is precious*, rejoice in it."

After leaving the palace Marty, Nick, and Amy descended back to the bridge in silence until Nick looked down at his watch, "Hey! Grisele did *it*! It's 11:29 and 30 seconds!"

With that, they stepped through the portal back into Marty's room and returned to reality with the simple click of the key.

Stashing the solitary remaining key in his drawer, Marty turned to Nick and Amy, "Want some milk?"

Chuckling they grabbed the glasses of milk, amazingly still cold, off of the dresser and were about to drink when Nick said, "A toast!"

They all stopped, "To us!" he held out his cup and the other two clinked their glasses with it, repeating "To us!" in unison.

After that day the rest of the school year went by quickly: finals, yearbook signing, and cleaning out their lockers. Summer was filled with hours of fun as they played night games like kick-the-can, and steal the flag. In these games they were joined by other neighborhood kids but Marty, Nick, and Amy stayed true to their word, and to each other. They read many books and went on literary adventures dreaming of the next time they could go on another *real* adventure in the land of books.

Chapter 37
Return to the Beginning

Friday, May 24, 2075

Nicholas closed the age-worn book and peered over the top at the children's enraptured gazes.

"So, how did you like it?" he asked as he placed the book on the table off to the side of his chair.

Chante couldn't hold back her excitement, "Are you *really* Marty's Nick?"

Nick chuckled, "Yes, Chante I was the boy who became close friends with Marty Whimpel. We were inseparable."

"Amy was thirteen when that story took place? *Right*?" Nisha wondered aloud.

Secretly she was bursting, she had just turned thirteen, too.

"Yes, I believe so, let's see, I turned thirteen in October that school year, and Marty didn't turn thirteen until August the following year, just before eighth grade, so yes, Amy would have turned thirteen the week after the story ends."

"What day?" Nisha was getting excited.

"May the seventeenth," Nick recalled.

"*REALLY?* That's my birthday too!" Nisha was over-joyed.

This was a good omen apparently because they all looked at Nisha as if she would declare she was a *Shenahnger* right then, because of the similar birth date.

Looking past the excitement of the majority Nicholas looked over at Kimber Nayshon, the pixie-like brunette, who had been like a stick of dynamite earlier but now sat like a soggy glove after a snowball fight. She was quietly turning the pages of *Tom Thumb* that Nick had handed her when they had entered.

Venturing into her thoughts he said, "Hard to believe, Kimber?"

Starting, she had not been aware of his gaze, she laid the book in her lap and after a quick look around at her friends she nodded sheepishly.

Smiling, Nick reassured her, "It's *okay*, not everyone can have the faith of Amy, don't think that you're less of a person because of it. Remember Monica?"

Here Kimber perked up, "Yeah, I liked her. I could really relate with how she felt."

"Well, she still stayed very close, even though she couldn't believe in the concept of story lands," Nick soothed.

"So, it doesn't make me *uncool*?" another sweeping glance at her friends as they shook their heads gave her the added support she needed.

"No Kimber, I'm having a hard time swallowing it too," Billy said.

"*Really*, Billy?" Kimber now felt validated, Billy was looked up to by all of the others, and not just because he was taller, he was an officer at their school, one of the chosen, responsible for upkeep of the android staff.

Billy nodded, "No offense, Mr. Chrismon, it was a nice story, but I don't know if I can believe in the portal doors, and magic keys idea."

Then without warning he stood, "C'mon Kimber, let's head back home."

Smiling she joined him and as they left they passed through their friend's hurt looks. Brushing them aside like cobwebs. As the front door closed after them, those remaining turned back to Nick, looking for guidance.

"Everyone is given a choice," Nick said quietly, as he noticed Kimber's *Tom Thumb* and Billy's copy of *The Emperor's New Clothes* remained on the carpet where they had been sitting.

"I tell you these stories because I have reason to believe there is one among you who should take my place as the Eyahge'er."

This statement brought curious glances among the youth. One of them could become the next story teller? Several felt the prickle at the base of their neck just where the hair starts, *what if it's me?* They asked themselves.

Looks of secret hope glanced back at Nick out of the eyes of each of the friends present. He nodded thinking, *Yes, it is best to weed out the non-believers as they crop up, that way we'll be left with the faithful, if not the next Eyahge'er.*

Although his heart ached to lose Billy and Kimber so early, it may have been for the best. Looking at the upturned faces he couldn't help but think, *I wonder who else we'll lose before we're through?*

Speaking again, he glanced at each face in turn, "Do you remember what Bismorda challenged us there at the end of the story?"

Nick selected Weston Mils, "Can *you* tell me what she said?"

"To read lots of books, enjoy freedom, and to come back to share your adventures of summer break," he responded energetically.

"That's correct," Nick smiled, "Now, which one of you can tell me what Amy, Marty and I did?"

Menalee's face lit up, but she didn't raise her hand instead she looked around the group to see if anyone else would speak first.

Seeing this, Nick almost asked her, but Alden blurted out, "You played kick-the-can!"

Then Josh added, "And steal the flag!"

"And read books!" Saul answered.

Each of these responses were accepted by Nick with a smile and a nod, then he addressed Menalee, "I think you know what I *really* mean, don't you dear?"

Menalee nodded, her eyes sparkling as quietly she said, "You went back."

The whole group looked at her, wondering what she meant by that. Nick's voice startled the young people into turning again to face him, "She is absolutely right, we *did* go back. We went to see Bismorda after that first summer break, and I hope you will all come back here to see me after *your* summer break as well. I would love to hear of your adventures, and if you're interested, I would love to share more of our adventures."

Each face filled with excitement and took on a glow, the glow of curiosity, the glow of anticipation, the glow of *youth*. Nick smiled at the group and thought to himself, *I do hope you will come back, that is what I depend on.*

As he finished, the children, each clasping the book he had given them, waited for him to join them on their way out of his home.

Standing slowly, Nick joined them, again looking each in the eye and smiling, "Thank you for coming to visit today, it has been wonderful."

The train of people slowly moved out of the library, down the hall past the boxes and shelves of books, Chante retrieved her tabby cat, and Alden opened the front door. As the single-file line emerged again on the ancient wood porch they waited for those following them until there were seven in a cluster. Looking back over their shoulders they saw one left standing near Nick.

Menalee had paused before she stepped out with her peers, turning to Nick she threw her arms around his neck and whispered something in his ear, this is what she said, "*I believe in the Yulesaychaater, the Eyahge'er, and everything else you told us. I wouldn't miss the next adventure for anything!*"

Nick hugged her and then she pulled away. Moving out to join the group they all waved, made their way across the porch, down the stairs, over the stepping stones and out at the gate. Menalee turned and pulled the gate shut behind them, smiling again at Nick as he stood in his doorway.

Standing, watching, until the retreating figures have disappeared from view Nick slowly shut the front door and moved along his hallway, pausing to touch various books, look at covers, and remember the words of wisdom he had gained from the volumes lining his home. He made his way slowly back to his library. Re-entering the now empty library he stood in the doorway absorbing the energy that was now floating in the air. Stooping slowly, he retrieved the forgotten books of Billy and Kimber. A momentary pang of regret at more lost believers tugged at his heart, then straightening as best he could he moved to his trusty chair.

Lowering himself into the chair brought sounds of creaking bones and tired muscles. "Oh Marty, *could* one of them be my replacement?"

"*Nick, didn't you* feel *it?*"

Again Nick looked to see if he could find Marty, but even as he did, he knew he wasn't there. Settling again he thought, *Feel? I have looked so long and now that more children have come, I don't know if I can feel more than their curiosity.*

"Yes, they each had that, but a few of them had more," Marty's voice floated from nowhere.

"A *few?*" Nick was surprised, "Isn't there just one Eyahge'er?"

Then, before Marty's voice could answer Nick, he answered himself, "You mean Shenahngers? Yes, there must be some believers in the group too."

Trying to remember whose eyes had given off that spark the only images that would come to his mind were Amy and Marty, so excited, their group playing in the twilight on those long ago summer evenings.

With these happy memories dancing before his eyes, Nick nodded off to sleep a satisfied smile playing on his lips.

Among those who have just left Mr. Chrismon's house there is a sense of excitement. Chante bobbed along, her red curls bouncing. The others each had a slight smile and if anyone had seen them they may have wondered where these eight pre-teens had just been to make them so excited.

When they passed the sign and crossed back into their neighborhood they split to go their own ways, but before they walked away Menalee spoke, startling them all into turning their focus back to her, "What would you guys think about getting together to play kick-the-can later?"

Without question seven other heads nodded in agreement. Later that evening the eight of them gathered again on the edge of town, behind the force field they now knew was nothing more than a wall, the only area that had places to hide, among the run-down rambler homes from the old Scat-town.

They had passed these homes earlier that day.

None of them knew any rules to kick-the-can so they made them up as they went along. It was the beginning of an exciting and memorable summer where they would take turns being the Yulesaychaater, the Eyahge'er and the remaining ones would be Shenahngers.

Each child read the book that had been given them, then they traded among their group until each book had been read, expanding their field of adventure for new missions and new games. At night they would part with promises of staying true to each other and their quest for learning.

That was the first summer after the return of the books.

THE END

...or was it just *THE BEGINNING?*

Coming Soon:

Marty Whimpel
And the
Darkness of Indifference
Book 2

WRITTEN AND ILLUSTRATED BY
Jim Tatton

The adventures continue with Marty, Nick, and Amy as they battle against the crippling power of The Darkness that has contaminated his world and is now affecting the world of books. New characters join forces with the friends as they try to create a barrier against this mind-numbing force that continues to grow stronger. Will they be able to stop its influence before it destroys both the land of books and the world as we know it?

CPSIA information can be obtained at www.ICGtesting.com
Printed in the USA
BVOW08s1544050813

327883BV00014B/346/P